THE
LODGE

By Colleen Mahan

THE LODGE
MOVIOLA MAN (with Bill Mahan)

COLLEEN MAHAN

THE LODGE

DOUBLEDAY & COMPANY, INC.
Garden City, New York

COLLEEN MAHAN

THE
LODGE

DOUBLEDAY & COMPANY, INC.
Garden City, New York

For G.

What is life? a tale that is told;
What is life? a frenzy extreme,
A shadow of things that seem;
And the greatest good is but small,
That all life is a dream to all,
And that dreams themselves are a dream.

Pedro Calderón de la Barca

Dear Friends and Kind Strangers,
welcome to my Lodge. Be merry,
rattle and shake with me—but if
you die, the Fault is not mine.

The legend inscribed in the redwood lintel
above the main entrance to Kirbo's Lodge.

Flying at only twenty-five hundred feet, the Twin Otter bounced uncomfortably in the updrafts from the wide, flat valley which lay between the awesome escarpment of the Sierra Nevada on the west and the bald massif of the White Range on the east.

In the plane, Cabot Markey pressed his forehead against the cold pane of the porthole and looked down upon the brown valley. In places it was smeared with the gaudy yellow of autumn-blooming rabbit bush, and from the dark mouths of the Sierra canyons there licked bright tongues of yellow aspen. Orange necklaces of cottonwood trees curled alongside the streams flowing from the mountains, and sunlight caught and flashed in the tumbling waters. Markey looked up and watched the snow-dusted peaks of the escarpment parading far above the laboring, jolting aircraft. He knew the names of those peaks—Whitney, Darwin, Tyndall, Russell, Langley—as he knew the names of old friends. He had climbed them all, slept on their bosoms, melted their snows to drink, listened to the voices of their winds. Though he was nauseous from the rough flight and felt dried and stiff from the long hours in the air, the sight of those whitened heights produced a sharp, pleasurable anticipation. He would soon be among those granite towers and their fresh, drifting mists.

Markey had come over the pole from London and, in San Francisco, had changed, without resting, to the lighter, prop-driven air-liner which serviced the small cities of the northern deserts of California. They had landed twice at remote airports and would shortly glide down to a third stop, this one called Kirbo's Landing, a terminal which existed almost exclusively for the guests of Kirbo's Lodge. There, Markey would leave the plane, retrieve his big, travel-scarred bag from the luggage compartment, and the terminal porter would see that it was promptly delivered to the lodge's airport limousine. In the bag were good tweeds, quiet woolen ties, tailored shirts and a .38 caliber revolver he had picked up, between planes, from the apartment he kept in San Francisco.

There were twelve passengers on the Twin Otter, but only three would disembark at Kirbo's Landing—Markey and Dr. Alfred Friendly and wife. Dr. Friendly was fifty-eight years old. His wife was twenty-two. Her name was Jessica. The doctor was a squarely built man with cautious gray eyes behind rimless glasses. His hair was a carefully dyed dark brown, but with stylish gray at the temples. He tinted it himself, pasting out the gray with Vaseline before he artfully applied the tint. He was artful in all that he did. His surgery was exquisite, as it had to be, for his specialty was removing lumps from the breasts of terrified women. The famously minute scars left in that tender flesh had made him a wealthy man.

Friendly carefully touched his wife's arm to awaken her. He rarely touched her in public. "I don't want people to think I'm a lecherous old goat," he had told Jessica.

"Always hiding the truth," had been Jessica's reply.

At his touch, Jessica opened her sleepy eyes and squinted at him. "We'll be landing soon," he said.

"Fuck off," whispered Jessica, and shut her eyes. Friendly glanced warily about to see if she had been heard by their neighbors.

Jessica grinned her crooked grin without reopening her eyes. "Nobody heard me," she said. "Everybody's deaf from those goddam props." She playfully jabbed her elbow into his ribs and Friendly suppressed a smile. He adored Jessica.

The plane's propellers softened their din as the pilot powered back for the descent. The stewardess delivered Markey's old reversible Burberry and he buttoned the collar of his shirt and moved his tie into place. He ran his fingers through his short beard and took a beret from the pocket of the Burberry, pulled it over his rope-colored hair. He collected his carry-on bag from under his seat and thought of the gleaming blue steel revolver riding in the big case in the luggage compartment. It was less than a thought, a consciousness that the gun was there, waiting.

On the ground near the A-frame passenger terminal for Kirbo's Landing, its porter was watching the incoming plane. He was an ageless Latino who had been the porter for Kirbo's Landing when it was in fact a steamboat landing on the western shore of Owens Lake before that lake was drained to fill the swimming pools of distant Los Angeles. He was also watching the woman who stood near him, her face lifted to the sky.

A dozen guests departing the lodge were waiting for the plane, but they were inside the terminal by the blazing logs in its fireplace, protecting themselves from the cold autumn wind. This one, this slender female in the black ski pants and black, fur-trimmed boots and short, black mink jacket, preferred to stand on the tarmac in the wind and watch the Twin Otter sideslip its way down to the runway. It was the third day in a row that she had made the fifteen-mile journey from the lodge to meet the afternoon flight from San Francisco. Twice now she had returned alone to the lodge.

The ageless Latino hoped she would not be disappointed this time. He coveted her strong legs and the curve of her in the tight black pants. He studied the flawless profile of her face. Never before had he seen such a beautiful woman. What man would be so foolish as to disappoint this woman? He was an old lover and for that reason knew that it was a man she was waiting for. He was a little embarrassed to find that he was wishing that he could be that man and was imagining the curve of her in his hands. He rubbed their wrinkled palms together against the snapping cold and the frustration of his years.

The plane, its motors revving, hit the runway, kited for a few yards and settled to roll to a stop before the terminal. The Latino pushed the carpeted steps to meet the passengers' door as it opened. The propellers became still and one engine backfired grumpily. First there appeared a blond young woman in a thick sable coat and, behind her, an older man in rimless glasses; next, a tall, lanky man with a trimmed beard, wearing a Basque beret. He waved to the porter and the porter smiled and called out, "Hello there, Mr. Markey." The co-pilot trotted down the steps, unlocked the baggage compartment and dealt the tagged luggage into the porter's cart.

Clarice Hammond Donner Cones Bishop pulled her black mink

jacket closer about her trim body and walked with head down to the airport limousine, opened a door and slipped inside. She fumbled a cigarette from her pocket, lighted it with a jeweled lighter and sat with it in her fingers, not smoking it. She did not look again toward the plane. Working with the luggage, the porter had seen her go alone to the limousine and he was sad for that woman with the beautiful face and the admirable bottom.

2

From the mouth of Kirbo's Canyon a cheerful creek, which in the spring became a snarling torrent, wound down across the long, gentle slope from the base of the escarpment to the center of the valley, feeding finally into the Owens River. Alongside it grew those golden cottonwoods which, from the plane, had looked like a necklace carefully strung upon the land. The airport limousine sped beside the gurgling water and the wind brushed bright fallen leaves across the black pavement in front of the big green vehicle.

In the limousine, Dr. Friendly and Jessica were in the seat behind the driver. Jessica sat too close to the doctor for his comfort. He was sure the young man behind the wheel, who now and then glanced into the rearview mirror, was censuring him for being, at his age, in the company of so young a woman. He attempted to lift that imagined onus by rather loudly and in a fatherly way lecturing Jessica on the creation of the Sierra. As he spoke knowledgeably of the movements of the earth's crust which had thrust the mountains up from the primordial plain a million years before, Jessica wriggled her hand into his crotch and squeezed. The doctor suddenly developed a fit of coughing.

Behind that merry scene sat Lorenzo Dante and his bridge partner, Cora McElvain. As the doctor coughed, Lorenzo snatched out a white handkerchief and covered his prominent Mediterranean nose. Cora glanced at him with disgust. Among the endless number of things she detested in Lorenzo was his pathological fear of germs. Lorenzo and Cora had not spoken to each other for seven hours— that is, unnecessarily. It was their common condition. On the long drive from Los Angeles in Lorenzo's yellow Cadillac, they had exchanged perhaps twenty words, the longest passage being when Cora had pleaded with him to stop at a gas station. "For Chrissake, I got to go to the loo!"

And Lorenzo had replied, "Piss in your pants, my dear."

Lorenzo in appearance was an elegant man, impeccable, sanitized. Cora was his opposite, dumpy, frumpy, her spectacles always down on the end of her button nose, her slip showing when she wore a skirt or the seat of her slacks bagging unhappily when she wore pants. Each hated everything the other was and yet they were indispensable to one another. At the bridge table they could look at each other through their hatred and, by some curious and contradictory meeting of minds, bid their hands with uncanny accuracy. It did not always permit them to win, because they were both plungers, trying always for the slams, the big gains.

Lorenzo and Cora were en route to Kirbo's Lodge because there, at that time of the year between the summer and winter seasons when that almost incredibly expensive and exclusive hostelry had its fewest guests, there was traditionally gathered a rare collection of the world's most viciously addicted bridge players. In the ornate gold and pink cardroom, which was sealed off from sound and light except for the deadly riffle of cards and the pale, violet glare of low-hanging table lamps, fortunes were won and lost each autumn.

Dr. Friendly succeeded in extracting his privates from Jessica's red-tipped clutches and his coughing stopped, his lecture continued. Jessica grinned that deliciously crooked grin and Lorenzo was reprieved from the danger of germs. He tucked his handkerchief away and Cora wished nothing for him but double pneumonia.

The entrance to Kirbo's Canyon was closed by a long wrought iron gate. The guard in the station beside the gate pressed a button as the airport limousine approached, and the gate slowly opened upon the narrow pavement which snaked steeply up the wall of the canyon into the granite fastness of the Sierra escarpment.

Only lodge vehicles or delivery trucks were allowed to ascend the canyon. Guests like Lorenzo and Cora who had arrived by highway were required to park their cars in the airport garage and take the limousines up the winding road to the eight-thousand-foot level. There the aerial tram collected them for the rest of the journey and whispered up its black cables across the dizzying chasm of the glacial gorge to the nine-thousand-foot level, where Kirbo's Lodge crouched in its green eyrie of ancient sugar pines below the massive white sweep of the trapped glacier called the Gornaad.

Cabot Markey looked back over his shoulder through the window of the limousine and watched the iron gate close. Beyond it, he could see the ribbon of yellow cottonwoods descending to the valley, where diesel trucks smoked along the interstate highway and where Kirbo's Landing flew its red wind sock. The plane on which he had arrived was taking off.

It was an ending for Markey and the closing gate was like a curtain being drawn.

He looked down with comforting pleasure into the canyon, where the cottonwoods had been replaced by the ocherous aspens of that higher altitude. His neck no longer ached and he felt less weary.

Markey was aware of the silent woman beside him at the other end of the long limousine seat. It was impossible not to be aware of her. She had glanced at him and nodded politely when he had climbed into the car, and the clear peacock blue of her eyes had been startling. On the ride up the slope to the canyon he had, like the porter, secretly considered her. She was slumped in the corner, one straight, perfect leg stretched out with its fur boot on the footrest. The other leg was drawn up, the heel of the boot caught on the edge of the seat, her gloved hands clasped about the knee. She had altered this position from time to time by pushing the bent leg out and drawing up the other to clasp it, or by stretching both legs and resting her hands flat upon the firm, round thighs.

It was not being done for him, he knew. One knows when a woman is preening herself for inspection. Her thoughts were not of him. Her movements were symptomatic of an inner tension, her gaze was straight ahead and unseeing. She was within herself completely and unconscious of herself. In any case, Markey's interest was an artist's interest. He admired the woman without wanting her. He was, he believed, beyond that. At another time in his life, being a man with an abiding curiosity, he would have spoken to her and adroitly engaged her in a dialogue which might have explained her distress. But Markey's interest now was fleeting, and having noted this unknown, handsome woman beside him and her ill-concealed pain, he easily shifted his contemplation to the beauty of the turning aspens.

Paul Binns had the last seat in the limousine to himself and he had made himself comfortable, legs up, head against the armrest. He hadn't slept in forty-eight hours except for short naps on the side of the highway behind the wheel of his Volkswagen on the long drive from Wyoming. At Kirbo's Landing he had guided the battered little car into the garage, shaken hands with the attendant who guarded the Cadillacs and Rolls Royces of the lodge guests, gone to the men's room, shaved, given his tumbled dark hair a good combing, pulled on a blue turtleneck sweater and a plaid windbreaker, and delivered himself and canvas val-pak to the airport limousine for the trip up the mountain.

He had been seated as the plane from San Francisco touched down and he had seen the woman in the black ski pants and fur boots stride alone from the tarmac to the car, take her place two seats ahead of him and light a cigarette. He had sleepily observed the easy, athletic swing of her body but no more than that. He was too tired for details. They were alone in the limousine and, with the sound of the wind that rushed over the car, Paul heard a soft, throaty gasp which might have been a sob. He looked at the back of her head. Her head was upright, she took a draw from her cigarette. Paul had yawned and closed his eyes. He was almost asleep when the limousine doors began to slam as the other passengers got in. His door opened and the pink-faced driver leaned in and asked, "What's your name, sir?"

Paul said, "I'm the snowtime bartender, sir."

"Oh, yeah," the driver said. "We been expecting you. Jesus, you look half dead."

"I'm all dead. Get me up the hill for burial, man."

The driver grinned and closed the door. In a moment the motor started and the car moved. Paul dozed again. It was to be his second winter season at that log, stone, glass and steel fantasy in the mountains called Kirbo's Lodge.

In the chilly doldrums of autumn when the lodge was no longer a resort to escape the heat of summer, and the snows which dusted the higher pinnacles had not yet descended to the lower levels, the lodge began to change its character. The stables were deprived of their sleek riding horses, the animals being led out over the Gornaad Pass on a three-day pack trip down to winter pastures. Great stacks of firewood were built in the shelter at the south end of the main building. The general store off the lobby put away its summer sporting goods, and the shelves and racks began to fill with bright woolens, padded jackets, fur-lined gloves, wind goggles, shining skis and French ski boots. And with all this came a slow change in personnel.

Those polished, severe and deferential servants who so much delighted the generally middle-aged guests of the quiet summer days gradually disappeared from the staff dormitory and their places began to fill with smiling younger faces; slim girls with loose hair, tall youths with broad shoulders and flat stomachs who went about their duties with an insouciance that spoke of their equality with the winter guests, the skiing crowd. Indeed, when they were not about their duties in the lodge they could be found on the slopes with those they served, as they were expected to be by Arly Kirbo, that shrewd, renowned innkeeper of the famous hotel.

Paul Binns, asleep on the last seat of the airport limousine as it passed a road maintenance station where the snowplows were being greased and tuned, was one of those easy-mannered employees whom Miss Kirbo brought in to handle the singles, the young marrieds or the young living-togethers who filled the lodge from November till March, who came to ski, drink, sing, dance, smoke grass and fornicate, all in a very tumbled order.

Nominally, Paul's job was tending the snowtime bar, as it was called—a temporary arrangement in the great sedate hall where, in the summer, tea was served and chamber music played in the late afternoon, but where in the winter at dusk a rock group rattled the rafters, a fire roared in the huge fireplace and the thick rugs were as much used for sitting or lying upon as were the deep sofas and chairs.

He had made an auspicious debut in that job in the last year. Working in a baggy sweater and worn jeans, he had kept the trays of the cocktail waitresses loaded with drinks, the glasses of those customers who sat at the bar filled, carried on a dozen conversations seemingly at the same time, and demonstrated an astounding memory for the first names of the guests. His command of French was more than adequate (a requirement for all contact personnel in the lodge, its clientele being international) and he had a good smattering of Italian and German.

There was no wasted motion in his work. He shambled about quickly on the balls of his feet, grinning his friendly, infectious grin, his brown eyes shuttered by thick lashes and with something behind them that was as hard and sharp as obsidian. He expected friend-liness in return for his friendliness and usually got it.

On the runs behind the lodge which were served by the lifts that carried the skiers up the mile-long slope to the lower lip of the Gor-naad, Paul could hold his own even against the professionals, and this added to the respect he was given.

For Miss Kirbo's purpose, he was perfect. He mixed drinks as well as he mixed with the guests. His discretion was faultless. If there had been a connection between Paul and a woman, guest or staff, in that first winter, it was not known. He was also mysterious. He deflected personal questions with a simple, smiling grace and neatly engaged the other party in a confession about himself or her-self. When he retired to his room in the dormitory, he closed the door and no one was invited in. Those men who had been in the shower room with him when he bathed, which was always in the quiet of early morning, had reported that he carried two livid scars on his body, one across his breast and the other on his right thigh. "An accident," had been his explanation, and it had been instantly concluded that they were war wounds. That had contributed further to his charisma.

Those splendidly cared-for, handsome young people whose wealth permitted them to pay the prices at Kirbo's Lodge and ski on its twisting, blindingly beautiful runs, found themselves currying the favor of a bartender whose worldly possessions seemed to consist of an old Volkswagen, worn jeans and a collection of sweaters with patched elbows. If they themselves dressed in much the same way, it was for style, while with Paul it was all he had.

None of this had been lost on Arly Kirbo. At the season's end, she had given him a substantial bonus and a promise of doubled wages if he returned the following year.

The airport limousine rolled into the carport of the tram sta-tion, where nine similar long vehicles were parked and where the lodge's ambulances were kept for emergencies. As the tram porter began to unload the luggage from the rear compartment of the lim-ousine, its passengers got out and walked through the station to where the red tram car hung on its cables a thousand feet above the ice-blue lake in the glacial gorge. Carved through granite domes by ages of moving ice, the gorge lay in deep grandeur, its slick gray walls shining in the afternoon sunlight.

asked Harry Ames, the general manager, to send Paul to her apartment. She had plans for him that she hoped would encourage him to build his future around the lodge.

Paul had come to her through a reference from the manager of a resort lodge in Vail, Colorado. The manager had said, "Arly, I'd like to keep him because he's a natural in our business. He's an oddball, but you can trust him while you've got him—which won't be long. If he comes back for a second season, you can thank your lucky stars."

Well, Paul was back for a second season. He had written her from Greece asking for his job again. He had given his address as *poste restante* in Itea. It was the access port to Delphi, the place of the Grecian oracles. His short note had given no explanation for his location. It had been as if he were writing from Sacramento. She had answered him in kind, stating that his place was open if he could make an appearance by the middle of October.

Another woman had seen Paul arrive on the tram. From the window of her room in the dormitory, Diane Haynes, a third-year winter employee, had watched Paul make his shambling, leisurely way toward the lodge. She hadn't known that he would be returning for a second season. She had not had a word from him since they rode down the canyon in the limousine on a rainy day in April and he had said, "Well, so long, pal," and left her at the airstrip terminal to wait alone for the plane to Los Angeles. He had driven away to the north in his Volkswagen. Diane had hidden herself in the women's lounge and let the tears flow unchecked.

From the tram station the cables crossed a corner of the gorge, rising toward the distant, locked-in forest of pines where the peaked roofs of the lodge could be seen among the trees. Beyond the lodge the trees thinned on the steepening slope and, finally, only a few gnarled survivors clung about the course of the plunging Gornaad Creek, and there above all lay the Gornaad itself, a gigantean saucer of imprisoned ice, its far perimeter tilted high and frozen forever against a saddle between two snowcapped peaks.

Clarice Bishop had immediately entered the tram car and gone to sit alone in a rear seat, but the other passengers had remained on the platform in silent study of the magnificent spectacle. All had seen it before, but each time they returned to the lodge they found it necessary to pause here in wordless wonder.

Jessica had both arms hugged about one of Dr. Friendly's, Cora's mouth hung open, her tongue resting on the lower lip, Lorenzo's long fingers were touched together prayerfully, Paul rubbed his bloodshot eyes and breathed deeply of the rarified air, and Markey, who loved it most of all, had tears in his eyes.

With the luggage stowed, the porter ushered the passengers aboard the tram and closed the doors. He pressed the red button that signaled the control engineer in the steel tower near the station and the red tram slid noiselessly out on the breathless eight-minute journey across the gorge.

Lorenzo, who perspired every inch of the way across the depths, was huddled in a seat with his wet hands between his knees, his eyes closed, mutely beseeching Jesus, Mary and St. Christopher to keep him safe. Only the prospect of the bridge tourney which lay at the other end of the cables gave him the courage to make the crossing.

Cora was none too secure herself, but so contemptuous of her trembling partner was she that she stood in the front of the tram with her short legs spread for balance, her hands folded across her plump behind in the best captain-of-the-ship manner and stared deliberately down into the chasm.

Markey was exhilarated by heights as becomes a mountain climber and Jessica was, of course, fearless. Dr. Friendly was not fearless, but his profession had made him a fatalist and, besides, his good sense told him that the machinery of the aerial tram was scrupulously maintained by the management of the lodge. One did not pay five hundred and fifty dollars a night for a double room unless the innkeeper kept her plant in perfect working order.

The tram docked under the sloping roof of the upper station and the porters were waiting to take the luggage and escort the guests to the lobby.

On the terrace which faced out upon the gorge and was screened from the wind by glass, where luncheon could be had while watching the trams slide up and down their cables, Emil von Rothke was allowing his shaved head to turn pink in the warm afternoon sun as he stuffed himself with rare filet mignon, candied yams, sauerkraut, limestone lettuce, garlic bread and, eventually, a thick slice of lemon cream pie, all washed down by red bordeaux. Surprisingly, Emil was not fat. He was barrel-chested and solid, but not fat, and his secret was that he ate only this one complete meal a day. After the meal, he would rest from his gustatory exertions for two hours, take an ice cold shower, present himself perfectly groomed at the bridge tables and there he would have the stamina to remain for ten to twelve hours with only an infrequent snack and without once retiring to use the toilet.

Emil von Rothke's column was syndicated around the world in twenty-four languages. "Von Rothke on Bridge" was eagerly read by every man and woman, black, white, brown or yellow who had ever finessed a jack. He was also ardently hated and feared by every professional player with whom he had played, and that was most of them, because he had no hesitation about attacking them and their game styles in his column. It was, in fact, part of his own style to make his opponents fear his ridicule. It caused them to play too cautiously.

Across the white-clothed table sat his partner, a small, gray-faced, sharp-nosed fox of a man named Archie Epstein. Archie picked at a broiled trout and carrots and sipped black coffee. He was rarely known to speak except for the necessaries at the bridge table, but so relentless and accurate was his game that the great Von Rothke had never been known to criticize his partner's play.

Said Emil, "Do I see Lorenzo and Cora? Yes?"

Archie looked and nodded. Emil rose, napkin tucked into his collar, a fork with yams on it in one hand and a knife in the other, strode to the edge of the terrace and peered over the glass windscreen. "Lorenzo, Cora, my friends!" Emil bellowed.

On the curl of stairs which climbed from the dock to the lodge porch, Cora and Lorenzo stopped and looked up. "It's that g Nazi," Cora said. Lorenzo bowed and smiled.

"We have the game tonight, yes?" shouted Emil.

"Not tonight with that goddam Nazi," muttered Cora.

"Of course, Emil," Lorenzo called. "Our pleasure."

"Good, good," roared Emil, and returned to his table.

"You damn fool, we're too tired," Cora said.

"Just one little rubber, Cora, dear?" begged Lorenzo, the pation gleaming in his eyes.

"We'll lose our ass," said Cora.

From the windows of her apartment, Arlene Kirbo had w Markey and the others arrive on the tram. She looked fe eagerly to tea with Markey that afternoon. The artist was go her lonely soul and perhaps the only person she knew who stood that hers was a lonely soul. It was not a subject of disc between them, rather that all-seeing talent of his made her kn grasped the truth about her. In his presence she did not fee she was hiding.

Arly shook her head in sad amusement as she watched and Lorenzo come up the steps from the station. They had bee ular guests in this season for a number of years and she had their running battles in their rooms many times. She always sa they were housed near the very end of the west wing and, if po arranged for an empty room between them and their nearest bors.

Arly observed that Clarice Bishop had not brought bac man for whom she had kept an adjoining room for almost a Arly momentarily expected a cancellation of that extra room. Clarice. For all her beauty and money she was such a hapless ture.

Dr. Friendly's young wife pleased Arly. Possibly she had ried him for his money and prestige. But no matter. Friendl become a changed man. He looked ten years younger and his went a pleased pink when Jessica clung to his arm. Before h married her, he had always come alone to the lodge to rest. H been stooped and pale, but now his stride was firm, his sho back, the tint on his hair becoming. Arly suspected that Jessica him something he had never before had in his distinguished Whatever it was, she was all for it. He deserved it.

As Arly saw Paul Binns step off the tram she rang the desl

3

Caiphus Clark Kirbo, at one time in his life, was thought to be and, in fact, was, one of the richest men in the world. His fortune was founded upon an item sold in drugstores and labeled Kirbo's Skinnays.

Skinnays were a silky, thin contraceptive manufactured from the skin of carp fish and were better known as "fishskins." Promoted by his father, George Freestate Kirbo, they were a somewhat more expensive device than the common rubber condom. The thing about them that held George Freestate's estate down to a mere half-million dollars was that the Skinnay had to be dampened before use. One couldn't just be snapped on at the hot physiological moment; its user had to have water to soften it. It sold well until the backseats of automobiles became the most active trysting sites. Draining water from the car's radiator to make the Skinnay pliable was not conducive to instant seduction. Still, son Caiphus inherited enough money to start him on his way to a fortune.

He plowed the inheritance into a newfangled invention, the innerspring mattress, a rather logical step from contraceptives. Those leaky sleeves which served birth control so inadequately were operative in producing a bed whose squeaking springs did not disturb the children as the Skinnay-clad head of the house lunged about in what he believed to be a baby-safe ejaculation.

From this basic need of civilized America, Caiphus went on to other basic needs—a no-split toilet seat, rolled toilet paper and its cute snap-in wall fixture, a hot-patch kit for punctured tires, dental material for false teeth that Bourbon whiskey wouldn't turn black and, finally coming a full circle, he was the first to market a vaginal diaphragm. All of this led to vast holdings in real estate and oil wells, and all of that led to huge and monstrously profitable speculations in the stock market. And made Kirbo's Lodge possible.

With a bunch of his cronies, he was on a fishing trip in the high Sierra, where the guides did most of the fishing while the sportsmen played poker at the camp tables and drank Bourbon before breakfast. It was here that Caiphus one day at noon left his boozy companions and rode off with the guide foreman to see what the foreman called "the damndest place you'll ever see in these mountains."

For two hours, they urged their mounts higher and higher on a faint track over ridges and through flowering meadows and beside cool tarns until they reached a point which looked down upon that glacier that had first been named Gornaad's glacier, after the Swiss explorer who had found it in the early nineteenth century, but for whatever reason had lost its possessive character and was now simply *the* Gornaad.

The guide led Caiphus down along a razorbacked ridge beside the vast, smoking sea of ice until they came to its lower rim, where, thousands of years before, a mighty earthquake had tumbled half a mountain into the glacial gorge at a time when the glacier had withdrawn to its highest level. Then the earth had turned colder and the Gornaad had begun to swell and move again into the gorge, only to find itself blocked by the crumpled mountain. It could do no more than trickle its melt over and through the dam into the lower gorge, where that trickle formed a lake. The lake was formed because the lower gorge was also blocked, first by crashing peaks in the same earthquake and then by the inexorable rising of the Sierra escarpment. So here they were, glacier and lake, caught forever in a granite prison.

The dam in the gorge had been worn and smoothed by two hundred centuries and halfway down its slope was the hidden, forested flat of about fifteen acres which hung magically between the mists on the glacier and the lake far below. "That's it, Mr. Kirbo," said the guide.

They rode down the mile-long slope beside the rushing Gornaad Creek through the talus of the fallen mountains and reached that petite meadow covered with montane flowers and surrounded by towering sugar pines. In its center, concealed from the view above, there was a perfectly round pond of steaming hot water. "That water don't come from the glacier," the guide explained.

"They's a vent somewhere in the old gorge walls that feeds that hot water from way down in the mountains."

Caiphus stood in wonder beside the pond and lifted his eyes to the concave wall that rose for almost two thousand feet on one side of the meadow. "God must have used his ice cream scooper to make that cliff," he had said.

"Danged if he didn't," agreed the guide.

And that wall became known as The Scoop to the rock climbers who later came to Kirbo's Lodge. But at this moment, Caiphus had not yet conceived of the lodge. It took him another ten minutes. He shucked his clothing and waded into the hot pond. It was there, while steaming the Bourbon whiskey out of his pores, that he knew what he had to do.

Within weeks a team of engineers was camped beside the pond of hot water and had begun exploration into the problem given them by Caiphus. Since the glacial gorge did not debouch upon the valley between the Sierra and the White ranges, there was no access to the meadow except as Caiphus had first come—over miles of narrow trails deep inside the Sierra. It was not practical to bring building materials through those primitive paths and, besides, Caiphus wanted to be able to drive his Pierce-Arrow touring car to the lodge's front door.

The engineers mapped a route up from the valley floor through a twisting canyon, over ridges into other canyons, a route that would require bridges and tunnels but would finally arrive at the precipice above the glacial gorge. But here the roadway must stop. Mr. Kirbo would not be able to drive to his front door. The best they could do was to propose that from the end of the road an aerial cable car would deliver Mr. Kirbo across the gorge to the magic meadow.

Caiphus was not deterred. If anything, he was delighted. That small, rotund man with the determined chin and scheming eyes who had dealt with the sophistications of no-split toilet seats was not to be put off by the common likes of mountain roads and aerial cables.

Through friends in high places and discreet drops of cash, he obtained the necessary inholding rights for his lodge and its access roadway. Next he caused a landing to be constructed on the shore of the lake in the valley and into the lake he put a paddle-wheel steamer which would connect with the railroad which ran on the other side of the lake and would ferry machinery and mules and men and materials to the landing called Kirbo's. There he built a temporary village of tar paper houses to shelter the work force and the work began in the spring of 1920.

In the fall of 1924 the roadway reached the terminal above the glacial gorge. The Swiss aerial cable experts began their chores in the following spring after the snow pack had melted, were delayed by the succeeding winter, but in the spring of 1926 the first tram whizzed across the chasm and, in that same summer, architects ordered the pouring of the first concrete for the foundations of the lodge. In the fall of 1927, Caiphus took possession of the three-story, forty-room palace below the Gornaad.

From start to finish he had spent nineteen and one half million dollars on his dream and that at a time when the only thing harder than the American dollar was the granite of the Sierra.

No sooner had he claimed his spacious, thick-walled castle than a geological survey conducted by the government reported to Mr. Kirbo that he had built his lodge precisely astraddle a main tributary of the Sierra Nevada earthquake fault.

Now, the celebrated San Andreas fault, which streaks through California from San Francisco in the north to the Sea of Cortés on the south, is spectacular mainly because it can be seen as it races through lush vineyards, tracks vividly across the Carrizo Plains, slashes like a mighty sword through the rotten San Gabriel Mountains and rips on to meet the Colorado River where the river meets the sea—and because it once trashed a young and rickety San Francisco. Its works are great and its final splitting of the continent some millions of years hence will no doubt be newsworthy, but until that time the works of the Sierra Nevada fault must stand as the most inspiring monument to a moving crack in the crust of our globe. The Sierra Nevada fault has created the high Sierra.

The fault and its tributaries cannot be seen so plainly as the San Andreas complex, but in its secret, crooked way it has sculpted those granite temples of the Sierra. Rarely does it make a display of its power, preferring to nudge and chip and gently jack its peaks closer to the sky, but that temblor which stopped a ponderous glacier in its own gorge must have been a corker.

As reported to Caiphus, the last quake of note had occurred in March of 1872 and that must also have been something to behold. Mt. Whitney, that prize among the growing alpine crags, was punched fifty feet higher in one staggering moment on that cold March night of the last century.

Over in the Yosemite gorge, John Muir, the naturalist who claimed the Sierra as his own personal love, was present for that fearful quaking instant. "The shocks were so violent and varied," he wrote, "and succeeded one another so closely, that I had to balance myself carefully in walking, as if on the deck of a ship among waves. . . . Suddenly there came a tremendous roar. The Eagle Rock on the south wall gave way and I saw it falling in thousands of great boulders . . . pouring to the valley floor in a free curve luminous from friction, making a terribly sublime spectacle—an arc of glowing, passionate fire fifteen hundred feet in its span. . . . The sound was so tremendously deep and broad and earnest, the whole earth, like a living creature, seemed to have at last found a voice and to be calling to her sister planets. In trying to tell something of the size of this awful sound, it seems to me that if all the thunder of all the storms I had ever heard were condensed into one roar, it would not equal that rock-roar."

Caiphus was having a light dinner of fried ham and biscuits with red-eye gravy in his stateroom aboard the steamboat when the news of his appalling mistake was handed him. He slopped his last biscuit into the crimson gravy, munched it with thoughtful relish and asked, "Well, what's my chances?"

"Mr. Kirbo," the geologist said, "the mountains might move again tomorrow or in the next minute or they might not move again for a thousand years."

"Them's chances," Caiphus said in his best sixth grade grammar, which was all he had since his father had believed in the work ethic and not in the education ethic, "them's chances I'll take." And he promptly hired a wood-carver to hew the prophetic legend into the beam above the door of the lodge. The first part, which read, "Dear Friends and Kind Strangers, welcome to my Lodge. Be merry, rattle and shake with me" was actually conceived by a boozy newspaperman in Caiphus' retinue. But it was Caiphus who added the last words, "if you die, the Fault is not mine." The play upon the word "fault" afforded large amusement to Caiphus.

4

A knock sounded on the door of Arly's apartment—the same apartment her father had had constructed especially for her when the lodge was built, small and intimate quarters for the young girl she then was, and she had not changed it through the years. Arly opened the door for Paul Binns. They shook hands and she asked him to sit, told him he looked well.

"So do you, Miss Kirbo," said Paul.

"Shall we drop the Miss Kirbo for this season, Paul? In honor of your second season with me, why don't you call me Arly?"

And Paul realized that he had been admitted to the inner circle of the big staff that flowed about this small, square-shouldered woman with calculating eyes. His only answer was a polite "Thanks, Arly."

It was an answer that pleased her, indicative of the security he had in himself, which was one of the reasons she liked him. A tough mind was behind his wry face and her own sinewy intellect responded to it.

"Until the snow falls, I'd like you to fill a shift in the Earthquake Room, if you don't object."

"Sure."

"But would you object to wearing the Earthquake Room bartender's uniform—the white jacket and black trousers?"

"I guess I can stand it for a couple of weeks," Paul said.

"Good. I'm giving you an apartment in the dormitory. You seem to collect so many friends, I thought you might like to have space for them if you should care to use it."

The two-room apartments in the staff dormitory were usually reserved for the supervisory personnel of the lodge.

creaked and groaned and at times, far up against the
he friction between the moving fissures in its surface
ange and echoing shrieks of agony.

or beast hurts," Markey had said to Arly.

only a frozen snow pack," she had replied.

think of it as *only*," said Markey. "It's just that we don't
hat else things are."

Malraux, in an article about Markey's works, had
n the artist's perception and had concluded his observa-
e following: "We cannot understand why Cabot Markey
does and, try as he might, he cannot truly articulate the
f. We, and he, must be satisfied with the end result and
describe: it is the energy, the force of creation. He
ere is life in a stone or in ice or in wind. As Van Gogh
sun as an explosion in the sky, so Markey paints a
a gnarled fist thrust up from the living musculature of
Ve must call it genius. What else?"

had completed the painting of the Gornaad in the end
's greenhouse, where Arly had had space cleared for him
e was the first to see it, its final touches of oil not yet
was not a pretender to artistic sensitivity and from that
n standing before the huge canvas there came not one
amation. Said she, "Name your price. I want it."

his perch on the top of the stepladder beside the painting,
looked down into her earnest face. He had become
ly. Above all things, he admired courage, and Arly was
that. "Will you hang it where the light's good?"

orangery," said she.

it's a gift," said Markey.

Paul Binns, Arly didn't go on unnecessarily about any-
stared up at the lean man on the ladder just long enough
nced that he meant the offer, and then said, "Thanks."

later, when Markey returned to the lodge from one of
s to the odd ends of the earth, he had found not his usual
waiting for him, but a studio built on top of the lodge's
—his studio.

like it, Cabot?" Arly had found him in the orangery. He
the painting with a wave of his hand and bent to kiss her
ek. Arly squeezed his hand and felt the hard stubs of his
little fingers where he had lost their first joints from frost-

"I wouldn't want to waste it," Paul replied. "Generally, all I
need is a place to sleep. I liked my single room from last year."

"Take it anyway," said Arly. He nodded. She smiled, her teeth
white and even, her skin smooth, with tiny spider tracks about her
eyes and the corners of her mouth. She looked forty. She was sixty.
"Did you like Greece?" she asked. He nodded again. "Your letter
came from Itea. I was there once. On a yacht. We anchored there
and took a bus to Delphi. I remember it vividly." She waited. If he
wanted to talk about himself, she had opened the way.

"I was there all summer," Paul volunteered. "I had a job with a
touring agency, guiding American tourists through the Delphi
ruins."

"I remember we had an American student take us through
Delphi." Take us. Take Arlene and Elsa. She remembered Elsa
more than she remembered Delphi.

"You know," said Paul, "this place is like Delphi must have
been. The richest Romans coming to take the baths and drink the
wine and consult the oracles in the most expensive resort on earth."

"And who's Pythia here? Not I."

"You're probably smarter than Pythia ever was. Another thing.
Delphi was built on a big fault just like this lodge."

Arly laughed. "And was destroyed. Well, until the big shake
comes, let's make the most of our Delphi."

"I'm with you, Arly," said Paul. "For another season anyway."

"I'd like to discuss that with you sometime this year. Not just
another season, Paul."

"We can talk," he said.

When he had gone, Arly again thought of Elsa and that led her
to thoughts of Tati and Jeannette and brought her forward in time to
Francine. Yes, she must determine what to do about Francine.

In her bathroom, Clarice Bishop stepped off the scales. One
hundred and twelve pounds. Perfect. She looked at herself in the
full-length mirror. Perfect. Now, because that architect in San
Francisco had disappointed her, three times promising to be on the
plane from San Francisco (she wouldn't call the bastard again), she
would eat too much and drink too much and get fat. It always happened. And smoke too much and cough. He wasn't worth it.

She went down the steps into the sunken bath and turned on the overhead jets and let the hot water sting her skin and pour into her hair. For ten minutes she stood in the shower and now, swathed in the thick white body towel the lodge provided for its guests, sat in the hair-drying chair, brushing her gold-red hair under the hot, rushing air.

Having accomplished all of this, she padded, barefooted, into the bed-sitting room. She opened the wall refrigerator, filled a dish with caviar, popped the cork on a split of champagne and sprawled into a deep chair to wolf down the caviar and gulp the wine. Clarice was starved most of the time. If she let herself go completely, she would be a balloon and a drunk. But she couldn't stand to be either of those things so, as a rule, she suffered. But not at this moment. And she knew exactly what she was going to do next—what she had to do next—but she delayed it. She had more caviar and champagne, smoking a cigarette between swallows. She snapped the television remote control and dialed in a daytime game show, snapped off the set and dialed music into the room. She lay down on the sofa and stared at the ceiling. Enough of that. She rose and pressed the switch that brought the room separator from its wall recess. The big pink curtain slid slowly and silently across the room, shutting off the afternoon light from that end of the room where sat the wide, deep bed.

From a secret compartment in one of her hand-tooled bags, she brought forth a small white instrument. She dumped its old batteries and put in fresh ones and, dropping the towel on the floor, she lay on the bed, touched the button on the mechanism and felt it come alive in her fingers. She moved its vibrating tip over her breasts and stomach and pressed it into her body. She cried out softly as the whirring little dildo did its work and left it there until she and its batteries were exhausted.

Now she wept and, finally, slept. One round arm was bent beneath her head, her body twisted at the waist, one long, fine leg scissored across the other. Her delicately curved belly moved pliantly with her quiet breathing. The true line of her hip and buttock could not have been duplicated by Scopas himself and her breasts were like Rosalind's orbs of heavenly frame. Perfect.

In the big studio atop the lodge's west wing, Cabot Markey had fallen asleep almost immediately after his arrival. Two hours later,

---

he awakened with some sense of pression of jet lag. He bathed an moved to the high, slanted wind meadow toward the north and t late sunlight made that hard gray sculpture, indeed as if a giant sp ange ice cream. From its base to the most challenging climbs in the Markey's first visit to the lodge son

It began with a gentle slope t halfway up, its wall began to lean version. For that distance the clim ropes and pitons, and for the las working at almost a forty-five de wall.

Markey had made the ascent done it alone. Except for those fe upon the summit of Mount Ever had given him his most profound se

He turned from the windows short flight of private stairs into th the west wing, past the door to the asleep in all her naked beauty, an with him down the wide stairs into t

He walked through the lobby was to meet Arly for tea. She was ceeded through that long, high-bea where hung his painting of the Gor room, placed on the wide wall whi fifteen-by-twenty-foot canvas, it wa lodge. In the summer, Arly allowed lovers to visit the painting and then take the lift to the glacier and see the

Markey studied the work. The l his paintings by natural light. Lying seemed to be a living, suffering fossi been allowed to die. One could al Markey had heard them in the early settling miserably down into its bo

---

summer. It mountains, produced st

"The po
"But it'
"Don't always see

André dwelled upc tions with t paints as he thing himse that we ca shows us th painted the mountain a the earth.

Marke of the lodg to work. S dry. Arly small persc phony excl

From Markey ha fond of A the soul of

"In th
"Ther

Like thing. She to be conv

A yea his journey single roo west wing

"Still dismissed on the ch third and

bite on a climb in the Himalayas. Arly didn't understand why some men climbed mountains, though she had seen enough of them in the lodge, until Markey had given her a quite simple explanation by asking her a question. "What do you do to make yourself feel more alive, more conscious of living? Nothing?" She had had no answer to give him, but afterward she had reflected upon it and had known when she had been the most conscious of living. It had been when she was in love, as she now was. It struck her that if Markey had to climb mountains to find that feeling, then for all his great talent, his adventures, his fame and insight, he was in some secret part of him a failure.

They moved from the orangery into the great hall and to a tea table which had been set for them. There were other guests in the hall, four Japanese gentlemen in traditional lounging dress who later would change to black ties and dinner jackets and take their places at bridge tables in the cardroom; a table of wealthy, white-haired widows; an Arab prince from one of the emirates and his bridge partner; a British planter from Rhodesia; and in a secluded corner, Dr. Friendly and Jessica, to whom Arly had already paid her respects. One of the white-haired widows recognized Markey and told her companions and shortly all four went in the orangery to view the painting of the Gornaad with more intimate interest since the artist was now in residence.

As tea was served, Markey squinted at Arly as he might squint at a detail of a work in progress. "What's going on?" he asked.

Arly busied herself with the teapot and felt a flush come into her cheeks. "How do you know something's going on? How do you know those things?"

"I don't know, Arly. I can't help it."

"Yes, something's going on."

"Are you being careful?"

"Oh, god, yes." She had an exceptionally happy look and a quickness in her movements that Markey knew had an origin in something more than his return to the lodge. Once before in the years he had known her, he had sensed an expanding of her spirit and had watched it fade and seep away. Somewhere in her past, Arly had been treated cruelly and, for all her toughness, Markey understood that she was extremely cautious with her emotions.

"The most extraordinary woman rode up with me in the limo today," said Markey, and watched Arly closely as he said it.

"Clarice Bishop," she said. "Poor Clarice."

No, Clarice Bishop wasn't the one. "Poor? Why poor?"

"She's such a mess. I've known her for a few years. She's been here occasionally, but never when you were here or you'd know her and understand. In her own way, she's as freaky as I am."

"I can't think of you as freaky."

"But you know damn well I am—or sometimes I am. Clarice always is. She spends a fortune calling her psychiatrist. Her problem is that she can't keep a man. Oh, she could buy one, but that won't do for her. She chooses men who can't be bought and they very quickly don't want her."

"That's hard to believe, to look at her."

"You'll meet her—or she'll meet you. You're exactly the sort she's drawn to. And you'll see what I mean. Oh, you, of course, will see a great deal more, but the first thing you'll note is that she's an incredible narcissist."

They went on to talk of other matters, the lodge, her plans for its future, his journey to Europe. But she had aroused his interest in Clarice Bishop. Markey was interested in difficult people. Arly, in her own charming way, was difficult. But he would have no time to devote to that amazingly beautiful woman named Clarice.

"I'm tired, Arly. I think I'll have another nap before dinner."

"Yes, do. Your hand shook with that teacup."

He realized that as he had been scrutinizing her, she had been giving him the same treatment. "My hands always shake," he said.

"No, they don't. You've been ill."

"As a matter of fact, I have. In London."

"Well, this is home. You rest. I'll look after you."

He smiled and rose from his chair. He bent to kiss her cheek again and left the hall. Arly noticed the slight stoop in his broad shoulders and the slowness of his step. He not only had been ill, he was now. Well, he would explain more in his own time. He trusted her. She poured another spot of tea for herself and worried, not about Markey, because to worry about him was pointless, this man who had deliberately spent much of his life courting death. She had, after all, through binoculars, watched him inch his way alone and unaided up the face of the Scoop, heard the ring of his hammer as he confidently drove pitons into cracks in the granite wall and had seen him swing out over that awful depth to catch a crevice by that hand with the chopped fingers. Arly's worry was about herself, whether or not at this hour to pay another casual visit to the accounting office behind the main desk in the lobby. It was, she knew, an absurd worry. It was her lodge and her accounting office and Francine was her employee. But Arly was, in this delicate area of her life, as shy as a child. She had to be, as she had told Markey she was, careful.

As Arly sipped her cooling tea and fretted, in the far corner of the hall Jessica Friendly looked at her happy, past-middle-aged husband over her own cup of tea and decided it was time for his afternoon amusement. "Daddy," said she, "take me upstairs and do things to me."

5

When Diane Haynes had seen Paul Binns come from the tram station, she had waited at the window, knowing he had likely been sent directly to Arlene Kirbo's apartment but would again appear, this time on the walkway from the main building of the lodge to the entrance of the employees' dormitory. Appear he did, scuffling along with his canvas val-pak, and Diane gave her hair a quick shake before the mirror to loosen it about her face and ran down the stairs to stand forthrightly in the dormitory foyer. Through the open door she could see Paul. He had been stopped by another employee of the lodge, a sub-chef, and was shaking hands with the man.

Diane seized the opportunity to hitch up her slacks and smooth her sweater over her hips. Paul came on toward the dormitory and entered. Diane was squarely in the middle of the corridor in a militant stance, legs apart, head up and with her eyes seeking Paul's. He glanced at her, looked away and passed her. He didn't even remember her. Diane felt as if she were crumbling like a pillar of sand.

His voice came from over her shoulder. "What are you doing, pal? Directing traffic?"

She spun around into his wide smile. "Damn you!" said Diane.

"Hey, I've got an apartment this time," Paul said. "Let's take a look at it." He walked on to the stairs and Diane obediently followed.

Diane was a tall girl and slender. She wore glasses for her nearsighted brown eyes, but her eyes were wide apart and her cheekbones broad beside her rather nice nose, and the glasses, as sometimes happens, added to her attractiveness. She was outgoing and hardworking in her winter job as one of the cocktail waitresses in the great hall, where Paul had reigned behind the snowtime bar.

She had fallen in love with him, or at least as much in love as one can fall when receiving no encouragement from the object of that love. In that winter she had lived in a perpetual state of anger at herself.

Diane was a well-ordered young woman with considerable certainty about herself and what she wanted from life. First, she wanted to be a teacher and to that end she gathered the necessary education at the University of California in Santa Barbara in the summer. She had her B.A. degree and was working on her M.A. At some point along the way before she was thirty, she expected to add a husband and at least one child, but not at the expense of her career. She was her own support and, with the generous tips she made in the winter at the lodge, she even was able to contribute to the support of a younger brother and sister in Los Angeles, where her mother worked as a secretary.

Diane had lied about her age and gone to work as a part-time waitress in a pie shop, pushing on through high school and into college. In her second year of college, she had made the connection with Kirbo's Lodge, and now her life was ordered to winters of work and summers of study.

Those unhappy years in America, the late sixties and early seventies, the years of the drug scene, of dropping acid and dropping out, which had swept up so many young people in their ugly tides, had hardly dampened the firmly planted feet of young Diane Haynes. She had lost her virginity at sixteen, but nothing more damaging than that had been permitted.

So one can understand the humiliation of this rock of a young lady when she had realized as she stood at the service section of the snowtime bar waiting for that shambling young man with the hard eyes and ragged sweaters to make drinks for her tray, that she was like a supplicant waiting for the high priest to notice her. When he would place the filled glasses on her tray and smile, she would find herself not breathing, and all the way across the great hall to the group she was serving she would curse herself for being the poor fool she was.

Diane was not a good skier, but she made the effort to be part of the activity and mingle with the guests as Miss Kirbo had decreed. Through the windows of the ski shack near the lifts where one could watch the skiers come flying into view on the lower slopes of the runs, Diane had many times watched Paul Binns rocket into the last turn of Number Three, the fastest run in the complex. He always did it with style, crouched over, clouds of powder rising from under his skis, his sticks caught back under his arms. None, not even the professionals, could take Number Three with better style than Paul. "Yes, he's good," she had heard one of them say. "But," he added, "it's too easy for him. He won't work at it." And Diane had thought that, yes, it was too easy, that everything he did was too easy, and she determined that she would not be that easy for him. But then, in the shack, a laughing group would be gathered about Paul near the fire which roared up its flue in the center of the shelter, and from across the room he would see her and lift his thumb and grin and her breath would stop, as usual.

On a Sunday night in February, when the business in the snowtime bar was slow because so many skiers ended their week's reservations on Sunday, Paul had waved her to the bar from her idle station. "You're putting yourself through school—right?" he'd asked. She had nodded.

"Tell me about it."

"Why?"

"Because I'm interested." And he had looked interested. Diane, feeling that a *deus ex machina* had finally descended to rescue her from her misery, found herself blindly babbling the history of her life and seemed unable to stop the tumble of words. When at last she panted out her aims for the future, Paul had said, "Good. You've got a direction. I envy you."

"Don't you have one?"

"I wouldn't know one if it poked me in the eye." And he had moved away to an Italian miss at the bar who was wearing a three-hundred-dollar English cashmere sweater and was calling for an Irish coffee in bad French but who actually wanted attention from the American bartender. As Paul mixed the hot drink, he had flicked a wink in Diane's direction. It was all the encouragement Diane needed, she being a convinced believer in women's liberation.

Was she not making her own way, educating herself, preparing to meet life on her own terms? Need she wait to be ravished?

When the snowtime bar closed at 2 A.M., Diane girded herself to do an act of liberation. She bathed and scented her body, donned pink pajamas and a white robe and slipped through the quiet halls of the dormitory to Paul's door. And knocked.

The door had opened. He had been dressed in a grubby terry

cloth robe and had a book in his hand. He had stared at her and seemed not too pleased. "What's up?" asked Paul.

"I'd like to come in. That's what's up." She knew she was glaring at him through her glasses.

"It's too late, pal," said Paul. She had the feeling he was not speaking of the hour. Without another word, she turned and marched away, feeling her disgrace rising in great, hot waves from her face into her scalp. In her room, she had not wept, but sat shivering with anger on her bed. It had been daylight before she fell asleep.

On that Monday afternoon, a new snow had begun to drift down from the dark, low clouds, and Diane had gone to the lodge's library, that big, peaceful room with its tall windows, stacks of books to its high ceiling and ladders to climb and polished oak tables for its readers to sit by. She had found Paul there hunched over a volume in the light of a green-shaded table lamp.

She had quickly turned to leave, but his "Diane," in a loud whisper, had stopped her. He motioned her to the chair across the table from his. "You're sore at me," he suggested.

"It's nothing. Just a matter of murder." They were talking in whispers. There were a few guests in the library.

"We can't have that. We have to work together."

"We'll manage. You make the drinks and I'll ferry them."

"We should talk it out."

"Okay," said Diane. "I'm for that." She leaned across the table. "I'm a fair sort and I'm affectionate and it seems to me when a fair sort like me offers herself to a fellow who's not a damn bit better than I am, the least he can do is not make some stupid excuse about it being too late."

"I didn't handle it too well, did I?"

"You can bet your teeth you didn't."

"Let's take a walk," said Paul. He pulled on a wool cap and an old Navy pea coat and waited for her response. She rose and wrapped her scarf over her head and zipped her padded ski jacket.

They had walked silently for a few minutes in the windless day through the dry, falling snow. Paul had said, "Listen, I'll tell you the truth. I was in pain last night. I have lots of pain."

She remembered the stories she had heard of the cruel scars on his body. "All of the time?" she asked.

"Not all of the time," he had answered, "but last night was one of them." They continued to walk; the path led them through the pines to the bank of the hot, smoking pond. On the bank Paul turned to her, took her face in his gloved hands and kissed her. "I'm sorry," he said. He kissed her again. Warm breath came through their noses and steamed her glasses. She turned from him, sought a tissue in her pocket.

"Goddamit," said Diane, "here I am kissing Jesus and I can't even see him." And they laughed.

But he had not taken her to his bed and she had not presented herself again. She had to content herself with his friendship, with that straw of satisfaction. And now it was the second year and in the intervening months she had not known whether he was alive or dead or whether she would ever see him again.

She followed him up the stairs. "What did you do with the summer?" she inquired.

"Went to Greece," said he. No further explanation. He went to Greece. Everyone goes to Greece. Of course. Silly question.

"What does Arly have you doing?"

"In the Earthquake Room till snow."

"So am I. Maybe we'll have the same shift."

He found his assigned quarters and they went in. The apartment was small and plain but not without charm. "Look! How about that? I've even got a kitchen," said Paul, and tested the oven door, then peered into the refrigerator. "I'll cook for us."

"Us including me?" Diane was dubious.

"You don't think I can cook?"

"I'd bet my teeth you can cook. You can probably show the French chefs a trick or two."

He turned to her and studied her for a moment. "Are you going to be in love with me again?"

"Certainly not. I scarcely know you."

"That's true. You scarcely know me."

"See you in the Earthquake Room," said Diane, thumbed her nose at him and left the apartment. It hadn't been so bad. She felt buoyant and cheerful. It would be a good winter and there would be fun and laughs and, if she went about it in just the right, neat way, he might come around.

6

Arly had finished her tea and gone into the lobby, where she conferred with Harry Ames in reception. He had briefed her on the current reservations, his choice of rooms or suites for certain incoming guests, and she had made a few suggestions which he had duly noted but would probably ignore, because Harry was the unerring master of hotel reception and knew it. He had learned his trade at Claridge's in London, and besides, he had been with Arly for twenty years and knew the guests of Kirbo's Lodge as well, if not better, than did she. That tall, dapper man with the pencil moustache and twitching nose, deploying his staff like chessmen, played the game of cajoling the egos of the lodge's rich, spoiled clients with the swift calculation of a mathematician. Complaints were rare under Harry's management.

Having dutifully listened to Harry's recitation of futures, Arly went directly into the accounting room and to a file cabinet, which she unlocked with a key from the pocket of her white blazer. She thumbed authoritatively into the file, but in her side vision she took account of Francine Sharpe. Francine was wearing a simple gray dress that struck her just below her slim knees, gray suede shoes with low heels, a lavender scarf about her neck and small pearl earrings in the lobes of her precious ears. Her ash-blond hair was pinned up off the back of her white neck, her lipstick was a pale pink, she had a white-gold ring with a tiny opal on the third finger of her right hand, her nail polish was pink and, as she stood before the computer studying the print-out, she blinked one eye as if a lash were caught and brushed at it with a blue Kleenex tissue. All of this Arly grasped hungrily.

She closed the file, locked it, glanced about the spacious room (all rooms were spacious in the lodge, nothing cramped) and at its half-dozen employees, noted their industry over their typewriters or their adding machines, and casually moved to beside Francine. "Is dumbo behaving?" she asked. Because the computer sometimes produced addled figures, it was called "dumbo."

Francine turned her cool green eyes upon Arly and smiled. "Not one mistake today," said she. She was the computer programmer for the office, age twenty-seven, from Chicago, unmarried, no family in California, worked for four years with an oil company before being sent to Arly from San Francisco. All this Arly had learned when she had interviewed Francine two months before.

Francine had been wearing a little pillbox hat, white gloves and had held her knees together with her toes pointed straight. She had been shy but demurely proud and her gaze had not left Arly's face as they talked. She had seemed to Arly like a young woman from another time, from the 1930s, when jobs were scarce and applicants dressed appropriately and conducted themselves to persuade you of their well-bred respectability. Francine had been like a pretty wind-up porcelain doll from that distant period and Arly had felt the desire to touch her as one wants to touch those delicate figurines.

Arly had hired her quickly and had been rewarded with a blushing smile and an extended white-gloved hand that lay in her own small hand like a weightless white flower. And now Arly for these past two months had been like a grower of orchids, watching this most rare blossom breathe, circling it, peering at it, shielding it, feeding it with nourishing encouragement, but never once daring to caress it for fear that it might wilt.

The best that she could do at this moment in the accounting office was to say, probably for the twentieth time, "It's given us much less trouble since you came, Francine."

And Francine said, "Thank you."

Arly remained beside Francine, watching the computer machine-gun its collected information. She was headily aware of the scent of L'Air du Temps emanating from the pristine young woman.

"According to the time sheets, you've been working late," said Arly.

"Just now and then, Miss Kirbo."

"Tonight?"

"Yes, ma'am. Till about eight-thirty."

Arly could feel a vein pulsing in her throat and her mouth was dry. "Francine," said she, "before you leave, stop by my apartment, will you, please?"

Francine turned her face to Arly and Arly could see alarm in the parted lips. "I've a suggestion that may make your work easier," Arly hastened to explain. Francine nodded and obediently agreed to stop by the apartment. Arly left the accounting office and inwardly she was trembling, the palms of her hands damp.

* * *

On a rainy night in the late spring of 1936, Caiphus Kirbo fell to his death from the open door of his own aerial tram. His body was never recovered from the icy deeps of the gorge lake, but that he went in was beyond a doubt. He had driven alone up the road from the valley in a Cord convertible and stumbled, drunk and singing, into the tram. He had signaled the engineer in the control tower and the tram had been sent whizzing out into the darkness. It had arrived at the lodge's dock sans Caiphus Kirbo. The control engineer reported that he had heard a cry from the spaces over the lake —not a scream of terror, but an insanely joyous whooping.

"Just like a fellow riding a bucking horse," he had described it.

In the aftermath of the plunge, it was discovered that the Kirbo fortune was collapsing in a huge heap of financial rubble as so many other fortunes had done in those years. The insurance companies tried desperately to prove that Caiphus had committed suicide, because he had left double indemnity policies totaling more than a million dollars to his sixteen-year-old daughter, Arlene Kirbo.

Arlene, not yet of legal age, had instructed her attorneys to hold fast, make no compromises, demand payment, and all the batteries of insurance investigators and threats of insurance lawyers could not put the fear of anything in young Miss Kirbo's knot-headed determination to get what was rightfully hers. It was beside the point that she alone knew her father had killed himself. A note she had found in a safe-deposit box in San Francisco had given her instructions:

Honey, I am sick the sawbones tells me, my liver he says and besides I am not as smart as I thought I was and that is hard to take. Just don't let the insurance lawyers screw you out of one nickel. Stand up to them and kick ass. Forgive me honey. I love you the best.

                                                            Dad.

Arly had burned the note and kicked ass and collected more than two million in cash.

Armed with an education from expensive European schools where her father had placed her upon the early death of her mother, and with an inherited wile for business, Arly had engaged the realities of the Great Depression with her razor-sharp wits.

Her growing-up years in Europe, where her school chums lived in palazzos and châteaus, where she had summered as a guest in grand villas on the Côte d'Azur or sailed the Mediterranean in white yachts, had given her a steady faith in the very rich. She believed, her father notwithstanding, that the rich would remain rich even through the worst of times.

Arly set about converting Kirbo's Lodge from a private dwelling into a public dwelling, but only for those of the public who could afford that exquisite retreat hidden behind the colossal escarpment of the high Sierra.

She enlarged the swimming pool (fed by the hot spring from the round pond) and the stables, reconstructed the interior of the main lodge to satisfy the purposes of a hotel, added a north wing with eighty more rooms and/or suites, built a staff dormitory, bulldozed ski runs into the slopes that rose to the glacier and, while all this was being done, she herself took a crash course in hotel management at an eastern university.

When all was ready, Arly hired a small troop of experienced personnel and one summer morning in 1938 walked to the tram station and from its platform hurled the key to the lodge's front door into the gorge where her father had died.

In the history of innkeeping, never had there been an inn to compare to Arly's lodge—and it is not likely one will ever again appear. While soup kitchens were feeding the unemployed across America and Hitler was consolidating his power in hungry Germany; while governments were toppling and Communism was the fairest word of the day; while the grapes of wrath were being stamped out in the Kansas dust bowl and the rich were hoarding gold and diamonds in New York, London and Paris, Arly Kirbo let it be known in fashionable international publications that those who wished could find a super-exclusive retreat from the sights of poverty and the fears of revolution high in the western mountains of the United States for the modest price of thirty dollars a night for two and sixty dollars for suites, European plan, of course.

By the time Franklin Delano Roosevelt was campaigning for his third term, Arly had found it necessary to establish a system of reservations by reference. If you had stayed in the lodge before, you could obtain a reservation. But if you were a newcomer, your request would be in vain unless it was accompanied by a reference from one of those on the approved list of guests. And a double room by the night had jumped to fifty dollars, the suites to one hundred.

After World War II, a west wing was built with fifty-five rooms and ten suites. It was now one hundred dollars per room and two hundred for the larger accommodations.

The lake in the valley had long since disappeared into the aqueducts to Los Angeles, the steamboat had been sold and the railroad had died, but paved highways reached Kirbo's Landing from the north and south, and Arly had caused the first airstrip to be laid. Until a commercial charter was granted, she provided private air transport from San Francisco and Los Angeles. With the commercial charter and the burgeoning industry of private plane manufacturing, the airport at Kirbo's Landing became a thriving little terminal. A long row of hangars went up for private planes and a field was set aside for plane anchorage, and the big heated garage for guests' cars was built. With all of this the prices were rising at the lodge—one hundred and fifty for a double room, three hundred for a suite.

By the middle sixties, Arly had added the Swiss chalets among the pines, used only in the winter for skiers—four to a room in the chalets, one hundred dollars a night per person—while in the main lodge it is needless to say that the prices were mounting. By the year 1979, two people could take their ease for one night for three hundred and fifty dollars and up, and the suites rented for six hundred to one thousand.

The prices of food and drink had increased proportionately. A dinner for two in the main dining room was never less than a hundred dollars (wine or drinks not included), although one could save a bit by eating in the coffee shop, where the cost of a steak sandwich was a modest nineteen-fifty.

According to the figures of the Internal Revenue Service, Kirbo's Lodge Corporation was grossing almost forty million dollars a year. And it was, relatively, still a small resort hotel.

Arly's faith in the rich had remained steadfast and they had not let her down. She was turning them away.

Was the lodge truly deserving of its prodigious success? Yes, if you accept the value of a painting by Van Gogh or Cabot Markey; if you find that originality meaningful; if you understand that Van Gogh's sun or Markey's mountains did not exist until they painted those subjects; and that while imitations can now be had, they must remain imitations, then you will understand the success of Kirbo's Lodge. Unlike those paintings, it cannot be imitated. It can only be remembered by those who once stayed there. This is what they remember: the palatial rooms, the splendrous suites, the happy fires laid in the bedroom fireplaces, the bowls of fresh-cut flowers from the lodge's own greenhouse; the champagne and caviar and icy white grapes in the refrigerators, the red buttons one pressed for service, which service was instantly at the door twenty-four hours a day; the snapping clear water from golden taps, the glittering hot swimming pool with snow-laden pines just outside its glass windscreens; the bathhouses where tired old bodies or abused young ones could be kneaded and slapped and steamed into condition; the horseback safaris to the chain of mirror lakes beyond the Gornaad, where golden trout leaped to the angler's cast and where plump blue grouse awaited the hunters' guns; motion pictures in the great hall after dinner that had not yet been seen outside the Hollywood studio projection rooms, obtained by Arly Kirbo because she had symbiotic connections with movie moguls—they got reservations if she got pictures—the baccarat tables which were uncovered at night in the baroque casino (a lodge such as this was beyond the law); the upper pavilion on the edge of the glacier where one could dine in the summer by the light of the full moon and watch skaters on a rink cut from ice that had witnessed the demise of the woolly mammoth; but most of all, one remembered the remoteness of the lodge, remembered its majestic, magical place on earth, remembered it as one remembers a fairy tale from childhood. And that memory is all that is left.

The road which twisted up into the canyons is impenetrable now, its tunnels crashed, its bridges wrecked, and if you take a plane over the Sierra peaks and look down into that depth where the lodge was once such a merry place, there is nothing to be seen—no ruins —nothing remains of Kirbo's Lodge—nothing.

At 8 P.M. Jessica and Dr. Friendly were dining in their room by candlelight. The waiter who usually stood by to serve from the hot cabinet beneath the table had been dismissed that they might have privacy. Friendly was rosy-cheeked and comfortable in cotton slacks, turtleneck sweater and slippers, and Jessica was naked. It pleased the doctor to dine with her in that manner.

In the cardroom, Lorenzo and Cora were sitting down with Emil von Rothke and Archie Epstein, much against Cora's better judgment. The true gambler instinctively knows when his luck is running and Cora was a truer gambler than Lorenzo. He had no instinct at all. To joust with Emil and Archie required more than skill; the stars had to be just right. When Cora picked up her first hand of cards, she knew the stars were wrong.

At the same time that Jessica's pretty breasts were bouncing as she attacked a savory steak and Cora was glumly studying her luckless cards, Cabot Markey was stirring from another few hours of restless sleep. His dreams had been scattershot dreams, pointless flashes of faces and movement—faces he did not know in places he had never seen.

He opened his eyes and stared up at the beamed ceiling of his studio bedroom. Light reflected from the surface of the lighted swimming pool which lay outside the west wing came through his windows and flitted across the dark beams and seemed to make them wriggle. Markey listened to the beating of his heart, a habit he had never had and disliked intensely. But still he listened until, impatient with his indulgence, he rolled to his feet, went into the bathroom and laved cold water over his face and neck and stopped the sound of his heart.

He dressed and walked to the lobby and then up the red-carpeted stairs to the Earthquake Room. There were not many guests in that famous lounge at this hour. A tall young cocktail waitress spoke to him. He could not recall her name, though he knew her face, but she was kind enough to give her name.

"Diane Haynes, Mr. Markey."

"Yes, of course," said Markey. "Back for another winter, are you?"

She smiled and agreed that that was the case. "Do you want a table?" she asked. Markey chose to go to the bar. He ordered a vermouth cassis from the bartender and knew that he had also seen this face before.

"My name's Cabot Markey," he said.

"Yes, sir. We met last winter," said the bartender, "and we rode up in the limousine today."

"Of course," said Markey.

"I'm Paul Binns."

Paul Binns. Arly's prize. At tea she had told Markey with some elation that the mysterious Paul Binns had returned for another winter—from Greece or some such place.

"Yes. You're the snowtime bartender," said Markey.

Paul smiled, the smile crinkling his face, and Markey found himself smiling in return. It was contagious.

"I may be snowtiming in a couple of days or sooner," said Paul as he deftly mixed the drink. "There's a low pressure moving in, according to the reports, and not a weak one."

As Markey sipped the vermouth cassis, they discussed the snow records of the past. It was early for important snow, but there had been those years when blizzards tore across the western states in October. Paul recalled that in Wyoming, where he had grown up and learned to ski, he had once been on the boards in September.

As he talked, Markey considered the young man's angular face and the curiously thick eyelashes which shuttered his direct eyes. Cold eyes, thought Markey. Binns was a man who would protect himself first, so Markey's ever sensitive antennae told him. Not a man to have on a rope. Not a team man. A loner.

Diane came to the service gate and gave an order. Markey noted the way her attention was worshipfully upon Paul as he mixed the order. Pity the girl who involved herself with that young man. Yet Arly had said that Paul involved himself with no one. Odd. Markey would guess him to be an opportunist with women. He had

the look, the confidence of a youth who had a sure and callous hand with the other sex.

Several more people had arrived at the bar and Paul was busy. Markey occupied himself with details of the Earthquake Room, as it had pleased him to do many times. Arly had not tried to conceal the lodge's precarious situation—she had capitalized on it. All around the walls of the lounge were large back-lighted photographs of earthquake results—some in color, as was the wreckage of Anchorage, Alaska; older photos in black and white, the smoking ruins of San Francisco and Tokyo.

The drink menus featured exotic concoctions named Tsunami Wave, Assam Slam, Sanriku Shake—and in the center of the lounge, in a glassed-in case and ominous blue light, sat a seismograph, its spidery claws recording the movements of the mountains.

Stacked in a specially built cove behind the bar was a pyramid of big, thin wine glasses, over which there glowed a green light. When a quiver was passed through the mountains by the Sierra Nevada fault, those wine glasses would ring out as they trembled and the green light would change to red and the drinks were then on the house. It had not happened too often, but when it did, it was a gala occasion in the Earthquake Room, and guests who had been coming for years to the lodge remembered those occasions with great affection. Those who had not experienced those exciting moments, always—at least once a night—repaired to the lounge with hopes of becoming initiated during their stay on that meadow below the Gornaad.

When Markey had first come to the lodge, he had marveled at the seeming lack of fear of its guests, at their eagerness to feel a quake beneath their feet and to hear the wine glasses ring out. He had soon realized that they simply did not believe in the danger and saw only a multimillion-dollar establishment that (despite Caiphus Kirbo's warning on the lintel) would never have been constructed if there had been the remotest chance of disaster. Oh, perhaps a small chance. But small chances make life interesting for the bored and sated, as were so many of the visitors to that hotel.

Among all the people who came to vacation at the lodge or worked there, Markey knew of at least one who did not treat the matter of an earthquake lightly. Arly.

The seismograph in the lounge was a real one, but not accurate because it was not seated in bedrock. There was another, and only one of several instruments, that lay at the end of a long tunnel beneath the lodge—in a room quarried into the wall of the glacial gorge. Markey had gone into that damp, secret room with Arly and the team from Caltech's seismological laboratory who came every three months to take the pulse of the mountains. Besides an accurately working seismograph, there was a tiltmeter, a scintillation counter and a magnetometer.

If it was possible to predict a major quake, Arly intended to take advantage of that possibility and close the lodge before the quake could happen. She was kept abreast of all the newest theories by the experts from Caltech and did not hesitate to invest in the latest equipment to measure the shudders of the mountains that could not be detected except by the most sensitive of machines. So far, the Caltech people had not been able to tell Arly more than Caiphus had been told years before, that it could happen in the next minute or not for a thousand years.

Markey saw that the doors to the casino, which opened off the lounge, had been closed for the season. Arly was not in the business of gambling and operated the casino only during the peak months of the summer, and even then took no cut of the action for the lodge.

Markey had thought to distract himself for a little while at the tables, but now he knew it would have been pointless. There was no real distraction for him.

The cocktail he was drinking was biting into his stomach and reminded him that he had not eaten since morning. He beckoned to Paul. "Is the upper pavilion still open?" he asked. He was told that it was serving until ten-thirty, buffet only.

He paid for the drink, left a tip and moved through the lounge and out upon its terrace. The terrace was deserted, the umbrellas above its luncheon tables folded for the night. Markey paused at its railing and watched the lighted cars of the aerial cable winging their way above the gorge. They looked frail and tiny in the huge darkness. He was always gratified by the boldness of his species. How undaunted was man by the awful reality of his condition. He did not cower upon this trembling, stormy planet, oppressed by the inexplicable vastness of the universe; instead, he challenged it all—strung cables across chasms, hurled rockets into the sky, built cities that must finally be dust, and lived as if he would endure forever, refusing to believe that he was nothing more than an accident.

Markey had a clear, literal belief in a Creator, but it was, like his paintings, his own peculiar conception. He believed that life was an accident, something the Creator had not intended to happen—a careless slip in the cosmic laboratory, a piece of bubbling mold tossed into the refuse bin, where it had clung desperately to its slimy existence unnoticed through eternity.

Markey had been asked why so many of his paintings were gigantic in size. "So God might see them" was his answer. He had cheered the thrust into outer space. Perhaps those machines ripping through the cold vacuum beyond the earth might call attention to what was germinating here in the wastebasket. It was told of him that when he reached the summit of Mt. Everest he shook his mittened fist into the shrieking wind and shouted, "Here we are, you clumsy bastard! Look at us!"

Markey left the terrace, went to his room and tugged on his Burberry reversible, let himself out of his studio's garden exit and descended to the path which led through the pines to the ski tram. He walked with deliberate slowness and was contemptuous of himself for doing so. Had he not yet had enough of life? Why should he guard himself against the inevitable? Still, he walked slowly and consciously fed his lungs with deep breaths of the thin mountain air.

He passed the hot pond and paused, his attention caught by the movement in the water, as if a current were running. It was always still water, a slow seep from its source beneath the mountains and was heated by exposure to the earth's hot mantle. As Markey watched the pond, its surface again became placid. He concluded the movement had been an illusion of the night and he went on toward the lift depot.

In the depot, the attendant brought the cables to a halt and opened the door of a gondola for Markey. He stepped into the dark interior and seated himself in the rear that he might look back down the slopes as the lift carried him up toward the glacier level. It presented a splendid view of Kirbo's Lodge—the shielded lamps on the paths through the pines, the Olympic pool with its underwater glow, the gabled old main building of the lodge and the long arms of its added wings, most of the windows bright in the night; below the now black wall of the Scoop, the dormitory windows were also lighted and, as the lift rose higher and higher, one could see into the gorge and the lake, where reflections from the lodge were like distant, myriad fireflies. The moving trams were even tinier now and the lighted tram station on the far side of the gorge seemed many miles away; beyond the station, the blue mercury lamps on the road to the valley wound off through the mountains and were finally lost in a canyon.

The spectacle took Markey out of himself and he was no longer conscious of his own breathing. This was his natural element, high and alone, his artist's eye arranging the patterns of light and darkness.

But far below, with none to see, the current was running again in the hot pond.

In the bar lounge, Paul went easily about his work, chatting with customers who remembered him from the first winter. He was not disappointed that Markey had not lingered at the bar. He was uncomfortable with the artist. The man looked at one too closely. Most people didn't *look* at you; they responded to you. Markey inspected you as if you were an object. Even as he was talking to you, he was reading you. Paul knew from Markey's quick glance that he had made the connection between Diane and himself when she had come to place a drink order. Paul was annoyed by that canny observation. He felt his privacy had been invaded. Not that Markey was a threat. His interest was in passing. He might never look at Paul again. It was just that Paul had formed a carapace about himself and he did not want people poking about underneath it. He wanted all his relationships to be bright and superficial. Stay out. No entry. In here I'm secure and content. Leave me be.

He endured Diane—even liked her. She bounced off him like a ball against a board fence and she was none the worse for it. He knew that soft as her heart was, it would not break easily. He need not feel responsibility for her any more than he felt it for those other admirers he collected.

The past summer in Greece he had lived with a wealthy Englishwoman who was, like him, emotionally unattached. It had been entirely satisfactory for both. He had amused her and made her happy in bed and she had been more than liberal. When it had come time for him to go, as she had known he would, her eyes had become moist and she had stuffed money into his pockets, driven him to the airport in Athens, kissed him on the cheek and not waited to see him board the plane. That was the only kind of relationship Paul wanted. He had had too much of the other kind, and too soon in his life.

In Dr. Friendly's room, Jessica was lying stomach down on the bed and her loving husband was massaging the small of her back with many a kiss upon and gentle nibble at the flesh of her fetchingly rounded posterior. She had complained of low back pain where none existed, simply to make an excuse for him to administer to her body. She knew that he knew there was no pain, that she was leading him. From the beginning, Jessica had had to lead the doctor, so shy was he and mindful of the difference in their ages. She was at all times the aggressor, the seducer. In a few moments she would roll over on her back and delight him by drawing his head down to between her spread thighs.

In the cardroom, Lorenzo and Cora were losing. Emil and his lethal partner, Archie, were forty-five thousand dollars richer and, as Archie silently played the hand they had bid, Emil further unnerved pale Lorenzo and angry, red-faced Cora by calmly munching a snack of fried potato skins filled with caviar, which he helped down his gullet with great drafts of ice-cold vodka. Only a fool or a man of supreme confidence would drink liquor in a game like this. Emil was no fool.

Every table in the elegant, soundproofed chamber was teamed. This was not a card party of laughter, gossip and cheerful losers, nor was it a bridge tournament where the skills of the players are admired and the fall of the cards discussed with intellectual enthusiasm. The games in this room were for blood and the blood was money. Except for murmured bids, carefully shuffled cards, an occasional cough, the snap of a cigarette lighter, the players might have been robots placed upright at the tables. Even the cigarette smoke was tense as it was jerked through the pyramids of light above the tables on its way to the exhaust fans in the ceiling.

The waiters who stood like sentinels about the room did not move unless a hand signal moved them to bring food or drink or new decks of cards.

The faces of the players described the nationalities of half the world. A team from Peru with the dark skins of the Inca faced two rosy-cheeked Scots. Two Japanese in big horn-rimmed glasses played against a long-jawed Swede and his fat Spanish partner. A Lebanese was coupled with a redheaded Pole, and a woman from London who wore a wide-brimmed gardening hat to shield her eyes from the light sat opposite a squat, beetle-browed Turk from Istanbul. Two Chinese merchant gamblers from Singapore, dressed in black silk suits, engaged the turbaned prince from the emirates and his Rhodesian partner, and if a census were taken of all the players' origins, the names of Montreal and Marrakesh, Paris, France, and Paris, Illinois, Rotterdam and Rochester, Haiti and Houston would not have been in the least surprising.

Nor was it surprising that in this room so rapt were its players that they ignored the little quake which, in the Earthquake Room, made the wine glasses sing and the claws of the seismograph scribble and brought cheers from the guests as Paul announced that drinks were on the house.

Nor did it disturb Friendly and Jessica on their bed, her legs about his shoulders, or Markey riding in the lift to the upper pavilion, where he would again see that extraordinary beauty named Clarice Bishop.

And in the hot pond the current ran faster and bubbles of steam burst on its surface.

8

Arly had so many times in the past forty-odd years felt the mountains move that she could guess the Richter scale measurements. The light tremor that had just occurred she would place at 2.5 to 3 magnitude. The strongest she had experienced had been in 1952—a 4.8 rumble and nothing to fear. It had caused no damage and had more than pleased the habitués of the Earthquake Room. The old-timers among her guests still spoke knowingly of the Quake of '52, and told how the wine glasses had actually collapsed in a crystal heap. Thrilling.

The original lodge was rock-solid and Arly had had the new wings built to structural specifications for any shake up to 7.5 on the scale, which was the limit to which any architect would commit himself. Since the force of an earthquake multiplies almost incredibly with each point on the scale, there was no way to insure against the bludgeoning that would transpire if the magnitude reached 8 or more. There lay the risk for the lodge, but the risk was small. Few quakes in recorded history had touched 8.

Arly straightened a Steuben bud vase which had fallen over on her desk in the light rattle of moments before and again took up her vigil for Francine. It was eight-forty now and Francine had said she would be leaving the accounting room by eight-thirty.

Only the contact personnel lived at the lodge. The office help, maintenance people, kitchen workers, most behind-the-scene employees had their own quarters in the towns of Lone Pine and Bishop not far from Kirbo's Landing. It was the same Lone Pine that had been devastated by the quake of 1872.

When Francine finished work, she had to take the tram and the employees' limousine to the valley, where she drove in her own car from the Landing to Lone Pine.

The doorbell chimed softly and Arly took a last look in the mirror. She had bathed and dressed in a black, slimming pants suit, applied a makeup for the lights of evening, brushed her becoming short hair until it fell just so over her ears and forehead—and was utterly depressed by her anticipation of Francine's visit. Her mouth was still dry and her hands damp.

She opened the door and Francine was there, looking dainty in her white gloves, little fur hat and fur-collared tweed coat.

"I'm sorry to keep you waiting," said she.

"Oh, Francine!" exclaimed Arly. "I'd almost forgotten. Please come in." She could hear the quaver in her voice and knew, though Francine might not, how ridiculous she was. No matter how she appeared, she was sixty years old and foolishly infatuated with this demure young creature in white gloves. Arly would have liked to take those quaintly sheathed hands in her own and kiss their freshly laundered palms. Instead she said, "Sit down, dear. Could I give you something to drink?" And her voice was firm again.

"I'm not much for cocktails," said Francine.

"I'm having cold white wine." Arly indicated a glass on the desk.

"I think I'd like that," Francine agreed.

Arly poured from the bottle in the wine cooler and brought it to Francine's white glove. Their fingers touched and Arly coveted the moment. Why could she not be a man? It would be so simple. Dr. Friendly had a young wife—many older men had young wives or mistresses. It was not simple for an aging homosexual, and a closet one at that.

"Francine, I'm going to suggest that you live here at the lodge," she said. "Working late as you do and living in Lone Pine is not easy for a woman. Especially with winter coming."

"I don't really mind the trip to Lone Pine."

"You will. You haven't seen our winter yet."

"But what would be the difference in my pay if I stayed here?" asked Francine very sensibly.

"None," said Arly. "But the dormitory will be full. You'd have a single room here in the main building. In fact, a room next to my apartment that I keep vacant for personal use—a friend now and then." She had said it. It was out. There was no way for Francine not to understand. Arly had managed to be looking away as she made the proposition and she was afraid now to engage Francine's eyes. She poured more wine for herself. A silence swelled in the room. Finally, Arly turned to Francine. The young woman's clear eyes were exactly upon hers, unblinking and thoughtful and without alarm.

"That's very kind of you, Miss Kirbo," said Francine.

"Nonsense. You're the only one who's been able to make dumbo behave. You've become indispensable, my dear." Arly walked to the window and looked out into the gorge, where the trams were swinging along like lighted matchboxes above the lake. She was now, curiously, at ease. What was done was done. Proceed. "It's up to you, Francine. I only thought it might be easier for you to live here." And she realized Francine had not refused or even suggested hesitancy. She glanced over her shoulder and the other was sitting with her gloved hands clasped on her knees, her head bowed, the top of her hat presented to Arly.

"That's the sum of what I had to suggest," said Arly.

Francine remained still. Her glass of wine, almost untouched, sat beneath the yellow lamp on the table beside the sofa.

"May I see the room?"

At the question, Arly's throat closed. She wanted to laugh, but no sound would come. She strode to her desk, took a key from a drawer and turned to Francine. Francine was standing, waiting, her face still and kind.

Arly beckoned her to follow and led her across the living room, where she unlocked a door and stood back for Francine to precede her into the adjoining room. The breath of her cologne was close. Arly came behind her and snapped on a lamp in the room.

"It's charming," said Francine. Arly waited. Francine turned to her. "Are you sure?"

"Of course I'm sure." What did Francine mean? That there would be talk about them or simply sure that she wanted Francine to have the room? Arly was afraid to ask for clarification. Perhaps Francine did not understand. "Move in tomorrow if you like," said Arly.

"Thank you. I will."

"You can go out this way." Arly opened the door into the lodge corridor. "Good night."

"Good night."

Francine stepped into the corridor and turned back. Again those clear eyes were fixed upon Arly's face. "I may not, you know," she said. "I may change my mind."

"If you do, please consider the offer a friendly gesture and forget I made it."

"I understand," said Francine, and walked away down the corridor.

Arly closed the door and did something she had not done in many years. She sat on the bed and burst into tears, her knuckles pressed childishly against her wet eyelids.

The buffet table was arranged in the center of the upper pavilion. At one end, a chef in a white uniform and tall cap waited to carve roast beef or lamb or ladle out a fricassee of chicken. Diners could approach the hot food service from either side of the long table, selecting salads, fruits and exotics as they moved toward the chef.

Markey was carefully picking small portions of delicacies for his plate, avoiding shellfish and worrying about the salt content of everything else, when he became aware, through the hanging pink lights above the table, of the woman keeping pace with him on the other side. He first saw the emeralds and diamonds on fingers which spooned gourmand helpings for her plate, piling salad upon salad, jell upon jell; the plate was a mound of food and still she piled on more. Wondering at this greed, Markey bent his head to peer under the pink lights and discovered Clarice Bishop. Her eyes, a glossy purple in the pink light, for a moment locked into his and went immediately back to the appetizing delights on the table.

They continued to move together until they reached the chef. Markey waited politely for Clarice to make her selection. She chose the red roast beef and, as the chef carved, she glanced again at Markey. He smiled and nodded and received no response but a remote stare.

A waiter took Clarice's stacked plate and the plate with the cut of beef, adjusted them on his tray and led her away toward a table by the wide windows which looked out on the glacier. Markey marveled at her slim figure in contrast to the gluttonous plate she had built. She was dressed in a pale blue pants suit trimmed in white ermine. Her hair was piled carelessly on top of her head. She walked with an almost exaggerated swing of her hips and, as she crossed the pavilion, attention trailed behind her and there was not a person there who did not watch her progress. At the table she tucked the big white napkin into the collar of her jacket and let it fall like a lobster bib across her front. She instantly attacked the food, bending over her plates, both hands working hungrily.

Markey was guided to a table not far from Clarice's place and found that, by a casual turn of his head, he could observe her without being obvious. He watched, fascinated, as that great heap of food disappeared into Clarice's rose-painted mouth. A waiter stood by, replenishing her glass with a ruby wine as she gulped it behind each unchewed swallow.

She was finished long before Markey and shifted her chair that she might face the windows. Lighting a long brown cigarette, she expelled a cloud of smoke which curled against the pane like fog.

The pavilion was not crowded on this night, most of the guests preferring to stay in the main dining room of the lodge rather than take the chilly trip to the glacier in the gondola. Bright spotlights outside the pavilion illuminated the glacier and on the skating rink a family of four, man and wife and two small daughters, glided about like shadows against the silvery ice.

Markey sat for a little after his meal, watching the skaters, then collected his coat from the checkroom and walked out on the decking of the pavilion. He passed the window behind which Clarice sat smoking and went down the steps to the narrow boardwalk which stretched out upon the Gornaad like a pier. He strolled on the boardwalk until he reached the darkness beyond the lights of the pavilion and continued to the small observation platform at the very end of the walkway. Here he sat on a bench and listened.

The glacier was making little creaking sounds, unhappy murmurs at its plight. Markey noted that the ski-path flags had been placed on the ice. When snow came, big snowmobiles would carry skiers across the glacier and up to the saddle in the mountains at the far edge of the ice, and from there they could come racing down, guided away from dangerous crevasses by the flags. The glacier run fed into the slope run, Number Three, and from the saddle to the lift depot the distance was, for experienced skiers, a wild, swift flight of almost three miles.

Markey pushed his legs out, crossed his ankles and leaned back upon the bench to look into the sky. There was a gibbous moon and high clouds were being swept across its face by a northwest wind.

He was reminded that Paul had said a storm was brewing. That wind could be its beginning.

All about the glacier towered the mountains and in the moonlight their peaks were frosty white. We think of mountains as always being there. But like everything else on this planet, the planet itself and its sun, mountains have a life-span. The Sierra was probably several million years old—an infant among mountains, and growing. In the valley near Lone Pine were some low red-rock hills which were eras older than the Sierra. Once they had been giants on the landscape and, in another age or so, would be pebbles in the sand, while the Sierra might match the Himalayas. This passage of the mountains through time had always inspired Markey. It was the thing that he painted, and that he could paint it made him feel less insignificant in the accident of life. Markey knew he was not a candidate for the Button Molder. He would be remembered at least for a while in that flash of centuries in which man would inhabit the world.

Far out on the Gornaad a crevasse of unknown depth split down through the blue interior silence of the glacier to perhaps its very bottom. There was where Markey planned to complete his cycle. When it suited him, as it soon would, he would make his way alone at night (perhaps a snowy night, since a storm was threatening) and stand with his back to the crevasse, the gun in his mouth. The shot would send him, gun and all, falling into that blue silence. His end would not be known. For some reason that he had not yet explained to himself, a peculiar madness, the notion of disappearance pleased him.

Markey heard footsteps on the boardwalk. He did not look around, but from the sharp heel sounds he knew the intruder was a woman.

Clarice Bishop moved out onto the platform and sat on a bench near him. She was wrapped in a thick black mink coat which had a hood that covered her head, leaving only her face in the moonlight. She lighted a cigarette and, letting it dangle in her mouth, buried her hands in the deep pockets of the coat.

She said, "You're Cabot Markey." The cigarette bobbed in her lips as she spoke.

"And you?" Markey suggested.

"I'm sure you know who I am. If you don't, you have no curiosity at all."

"I know your name," Markey said. "And I know you have an astonishing appetite."

"You watched that, huh? I do that sometimes. Overdo. Stuff and get drunk, lie about like a pig."

"Not too often, I'm sure."

"No. Not too often."

"What brings it on?"

"Disappointment."

"That's ordinary enough."

She looked up at the moon and her face was like white marble, her lips blue and her eyes black pits.

"That's a deathly light. It doesn't do you justice, Mrs. Bishop."

"Nothing does," said Clarice. She pulled the fur hood over her brow and shut out the moon. "Do you think I'm beautiful?"

"Yes."

"How beautiful?"

"Like your appetite. Astonishing. But why ask a question when you know the answer?"

"You're Cabot Markey!"

"So you've established."

"If I'm that beautiful, wouldn't you like to paint me?"

"I haven't painted a portrait in many years. I'd be too rusty at it, Mrs. Bishop."

"I've seen portraits you've done. At least one. In the Tate in London. Lady someone or the other."

"A special case."

"For a whole, huge lot of money? I can pay, you know."

"I meant, she was special."

"You were in love?"

Markey saw no reason to develop the conversation along those personal lines and he was silent. They were both silent for a time. Clarice drew on the cigarette and tossed it over the platform railing.

"I've never been painted by anyone really worthwhile," said she.

"But you've been painted, I'm sure. Many times."

"Junk paintings."

"Never done you justice?"

Clarice dismissed justice with a wave of her hand.

"And photographs?"

"Thousands. I've a library."

"That should be enough of one's self," said Markey.

"I don't really care what you think about it, or anyone." She sulked back into the cave of black fur.

Markey waited.

"What would be your price for painting me?"

"I can't be commissioned, Mrs. Bishop."

"How can I persuade you then?"

"You can't."

"Wouldn't you be interested if I'd pose in the nude?"

Markey almost laughed. Arly had been right. The woman was ridiculously in love with herself. How, he thought, could there be such hollowness under all that beauty?

"I don't really care if you think I'm foolish," said Clarice. "I'm used to it."

"You knew I was thinking that?"

"Of course."

Then she was not so foolish. Her presentation of herself was deliberate. Markey encouraged her. "Is your body good?"

"Unbelievable."

"I'm sure."

"No, I mean it. I'd be glad to give you a preview. Now, if you like."

"Not here, surely."

"My room—or yours?"

"I'll take your word for it. But the answer's still no, Mrs. Bishop."

"You're a coy sonofabitch, Mr. Markey."

"It wasn't fair of me to tease you."

"I'm used to that, too." She lighted another cigarette. The wind coming off the peaks stirred the fur of her coat. The temperature was dropping by the moment. She rose and stood looking down at him. "I'm going in," she said, and walked slowly away, the wind snatching at the smoke of her cigarette.

"I'll go with you," said Markey. She paused and he joined her. They walked back toward the lights of the pavilion. Why not paint her? thought Markey. There was no unfinished work on the easels in his studio. He could leave an unfinished work. A nude woman. It would go well with his disappearance. In a hundred years it would be called Cabot Markey's "Unfinished Woman." The name of the model would be lost and only the legend of it being Markey's last work would remain.

"You understand that if I painted you, the canvas would be mine, not yours, don't you?"

"I'd expect to buy it."

"No. It wouldn't be for sale."

"I'd just be the model?"

"Nothing more."

She threw her cigarette away. He wondered why she lighted them. A few idle puffs and they were tossed aside.

"You'd have to sign a paper that you had no claim on the painting."

She was thinking this over as they walked. It was not part of her plan not to own the painting.

"Who'd see it?" she asked.

"It would be hung. Never fear."

"I wouldn't fear, but I'd like it to be seen by as many people as possible."

"I'd arrange for it to go to a museum where thousands of people would pass by and look at it."

"I'd like that," said Clarice.

Markey could sense that she was rolling the idea about like a taste of almond divinity: Clarice Bishop, nude, on a special gallery wall of the Metropolitan, forever.

"Be in my studio at eight in the morning. We'll begin."

"Eight—in the morning?" It was a gasp.

"The light's best in the morning."

"Well, my god, I'm not."

"I won't paint the morning circles under your eyes."

"I don't have morning circles."

"No, I suppose you don't."

"I look the same, morning, noon or night. And I don't need makeup. Lipstick is all I use. My lips are too pale."

"Your only flaw."

"One other. I have a birthmark under my left breast."

"Good. I'll paint it. We'll call the painting 'The Birthmark.'"

Clarice laughed. Its tone surprised him, a low, gurgling laugh and not unappealing. It would be interesting, thought Markey, to discover what else this woman was. But that might take a long time and he had none to spare.

Lorenzo mopped his face and played the wrong card, which Archie promptly trumped and took the lead to a slam bid that Cora had doubled. Without finishing the hand, Cora threw her cards across the table into Lorenzo's face and stumped from the room on her short legs.

This wordless altercation caused only a moment's nervous pause in the games in the room. Lorenzo apologized in whispers to Emil and Archie and followed her. Emil and Archie bent over their scores and calculated their winnings. Seventy-three thousand dollars.

Lorenzo stormed into the suite he occupied with Cora and found her sitting calmly in front of the television set, shoes off, a bottle of beer on the table beside her chair.

"You have humiliated me for the last time!" he shouted.

Cora tipped the bottle of beer to her mouth. He snatched the bottle away and hurled it across the room, where it bounced and spewed foam in protest.

"Pay attention when I speak!" cried Lorenzo.

"You led with a diamond, you goddam senile wop," commented Cora.

"I didn't double. You doubled, you smelly old bitch!"

"Shit on you. I'm going to bed."

"We'll see who shits on who," yelled Lorenzo. "If there's any shitting, it's going to be my shit!"

"Well, you've got enough of it for sixteen people," muttered Cora.

Lorenzo hurled a vase of fresh white roses at Cora. Water splashed in her face and the roses spilled and caught in her cardigan sweater by their tiny thorns. She came from the chair, her bosom decorated by long-stemmed beauties, and feinted a kick at Lorenzo's crotch. When he dropped his hands to shield that vital part, Cora caught him high on the left cheek with a roundhouse swing of her fist, and thin, lightweight Lorenzo fell over a hassock that had a thunderbird design in its cloth and landed on his back on an antique Navajo rug (they had the suite called Piute, which featured an American Indian motif).

As Lorenzo tried to get his Gucci-shod feet under his scrawny legs, Cora delivered a barefooted kick to his rump, which straightened him out on the floor and deposited his head in a bookshelf beneath the television set. A wooden bust of Sitting Bull fell from above the set and landed on Lorenzo's neck at the same time two heavy volumes of Catlin's engravings of Sioux Indians collapsed on his head. On the television screen a band of Comanche was pursuing the hero of an old western flick as Cora counted coup on Lorenzo by opening the refrigerator, grabbing a pitcher of yogurt (which he fancied as a bedtime tranquilizer), pouring it on the seat of his pants, and shouting, "Stuff your yogurt up your ass!" as if the yogurt had been the reason for their fight. She thrashed into her bedroom, locked the door and left Lorenzo groaning in the bookcase.

In another part of the west wing, Archie and Emil entered their suite.

"Do you want a nightcap?" Emil spoke in German. When they were alone, they always spoke in German. The shadings of their native language permitted a better understanding between them, or as much understanding as was possible between these disparate men and their ultimate characters.

Archie didn't answer Emil. It was not necessary. Emil had asked the question knowing he would not receive an answer. Archie never took a nightcap.

Archie walked to the windows and pressed the button which activated the silent electric motor that opened or closed the drapes. The drapes slid open and Archie unlatched a window and pushed it outward. He breathed deeply of the night air. "Too much smoke in card games. Why do they smoke?"

Emil volunteered no answer to this question, as Archie knew he would not. Emil stirred scotch into milk and dropped in an ice cube.

"The sky is clouding," said Archie.

"It's going to snow," Emil said.

Archie closed the window, but remained there, looking out. What is he seeing? Emil wondered. Is he seeing Bavaria in the winter?—beautiful, white Bavaria—or is he seeing other things? Emil hoped Archie was seeing beautiful Bavaria and not other things.

And Archie thought, He knows what I'm seeing. How can I not see it, the snow in Belsen, the frozen bodies like stacked cords of wood? If it rained, Archie saw the rain falling in Belsen. Or if the sun was shining, it was shining on the metal helmets of the German guards in Belsen.

"I'm going to bed, Herr von Rothke," said Archie.

Emil clicked his heels and bowed, extending his hand. Archie accepted the hand in his.

"Good night, Herr Epstein," said Emil.

Archie's mouth formed what might have been a smile had its shape been more pronounced. He released the hand and went into his room, closing the door behind him.

Emil sat in a chair beneath a standing lamp and sipped his scotch and milk and sighed heavily as a man does whose burden is eternal.

In his bedroom Archie sat upon his bed, his head bowed, his hands dangling between his legs as a man does whose search for forgiveness has left him exhausted.

9

When she left Arly in the lodge's corridor, Francine Sharpe felt the triumph an actress might feel at having given the consummate performance of her career. Alone in the tram as it carried her across the gorge, Francine sang aloud and stamped her little feet in delight. Arly Kirbo, that famous innkeeper and wealthy woman of the world, had finally capitulated.

If Francine could remain prudent and keep the image of purity she had established with Arly, she would reap—oh, who could even project?—rewards of immeasurable value: money, gifts, travel and then inheritance—maybe the lodge itself.

For as long as she could remember, Francine had felt deprived. An only child, she had always lived in railroad apartments, the kind with all the rooms off one side of the long hallway and the narrow toilet at the end, because her father, the credit manager of a small department store, had never been able to accumulate the down payment necessary to buy a house. She lived with her parents in the same building for fifteen years and they stayed there mainly because the owner was willing to accept one quiet little girl. In return for this tolerant attitude, he felt it was unnecessary to invest in any upkeep of the apartment.

It was Francine's misfortune that the old building in which she lived was barely within the school district that encompassed one of the most affluent areas of the city and so her classmates were the children of prosperous parents. They lived in big, expensive homes and their mothers were active in chic charity work, their fathers, doctors, lawyers, advertising men and chairmen of the boards of large companies. In class or outside, whenever the subject of her father's profession came up, Francine always said he was dead—killed in the foreign service—and that she lived with her mother, who was a cousin to the King of the Belgians.

She was a pretty little girl and might have been popular with her peers except for her completely humorless and self-defeating determination to be what she was not. By the time she was twelve years old, Francine had become the worst kind of snob. At eighteen, what she wanted was what Clarice Bishop and Jessica Friendly had been born to and accepted without question as a normal way of life —not just money but social status.

Upon graduation from high school, she watched with grim envy as her classmates—no more attractive, no smarter than she—went off to Radcliffe and Smith, to Bryn Mawr and Vassar and, in the fall, she registered at a business college in the city, which was all her father could afford. It did not interest Francine that she could earn her own way at a good university. An education was not her goal. She wanted a beautiful home, the Junior League and a country club membership, and she wanted her picture in the society columns, described as the lovely wife of anybody who could give her those things.

Francine desperately wanted a life that had gone out of fashion in the 1960s.

When she finished her computer training, she found a job with the SoMo Oil Company in Chicago and a year later frantically threw herself at a vice-president of the company, a short, round-faced man in his forties who had all the right credentials and a wife and three children. The befuddled v.p. became so enamored of the young and fragile Francine that he lost all reason and asked his wife for a divorce. His wife spoke to her first cousin, who, it turned out, was the president of the company, and he summoned Francine to his office. She had a choice, he told her, immediate termination or a transfer to the San Francisco office. Francine accepted the transfer.

In San Francisco she repeated her mistake, offering herself to the chief legal counsel, a handsome womanizer, also married, whose susceptibility was limited to the bedroom. After two years of motels and an occasional movie, Francine recognized that what she had was all she would get and she registered at the finest employment agency in the city and that step led her to Kirbo's Lodge. Her attorney friend gave her a splendid recommendation and wished her good luck.

She was still young but experienced enough now to know that

the prize did not always go to the eager, anxious early bird but sometimes to the one who watched and waited. With Arly she had watched and waited.

In the limousine to the valley, Francine lay her head back against the seat, closed her eyes and schemed. She must keep Arly off balance for a time; let her be still undecided about pressing her suit further or whether Francine had really understood the nature of the offer of the room. She would not lock the door between her room and Arly's apartment, but she would not open it. When she had some communication for Arly (which she would devise), she would go into the corridor and ring the bell to Arly's apartment. She would take care that her small wardrobe was always neatly hung in the room's closets, her intimate things folded fastidiously in the cupboard drawers, for it was likely that Arly would prowl about the room when Francine was not there.

Francine would see that the room was always sweetly scented, and she would demonstrate her orderly ways by placing a fresh lacy nightdress across the foot of her bed, with her soft white slippers arranged on the rug beneath it.

On the bedside table she would keep an ounce of L'Air du Temps, a box of monogrammed scented handkerchiefs and in the drawer a much marked copy of Lobel's translation of Sappho's lyrics. Under the Sappho would be several current magazines and under the magazines, as if it were buried there in shame, would be found a frail old copy of that famous novel of lesbian love, *The Well of Loneliness*.

Francine, as the limo rolled down the lighted canyon road, imagined Arly opening the cupboard drawer and fondling the silken underthings—or cradling the nightdress in her arms—or reading the scored passages of Sappho's verses and then, breathlessly, discovering the novel of homosexual sorrows. She would, indeed, have Arly going.

Francine had known from the first interview that Arly saw her as someone very special, and she had observed how the older woman's visits to the office had rarely ended until Arly found some excuse to bend over Francine's desk or stand beside her at the computer. Francine, through the weeks, had made casual inquiries of senior employees about Miss Kirbo and had put together in her mind a dossier on that brilliant, graceful woman. Miss Kirbo had never married; Miss Kirbo had no relatives; Miss Kirbo had had a dear friend who, some years ago, visited the lodge frequently but had gotten married and moved to Europe; Miss Kirbo had been the patron of a young woman novelist and allowed her to live at the lodge while she was writing her novel; the novel had sold to Hollywood, and the novelist had gone to Hollywood with it; Miss Kirbo did not often leave the lodge any more—only to go to San Francisco for business or to replenish her wardrobe; Miss Kirbo was thought to be lonely, despite the many guests who were her personal friends; Miss Kirbo's only real confidant was the artist Cabot Markey, or, perhaps, Harry Ames.

Francine had never seen Markey until he had arrived earlier that day, and she was afraid of Harry Ames. Once she had coffee with him in the office and had asked a question about Miss Kirbo. She had received a cold stare and no answer.

Driving in her old Chevrolet through the windy night from the Landing to Lone Pine, Francine continued to develop the scenario for her affair with Arly.

In the next few weeks, Arly would one night knock on the connecting door between their rooms and Francine would open it. Francine would be wearing the nightdress and soft slippers. The bodice fitted closely and the points of her breasts would be outlined beneath it. Its skirt was sheer and the light from the bed lamp would shine through it to reveal her straight legs and full thighs. Arly would say, "Did I wake you?" and Francine would say, "I was reading."

"What are you reading?"

"I always read a little poetry before I go to sleep."

"Well, please go back to bed. I'm sorry I disturbed you."

"No, it's quite all right, Miss Kirbo."

"Get under the covers anyway."

And Francine would get into the bed and Arly would sit beside her. Francine would read a passage from Sappho and Arly would comment favorably. They would chat about the work in the office and the weather and finally Arly would say, "I'm glad you're next door to me. Sometimes I'm lonely."

"I'm afraid I'm not much company for you."

"More than you'd think. Good night, Francine."

"Good night, Miss Kirbo."

Arly would kiss her on the forehead and rise and Francine would catch Arly's hand and draw her down and kiss her gently on the lips. "You're very kind to me," Francine would say, and Arly would hug her and leave, looking back with a smile before she closed the door.

That's the way it will begin, thought Francine as she watched the black highway unreel under the headlamps of her car. And from there it won't be long before she'll have my nightdress off and I'll let her and then weep for shame afterward and she'll try to make amends and I'll let her do that, too.

Francine's white-gloved hands squeezed the steering wheel tightly and she began to sing again, la-la-ing a Romberg sentiment. Her voice, like her eyes, was clear and gentle.

Arly, after she had stopped her tears, had gone to the reception desk and, in private, told Harry Ames that Francine would be taking the single room next to Arly's apartment. With lowered eyelids, Harry had listened attentively to her instructions about the room. She wanted a new bedspread immediately, a very feminine white spread with pastel flowered design, and bed linen with lace edging on the pillow slips. She wanted the whitest, thickest towels and mats for the bath—and, oh yes, white drapes and white throw rugs, and it was all to be in place by nine the next morning.

Harry nodded obediently and said that he would personally instruct the night housekeeper. Not even by a twitch of his nose did he comment upon his mistress' orders, but behind his icy efficiency he felt a very warm sorrow. Twice he had seen Arly's fragile happiness splintered and he feared that it might happen again. His respect for and loyalty to Arly were boundless. Twenty years before, in London, from among dozens of applicants, she had chosen him and that choice had changed his life, not just for the better, which he had desperately needed, but had transported him and his family to the magic world of Kirbo's Lodge. His three children were now Americans with careers of their own. His ailing wife had had a few good, happy years before she died here in the mountains, and he, himself, had found honor and position and authority in a renowned hotel.

There was no sin, even murder, that Harry would not have forgiven Arly, and certainly his tolerance for her frailties, which were few, was wide and deep. Yet he had instant reservations about Francine Sharpe. First, she was an employee and there would be talk, and, second, he felt that Miss Sharpe was sly. She had asked him a question about Arly that he had not liked—had the novelist, Tati

Leyva, when she had lived at the lodge, had she lived with Miss Kirbo? He had not answered.

But he knew Arly was sixty now and that she was, for all the hundreds of people about her, sadly alone. So, thought Harry, let there be talk and be damned to it, and if Miss Sharpe believed herself a match for shrewd Arly Kirbo, she'd get a bit of a shock at the proper time.

He rang for the night housekeeper and went with her to the storage room where a vast assortment of linens and towels and spreads was stacked, and carefully selected the fittings for Francine's room. If the housekeeper wondered at the luxurious selections for a single room in which an office clerk would be staying, she kept those questions to herself in the stern presence of Mr. Ames.

In her apartment, Arly opened the door to the single room and stood there, considering how else she could add to Francine's pleasure and comfort. A different vase on the table by the window, a white leather stationery folder on the desk—and throw pillows for the bed. How could she have forgotten throw pillows? She would pick those out herself, from the pillow bins in the morning; small velvet pillows of different shapes—round, square, triangular—a nest of pillows in which Francine could play kitten . . .

While Arly, in the main lounge, was juggling hope with doubt about her young lady, in his room in the west wing Dr. Friendly was watching his young one sleep.

Jessica slept in a sprawl, her legs wide apart, a pillow clutched in her arms, her hair in her face, her mouth open and one slender foot and ankle out from under the covers. That exposed foot and ankle distressed Friendly. He feared that she might take cold. But if he covered that extremity, Jessica would instantly awake and say, "Dammit, leave my foot alone." She wanted it out. She had always slept that way.

Friendly sighed happily and watched her as if she were newborn. Jessica was not exceptionally pretty. She was slim enough and her legs were good, but her nose was rather flat, her eyes a dull gray, her ears protruded too much and had to be concealed by her hair, and she had a tiny, congenital double chin. But when she smiled her curiously provocative smile, you were given a clue to the person behind that pudding face. It would come slowly, askewly, to her full lips and in it could be read humor, intelligence and a rare sensuality.

It was the thing about her that had caught him, but only after a determined chase by Jessica.

And if it had not caught him, it would have nailed another man with money and prestige just as easily—more easily. Why him? Friendly had quite naturally questioned. He had a shy manner that consisted of ducking his head when he spoke, as if he were afraid of offending with his words. You would not have known he was a famous surgeon or a famous anything, for that matter. He disappeared against the scenery—a nondescript face among the supernumeraries of the world.

But catch him she did, and he was deeply grateful for her predatism. She had managed him well, tortured him gently and given him a profound pleasure that he had not ever had until she came into his life via a minor lump which he had excised from her small right breast.

He was not a foolish man. At some time he knew she would leave him—or he thought she would, being unable to believe she would endure the inevitable aging process of a man more than thirty years her senior. He had accepted that probability when he had married her. He knew he was having the best of his life now and that sooner or later she would end it. She would take with her her youth and a handsome settlement and he was prepared to let her go when that moment came.

In the meanwhile, she was faithful to him—that he knew—and for some reason which escaped him, truly enjoyed his company. He counted the days and the hours with her like Midas with his gold, but unlike Midas, the doctor would not ask the gods to take back the favor.

Alfred Friendly was a woman's man, a totally, unequivocally heterosexual individual. He was passionately devoted to women and their bodies, a passion which had much to do with his success as a women's surgeon. To save a woman's breast and her life from the assault of cancer was not just a lucrative specialization of his considerable talents; it was as agonizingly creative an act for the doctor as were Markey's paintings of his beloved mountains for the artist.

When the need to amputate was indicated, the doctor suffered a deep sorrow at the mutilation he was performing on that living canvas which lay on his operating table. Young, middle-aged or old, women were works of art to Friendly. But until he had met Jessica, he had not once in his whole useful life been given the opportunity to love a woman as he had wanted—to lavish affection upon her, to serve her, to use his great knowledge of her psychical or physical responses for her pleasure and contentment.

Being what he was, it was one of those awful quirks of fate that Friendly had not been attractive to women. He was not ugly. Rather, he was more ordinary than normally ordinary men. To add to those problems, he was shy, uncommunicative, introverted and completely unable to be aggressive. He could be assertive enough as a surgeon, even tyrannical, but outside the operating theater or the examination room he had been hopelessly inadequate with women.

Because in his youth his numerous attempts to present himself favorably to the opposite sex had either been repulsed or ignored, he had remained a virgin until he had married at the age of twenty-eight. Once he had gone with a college chum to a brothel—but once only. He had proved to be impotent with the worried, hard-working prostitute who had tried to stimulate him. His impotence had been caused by his pity for her. If his pity was undeserved, it did not change matters. He was born to be a lover, to give more than he got, and that distressed woman, trying to earn her fee by arousing him, had lost her temper, called him a fairy and then been baffled by his laughter.

Now Friendly, in this second marriage, had found in Jessica the touchstone to judge himself as a man, and he had not been disappointed in himself. As he watched her sleeping there in the luxurious room, he felt that if he should die in the next instant, his life would have been done well, with grace and completion. He loved, and while to be loved might have been one more added grace, to love and have that love appreciated was quite enough.

In this respect, Dr. Friendly and Arly Kirbo were of similar philosophies.

In Markey's darkened studio, the artist was not asleep. He was sitting in a deep chair looking up through the wide, slanted windows into the sky, where, now and again, the moon appeared from behind swarming clouds. He was remembering the woman whose portrait hung in the museum in London. He was remembering her limp body on the end of a rope, swinging slowly back and forth against a granite rock face in the French Alps. He had himself gone down the wall and carried the body up where the other climbers silently waited, and with their help he had brought it in to Chamonix. She had been a good climber, a strong-limbed woman with quick reflexes. Nothing could detract from her rare depth of beauty—not chapped lips or wind-roughened cheeks. The perfect conformations of Clarice Bishop were only perfect conformations. Beauty exploded from within the woman who had died that summer's day on the end of a nylon rope.

Markey had painted the portrait from memory. He could, he thought, even now remember every detail of her so clearly that he could paint a thousand canvases of her and not one would be like the other in that each would be a separate memory.

Seven years had passed since her death, yet he knew that day as if it had been this day. They were a rope of four, Markey first on the rope and she had been third. Her fall had not been a long one, no more than fifteen feet, but her line was caught under one leg and the result was that she spun as she went down and, when the rope stopped her fall, the spin had smashed her head against the wall. She had died instantly.

At the beginning of the fall, she had known that the line was dangerously entangled about her leg and she had cried out, "Cabot!" It had not been a cry for help or even of fear, but a statement of love. And Markey had shouted her name in answer and knew that she had heard before she died.

The gibbous moon leaped from behind a black cloud and its light flashed through the studio windows, and Markey, under the hypnosis of his memory, whispered her name to the moon: "Jael!"

The moon raced to the cover of another black cloud and the studio was dark again.

Clarice, having returned to her room from her encounter with Cabot Markey, was again naked before the full-length mirrors—not an unusual occupation for her, but this time she was working out poses to offer Markey in his studio come morning.

She considered the view of her back as she seductively peeked over her white shoulder; turning, she presented a profile with arms and hands flung out in a ballet gesture; now she bent forward, hands on knees, a cute, tantalizing position; then, straightening, she faced the mirrors and spread her legs mannishly, fists on hips, delightfully truculent. She lay upon a divan in the classic odalisque posture but was not pleased with the way her breasts were flattened, and rolled upon her side to fancy her body as a Modigliani ellipsoid. She rolled again, this time upon her stomach, and bent her calves back above her thighs, with toes pointed, and her chin cupped in her hands. She was charmed with this configuration but continued to experiment, kneeling, standing, lying in every conceivable arrangement of her parts, and, as usual, she began to feel desire for herself.

Clarice needed no sexual fantasies; she alone was fantasy enough for stimulation. She found it amusing and exciting to assume pornographical poses and now she was on the floor, her back resting against the divan, her legs apart, her breasts caught in her hands, pelvis describing small, lewd circles. Lubricious surfaces were reflected in the mirror and this brought an anticipating quiver to her loins. She moved her fingers down from her breasts and quickly satisfied herself, watching her face all the while with a voyeur's fascination.

Having completed the self-copulation, she draped a robe about her shoulders, opened a split of champagne and drank from the bottle. Sitting by the telephone, she dialed a San Francisco number and aroused her psychiatrist.

"Oh, my god, Clarice, don't you know what time it is?" said a sleep-numbed voice.

"But I'm doing the damned thing again," said she. "I've been doing the damned thing all day."

"Tell me about it," was his plaintive response.

And Clarice began to tell him all.

The Earthquake Room closed at 3 A.M. and Paul walked with Diane through the underground corridor that joined the dormitory and the central lodge.

"Let's get some mountain air," Paul suggested, and they climbed the steps of an exit in the corridor and emerged into the breezy darkness of the lodge's gardens. The tops of the trees were nodding in response to the whispers of the coming storm and the night had become damp with the threat of snow.

"This place'll be romping by the weekend," said Paul.

"You bet," Diane said.

She pulled her sweater up about her throat and Paul, seeing her reflex to the sharpening cold, put his arm about her as they walked through the gardens.

"Don't start something you're not going to finish," said she.

He laughed. "Sorry I'm not a finisher," he said.

There are those rare people who are exactly what they seem to be and Diane was one of those. She was straightforward, honest, guileless and decent. And being one of those, it was not comprehensible to her that a person whom she admired could be anything but what he seemed. And of all the possible young men to whom she might have been attracted, she had managed to choose one who was nothing that he seemed to be.

This unmatched pair moved comfortably together in the night until they reached the place beside the hot pond where he had kissed her that one time last year. He did not kiss her on this night. They followed the path around the pond, his arm still about her.

"What were you doing in Greece?" she finally asked.

"Guiding tourists."

"I've never been anywhere."

"You will."

"I don't know about that."

"There's lots of time."

"Do I bore you?"

"Of course not."

"Well then, why don't you sparkle with me? You sparkle plenty with the guests—especially with the girls."

"That's what I'm paid to do. That's a funny word—sparkle."

"That's the way I talk. I don't sparkle."

"Blessed be those who don't sparkle."

And they walked on, not sparkling, and Diane felt blessed by the arm about her shoulders and Paul felt secure in his shell.

The pond was still, again a slow seep from the hot river deep in the fractured crust of the Sierra. It was waiting.

Above the nodding pines, behind the slopes of its imprisoning dam, the Gornaad was waiting.

Almost invisibly, snow began to fall.

10

Floating in the cold air, snow is formed in trigonal symmetry and silently these feathery crystals fall upon the mountains and the valleys and bury them and where there is enough of this fall its lower layers compact and become granulated and as the granulation is packed tighter and tighter a clear blue ice is made and now under the tremendous pressure of hundreds of feet of this ice its lowest layer becomes like a soft plastic which allows that great mass above to flow and as it flows it is called a glacier.

JESSICA

Jessica Ellen Martin crouched in the bower she had made for herself in the rose garden behind the big, pink house on Beverly Drive in Beverly Hills, California. The bower opened against the chain-link fence that ended the Martin property on the alley which split the block of expensive homes. Jessica was lying in wait for Joseph Baum, age eleven, who practiced on his skateboard in the smooth, paved alley and lived three houses to the south.

Jessica was nine, her I.Q. was 150, she had recently lost the classic two front teeth and she was wearing no pants or anything else under the short terry cloth shift she had donned after a swim in the Martin pool. Jessica swam like a dolphin, oddly graceful for a child, curiously mature in her manner and movement, and her head was full of interests that should not have been there at age nine.

She heard the rattle of Joseph's skate wheels and scooted forward to the link fence. As the boy raced by, she called out, "Hey, shithead!" And Joseph stopped his board. "Who you calling shithead?"

"You."

"If you was a boy, you wouldn't. I'd kick your butt."

"Come over here."

"Not if you're going to call me shithead."

"I take it back. Come in here."

"For what?"

"I want to show you something."

"Like what?"

"You'll see what."

Joseph skated his board close to the fence and peered through the links. "What?"

"I said, come in here—if you want to see."

Joseph picked up his board and unhooked the gate in the fence and crawled through the rose briars until he reached Jessica's cozy little nest. "Okay, what?"

"You've got to show me yours if I show you mine."

"Show you what?"

"Your thing. Here's mine." Jessica sat back and lifted the shift, exposing her rosy little crotch.

Joseph's face became scarlet and he scratched his way through the briars and out through the gate and raced off down the alley. Later that afternoon, he told his mother and Mrs. Baum called Mrs. Martin and they laughed adult laughter and Mrs. Martin said she'd speak to Jessica. But she didn't. She did tell Mr. Martin, who pretended to be shocked, but he didn't speak to Jessica either. They were very healthy people with healthy minds and, besides, they didn't quite know how to *speak* to their daughter. Their two older children were as children should be, but how does one advise or reprimand a strangely grown-up little girl who at the age of six had objected to Sunday School teachings, especially that nonsense, as she put it, about the virgin birth.

"Mother," Jessica had said, "you may not realize this, but there is only one way to beget and that is the way I was begot. Daddy fertilized you with his thing and no way—and I mean no way—do babies get born any other way—except, of course, by artificial insemination and I doubt if Jesus was a test tube baby."

"I'll tell you what she'll say if I *speak* to her," Mr. Martin said, "or if you *speak* to her. She'll say the purpose of the body is to procreate and there's nothing shameful about the human genitals any more than there is about Mobby's genitals"—Mobby was the family dog—"and Mobby is always rolling over and showing his. That's what our daughter will say," he concluded.

So they let it lie and hoped that Jessica, because she was bright to the point of dazzling, would see the need to conform to accepted social customs and not go through life lifting her skirt at will—at least not in public places.

"Please, God," said Mrs. Martin, "let her be married when she's fifteen. Maybe that'll keep her on a decent track."

But Jessica not only didn't marry when she was fifteen, she remained a virgin until she was eighteen. That is not to say that she didn't masturbate. She was hearty about that and just as hearty about masturbating boys. When Joseph Baum was thirteen, he was not so reluctant when again propositioned by Jessica and, in the backseat of the Baums's Rolls Royce in the dark of the garage, he unzipped his pants and let Jessica seize him. She pumped him wickedly and giggled in delight when he spurted all over the rich beige of the seat.

She graduated from her private academy at fourteen and was in college—UCLA—the following year. There she made straight As and had dozens of young men following her about to gain her attention. She jacked them off, one and all, but nothing more. As she explained it to a girl friend: "Don't you see, they're all so brainless. If I ever find a man with a brain, I'll go to bed with him. Meanwhile, dear, it's fun to make them squirt and wiggle—and it keeps them from trying to rape me. They're really very sweet and do enjoy it so much. I like men to enjoy themselves."

Mr. and Mrs. Martin got wind of Jessica's outrageous reputation at UCLA and shipped her off to Vassar. There she kept a lower profile but, nevertheless, her little fist was busy on a variety of Yalies. Through it all her scholastic records were dashing and she exhibited a talent for dramatic acting that was clearly of professional caliber and led her to New York City upon graduation from Vassar. For a year and a half she played about with acting (but not seriously) and, at eighteen, met Glenn.

His last name is unimportant. What is important is that Jessica Martin went to bed with him. He was not a poet, actor, painter, professor, scientist or doctor. He was a lowly seaman 1st class in the U. S. Navy. A gob.

Jessica was performing in an off-Broadway musical—a bit of comic fluff about the sexual liberation of women with much nudity and protest rhyming. Stark naked and endearingly fresh, if not the most perfectly formed of the group, she leaped about the stage in several ensemble numbers. Her lopsided grin was perhaps the best asset the show had to offer and the choreography was deftly arranged to keep her in the eye of the audience as the mildly dirty verses of the songs were projected. Jessica's grin made them seem dirtier than they were.

The show closed after forty-two performances and on its closing night the cast and crew partied at a Village disco, and there in the hard rock din and psychopetal lights Jessica found herself dancing opposite a vacant-faced young sailor whose vacuity was relentlessly centered upon her bumping pelvis.

One can say that it was a meeting in exactly the right place at precisely the right time between two perfectly suited people and be almost correct with that romantic conclusion. But Jessica did not deserve Glenn. She had never done anything to deserve Glenn. And she could never explain to herself the totally mindless, but brief, attraction he had for her.

She took him to her apartment for two days and nights. Anything that could be done with the human body they succeeded in doing. There was no communication of any kind except that tactile speech of flesh. Indeed, young Glenn was incapable of anything else, but in that area he was monstrously responsive. Priapism was his sole contribution. He seemed to have a permanent erection. No sooner would he ejaculate into one of Jessica's orifices than he would withdraw and plunge into another. Even when he slept, his penis remained hard.

Jessica loathed him as much as she was fascinated by his total concentration on her parts. He slavered, panted, heaved and groaned, belched and farted, but never except to gorge a hamburger now and then, sleep or go to the toilet, did he stop either chewing on her or thrusting into her. She began to understand that he would have been as passionate with a knothole in a fence or a plugged watermelon, but she could not seem to resist his untiring onslaught.

Finally, on the morning of the third day, she waked and vomited, persuaded Glenn to go to the neighborhood deli for beer (which he could drink by the gallon) and locked the door behind him.

When he returned, she did not answer the ring and after a while he went away. He didn't go far. Only to Washington Square, where he sat on a bench and drank beer and got himself picked up by a middle-aged gay who was, perhaps as much as Jessica, finally horrified by Glenn's irreducible member.

Frantically, Jessica returned to California and the quiet office of the Martin family's amiable psychiatrist. The doctor listened patiently to her sad tale of abuse and said, "Well, honey, you got yourself screwed. It's no big deal."

"But it's what he *was*," Jessica whined. "What's the matter with me?"

"You've always been peculiar."

"Some shrink you are," said Jessica.

"We have our limits. You're one of them." He patted her on the cheek and sent her home.

For the next two weeks, she spent her days jogging around the Beverly Hills High School playing field and staring at television at night. Then she flew to San Francisco, took an apartment and opened a bookstore.

The business venture was eminently successful. The shop became a hangout for young artists and intellectuals—those with trimmed beards and clean feet—and Jessica was suddenly twenty-one, popular, loved, admired, envied and desired but very much her own person again. And this time she kept her hands off the boys and theirs off her. "I'm quite sexless, you know," she said of herself, and was pleased with her abstention. Then she found a small lump on the underside of her right breast and the last year in her not unhappy life began.

Dr. Friendly had performed three operations that morning and the tension of the operating theater was still pressing him; that plus the knowledge that the third operation had been a final solution for a pretty forty-year-old patient on whom he had worked several times before but whose cysts kept recurring. That morning the biopsy had pronounced a malignancy and left him no alternative.

At two o'clock in the afternoon, his waiting room was crowded, his nurses efficiently ushering his patients in and out of the examination rooms, some going in with drawn, frightened faces and coming out with joyful smiles; others, not so lucky, with tear-red eyes and trembling hands.

Friendly slid open the door of room number three and nodded

in his shy way to the young woman who was seated on the white table with her bra loosened over her small breasts.

"Miss Martin? I'm Dr. Friendly."

Jessica was unable to answer, staring at him with terrified eyes. He studied the record already prepared by one of his nurses, placed it on a table, adjusted his glasses and said, "Please lie down."

Jessica lay back on the table and he gingerly pushed her bra up until it was under her throat and began to probe her left breast with his dry, surgeon's fingers.

"It's the other one," said Jessica.

"I know." He continued with the left breast until he was satisfied that it was clear and then turned his attention to the right one's problem.

Jessica watched his face, saw nothing there but kindness and concern and, even in the midst of her terror, knew that he was tired. "I'm sorry," she said.

"Pardon?"

"To be such a bother. I know it isn't much of a lump."

"No, it isn't. But it'll have to come out."

"With a needle?" she asked, hopefully.

"With a scalpel, my dear. You can sit up now." He turned to the record and made notes on it as Jessica fastened her bra.

"When will you do it?"

"Would Monday morning be agreeable?"

It was and he told her that arrangements would be made for her to enter the hospital on Sunday night. With the formalities settled, he stood for a moment silently considering her face. "You're going to be very brave. I can tell." And he opened the door and left the room.

And Jessica, being as peculiar as the family psychiatrist would have expected her to be, knew that she was in love for the first time and with a man older than her father.

On the appointed Monday, Jessica was wheeled into the operating room and, through the haze of the pre-operation drugs, saw Friendly's plain face above her. His surgical mask was not yet in place and he had not yet covered his hands with the sanitary gloves.

He cupped her exposed breast in his warm palm and said, "They're a perfect pair. I'll try to keep them that way." He smiled and nodded to the anesthetist and, a few moments later, Jessica felt her consciousness retreating to some tiny nook in her mind where it clicked off without a sound.

As it came back, also soundlessly and like a fuzzy caterpillar crawling from under a leaf, she knew she was back in her hospital room and the first thing she saw was Dr. Friendly's face. Again he smiled, slapped her gently on both cheeks to bring her full to, and said, "You still have a matching pair, Miss Martin."

She was discharged from the hospital on the following morning without seeing Friendly again, but with instructions by telephone from a nurse in his office to report on Monday morning next for a postoperative examination.

Jessica was prompt on that day and waited impatiently atop the examination table, swinging her legs and hating the dull, characterless music that seeped from the Muzak. Friendly entered, nodded shyly, peered at the already fading pink scar on her breast, then deftly removed the stitches.

"Fine," he said. "Well, that's all, Miss Martin. One thing, please, no exercise for that side for a while."

Knowing exactly what he meant, Jessica asked, "What do you mean?"

Friendly squinted at her through his glasses and said, "You know exactly what I mean."

And Jessica grinned. He had not seen that expression on her face before and, caught unaware by its unexpected wickedness, felt a flush rising into his face. He was not the sort of doctor his patients flirted with, or the sort of man any woman would flirt with or ever had.

"Can I take you to lunch?" asked Jessica.

"Lunch?"

"Don't you eat?"

"Eat?" He seemed greatly puzzled by the suggestion and Jessica was even more in love with him. There he stood before her, a famous doctor, said to be a genius, winner of the Nobel prize for research in surgical techniques, the plainest man she had ever seen, his short gray hair untidy, his pale gray eyes baffled behind his glasses, a blush on his smooth cheeks, trying to decipher a simple invitation to lunch as if it were a coded message from outer space.

"I'd be awfully pleased if you would," said Jessica, and she gave an enthusiastic little bounce on the table where she sat and her yet exposed breasts trembled prettily. Still trapped by the crooked smile, Friendly dumbly looked at those breasts and Jessica deliberately bounced again.

Friendly turned away to the washbasin and busily washed his hands. "I don't have much time for lunch," he mumbled. "I usually only go to the cafeteria downstairs for fifteen minutes or so."

"I'll go with you."

"I usually try to read a little of the newspaper while I have lunch."

"I won't talk."

"Well, I suppose there's no harm, Miss Martin, if you insist." He knew his embarrassment was absurd but the girl had got him out of his element and he was floundering. He scrubbed his hands with a paper towel and started from the room.

"What time?"

He didn't turn around. She had not covered herself and, while she might feel perfectly free to discuss lunch with a bare chest, she had made it impossible for him to look at her. "I usually go at one," he said.

"I'll wait in the waiting room," said Jessica.

"Oh, god, no," said Friendly. He could just see his nurses bending their heads together and tittering as old Dr. Friendly went off to lunch with that cute bit with the saucy nipples. "Please meet me there, if you don't mind."

Jessica didn't mind and she was waiting as he came into the crowded cafeteria. He glanced at her and passed her by in a state of shock, fumbled silverware onto a tray and went ahead into the serving line. Jessica grabbed her own tray and pushed along behind him. He blindly selected a pineapple and cottage cheese salad, soda crackers and coffee and got himself to a corner table where Jessica presently joined him with a generous helping of Irish stew, salad, rolls, butter, milk and pecan pie. Jessica was one of those fortunate people who seem able to eat anything and everything and never gain an ounce of weight.

She sat as close to him as the chairs would allow and said, "Go on—read your paper."

He placed the folded newspaper beside his plate and stared at it, seeing not a word of print. Jessica ate the pecan pie first and pretended to ignore him, but in her mind she was arranging all the things she had learned about him in the past week. She had had his nurses to dinner in her apartment, ostensibly to repay them for their courtesies, and had encouraged them to talk about Dr. Friendly. It was not too difficult; nurses love to talk about their doctors.

Dr. Friendly lived alone in a big apartment near Stanford University's medical college, where he frequently lectured. His wife lived in Cannes, France. They were not divorced but had been apart for many years. He had a son and a daughter. The daughter was married to an English lord named Botherstone and the son was in the American diplomatic service and presently stationed in Madrid. They rarely saw their father, which, the nurses opined, was all right with him. They suspected he didn't much like either of them.

The doctor had no social life the nurses were aware of—no appointments other than with his patients or at the university. Apart from work, what did he do? He looks at birds and goes walking on the shore or in the mountains, all by himself. I'll swear, he's a very, very peculiar man. He isn't queer, is he? He isn't anything. He's just a genius with a scalpel and that's all he is, I swear.

Once a year, Dr. Friendly took a vacation—two weeks—always at that place called Kirbo's Lodge. You've heard of it—way up in the mountains?

Jessica had been to Kirbo's Lodge, first with her parents when she was a child and later for skiing several times. There, she remembered, she had pulled the pud of the head ski instructor, a handsome French youth, and giggled with her friends about the small size of it.

What else was there to know about Dr. Friendly? Well, not much else that was not public knowledge. Jessica shoved the bites of steaming Irish stew into her mouth and watched him trying to read his newspaper.

"You're not eating," she observed.

He noticed it, too, and poked awkwardly at the cottage cheese.

"I want to tell you something about myself," said Jessica. "I don't want you to misunderstand. I'm not after your money."

"I didn't think you were after anything, Miss Martin. I thought nothing about it."

"You did. Of course, you did. You must be saying to yourself, what does she want?"

"Well, what do you want?"

"To be near you."

"Oh, my god," said Dr. Friendly.

"So please let me continue. I have an income of sixty thousand a year from a trust fund my grandmother left me and I have a good business at my bookstore. My parents are rich and they'll leave me a few million when they die, so you can see I'm not after your money. When I say I want to be near you, that's exactly what I mean."

He stared at her helplessly. She must be insane. That's it. She's under psychiatric care. "Are you under psychiatric care, Miss Martin?"

"I did see our family psychiatrist last year, but it was about getting balled by a sailor in New York City and he told me it was no big deal."

Dr. Friendly spilled cottage cheese on his jacket and swallowed his coffee wrong. Jessica grinned at him and again he was trapped. She's pulling my leg.

"I'm not pulling your leg," said Jessica. "When can I see you again?"

"I'm afraid that's quite impossible, Miss Martin. Well, it has been—yes—a very curious lunch."

"I won't give up," said Jessica.

"Good-by, Miss Martin." He left the table and hurried from the cafeteria. Jessica finished her stew and drank her milk and plotted.

On Sunday morning, she sat in her car and watched the entrance to his apartment house. Friendly came out, got into his car, which the doorman had waiting for him, and drove away. Jessica followed.

He drove directly to the shore, stepped from his car and, with binoculars about his neck, began to walk on the path along the high rocky bluff above the sea. Jessica followed.

Friendly reached a lonely head of land and sat on a boulder. Jessica made up the distance between them and sat down beside him.

"I was afraid that was you back there," the doctor said.

"I told you, I wouldn't give up."

"Miss Martin, I'm fifty-seven years old. I'm consumed by my work. There is no place in my life for a young girl."

"Do you have an old girl?"

"I will not discuss my personal life with you."

"I'm going to make you go to bed with me sooner or later."

"You're not going to make me do anything, Miss Martin. No one can make me do anything I don't wish to do. You'd best pay a return visit to your psychiatrist. You're completely mad."

He rose and plunged off down the steep trail to the sea. Jessica was astonished at his ability. It belied his plodding, stooped walk as he went about his office. Here, on the shore in the wind, he seemed a younger man. She let him go, but again had his nurses to dinner and discovered the date he planned to take his spring vacation.

When, in the spring, Friendly arrived at Kirbo's Lodge and looked from the window of his room down upon the swimming pool, there, sitting on the end of the diving board in a one-piece, flesh-colored swimsuit, was Jessica Martin. "Oh, my god," said he.

He cowered in his room until dawn, donned his hiking boots, slung his rucksack on his shoulders and slipped quietly out into the gray morning. He took the lift to the glacier and set off along the trail which climbed above the ice bowl and wound off into the wilderness where the chain of cold lakes lay steaming in the May morning. He looked back and was comforted to be alone. He had escaped her. But had he? The picture of her sitting on the diving board in that flesh-colored suit was fixed on the plate in his mind. She was provocative—and bold—but to be bold toward him was an absurdity. Why? What on earth did she *really* want with him? Even after they were married he would continue to ask himself that question. Fifty-seven years of being unwanted were not easily forgotten.

Within a few days after he married his first wife, he had known that his hopes were to be dashed. She was a handsome woman, and intelligent, but she had married him because he obviously had a distinguished future ahead of him. She had borne the babies without complaining, but there their sex life had ended, and knowing that he was not loved, he had drawn more and more into himself, shutting out even his children. They were hers, conceived without passion, as duty, and, in revenge, he had made them her total responsibility. He regretted that, wished now that he had not been so bitter, because as he became older, he became more lonely.

Friendly walked on into the day and at the first lake assembled his fishing rod from its aluminum tube and cast a green drake out into the blue water, let it float with the quick breeze and took a golden trout. He expertly brought the fish to the shore and held it, felt its trembling, shimmering body and carefully removed the hook and cast the pretty creature back into the water. He loved the idea of angling, the disciplined skill required, the solitude of the art, but he had long since lost satisfaction in the kill. Now he fished as he birded, to lose himself for a little while in the act of casting the fly or identifying the bird, and he had found it more rewarding than to eat his catch or look down the black barrel of a shotgun with death under his trigger finger. He was, he knew, too civilized a man.

"Hi, there." Her voice came to him from the top of the trail where it descended to the lake. He looked up and groaned aloud, but even as he did, he suddenly knew that he was pleased to see her.

She was wearing the smartest of hiking togs—green leather shorts, red knee-high stockings, Italian boots, a red windbreaker and Robin Hood cap with a white feather in it. On her back was a new rucksack from which protruded the shining cup-cap of a thermos jug. "I brought some cold white wine," said Jessica. "I thought you might like that."

"I never drink when I'm hiking."

"Do you ever drink any time?"

"No."

"What a shame. Do you ever fuck while you're hiking?"

"My dear Miss Martin—"

"Do you ever fuck any time?" And she grinned at him, but now he was not being embarrassed and his gaze was directly upon her and in it was the steel of his paradoxical character and now it was Jessica's turn to be embarrassed.

"I'm sorry," she murmured and looked away from him. "I'm being awfully cutesy," she went on, "and I know you're sick of it. But I'm serious about this and I don't really know how to persuade you that I am. So I fall back on bad jokes and things that seem to shock you."

She seemed to Friendly to be genuinely penitent, but he could not see any reason why this curiously charming young woman would pursue him unless she was deranged. No woman had ever pursued Dr. Friendly. "Miss Martin, you don't shock me at all and while I agree your jokes are bad jokes, you puzzle me more than anything else."

"You really think I'm crazy, don't you?"

"How would you explain it if you were me?"

"Perhaps I don't see you as you see yourself."

"How on earth do you see me?"

"As a man who deserves a lot more than he's ever had."

He laughed. "You couldn't know anything about me or what I've had or what I deserve. This conversation is making me feel foolish, Miss Martin. I'm too old for it." He was folding the fishing rod, putting it into its case. He thrust the case into his rucksack and swung the sack to his shoulders.

Jessica silently watched his efficient hands and was again aware of an unexpected youthfulness in the way he handled himself here in the outdoors as opposed to the way he presented himself in his office.

"You're not too old for anything," she said.

"I'm not too old to hike on to the next lake," said he, and, wanting her company but not wanting her to know it, he said, "It's a steep trail. It won't leave you much breath for talking, Miss Martin. I wouldn't advise it."

He set off along the trail, which shortly began a twist of switchbacks beside the creek which fed water from the unseen second lake into the first. He was pleased to hear Jessica panting along close behind him.

The walk took almost an hour and, when they reached the rocky banks of the second lake, Dr. Friendly sat down, opened his rucksack and produced the box lunch packed for him at the lodge. "I will try a little of your wine," said he.

Jessica unpacked her own box lunch, opened the thermos, poured wine into paper cups. Even though there were great patches of snow all about them, it was warm in the sun on the bank of the lake. They ate without talking at all, Jessica because she was afraid of offending him again and Friendly because he had nothing to say.

Lunch finished, Friendly turned his back to her, pillowed his head on his rucksack and dozed. Jessica unlaced her left boot, took it off, rolled down the heavy wool sock and inspected the angry, bleeding blister the walk had made on her heel.

"I don't suppose you have a Band-Aid, do you?" she asked very quietly.

He sat up and looked at her foot, brought a small first aid kit from his rucksack, took her foot in his lap, applied a red antiseptic to the wound, then a wide Band-Aid and, finally, a piece of soft moleskin. "Put your shoe on," he said, "and don't ever do that again. It's stupid not to complain when you feel a blister coming on. When we get back to the lodge, you'll see the nurse and get an antibiotic shot. That's a bad heel."

They came silently down from the heights at a slow pace, rode in the lift from the glacier to the lodge and, at the lodge's entrance, he said, "See the nurse," and left her without another word.

When, on a silver tray with its customary Waterford crystal creamer, sugar bowl and jelly dish, his breakfast was delivered to his room at seven o'clock the next morning, Dr. Friendly stared at the obviously expensive cream-colored envelope which rested against a Waterford crystal bud vase containing a perfect Reine des Violettes rosebud from the lodge's greenhouse, "Dr. Alfred Friendly" inscribed in a bold, distinctive hand across its face. The doctor knew immediately that the note was from Jessica and resolutely denied the urge to open it at once. Instead, he picked up a copy of a new medical journal and read while he ate his Spartan breakfast of Quaker's old-fashioned oatmeal, dry rye toast and hot camomile tea. It was an article about new techniques in breast implants, a subject in which the doctor was quite naturally interested, but he found himself finally unable to concentrate, tossed the article aside, picked up the envelope and opened it. The note read:

> "I'm sorry, Alfred. I had hoped you would understand me better. Please forgive me."

Dr. Friendly frowned. What an extraordinary young woman and what on earth had he been supposed to understand? He was not offended by her brave use of his Christian name and, in fact, had he allowed himself to feel anything at all, he would have been pleased. By addressing him as "Alfred," she had diminished the thirty-six years that separated them. Upon momentary reflection, the doctor now allowed himself a small feeling of pleasure. The entire situation was, however, ridiculous. He shrugged, tossed the note in a wastebasket and crossed to the window. The skies were clear and there was no wind. Friendly put on his hiking boots and outdoor woolens, determined to take a walk. At the door, he hesitated a moment, then turned and retrieved Jessica's note from the wastebasket and placed it on a small night table.

Outside he plunged off up a foot trail behind the lodge, walking swiftly against the early morning cold. The exertion soon warmed him and he strode on for several miles, occasionally permitting himself a glance over his shoulder. There was no sign of Jessica and that was a relief. That had been an ugly heel and, of course, she could not have walked today in any comfort. Had she visited the nurse as he had instructed? Perhaps he should have a look at her foot. It would be only courteous. She had, after all, rubbed her heel raw walking with him, uninvited though she had been.

Back at the lodge, he visited the swimming pool, but Jessica was not there. He wandered about, through the orangery, the general store, into the coffee shop and the library. Jessica was nowhere to be seen. He decided to have an early lunch on the terrace, where he picked at and hardly tasted a delicious quiche and surreptitiously watched the arrival and departure of other guests. Finally, he left the terrace and walked to the lobby. Completely self-convinced now that it would be impolite not to inquire about Jessica's small injury, he walked to a house phone in a far corner rather than risk an embarrassing face-to-face encounter with the desk clerk. He asked to be connected with Miss Martin's room.

"Miss Martin has checked out," the voice informed him. "She left last night."

Just as well and that was that, the doctor told himself, and retired to his room, where he spent the afternoon reading his medical journals. But skipping. And being bored.

To his dismay, the good doctor remained disturbed during the rest of his vacation. The solitary pleasures he had always enjoyed seemed somehow too solitary. He hiked miles by day and read for hours at night and always the memory of Jessica's reckless smile and young vitality prodded and pushed itself to the forefront of his disciplined mind.

It was with some relief that the doctor returned to his office at the end of his holiday, there to deal with the real business of life and death and to do the work he had been born to do. There was no room for thoughts of Jessica throughout his busy week and it wasn't until midday on Saturday that Dr. Friendly became aware once again of the peculiar restlessness that had bothered him at Kirbo's Lodge. It was just curiosity that made him check the classified section under bookstores and only coincidence that he decided that afternoon to take a drive.

The small town of Sausalito faces San Francisco from across Richardson Bay, its rustic and frequently expensive homes rising on the precipitous hillside. Its population of some seven thousand people includes artists, yachtsmen, fishermen and wealthy businessmen who live in the North Bay area and work in San Francisco. In good weather, the young are drawn to its beaches, where they come to play in the sun, and older people are attracted by its peaceful environs. The town's one business street is a string of unique, charming shops and waterside restaurants and it was not surprising to Dr. Friendly that Jessica Martin's bookstore should be located in Sausalito.

On this afternoon in early June, there was no fog and the sun was high and bright as he drove across the Golden Gate Bridge toward the Marin hills. Leaving the bridge behind, he turned north at the junction a few miles later and drove slowly into Sausalito. Sailboats of every type from cats to schooners busied the bay and he watched the agile footwork of the wind-surfers, wondering whether he was too old to learn this new sport which looked like such fun from the safety of his car.

Dr. Friendly was feeling more conspicuous than he had ever felt in his carefully inconspicuous life, and, as he turned into the street of shops and restaurants, he shrank lower behind the wheel. The traffic moved slowly down the narrow street and he spotted the small bookstore near the corner, "Martin's" in discreet gold lettering on the left-hand lower corner of the show window. At that very moment, a couple turned the approaching corner and walked swiftly toward the bookstore. Dr. Friendly caught a glimpse of a familiar small figure in jeans and red shirt, walking with a tall, athletic-looking blond youth. She turned her head toward the moving traffic and he had a panic-stricken conviction that Jessica had seen him. He slid even lower in the driver's seat and wheeled the big car around the corner. Feeling altogether ridiculous, he gunned the engine and headed for the Golden Gate Bridge.

If he had looked back, the doctor would have seen Jessica, wearing her wicked grin, stop dead still and look after his car. Her companion, who had never been the recipient of that delicious smile, looked at her curiously.

"Why're you smiling?" he asked.

Jessica's grin widened. "Was I?" she responded absently, then laughed out loud, hugged the bemused young man's arm and bounced down the two steps and into her bookstore.

Dr. Friendly spent his Sunday thinking about all the remarks he had ever heard about old fools and, during the following week, he used the same steely will that he had employed when, cold-turkey, he stopped smoking two packs of cigarettes a day, to vanquish Jessica forever—all of which made his second visit to Sausalito the next Saturday even more aggravating. This time he parked his car and walked along the waterfront across the street from the shops, stopping for lunch at an open-deck restaurant. He was not familiar with the area and found he liked its Mediterranean flavor, and that surprised him because, on his one visit to the Italian Riviera, he had not approved of the undisciplined mode of living. After lunch, he walked back toward Martin's bookstore, striving for the casual air of a man out for an aimless afternoon stroll.

He stood motionless at the display window, examining what seemed to him a surprising selection of books. There were no insignificant novels, but rather books on art, music, poetry and politics, all tastefully arranged. The store was not what he had expected it to be and he stood, confused, and continued to look into the window.

Inside, Jessica saw the doctor through the window, walked briskly to her small desk at the rear of the store and busied herself with her ledgers.

Dr. Friendly entered, interested enough now to compensate for his nervousness. There were a few customers browsing the tables and he stood for a moment studying the narrow, well-lighted room. One wall was covered with bright, modern prints for sale and lush plants were everywhere, above and on the floor. He reached up to touch a luxuriant Boston fern and was pleased to find it was alive. At the back of the room was a coffee machine and a small table and chairs where a group of casually dressed young men and women lounged about drinking coffee in the manner of country folk gathered about the stove in a general store. Dr. Friendly walked tentatively toward Jessica.

At her desk, she studiously checked a column of figures and neatly entered the total sum from a small stack of sales slips before she looked up and, with a charm and composure well learned at Vassar, combined with the slightest hint of surprise that came easily as a result of her acting experience, she said, "Why, Doctor! How nice to see you."

She stood and Dr. Friendly took her extended hand in his damp palm, his eyes behind their rimless spectacles registering the change in her appearance. Ash-blond hair pulled back in a smart chignon and dressed now in a simple navy knit and high-heeled pumps, she appeared poised and more mature than he remembered.

And Jessica observed the sturdy figure before her, gray suit and narrow dark tie, short gray hair neatly brushed, gray eyes blinking anxiously. "May I help you?" she asked, noting how out of place and time his solid presence was here in her store that courted the carefree young. Recognizing the courage it had taken to bring him this far, her emotions became even more entangled.

"I think you can," Dr. Friendly blurted. "Miss Martin—" He stopped, wordless as Jessica's irrepressible grin flickered. For a moment, he stared at her, wondering why he was where he was and what it was he wanted to say.

"Let me guess," Jessica came to his rescue, and the grin of his memory emerged full-blown, erasing the adult facade she had worn a moment before. "You've grown accustomed to my face!"

"Miss Martin," the doctor began faintly, and stopped, a flush tinting his smooth cheeks. "Yes," he said more firmly, "I guess I have."

"I hoped you would," said she, "and please call me Jessica."

"Jessica," Dr. Friendly tested the name, "would you be free for dinner tonight?"

"I'd be delighted, Alfred," Jessica answered, and took his arm. "Now let me show you around my shop."

In the weeks that followed, Dr. Friendly, who at the beginning had been attracted to this astonishing girl for the oldest and most basic reasons, discovered her very bright mind and found the most acute pleasure of his life in her company. He soon felt the difference in their ages increasingly unimportant, but still he continued to suffer embarrassment in public places. Often she cooked for him in her artfully comfortable apartment above the bookstore, but when they went out, he always chose the darkest restaurants, and one evening, while dining in a place where a pencil flashlight was necessary to read the menu, Jessica objected.

"I feel like a mole. I can't see anything," she complained. "Nobody really cares what kind of relationship we have, Alfred. They don't even notice." She squinted at him through the darkness. "Besides, since you've started coloring your hair you could be my older brother."

"Hardly, my dear," he said.

"Well," Jessica announced, "you're simply going to have to get over this stumbling around in the dark when we get married."

Dr. Friendly blinked. "I'm already married."

"Not really, Alfred," Jessica said firmly. "You've never *really* been married."

And that was the truth. So with the permission of his wife, her lawyers and his lawyers reaching satisfactory agreement, the doctor obtained a quick Mexican divorce and he and Jessica were married in the garden of her parents' home. To his surprise and pleasure, the doctor's son and daughter crossed the Atlantic to attend the ceremony, and those two young people looked at their father for the first time with real interest and some respect.

Jessica's mother was delighted and her father baffled.

"He's older than I am," her father exclaimed. "Who calls who Pop?"

"For heaven's sake, stop fussing. He's distinguished and brilliant and our daughter is married," Jessica's mother responded with triumphant relief. "Call him Al."

Now, after one happy year, in their big room at Kirbo's Lodge, Dr. Friendly looked down at his sleeping young wife, her right foot and ankle protruding from under the covers. Carefully, so as not to awaken her, he lifted the blanket and dropped it gently over her foot. Jessica mumbled in her sleep and thrust the foot free again. Dr. Friendly smiled, turned out the bedside light, opened the drapes and slipped into bed beside her. As he lay there in the comfort of the bed and his love for the young woman beside him, he could see the snow drifting down in the pale amber glow from the lights on the garden paths. He felt her move and her hand lay upon his shoulder. He smiled, closed his eyes and slept.

11

In the first tremors, the tall gray telephone poles that lined the interstate highway began to wave, their cables parting and whipping out into the night with a fiery display of electrical discharge. When the quake reached its full force, the poles cracked at their bases and, for thirty miles north and south of the epicenter, snapped off like breaking matchsticks.

In the communities of Lone Pine and Bishop and Independence, windows shattered, the fronts of brick buildings fell out on the streets and the pavement of the streets and highways when daylight came had the look of jigsaw puzzles put together. The domed roof of the courthouse in Independence crashed down, tombstones in the cemeteries were tossed about like dice, the aqueduct to Los Angeles was ruptured in a hundred places and its water ran joyously free into the desert.

Because the first and most violent quake came in the wee hours of the morning, most people in the towns nearest the epicenter were in their beds in one-story wood-frame houses and there were not many deaths. But so powerful was the quake that even in faraway Los Angeles the tall buildings did their much publicized swaying acts on their presumably quake-proof foundations. The real truth, however, occurred in the Sierra, where creeks and canyons and peaks and precipices were rearranged in such a scramble that it would take ten years of aerial photography and earthbound surveying before topographical maps were reasonably accurate again.

EMIL AND ARCHIE

Present on that historically indelible April afternoon in 1945 were the Chief's three secretaries, two generals, one vice-admiral, one ambassador, a major general, one doctor and the Chief's valet. In addition, but not in the immediate foreground, were the six young officers selected from the FBK personnel to stand by and, upon order, attend to the cremation of the bodies. Of these young officers, the Oberst was the elder and he was only twenty-four, the youngest colonel in the famous elite LAH division and prominent in the intelligence corp of those dashing regiments.

When the Chief had chosen to return to Berlin and take personal command of the defense of that battered city, three hundred of the LAH had been detached from the division and sent to assume the job of guarding the Chief in his bunker. The Oberst had been given command of that gallant three hundred—that is, command under the overall command of a major general.

And now, approximately thirty days after their arrival, the Oberst stood with his five subalterns waiting for the steel door of the Chief's private quarters to open. Waiting for the Chief to come forth and bid them adieu. Waiting for the end.

The man with the lopsided face and the lopsided walk came lopsidedly down the steps from the upper bunker. "Have they not come out?" he demanded to know, and seeing the answer in the faces, he stumped to the steel door and pounded upon it. "We are waiting!" he shouted, and pounded again.

They heard the latch turn and slowly the door swung open. The lopsided man stepped back and bowed, making himself very small as the aged Chief came through the open door with the *zaftig,* simpering young woman behind him all dressed in blue taffeta as if for an afternoon tea. Truly the Chief was only in his fifties but to the Oberst he looked like a very, very old man. His moustache was white and his eyes were sick and matter was stuck in the corner of the left one. His gray tunic had soup stains on its lapels and a darker gravy stain on the left breast where hung the Iron Cross from World War I.

The lopsided man said, "Forgive me for making noise on the door but we were frightened that we had lost you."

And the old Chief made a deprecating gesture with his crippled hand and said, "Not yet, Joseph, but soon," and lopsided Joseph's eyes filled with tears. The Chief shuffled forward and embraced the weeping man and now turned solemnly to shake hands with all the others in the room, or at least with his intimates, because he only nodded toward the Oberst and the chosen young officers.

The Oberst kept expecting the Chief to attempt to make some

memorable statement but none was forthcoming, which surprised the Oberst. The Chief, in the Oberst's opinion, was lacking in almost everything but a clarion voice, and that he had always had aplenty.

As the Chief and his lady passed near the Oberst, he could smell her perfume and with it her armpits. She smiled her simpering smile at the Oberst, no doubt thinking it was an expression of brave suffering. The Oberst automatically inclined his head forward on his stiff, Prussian neck in the proper salute for a lady, but he held his breath against the lingering reek of perfume and armpits. Peasants, both of them, the foolish woman and the bent old man with the soup stains on his tunic.

They turned back to the open steel door and at the door the Chief bowed his lady through and turned to lift his crippled hand and said, "My dear friends, my dear country, fare thee well," and went into the room beyond the door. His valet moved to close the door and now they waited in silence. For ten minutes, they waited in silence. The Oberst had to break wind but he tightened his sphincter muscles and pumped the gas back up into his bowels.

From somewhere through the concrete walls and steel hatches there came a faint thudding sound as if a heavy shoe had been dropped. They waited for the second shoe to drop. It didn't. The lopsided man gestured to the valet and the valet heaved against the steel door and pressed it open. He looked at the lopsided man for further orders and a nod of the lopsided head directed him to take a look in the Chief's apartment. Reluctantly, he moved through the door, thinking that it was a hell of a note that he, a mere servant, a person of no historical consequence, should be sent on this dismal errand. The lopsided man and the generals and admirals and Waffen SS assholes did not have the guts for the job. "You look first," the nod had said. "Be sure it's safe for us to look."

They waited. In a few moments, the valet returned, handkerchief held to his nose. He took the handkerchief away and coughed. "Yes," he said, and now the people of historical consequence entered the Chief's chambers.

The Oberst and his handsome young men were the last to enter, the Oberst leading. They went through the first room, which had served the secretaries, then the second room, which had served as a conference chamber and now into the sleeping room, where all the mourners had gathered with their hands over their noses because the pungence of cyanide and cordite was strong.

No one was doing anything but staring at the two bodies. She lay on a flowered sofa near a coffee table, her blue dress spread about her, a thick green mucus oozing from her nostrils. There was no blood on the Chief's silly lady. The Chief was sprawled in a chair opposite his lady, mouth hanging open, blood dripping from a hole in his temple, handgun on the floor beside the chair. The Oberst could see the gleam of a crushed blue cyanide capsule lying just inside the Chief's lower lip.

"He died like a German warrior," intoned the lopsided man.

The Oberst thought he had died like the madman he was, because of his madness, taking that stupid cunt with him, both thinking their deaths would martyr them as Caesar was martyred or Cleopatra. A soup-stained old *besserwisser,* a loudmouth, was what he was, and she an addlebrained half-whore.

"We will obey his orders," said the major general, and the Oberst and his strong boys stepped forward and gathered up the remains. The lady belched loudly as they lifted her body and the crushed blue capsule fell from the Chief's mouth as they lifted his. His was heavy, almost two hundred pounds of blubber. Four men carried the Chief, two the woman. Making as orderly a funeral procession as was possible in the narrow corridors of the bunker, they reached the stairs and toted the corpses up through the several flights until they reached the exit to the garden of the Chancellery, which was now nothing but rubble enclosed by bombed-out buildings. Here there was no mournful silence but the shriek and crash of Russian artillery shells coming into the wasted city. This Dämmerung was without beauty or Wagnerian glory and its gods were frightened, soiled men and women and two stinking cadavers.

The Oberst and his officers lowered those cadavers into the prepared trench. Russian shells screamed in and exploded a few hundred meters away and shrapnel rattled down into the garden and the gods scattered in panic, rushing back to the bunker door. But not the Oberst. He alone remained beside the trench, unconcerned with the howl of the shells or the hail of shrapnel bits. He lifted one of the lined-up cans of gasoline and poured the liquid upon the bodies, poured another and another, then stepping back, he took a small box of matches from his jacket pocket, struck one and with it fired the whole box and tossed the small torch into the trench.

"Bravo, Oberst," came the cries from the bunker exit and the

Oberst gave himself a silent bravo. *He* was burning the monster. Bravo, Oberst!

For the edification of the gods huddled in the shelter of the door, he snapped his hand out in the grandiloquent Nazi salute toward the roaring flames of the funeral trench and, the sound drowned by the thunder of shell bursts, farted.

Now, with shoulders back, he strode triumphantly to join the others and the lopsided man slapped him on the back and said again, "Bravo," adding, "Will you do the same for me, Herr Oberst?"

"If it is your wish, Herr Reich Chancellor Goebbels," replied the Oberst. But he knew he would not be there to do the same honors for the lopsided man, though it would have given him almost as much pleasure as had the firing of the monster's body.

The mourners drifted rather aimlessly back into the lower bunker, where they drank champagne and spoke of the good old days in Berchtesgaden before the Jews had become such a nuisance and when the world had trembled in fear of Nazi disapproval. The Oberst did not go with the party into the lower bunker but instead maneuvered through the labyrinth of the upper bunker, through the corridors which led past the living quarters of the lopsided man. A tiny little girl in polka dot rompers came skipping through an open door into the corridor and stopped to look up at the powerful, glowering young Oberst. She smiled and he smiled and touched his fingers to his lips, throwing her a kiss, and she hid her face behind her dimpled fingers. The statuesque wife of the lopsided man came from the apartment and said, "Come to me, Heidi!" And Heidi ran to her mother and was lifted into her arms.

The woman turned to the Oberst and he inclined his head properly. She seemed not to really see him with her cold, pale eyes and went back into the apartment with the child. The Oberst thought this, that he should have grabbed the little girl and gone quickly away with her, for he knew that the woman, like the Chief and the Reich Chancellor, was completely mad; he knew she had said that she would, like Medea, sacrifice her children, all six of them, to the memory of the glorious Third Reich and its glorious Chief, that soup-stained old *besserwisser*.

The Oberst stiffened his back and went on. He could no longer cope with madness. He had had enough of that in the past six years. He must now think only of himself and his orderly.

In his room in the upper bunker, a room large enough for two since he was a commandant, his orderly was waiting for him. As young as the Oberst, but slender and dark, of German-Spanish descent, so his identification papers said, he was sitting on his cot in the corner of the room as the Oberst entered. He did not rise.

"Is it over?" he asked.

"Done," said the Oberst. He looked at his watch. "One hour till dark. Then we go."

The Oberst knew that the major general planned to lead the bunker denizens, or at least those who were not idiotic enough to commit suicide with the lopsided man, in an attempted escape through the Russian lines to join the remnants of the German armies northwest of the city. The chances of getting through the Russians were slim and the Oberst knew that the larger the group, the more obvious, and the chances would narrow to impossible. Two men moving alone might make it—but not to the northwest and the relict Waffen SS; instead to the west and the British legions, for he had no intention, if he could help it, of falling prey to the Russian NKVD. Those bastards liked to crack bones and gouge eyes almost as much as Himmler's Gestapo, and while the British intelligence officers might pull one's fingernails out with pliers if need be, they did not enjoy doing it. The Oberst and his orderly would surrender to the British and their more tender mercies.

With the dark came a cessation in the artillery bombardment and now that the Russians were within the city, the British and American planes no longer came over at night with their bellies full of incendiary bombs, and into this relative silence crept the Oberst and his orderly.

They came up from the bunker into the Wilhelmplatz and ran to the subway entrance. Down into that darkness they plunged and came out onto the subway platform, where a jam of people huddled in candlelight with cots and blankets and dunnage and the malodor of feces and urine. The Oberst and the orderly moved as unobtrusively through this mob as they could, suffering the occasional grasp of a desperate hand or a voice mewing for help. At the end of the platform, they dropped off into the subway tunnel and, keeping carefully to the center of the track and away from the third rail, which might, for all the wreckage of the city, still be alive with voltage, they moved behind the muted beams of their small flashlights. In a little while, they passed through the Stadtmitte station and its horde of refugees, then to the Französische Strasse and more masses of fearful Berliners and finally neared the tube under the Spree River.

Moving more swiftly now, assured that the third rail was dead because a fall of steel girders from bomb penetration lay across the rails without accompanying electrical fireworks, they came closer to the entrance to the Spree tube. Ahead they could see electric torches and soon arrived at steel bulkheads which were closed and guarded by two soldiers.

"We must go through," said the Oberst.

"No one passes here," said a guard.

"Please stand aside," said the Oberst.

And the guard obdurately placed his hand on the butt of his pistol.

The orderly moved out from behind the Oberst and the skirt of the trench coat he was wearing lifted in front and the ugly snout of a Schmeisser poked out and fired. The two guards were flung back against the bulkhead and bounced forward, dead before they reached the ground.

"You did not have to shoot them!" bellowed the Oberst.

"Don't be a fool," his orderly softly replied, and he lifted the latch on the bulkhead and shoved. With his light weight it moved only a few feet, but that was enough. The orderly slipped through and the Oberst, still fuming, followed.

They made their way through the dripping S-Bahn tube beneath the river and surfacing they dodged through rubble along the Schiffbauer Damm, crossed the bridge over the Humboldt Harbor on their hands and knees and proceeded west on the Invalidenstrasse. Frequently, they had to take cover in blown-open cellars or bomb craters when Russian squads came trotting through the ruins. They backtracked and circled and climbed and crawled and, before the break of day, they were on the outskirts of Berlin. Then all that day they lay quietly, not sleeping and without food, in brush alongside a canal through which drifted the bloated bodies of German and Russian soldiers.

With the darkness they moved on, going west, and on the next morning they came upon a British bivouac beside the main highway to Berlin and they threw away their weapons and came into the British camp with hands raised. In his excellent English, the Oberst announced that he was an officer and asked for the commanding officer of the platoon. The commanding officer was awakened and came from a roadside cafe where he had spent the night sleeping on a dining table and managed to get his hand to his brow to return the Oberst's stiff salute.

"My name, Captain, is Colonel Emil von Rothke of the Waffen SS and the Leibstandarte Adolf Hitler. I surrender to you. The man is my orderly. His papers will tell you that he is Corporal Wilhelm Stanza, but his real name is Archimedes Epstein. He is a Jew."

In years to come, when Emil and Archie would have one of their rare quarrels, Archie would always harken back to that moment and say, "I was your passport. You used me—the Jew—a passport."

"What should I have done?" Emil would ask, and to that Archie had no answer and they would be silent and their tempers would ebb and soon Emil would say, "Forgive me, Herr Epstein," and Archie would say, "There is nothing to forgive, Herr von Rothke."

That mode of formal address between them began when they were fourteen years old, child prodigies both, enrolled in the college of higher mathematics at Heidelberg University and from most proper families. Archimedes derived from an old and honored line of musicians in the musical city of Leipzig. In the beginning his name was Johann, but when his father realized that the boy grasped multiplication and division at the age of four, he promptly changed his name to that of the Greek mathematician on the theory that an innate talent should be honored.

Emil was, of course, Prussian—from Brandenburg—of a family that could trace itself back to the Teutonic knights of the thirteenth century, and young Emil von Rothke was the last male of the line and great store was set in him by his aged grandfather, General Emil von Rothke. His father, Major General Emil von Rothke, had died shortly before Emil's birth of a lung cancer that had had its beginnings in a dose of mustard gas in World War I.

Emil and Archie were introduced to each other by the professor of analytic geometry at the university. "Herr von Rothke, I wish you to meet Herr Epstein," he had said, and that is the way it started, first as an amusement between them and then to become a habit.

They were dreadfully spoiled, aggravatingly brilliant and man- ifestly jealous of each other's brilliance, a jealousy that spurred each to best the other and finally brought them together in absolute respect. They were perfectly matched. One could not best the other in any test of mathematics, including tensor calculus, or in any game that depended upon cerebration. As for the games of tennis or soccer, they could do as well as any healthy lad but those activities bored them. They approached the activity of sex as they would any equation—a girl plus money equals satisfaction—and they journeyed to Munich on a chosen weekend, rented an apartment, went into the streets and found two fairly attractive and apparently clean prostitutes, took them to the apartment and there, at the age of fourteen and a half, Archie and Emil lost their virginities. Journeys to Munich became a ritual for them every other weekend during the three years they were together in Heidelberg.

They learned to sing in the beer gardens, graduated to the joys of schnapps, caught the clap, cured it and began the intellectual pursuit of theoretical physics.

It was now 1938 and Hitler was stronger and more manic. Being a Jew, Archie had to leave Heidelberg. He and Emil corresponded, a correspondence that consisted largely of a peculiar game of chess by letter. Taking turns, each would devise a game and give the other only the moves of black. From those moves the receiver had to work out the moves white had made to cause black's moves. It was a contest that would have baffled even Capablanca or Alekhine but it was for Archie and Emil an idle pastime, like doing a crossword puzzle.

With the winds of war blowing out of Hitler's big, loud mouth it became necessary, as a family duty, for Emil to involve himself with the German military. In 1939 he received training in the Reichsjugend and, because of his aptitudes, was immediately snapped up by the Waffen SS intelligence corps.

In 1940, his letters to Archie went unanswered and, on leave at home in Brandenburg, he made an overnight drive to Leipzig and found that the Epstein family had been gathered up, making a considerable dent in the Leipzig symphony (three violins, two cellos, one French horn and two flutes) and scattered to several concentration camps.

Emil returned quickly to Berlin and, using his not inconsiderable influence, learned that Archimedes Epstein, mother Epstein, flautist father Epstein and youngest sister, Sarah, had been sent to Belsen in north Germany. He gained access to the files and substituted a new card on Archimedes Epstein to show that Archie was an adopted child whose nationality was Spanish and whose name was Wilhelm Archimedes Stanza. Now, going directly to the commanding general of his division, he reported his personal knowledge of an injustice being done to a friend. Being a little in awe of Leutnant von Rothke, as were most people who knew him, the general arranged for the release of that poor Spanish lad and gave Leutnant von Rothke permission to go himself to Belsen and deliver the papers of release.

When Archie was brought into the office of the Belsen commandant, Emil stood and said, "Well, Herr Stanza, had you given up hope?"

And Archie, with no knowledge of the secret moves Emil had made to free him, instantly replied, "Almost, Herr Leutnant von Rothke, but I had faith that someone would discover the truth of my identity." Checkmate.

Emil drove away from the charnel stench of Belsen into the fresh winter air of north Germany. Beside him sat emaciated Archie, hollow-eyed and with malnutrition sores on his face.

"We will next get your family freed," said Emil.

"My family is dead," said Archie.

"I am sorry. How did you escape death?"

"I volunteered for certain unpleasant duties."

Emil did not ask what the duties were but drove in silence. Finally, "It is all madness," he said.

"A madness that Germany thrives upon," said Archie. "Look at you—an officer in the black uniform of the Schutzstaffel."

"You know about my family, Herr Epstein. We serve the fatherland. It is tradition. I cannot break my family's heart."

Said Archie quietly, "I knocked the gold out of my family's teeth."

Emil hastily, recklessly turned the car from the highway and braked to a stop, leaped out and vomited. Weakly, he sat back upon the auto's running board and feebly mopped the green bile off the toes of his polished boots with his handkerchief.

"Do you wish me to drive?" asked Archie.

"If you would be so kind," said Emil.

They drove on toward the south and Berlin and, for the rest of their lives, they never again spoke of those matters. It was not necessary to speak of them. Being together was enough to remind the two men of the horror, the horror of their pasts. They were inseparable, like two moons without a planet orbiting one another forever, held close by the gravity of their guilt.

On their surrender to the English, they were almost immediately sent on to London, where they went through many days of interrogation and were interned in separate prison camps until early 1946. They asked to remain in England and became British citizens. Archie found a position as an instructor of calculus at Cambridge and Emil was given employment in the British War Department, aiding in the historical reconstruction of the battles of the war.

On each Saturday night, they would meet in a pub near Notting Hill Gate, tank up on ale, catch a bus to Soho and find themselves women. Having completed these necessities, they would stumble along to Emil's bed-sitter on Bayswater Road and sleep it off, Emil on the floor on a pallet and his guest snoring in the lumpy, spring-sprung bed. It was not a productive period for them but it was a needed respite, a time to drift, to be caught in eddies and carried away again by gentle tides. Finally, though, these two fertile minds began to sprout restless tendrils that searched for anchor.

"Games," said Archie. "We were good at games."

Emil took a gulp of stout and agreed with this observation. They were in the pub near Notting Hill Gate. They were twenty-eight years old.

"I believe," said Archie, "that the games called 'chance' are as subject to the laws of mathematics as any other part or thing of the universe."

"Let us study that proposition," said Emil.

Six months later, two young men, one a powerful example of Teutonic physiognomy and the other a dangerous-looking Mediterranean type, both poorly dressed by comparison with the other players at the roulette table in Monte Carlo, were standing near the wheel end of the table intently watching the ball find colors and numbers. They were not taking notes as did the usual systems player, but their concentration on the wheel was like that of hungry wolves on a stray lamb. And they had been standing there for three hours, becoming objects of curiosity to the croupiers and punters.

Then at a given stop of the wheel, the dangerous one nodded to the Teuton and the big man stepped forward and tossed five five-hundred-franc chips on the table and said, *"À cheval huit, s'il vous plait, messieurs."*

A croupier obeyed by placing one chip on eight and the other four on the lines between eight and its surrounding numbers. The tourneur spun the wheel and the ivory ball, and the ball sizzled about in its groove and dropped into eight and the bank paid thirty to one for the eight and seventeen to one on the four chips circling eight.

A croupier stacked and raked the winnings to a place at the table where there was a vacant chair and gracefully gestured the blond young man toward that place. Emil sat and Archie stood behind him.

Now, to the bafflement of the gamesters, they made no further bets but again intently watched the wheel for another two hours before they obviously selected a precisely calculated moment in which Emil pushed all the chips forward and said, "*À cheval douze, s'il vous plait, messieurs,*" and twelve won, and by 3 A.M. the bank at Monte Carlo was broken and Emil von Rothke and Archimedes Epstein had begun a career in gambling that would make them wealthy before they were thirty years old.

"It is not a system," explained Archie. "It is a matter of covariant tensors. But please don't expect us to give you our equation."

And by the time they were thirty, they were barred from playing against the bank at every casino in the world and had turned to that final contest of contests—bridge. And usually they won.

And how did the accumulation of wealth and of years change their lives? They ate better food, lived in better hotels, dressed expensively, enjoyed a finer class of prostitute, were celebrated in their international circle of acquaintances and Emil became famous with his syndicated London *Times* column on bridge, but they, in secret, remained in bondage to those terrible years when each served his Nazi masters in his own unforgivable way.

When he was forty, Emil made an attempt to break free of that past and of Archie. He had developed an affection for a wealthy French widow of title.

"Herr Epstein, will you be my best man?"

"With pleasure," agreed Archie, and never looked happier than at the wedding. He danced with the bride at the reception held in the ballroom of the old casino in Monte Carlo, where their careers had begun, and he kissed Emil on both cheeks and drove in his Italian Maserati to the airport in Nice, took the first plane to Paris and thence to America. Emil did not hear from him, did not know where he was.

Six months passed. Emil came into his wife's bedroom in their suite in the Dorchester Hotel and sat on the side of her bed, admired her beauty, spoke of his love for her, presented her with a check for five million francs, asked that she get a divorce, drove to the London airport in his American Continental and flew to America.

Emil found Archie in the fabled Kirbo's Lodge in the high Sierra of California. They bowed and shook hands and Emil said, "I have come back. Please forgive me." And Archie replied, "As usual, Herr von Rothke, there is nothing to forgive."

By nightfall, they were engaged in a game of bridge with two very rich Egyptians who were, by dawn, a quarter of a million dollars poorer and the tradition of the autumn bridge tourney had begun at the lodge.

Now more years had passed and Archie and Emil were still orbiting one another and had come again to the great lodge for the tourney where fortunes were won and lost and they were, as always, winning. And in the afternoon of that day, while the blizzard was closing now upon the Sierra and after Emil had had his customary hearty lunch and a nap, they went into the soundproof cardroom and sat at a table with two Japanese challengers and began to play the last game they would ever play.

12

In the northern end of the valley between the Sierra and the Whites, where the Owens River was still a river just before it poured into the Los Angeles aqueducts, an astonishing thing happened on the first quake: the river ran backward, upstream to the north—and on the second, the river simply disappeared. There was no river. It had gone underground. Six days later, as if to prove a theory of seismologists that fractures in the earth are connected, a tremendous stream of water burst forth from the mouth of a cave in the Tehachapi Mountains—those mountains being several hundred miles to the west and south of Owens Valley. A test of the water proved that it contained certain vegetable matter found in the soil of Owens Valley and not found in the Tehachapis. The Los Angeles Water and Power Company promptly laid claim to the gushing spring as its lost river, and, in short time, despite the outrage of the residents of the dry Tehachapis who considered the fresh wild water a gift from heaven, was piping its bubbly essence into a nearby aqueduct and thence into the rainbird golf course sprinklers and marine blue jacuzzis and shocking pink commodes of the City of the Angels.

CORA AND LORENZO

"Daughter, you're putting too much goddam toilet water in that goop," said Mama.

"It's okay, Mama," said Cora, and poured another pint of Eau de Verbenia ($1.76 per pint at the Bessemer five-and-dime) into the tub of goop. Now she energetically stirred the goop with the old canoe paddle.

"Those poor ladies is going to smell just like a whorehouse," said Mama.

"Maybe that'll get their husbands all excited," said Cora, and Mama laughed and then squeaked with pain because the cigarette between the gnarls of her arthritic fingers had burned too short.

Cora reached over and knocked the cigarette from her mother's hand and stamped it out on the floor. "Mama, you're going to barbecue yourself one day with those goddam cigarettes!"

"How many pleasures I got left?" asked Mama. "Well, smoking cigarettes is one of 'em and by god I don't aim to stop smoking till the cows come home," she proclaimed.

"Okay, Mama," said Cora, and began to bottle the goop, painstakingly ladling it through a little tin funnel into the rows of twelve-ounce bottles on the back porch table. When the bottles were full, they were screw-capped and placed in bread cartons for storage and more bottles lined up on the table and filled from the tub of goop. When the tub was empty, Cora would set about labeling the bottles with her homemade labels, typed out on green paper and cut to size with kitchen shears, then stuck on the bottles with school desk glue —all phases of this manufacturing process being accomplished by the labor of Cora McElvain.

The goop, Cora's Pure Base, was sold exclusively to those customers who came to Miss Cora's Beauty Shoppe on Cherry Street in Bessemer, Alabama, a town where the steel mills roared and flashed their fires all night long, and Cora's customers were the wives and daughters and grandmothers of the men who worked in the mills.

"Listen," Cora would say in defense of her product, "it's the same goddam goop you'll buy at the corner drug and it costs you fifty per cent less. And it won't put no end to your wrinkles or pimples, but it'll cover 'em up and make you look nice and pink and healthy."

"Goddam," said Mama, "but all of Cora's customers look like they're blushing fit to be tied."

And Cora remembered that remark—the blushing part—and when she wanted a classier name for the goop, she called it Day Blush.

Madame Cara's Day Blush Products (Lorenzo had suggested that Cara was smarter than Cora—"Cora sounds like somebody doing dishes," he said) began on that back porch of the dirty little bungalow on Cherry Street where, in the front room, Cora had her

Beauty Shoppe—six chairs and driers and two shampoo basins—
and Cora was the sole owner and employee.

And from that humble beginning, as they say, came Madame
Cara's Day Blush lipsticks and Night Blush lipsticks, and Madame
Cara's hair tints and colognes, perfumes and bath oils and jewelry,
followed by scarfs and blouses and pants and sweaters and bras and
panties, and that slogan that had no successful equal in cosmetics
advertising, *MADAME CARA LOVES YOU, JUST YOU,* and its
signature, a tiny golden heart stamped on all of Madame Cara's
products or their packaging.

But in sixteen years—sixteen from the day Cora walked into
the Alabama Trust in Bessemer and placed a bottle of the goop on
an assistant cashier's desk and stated that she wanted a ten-
thousand-dollar loan to start a cosmetic manufacturing company—
the Cora who became Madame Cara had not changed in any way
except that she was rich and thirty-five pounds heavier. On that afternoon, as she sat at the bridge table in the cardroom at Kirbo's
Lodge, playing the hand to Lorenzo's dummy (their opponents
being the redheaded Pole now paired with the British lady in the
gardening hat), she was still about as her mother had described her,
"Poor little Cora got the shitty end of the stick when they was passing out looks but, my, they sure give that kid some balls."

Cora had taken the bid for the hand at five no trumps, was doubled and ballsed right in with a redouble and was now making the
bid with the ballsy kind of finesse play that had gotten her where she
was in life, Numero Uno in the field of cosmetics and able to win or
lose a million bucks at cards without turning one of her frowsy
hairs. She was tough.

"My son's a fucking fairy!" bellowed Papa Dante and his other
four sons, in their rubber shrimping aprons and rubber boots, stood
behind him with long, sad looks on their long, thin faces.

"Ai, Dio, Dio, my boy's a goddam hairdresser," wept Papa
Dante, and Lorenzo, hating the squashy deck of the wharf where the
shrimp were brought off the boats, feeling the ooze soiling the
pointed toes of his fawn-colored suede shoes, waited patiently for
his father to run out of breath, which he finally did.

"Papa, I'm not a fairy, just because I'm a hairdresser. It's no
different from a barber except I cut ladies' hair and make more
money."

But the father was not to be consoled. "Look, look at him!" he yelled. "I send him to New Orleans to a business school and the sonofabitch comes back a fucking hairdresser!"

Men from the other parts of the long wharf were gathering with big grins on their faces—shrimping men all, putting out into the gulf in the morning, chugging home in the twilight—grinning now because they knew the Dante family the way they knew the boats and the sea, all of their lives in Biloxi, Mississippi, where the Dante Wharf was built by grandfather Dante. And they were grinning because Papa Dante was too proud a man and had got himself a son who wouldn't walk the line, and if they privately thought young Lorenzo Dante was probably a fucking fairy, it amused them because of Papa Dante's rage.

"Get off my wharf," howled Papa Dante, and grabbed a handful of the tiny gulf shrimp from a wire basket and hurled them at his youngest son, who, with as much aplomb as he could muster, brushed the shrimp off the sleeves and shoulders of his pongee suit, shook them off the brim of his Borsalino hat and, tippy-toeing through the waste on the deck, left the wharf and climbed into his pink, secondhand '55 T-Bird and drove into Biloxi to see his mother. There he received better treatment and a nice lunch of preziosini al tomato and agnello brodettato with salad, coffee and then a pastiera di Pasqua because it was near Eastertime. Lorenzo could eat that wop stuff and never gain an ounce, which was another reason Cora hated him, or to be precise, his guts.

Lorenzo returned to New Orleans and his first job as a hairdresser in a cluttered little salon in the Quarter, where most of the customers were strippers from Bourbon Street or hookers from Canal Street or bar girls from any street. When he was not backcombing or beehiving platinum hair, he was rooting about in the Canal Street haberdasheries, looking for bargains to hang on his skinny back, and when he was not engaged in either of those important activities, he was playing bridge. He belonged to four bridge clubs and there was not a night in the week when Lorenzo wasn't propped up at a bridge table playing for a quarter cent a point, all he could afford.

As for his hairdressing, he was barely adequate but he made a great display of artistic expertise, waving his scissors about like a baton, standing back and viewing his work with loud ohs and ahs, and he was recognized for the natural born salesman he was by a sales representative of the Aphrodite Beauty Supplies Company (home office in Cincinnati, Ohio) and offered a job traveling for the company, selling hair driers, wigs, shampoos and a full line of beauty goops. He accepted and his territory included parts of Tennessee, Arkansas, Mississippi and Alabama, which first brought him to Miss Cora's Shoppe in Bessemer.

When he walked into the bungalow with his catalogues and black sample case, Cora thought, Jesus, what a prick this character is; look at those birds-egg blue shoes and that purple silk tie and that cute little moustache about the size of a mascara brush.

"Do you know," said Lorenzo, "that you have the most marvelously expressive eyes—just like Miss Bette Davis' eyes, only more so." And Cora thought what a pile of crap that was, but she placed an order for six blue-gray wigs and after he had gone, she studied herself in the mirror and began to see what the little man with the little mascara brush moustache had meant. There was, in that round, pudgy face, something about the eyes—her and Bette Davis. And that made her feel better about herself than she had in a long time, ever since Miss Gompers in the ninth grade had privately whispered to her that she was her favorite pupil out of that whole class in Home Ec.

It wasn't easy being Cora McElvain. Mama had started getting crippled up when she was only thirty and Cora, being too young to work, had to chase after her father for eating and rent money. He worked in the steel mill and made good wages, but he had another family and while he acknowledged that Cora was his child, he did not contribute much to her keep. When things were really desperate, Cora would wait outside the time office at the mill and, at the top of her lungs, yell, "I'm hungry and Mama's sick and you're going to let us starve to death!" when he would come out at the end of his shift. And she would follow him all the way to the Plunkett Beer Parlor, where he could not enjoy his glass of draft because she would push her nose against the screened door and let snot run through the screen as she cried. Finally, in shame, he would have to fork over twenty bucks or so and Cora would yell, "I hope you get your organ grinder cut off, you stingy sonofabitch!"

When Cora was fourteen, she got a job cleaning up the day's mess in a beauty salon in downtown Bessemer, and then she started doing a little part-time manicuring and shampoos and, when she was sixteen, she lied about her age and got a beauty operator's license and hung a shingle out in front of the dirty little bungalow on Cherry Street.

Anyway, the next time Lorenzo hit Bessemer, as drummers say, Cora handed him a bottle of her own concoction and asked his opinion and lived to regret that moment for the rest of her life or, as she put it, "That was the dumbest fucking thing I ever did, show that bastard my goop."

Behind his mascara brush moustache and small teeth and big nose and professional drummer's smile, Lorenzo was a man who could hang ten on the tide that would lead him to fortune. It was not the quality of Cora's goop that impressed him, it was Cora. He could see the tiger scratching at the cage door in that dirty little bungalow cage in Bessemer and he thought it might be worth his while to open that door. He suggested a partnership deal between them. He would take on Cora's Pure Base as an under-the-table item on his rounds and they would split fifty–fifty. Cora agreed to seventy–thirty, but gave Lorenzo a permanent partnership in her future and Lorenzo went all the way with her right to the cardroom at Kirbo's Lodge.

It was not a free ride. He contributed a large share toward the success of Madame Cara's products, more than 30 per cent, he claimed, but if it was not quite up to that, it was substantial, particularly in the field of packaging and advertising. It was Lorenzo who invented *MADAME CARA LOVES YOU, JUST YOU,* and the tiny golden heart.

You would have thought that two people who together started with nothing but spit and grit, built an empire of goops for my lady's face, folderols for her bosom and bottom, doodads for her ears and neck and wrists, and scent made from whale vomit to make her smell like violets, would have developed a genuine affection and comradeship for all the trouble and travail it took to build that empire. But with Cora and Lorenzo, it went exactly the other way. The closer they got to the top of the heap, the more they hated each other. It was only that odd turn of character they shared, the character of the gambler, the high roller, that kept them together. They could not resist the bet, the game, the chance. And early on in their relationship Cora, who had mastered poker before she was fifteen and become the *enfant terrible* of the Saturday night, three-dollar limit in the back end of Garth's Poolroom on the corner near the dirty little bungalow, was introduced to bridge by Lorenzo and she never looked back.

Since they were so well suited in many ways, it really would not have needed much to make them stick together as loving companions and sympathetic travelers through the vale, but now being halfway through, it was plain that they would never find that adhesive. Instead, they were both devoted not only to bridge but to longevity, each determined to outlive the other and dump on the other's grave.

Perhaps if there had been any sexual attraction between them, it would have ameliorated their devotion to hatred, but both were neuters, oddities one occasionally sees (though there may be more of them than meets the eye), who had no sex drive in any direction.

Still, Cora and Lorenzo were not without some admirable traits. Both loved their mothers. Mama McElvain, now no more than a poor, twisted old wire of a thing, was plugged into life supports in the big nursing room Cora had built for her in a mansion in Los Angeles. When wealth had come to Miss Cora of Bessemer, she had promptly moved West to that black hole in the firmament of the parvenu that gobbles up everything from rich Arabs to British rock stars, and Lorenzo, not to be outdone, had purchased an estate in the same city, a little more than a stone's throw (for protection) from Cora's place, and here he had installed his mother, complete with a St. Charles kitchen where she could to her heart's content cook up pots and pans of agnolotti, gnocchi, frittura piccata and beef garmugia Lucca style. Mother Dante had chosen to leave Biloxi, the shrimp, Papa Dante and her other four sons because they had never truly appreciated her culinary talents, actually preferring grits, okra and chicken fried steak, while Lorenzo doted on those steaming Italian plates of pasta and veal laced with piquant sauces and anchovy butter.

Lorenzo and Cora had never visited each other in their respective dwellings. When they invited another team for bridge, the game took place in a condominium they owned jointly in which there was a bridge table and four chairs and not another stick of furniture. When they traveled together, they sometimes occupied the same suite in a hotel, but only one that, like Kirbo's Lodge, offered suites of grand size with bedrooms well separated by the expanse of the suite, and even then they fought like two cats in a shoe box.

It is entirely possible that they enjoyed their endless duel, that it may have been a substitution neurosis for their obstructed sexual outlets or some other psychiatric snozzlewobble, but it is also improbable that either would have shed a tear had they been separated by death. The catastrophe at Kirbo's Lodge proved nothing, because they both survived, no doubt due to their perseverance against each other and the strength of their individual wills to be the survivor.

13

Our passion for measuring forces over which we have no control is one of those curious aspects of human nature. Much wealth and time and machinery is put to use obtaining the inches of rainfall, the feet of snowfall, the velocity of the wind and the energy involved in the shake of a quake. Most of this information is utterly useless and the most useless of all is the measurement of the force of our planet's quivering moments. We do not really know the absolute basic cause of the damned things, whether the earth is shrinking or expanding; we think we know the immediate causes and can draw all sorts of fancy diagrams of how faults move up and down or backward and forward, but actually it is no more than a lot of guesswork.

The Indians believed that we were riding on the back of a gigantic tortoise (which explained the curvature of the land toward the horizon) and when the tortoise took one of his occasional slow steps, he shook up the folks and their tepees on his back. Maybe the Indians had the whole thing right and we have got it all wrong.

ARLY

They were gathered on the green playing field in their white bloomers and blue middies, choosing up sides for the game of volleyball. Arly Kirbo because she was popular and a good organizer was one captain, and the Swedish girl who was the best athlete in school and whose father was a count was the other captain, and the girls stood about them yelling, "Choose me, Arly!" or, "Take me, Helga!" all in French, of course, because the main reason they were sent to the school was to learn French and become chic and terrifically continental.

There was a new girl who stood quietly apart from the rest and looked very trim and poised and above all the clamor. Her name was Elsa Geising and she was from Vienna and this was only her first year because her father, a very rich merchant, had been appointed ambassador to the League of Nations and had brought his family and moved them into a grand château in the Swiss countryside near Geneva.

Arly felt this new girl's eyes upon her, those curious green, brown-speckled eyes with their long lashes, and she suddenly turned and pointed to Elsa. "You, Elsa!" cried Arly, and Elsa smiled and Arly's heart beat faster. She did not know why it beat faster because she was only sixteen years old and innocent even for that.

Elsa was older than the other girls, almost eighteen, and because she was new and so coolly self-confident, her classmates made much of her, vying for her attention. She had a personal style and some of the girls began to let their hair grow longer, turning up the ends the way Elsa did hers. They admired her wardrobe of bright scarfs and English sweaters and began to dress casually, the way Elsa dressed. Arly was not an imitator, rather she possessed a sturdy independence and, in spite of her awareness of Elsa, the almost frightening sensitivity that made her conscious of the older girl's every move, she kept her distance, remained friendly but went her own way, as always. She did not change her regimented mode of dress and she continued to wear her dark hair in a curly halo about her face.

She had been exceedingly intelligent about herself even when she was a child. At the academy, where harmless and quite natural experiments in sex went on between any number of the girls who, like Arly, had grown up in that secluded school, the experiments were not harmless for Arly. She had realized long before her fifteenth birthday that she was not like the others and had ceased lending herself to those exploratory ticklings beneath the covers. She had become prudish and withdrawn and made a great pretense of being absorbed in her studies.

Her modesty had become the butt of jokes—friendly jokes because she was well liked. She would find all her panties stolen and would have to go red-faced to classes, naked under her skirts. Bananas were left in her bed and anonymous letters posted to her, presumably written by some youth at Le Rosay, the neighboring boys academy, that would make ornate, sexual suggestions.

Arly took it all with good humor but insisted upon her privacy and her prim behavior. None of her young companions understood that Arly was guarding a secret. She had experienced an excitement in herself she knew the other girls did not feel as they rolled about on each other and played at love-making. She had no interest in boys and surreptitiously she coveted the growing breasts of her classmates and wanted to kiss them, was fascinated with those round, peach-colored bottoms in the showers and the stirring of pubic hair at the triangles of soft bellies. She had desired them all and this unfocused desire now took shape and substance in the slender form of Elsa Geising. Arly became even more cautious.

Arly and Elsa both attended a class in Old English literature, Arly being an "A" student and Elsa an indifferent one, and finally Elsa came to Arly. They had been assigned a paper on *Beowulf*.

"I'm a complete dunce when it comes to poetry." Elsa smiled charmingly as if the admission excused her laziness. "Will you help me?"

They sat side by side on Arly's narrow bed as she bravely tried to explain the heroic poem to Elsa, describing the slaying by young Beowulf of the monster Grendel, conscious of her shaking hand as she turned the pages of the book. She spoke of the death of then King Beowulf in his old age, mortally wounded in his final savage battle with a monstrous dragon whom he defeated and slew before he died. The Austrian girl sat very close to Arly under the guise of reading the small print and, when Arly shifted uncomfortably, she moved closer and Arly fought the warmth that weakened her voice as she sat striving to overcome her own inner monster.

Elsa lingered for more than an hour. "You've helped me," she told Arly when finally she rose and prepared to leave. "Thank you." She studied the austere little room. "You must come to my home for tea. Tomorrow afternoon?"

She smiled at the entranced Arly, who happily agreed to come to tea and, as if impulsively, she suddenly kissed Arly's hand. "You're sweet," she said. "I'll send the car to pick you up at three-thirty."

The next day was a Saturday and Arly spent the morning studying her wardrobe, feverishly trying on and discarding clothes. Finally she chose a navy dress with a white Peter Pan collar and a full skirt that swirled about just below her knees. As the buzzer on the wall signaled the arrival of the car, she donned a wide-brimmed sailor hat and picked up her white doeskin gloves.

A gray-haired Swiss chauffeur, wearing a gray uniform and a closed, impassive expression on his rather gray face, waited in the visitors' lounge downstairs. "Mademoiselle Kirbo?"

Arly nodded and he led her to where a long gray Rolls Royce (matching the driver) waited at the curb. He opened the door and Arly stepped inside, leaned back against the pearl gray upholstery.

It was a bright day and they drove perhaps half an hour through the hills, out of the city into the early spring. They turned onto a narrow road and went on for almost a quarter of a mile before entering a high iron gate of intricate design, beyond which the eighteenth-century château could be seen surrounded by sweeping lawns and shaded by spreading oak, elm and linden trees. As the Rolls entered the circular driveway, the château door opened and the blond and lithesome Elsa, wearing a flowing white dress, stood framed in the doorway like the Coca-Cola girl on the back of American magazines. Knowing how she looked, she held the pose for the adoring Arly, who had stepped from the car.

"There you are!" cried Elsa. "Come quickly and meet my family."

Arly went to her and caught the fragrance of lilies of the valley and thought how perfect for the spring. Lovely. How lovely was Elsa. Elsa led her into the house, through the spacious rooms with their paneled and molded ceilings, their dark wood tones and Moroccan rugs into a graceful drawing room where wide windows opened on a garden.

"Mama, Papa," said Elsa, speaking in French, "may I present my dearest friend, Arlene Kirbo."

Arly shook hands with Mrs. Geising, a coiffed and manicured woman who might have been Elsa's older sister, and then blushed as Mr. Geising, a trim and distinguished-looking man wearing a blue-tinted monocle, murmured, "Fräulein," and kissed her outstretched fingers.

"You are so welcome," Mrs. Geising said. "Please—be comfortable. Sit down."

A maid served tea and small, delicious lemon cakes and Arly

kept her back straight as she had been taught, sipped her tea and admired the beautiful room with its pale gray walls and lettuce green drapes.

"You're American." Mr. Geising's French was pure, without accent. "Where is your home?"

"In California, San Francisco," said Arly with careful pronunciation.

"Ah, San Francisco," said he. "A marvelous city—very civilized."

"Elsa says you have helped her with her studies," Elsa's mother said.

"Only a little," said Arly, and glanced at Elsa, who made a soft and kissable moue.

"Oh yes," her father said. "She is beautiful, Miss Elsa, but very lazy." He patted her cheek and looked up as a tall, handsome youth, Elsa's brother, entered the room. "There you are, Erich! You must meet our pretty guest."

He introduced Arly, who acknowledged Erich politely but without the slightest hint of the flirtatious interest to be expected from a young girl in the presence of such an attractive young man.

"With regrets, I can't join you," said Erich, his look approving the fresh and pretty Arly. "Perhaps I'll see you again?"

Eyes only for Elsa, Arly barely nodded, and Elsa smiled a secret little smile. Just us, it said. You and me.

Arly was not impressed by wealth, for she had always had that, but Caiphus Kirbo had sent his beloved only child to Switzerland to make her a fine lady and Arly had developed taste. She could not help comparing the serene simplicity of Elsa's home, its Louis XV furniture and walls hung with Van Dyck portraits, seascapes by Vandevelde and paintings by Renoir and Vermeer to the house built by her grandfather on Nob Hill in San Francisco, in which her father still lived—a cupolaed monstrosity with bearskin rugs and mounted moose heads. Nor could she help but guiltily compare the polished sophistication of Mr. Geising with the earthy and exuberant coarseness of Caiphus Kirbo.

After they finished tea, the girls excused themselves and Elsa took Arly into the gardens. Enclosed by vine-covered walls, the grounds were a model of groomed formality with flowered terraces, sculptured fountains, splashing waterfalls and, here and there, a gardener bent over geometrical floral beds of blazing color.

In the center was a circular pond surrounded by bright yellow daffodils. They sat on a white iron bench beside the pool.

"Most girls think Erich very handsome," said Elsa. "Did you not find him so?"

"Oh yes," Arly answered quickly. "He is, but so are you all. And it's lovely here. You must be very happy."

"Erich is," said Elsa. "But he's so easily satisfied. The girls make much of him and he is content."

Arly did not look at Elsa as she spoke, rather stared into the water where Elsa's reflection shimmered in the sparkling clear pool.

"He brings his friends home to meet me—oh, he means to be nice—but boys are crude, I think, and mostly boring."

Hardly breathing, Arly dared not look at Elsa and did not respond.

"Sometimes I'm very lonely." Elsa's voice was soft and plaintive, but her shrewd glance at Arly's profile took in the rapidly beating pulse that fluttered at her temple. And Arly, who knew the real loneliness of being different, felt a rush of sympathy as Elsa intended that she should. A lightness of spirit danced through her at the unexpected revelation that the lovely Elsa was not as confident and whole as she appeared to be, that perhaps, like Arly, she too felt inexplicable yearnings and undefined discontent. In the pond she watched the sunlight on Elsa's golden hair as it curled about her shoulders, then turned and with her honest dark eyes looked directly at the Austrian girl.

"How could you ever be lonely?" asked Arly softly, and, in her sincerity, forgot her shyness. "You're as beautiful as—as those daffodils."

Overwhelmed by her boldness and fearful that she had betrayed herself, the innocent Arly looked back at the reflections in the water and did not see the coiled satisfaction in the eyes of the other girl.

Elsa's voice was silky. "You're so kind," said she, and patted Arly's hand. "Still, I am lonely. My parents love me, of course, but that is, after all, an extension of their own egos. And if acquaintances admire my clothes or my appearance, that is meaningless too. I need closeness and companionship—from someone who understands me. I have no one."

Overwhelmed by the confidences with which Elsa was entrusting her, Arly was silent.

"Perhaps it might be you, Arly," suggested Elsa. "You'd be

good for me. You're strong and all of a piece, not neurotic as I am, and I hope we shall become real friends."

Arm in arm, they walked back through the fragrant gardens and Elsa accompanied her to the waiting car. "We'll lunch together on Monday," said she.

On the trip back, Arly stared through the car windows without seeing, her mind and heart full of Elsa. She thought she had never been so happy.

She spent all of Sunday in giddy anticipation of lunch on Monday, full of things she wanted to discuss with Elsa. The girls shared only the class in Old English literature, which fell just before their lunch hour. Arly arrived early, and was dismayed when Elsa was not in her place as the class began. When she arrived ten minutes late and took her seat, she did not even glance at Arly. When class was dismissed, Arly gathered together her books and eagerly started toward Elsa, who was in a group of girls. As she approached them, Elsa linked her arms with two of the girls and they hurried from the room without a backward look at Arly, leaving her in pained bewilderment.

Poor Arly anguished through the balance of the day, going over and over the time she had spent with Elsa and wondering if she had in some way offended. She waited hopefully for a knock at her door in the late afternoon and that night she slept hardly at all. The next day she hurried to classes, hoping for a nod from Elsa, and when several more days passed without acknowledgment of any kind from the Austrian girl, she wrote a note, which she passed to her in class. "Dear Elsa," wrote Arly. "I have, I'm sure, been terribly stupid in some way. Whatever, it was not intended and I have only the warmest feelings for you."

In hot embarrassment, Arly rushed from the room when class was over without waiting for a response from Elsa. That night she was feverish and could not eat her dinner. She had no sleep and did not attend classes the following day. In the early afternoon a beribboned white box was delivered to Arly. Inside was a perfect red rose on a bed of white velvet and a pink, scented note. "You must forgive me," Arly read. "I am uncertain of my feelings about us—and I am a little bit afraid." It was signed "Affectionately, Elsa," and Arly's tears of relief spotted the note. That night she slept with the rose against her cheek and, in the morning, pressed it between the pages of *Beowulf*.

During the weeks that followed, Arly did not see Elsa alone and she was not invited again to the château, but Elsa smiled and chatted when they met and Arly walked through her days in a dreamlike trance. She was unaware of the other girl's sadistic nature and saw only the laughing, pretty face and winsome grace, and Elsa, recognizing the worship she engendered in the small, quaint girl with the large black eyes, wooed her expertly.

As summer approached and final examinations loomed, Elsa began to drop by to study with Arly. On a sunny afternoon a week before the school year ended, Arly stood at the open window in her little room, staring off and down toward the lake. Very soon now she would be going home to San Francisco for the summer, as she usually did, and the thought of separation from Elsa filled her with melancholy. She turned eagerly at a light tap on her door.

"Please come in!"

Elsa wore a slim beige skirt and soft beige cashmere sweater draped with a pale green scarf. Sunlight from the window fell across her gleaming honey-colored hair and the gentle and giving little Arly gazed with the purest wonder at this marvelous girl who was her friend.

"I've a ghastly appointment—with the dentist." Elsa shuddered elaborately. "So I can't stay."

Disappointment coursed through Arly and was reflected in her face.

"But I have a surprise." Elsa smiled in secure knowledge of the other girl's emotions. "I have my father's permission to invite you to accompany us on a cruise on our yacht. We sail in ten days and you must say you'll come or I shall perish on the spot." She swooned comically.

Arly's joy transformed her small face. "I'd love to come. Are you sure?"

"It's just the family," said Elsa, "and I'll be bored and lonely unless you're with us."

"I'll cable my father tonight," Arly promised, her voice bouncing with excitement and, when Elsa left, she hugged herself in dazed delight. Over all the other girls, the sought-after and admired Elsa had chosen Arly.

She cabled her father immediately and the loving Caiphus promptly sent his permission. He would miss her but, of course, she must have the marvelous trip.

The white yacht departed on schedule. There was a crew of five, Elsa's mother and father and her brother Erich. Arly and Elsa shared the same stateroom and, away from the academy, Elsa wasted no time. She did it very simply. She sat on the side of Arly's berth and said, "Arlene, you're different and so am I. We've known it from the first and there's no point in continuing this charade of being just friends." And she bent and kissed Arly with an open mouth and seeking tongue and Arly responded with bursting love.

For the next week as the yacht churned around the heel of Italy and into the Ionian Sea, bound for the Gulf of Corinth and Itea, Arly was lost in her own sea of love for Elsa.

She could not bear not to be by her side and was jealous of those hours they had to spend in the company of her family. When night fell and they were alone, Arly lavished her affection on Elsa and slept with her body wrapped about the other girl's naked form.

In the first days Erich, who was almost twenty, exercised his charm on Arly and, late one night when she awoke hungry and went to the galley, she found Erich there eating toast and eggs. He backed her against a wall and kissed her and Arly began to cry. "You're nothing but a big baby," Erich told her disgustedly, and he let her alone after that. Each time they were in port, he hurried ashore to find more susceptible companionship, leaving Elsa and Arly to amuse themselves.

In Itea a taxi took them to Delphi and there they slipped away from the family and the guide and found a hidden place among the ruins. Arly made a laurel wreath with which she crowned Elsa and Elsa played at being the high priestess Pythia and Arly, her slave. Arly bathed Elsa's feet from a warm spring and dried them in her hair.

On the yacht that night, Elsa stole a bottle of scotch whiskey from the galley and sneaked it into their stateroom. They drank until they were giggling and dizzy and Elsa decided to continue the game of slavery for Arly. Arly was giddy with happiness and did not see the ugly slackness of Elsa's mouth as she sat nude in a chair and commanded Arly to kneel between her legs. Arly gladly did so and cupped Elsa's breasts in her hands as she caressed the small clitoris with her tongue. Suddenly she felt a gush of hot liquid fill her mouth. Choking on the urine, she tried to pull away, but Elsa caught her by the hair and trapped her mouth.

"Drink it," Elsa whispered fiercely. "Goddam you, drink it!"

Arly fought free and fell back on her side. Confused and terrified, she tried to crawl away, but Elsa followed, kicking her and striking at her with her fingernails.

"You like it, you know you like it, you filthy little dyke!" she hissed.

Shocked by the twisted face above her, Arly cried out in pain as Elsa's fingernails bit into her shoulders. She lunged forward and seized Elsa's legs, tripped her and, before the other girl could recover, ran into the bathroom and locked the door. Elsa twisted the knob furiously, spitting out vile curses in German and threats in French, to which Arly closed her ears with her hands and spilled hot tears that mixed with the urine chilling on her breasts.

After a while Elsa recovered from her drunken temper and begged Arly to come forth and forgive her, but Arly remained locked inside.

Elsa ceased whimpering outside the door in the early hours of the morning and Arly quietly bathed, opened the door and found the other asleep on the floor with a quilt covering her. Arly dressed quickly, seized her purse and fled to the quarterdeck, where, for twenty dollars, the sailor on duty agreed to row her ashore.

She walked the dark streets of Itea until she found a church and inside huddled on a wooden bench, shaking and heartbroken, until daylight, when she took the first bus for Athens and in that city cabled her father. Within hours, five thousand dollars was waiting for her at the American Express office. She took the night boat to Brindisi, Italy, and the train to Genoa, where she bought clothes and booked passage on the first ship bound for America.

In the wide-brimmed Stetson and handmade boots he affected, Caiphus Kirbo stood firmly planted on the station platform when Arly stepped off the train in Oakland. She hurled herself at her father and Caiphus wrapped his arms around his small daughter, who buried her face in his shoulder and clung to him with relief and deepest love, grateful for his solid warmth and glad even for the familiar odor of cigar smoke and Bourbon whiskey.

On the ferry to San Francisco, his arm protectively around her, the wise and loving Caiphus asked only one question, the date when she must return to Switzerland.

"I'm not going back," said Arly. "I want to stay with you."

And Caiphus agreed to that, adding that he reckoned she was

smart enough already, and he left her to find her own balance,
which she quickly did.

Desperate transatlantic telephone calls from Elsa were refused
by Arly, and then letters and cables came in torrents but they were
burned unopened. Arly was baffled by the pointless pursuit and it
was only when she was older and wiser that she recognized Elsa had
been driven by that storm of remorse that so frequently howls in the
wake of the sadist.

It was almost twenty years before Arly again exposed her affec-
tions to the mercy of another woman.

As she matured, she wasted no time in grief over being
different. She consulted no analysts and did not exhaust herself
probing for the whys of her condition. She simply accepted herself
and set about living within her limitations as fully and with as much
joy as possible.

With her keen mind and the shrewd business instinct she
inherited from her father, she took stock of what she had and recognized she had a great deal. After Caiphus' death, all her energy, intelligence and enthusiasm were channeled toward the development of
the lodge, and the years brought her much satisfaction.

Arly was completely feminine in appearance and her deep-set
dark eyes and tidy little figure made her attractive to men, a problem she handled well, sidestepping awkward situations and turning
potential suitors into good friends. Only once was she tempted to try
an emotional relationship with a man.

When she was thirty, Horace Calley, the hotel wunderkind, sent
his emissaries to make an offer for the lodge. When they failed, he
came himself and, while he could not buy the lodge, he did his best
to sell himself to Arly.

Horace was a sophisticated forty-year-old, an aggressive bache-
lor who had been spoiled by many beautiful and accomplished
women, but he had never met a woman as natural and without
feminine guile as Arly. Challenged at first, he was soon genuinely
captivated by her warmth and intrigued by her independent spirit.
And she understood the hotel business. They had a common language.

When he came to understand that there was no possibility of
buying the lodge, he stayed on for several more weeks and had dinner every night with Arly. He worked hard to amuse her, regaled her
with tales of his adventures with his hotels around the world and

was rewarded by her laughter. On the night before his departure, Horace asked her to marry him.

"You're shameless," said Arly. "You'd even marry me to get the lodge."

"The lodge will remain yours. We'll put it in a contract," said Horace. "This is my first proposal, Arly. You're the only woman I've ever really wanted."

Recognizing that he was serious, she was silent.

"Think about it tonight," said Horace. "I'll be leaving in the morning."

And Arly thought about it, but not for long. She liked Horace Calley and he had offered her a new way of life, a passport to the heterosexuality from which she had excluded herself. Well, she might be able to fool him, but capacity for deceit was not a part of her nature and she could not fool herself. If she married Horace, she would be cheating him and she herself would be diminished.

"Horace," she told him, "everyone and everything belongs somewhere—you on a jet plane to Timbuktu, where you'll build a Calley Hotel. Me, I belong here in the rocks, with the marmots and the pikas. I'll never leave here, Horace. It's where I belong."

"Do you know President Eisenhower?"

The young woman with the delicate Asiatic face spoke to Arly in French and Arly answered automatically in kind.

"A little." The President and Mrs. Eisenhower had twice been guests at Kirbo's Lodge. Her invitation to the fund-raising dinner for his second term, held at the St. Francis Hotel in San Francisco, had come from the White House itself and Arly, who normally avoided such affairs, had felt her attendance was obligatory. "Why did you address me in French?" she questioned the girl in English.

Dinner over, most of the guests were dancing or collected about the room in conversational groups. Only Arly and the darkly exotic young woman opposite her remained seated at that end of the long banquet table.

"You look as if you speak French," the girl responded.

Eurasian, Arly decided as she studied the bone structure beneath the tight skin which glowed as if polished even in the muted light of the ballroom.

"I shouldn't even be here," said the Eurasian. "I'm a Democrat and I won't vote for him."

"And why are you?" asked Arly.

"I came with a congressman with whom I'm having an affair. He is out there somewhere"—she shrugged toward the circulating crowd—"courting votes. Sucking up, I call it."

Arly had been preparing to make her departure, but now she settled back, amused by the girl's frank conversation.

"Politics do not interest me. I'm writing a novel," she volunteered cheerfully, and offered her hand. "My name is Tati Leyva."

"Arlene Kirbo," said Arly, and took the small, soft hand with its green lacquered nails. "May I ask the background of your novel?"

"China—Shanghai, where I grew up. It's a love story. Love is what is important—all shapes of love—and that is what interests me most. Actually, it's about how I got born—my mother and father."

"How is it going?"

"Presently, I am stuck."

"Would it help to talk about it?" asked Arly.

"It might," said Tati.

Three weeks later, she dropped the congressman and came to Kirbo's Lodge to finish her novel, under Arly's patronage and in the room next to Arly's apartment.

Twenty-seven years old, the daughter of a Chinese mother and a White Russian father who had fled to China, Tati Leyva was a truly free spirit, not burdened by morals or anxieties, cheerful and engaging, soft and pliant, as happy, perhaps happier, in Arly's bed than she had been with the congressman or any of the others she had used or who might have used her. Silk and honey, she carried with her the scent of jasmine and, when she was not working on her novel, she enjoyed the luxurious life of the lodge to the fullest and could often be found in the greenhouse, where she spent hours creating feathery oriental flower arrangements which she brought to Arly with affection.

Despite Arly's awareness that the enchanting girl was a floater, her sunny nature and smoky beauty still charged Arly's life and for a time Arly was as happy as Tati. She stayed at the lodge for almost a year and, when the novel was finished, Arly gave it to a motion picture director who was vacationing at the lodge. He bought it in manuscript form before it was even submitted to a publisher and, when he returned to Hollywood, Tati went with him. That evening, Arly found an engaging arrangement of wild white azalea and Indian pinks in her room. There was a note from Tati: "Je regrette, darling."

No longer the vulnerable schoolgirl, Arly had known from the beginning that there would be no permanence with Tati and she allowed herself no sorrow. She was, instead, grateful.

Some years after Tati there occurred a short-lived affair with an unhappy divorcée named Jeannette Chalmers, whom Arly had met on a buying trip to San Francisco. Jeannette was employed as a saleswoman in a linen wholesale shop. She was a pleasant, dull young woman who meant no harm to Arly and tried to be a good friend and lover. But when she told Arly that she was to be married again, she made the gauche mistake of inviting her to the wedding. By this time Arly had developed a sense of humor about the lesbian problem and her reaction to Jeannette's announcement was uproarious laughter which not until later dissolved into tears.

Now there was Francine and not since those long-ago days in Geneva had Arly experienced such a helpless loss of emotional control. Unable to sleep, she stared into the darkness and wondered how soon, if ever, would Francine respond to her affection? How soon could she hold her close, sleep with her, bathe her, cover her with kisses, give her things she had never had, be mother, be slave, lover and friend? Francine need not be anything to Arly but receiving and grateful. Arly would expect no more than that.

14

In 1811 the tortoise took three steps over a period of three months and beginning at a place in Missouri called New Madrid, a chunk of land about one hundred and fifty miles long by fifty miles wide dropped nine feet. You can still see evidence of what happened there. It is called the Sunken Country, and it is the result of what may have been the greatest (we love being flabbergasted by the "greatest") quake to occur on the North American continent. The second greatest quake happened in Alaska in 1964 and measured 8.6 on the Richter scale—second, that is, until the recent tremble under Kirbo's Lodge.

The first lodge quake measured exactly 8.9, and except for the New Madrid quake, which was probably beyond the scope of any measuring device we have yet invented, is the strongest quake in recorded history anywhere.

It has actually upset the whole Richter theory of measurement because there are those seismologists who believe that shake and rattle was considerably beyond the 8.9 given to it by the dogmatic believers in the Richter system.

One eminent geologist was quoted as saying, "Mr. Richter is full of crap. That mother cracked the whole western half of the U.S.A. and you better by god believe it."

But so that you will be properly flabbergasted by the idea of even an 8.9 quake, it should be explained that by the Richter scale (which is not an instrument but an equation: $E=A+BM$), 8.9 is not just double the force of 4.5. A 4.5 shake will rattle the dishes. An 8.9 quake is about ten million times stronger than the 4.5, and what happened at Kirbo's Lodge happened for that reason.

Markey

That so many of Cabot Markey's paintings were laid upon huge canvases probably had not so much to do with God being able to see them as that Cabot's father was the last of the great barn sign painters. Cabot grew up watching his skinny, long-armed father, high on a ladder, slapping paint on the broad ends of middle-western barns, producing huge letters that, when completed, would proclaim CHEW SPARK PLUG TOBACCO or CARDUI FOR WOMEN, to the auto, buggy and wagon traffic passing on the dusty farm roads. Cabot came by the size of his paintings rightly. No one in the world painted bigger than Dock Markey. The bigger the barn, the bigger the sign, and no barn was too big. Dock said the largest sign he ever painted was over near Lexington, Kentucky, on a horse-breeding spread, and measured forty-five feet high and eighty feet wide and was done in yellow and blue—CARTER'S LITTLE LIVER PILLS. Dock said you could read the damned thing from five miles away.

In 1936, at about the same time Caiphus Kirbo's fortune was beginning to gasp for air in the sea of the Depression, Mr. Dockweiler Markey and his wife Delo were rattling through Iowa on a contract for DR. MILES NERVINE (black background with white letters) and were approaching the outskirts of a small city named Boone when Delo announced that her time had come. Dock accelerated the Chevy pickup and, with ladders clattering and paint cans dancing, he got Delo to the town's twenty-bed hospital and there Cabot Markey was born.

Now, if a child watches his father lay bricks, the child plays at laying bricks, or fishing, or doctoring or planting, or whatever his father does. Cabot played at painting signs and then, for whatever reason genius functions, began to paint his father painting signs, high on a ladder against the brown end of a barn with an azure sky and a weather vane against it.

"You see what this kid's doing?" Dock asked of Delo. Cabot was five. Delo nodded and took the piece of cardboard packing crate from Cabot and built a soft pine frame for it and hung it on the wall of the tourist cabin where they had based themselves while

Dock fulfilled a contract with TWENTY GRAND CIGARETTES (gold letters against a green background).

Said Delo, "Dock, I think our boy's a genius." And Dock opined that Cabot would make a fine sign painter. "Dock," Delo said, "he's going to paint more than signs. He's going to paint like Rembrandt painted, that kind of painter."

And Dock was all for it. Their money, what there was of it, and their love, were spent to develop Cabot's genius.

When Cabot got to be ten, his parents settled down in Chicago, where Dock opened a sign-painting shop and did as well as any sign-painting shop could do, enough to pay for Cabot's painting lessons while he was going to school and then enough, by some hard scrimping, to send him to study in Paris.

The young artist's first show was in Paris. He was nineteen. These early paintings were portraits in oil, a few charming nudes in gouache, some still life etchings of the usual pots and fruits and flowers, all conventionally impressionist and pleasantly decorative, but with a curious purity of line that caused one critic to write, "There is something here that belongs to no other. This young artist seems to see with a clarity denied to the rest of us."

Among the paintings exhibited in that little *rive gauche* gallery in the autumn of 1955 was a three-by-two oil in gray and green of a deserted park bench upon which lay a crumpled paper bag and a folded newspaper. It was not the most eye-catching of Markey's paintings, rather the least. But on the second day of the show, a well-known professional buyer named Phillip Bongart came to view the exhibit and stood before the gray and green piece for a concentrated fifteen minutes. He then removed his glasses, called the gallery owner to his side and bought the entire show for the equivalent in francs of eleven thousand, three hundred dollars.

Mr. Bongart was buying for a member of the Rothschild family and today that first show of Cabot Markey's hangs intact in the National Gallery in Washington, D.C. It was purchased from the Rothschild family for more than three million dollars. But eleven thousand dollars meant more to Markey in 1955 than three million would mean to a Rothschild. It paid some debts for him, bought him a plane ticket back to the states for a visit with his parents, made it possible for him to work comfortably for a whole year and was the beginning of the Cabot Markey legend. The fact that his first exhibited paintings had been purchased in one sweeping gesture by Phillip

Bongart brought his name to the attention of the art world, and especially to the attention of those who buy and sell the creations of others. Was it possible that a new master had been discovered? Would the name Markey ring out as clearly as the names Manet, Monet or Modigliani? It was and it did, for Markey discovered landscapes and no one before him had seen plains, rivers, hills and mountains with that strange, moving clarity. And added to this was the glamour of his adventurous spirit, his daring and a natural charisma that brought him fame he did not appear to court.

Markey did not affect an atelier in Paris or London or New York or any of the other places where artists colonize. He had no studio. Just as at Kirbo's Lodge, where he was perfectly content to place his easel in the greenhouse, he was also able to work comfortably in hotel rooms or chicken coops, and when he was bringing forth an especially large canvas, he enjoyed sloshing the paint about in the shelter of a big tent, pitched in some wild mountain meadow, its holding ropes grapevined against the rushing winds.

When he was not working, he was climbing granite spires, scuba diving into mysterious seas, following jungle rivers into their hearts of darkness or wandering aimlessly to places where only the rare tourist ventured, along the cold spine of Patagonia or the ice fields of Greenland or the black mountains of Afghanistan.

Markey was sometimes attracted to war and revolution, but because of the excitement they afforded his senses and not for political reasons. He was as apt to be found with the French legions in their debacle in Algeria as he was with Castro in the long hills of Cuba and was, in fact, found with both, sketching the bearded men and their landscapes or doing finger paintings of moments of violent action. Markey loved creating with that children's toy, the finger paints, but only a few of those instant pictures reached the market, because he claimed that if the artist couldn't catch the subject in five minutes flat, the painting was a dud, and his duds he burned. Those favored few who have visited Fidel Castro in his guarded house in Havana have been shown a finger painting which hangs in Fidel's study and which that fabled revolutionary delights in explaining that he obtained by plying the young artist with Cuban rum and, while Markey was sleeping it off, Fidel swiped the painting, which he knew was to be destroyed. It is of two men running from machine gun fire, one beginning to fall from a hit in his back. It is painted as if Markey's eye was the shutter of a camera snapping movement at one thousandth of a second. "The soldier who is falling," says Castro, "was named José Azana. He was sixteen years old. Cabot Markey brought him in his arms to the field hospital. He died." And Castro always affectionately touches the glass which covers the finger painting and says, "I'm glad I stole this painting. Cabot Markey caught the soul of that boy as he fell."

Much to Cabot's amusement, but not without some embarrassment, a biography was written of his life before he was thirty years old. "My god, I'm still wet behind the ears," he told the biographer, and refused to give the man any assistance. When asked why he was writing the biography of so young a celebrity, the biographer, an English journalist named Martin Galt, stated without humor that what with Cuba, the north face of the Eiger and the possibility of death by rapture of the depths, or a poison dart from an Amazonian blowgun, he doubted that Cabot Markey would live to be thirty-five, and he, the journalist, meant to be there with the first book ever written on the subject of that late, lamented genius.

The biography served to make Markey more famous and perhaps it shed some genetic light on the origins of the genius the biographer expected to come to some horrifying and untimely conclusion. The bloodline was not uninteresting. Dock Markey, the sign painter, came from a family of craftsmen. His father was a cabinet maker and his grandmother had been the daughter of a Boston silversmith whose father, in turn, was a contemporary silversmith and competitor of Paul Revere's. In England in the seventeenth century, great-great-great-grandfather Markey had been an engraver and, among collectors of old prints, particularly of birds, the name Markey is well known.

Delo Mapes, whom Dock Markey tumbled in the hayloft of her father's barn while his paintbrushes idled in their pots on the scaffolding outside the barn (VIRGINIA DARE TONIC in black letters with yellow background) and whom he married when she caught up with him forty miles away in Springfield, Tennessee, and told him she was pregnant, was astonishingly good with embroidery. When she was eleven years old, she had won a blue ribbon at the county fair for an original embroidered design of a golden ear of corn against green squash leaves with the word "Summertime" beneath, all stretched and framed in knobby willow. Delo's mother had been a seamstress before she married farmer Mapes and her grandmother had been a pretty good amateur portrait painter whose family portraits were treasured in Delo's family. Mr. Mapes, when not working in the rich black loam of northern Tennessee, was a wood-carver and an extraordinarily lively carving of a man plowing with a mule sat on Cabot Markey's desk in the studio at Kirbo's Lodge, a gift from his grandfather, carved in the last year of the old man's life. So, as you can see, genius is not altogether an accident. Rather, it is something that is passed along through breeding and suddenly, when the Muses decree the moment, all the crafts and talents of those who have gone before are ground into one mortar, liquefied by some fierce and secret fire, metamorphosed into genes and mixed in the womb of an unsuspecting mother.

Now the result of that mixture was standing before a drafting table scrawling quick studies in charcoal of a woman's nude body. The nude woman was Clarice Bishop. In the winter light from the north windows of his studio in Kirbo's Lodge she was sitting, standing, turning at his direction as he searched in charcoal for the painting he would begin but never finish—his "Unfinished Woman" that he would leave behind when he disappeared forever into the deep blue ice of the glacier.

Outside the windows an occasional light flurry of snow spilled down from the gray sky. The mass of the coming storm had been stalled somewhere just off the Oregon coast, and only the wet ends of its tentacles were reaching out into the Sierra.

"Will you explain to me what you're doing?" It was a demand more than a question.

"Turn your back to me, please," was Markey's answer. Clarice twisted about, hands on hips, and presented her perfectly formed bottom to the artist, who made a sketch beginning with her shoulders, slashing down to the slender calves of her legs, the lightning fast black lines trailing off as he reached her ankles. He tossed the charcoal stub into a bowl and leaned forward over the drafting table, hands flat on its edges, studying the busy page of rough sketches. Clarice looked at him from over her shoulder and, seeing him thus engrossed, turned toward him and impatiently crossed her arms over her exquisitely formed breasts. Clarice's body was almost as pale as the snow. No sunlight had ever been allowed to roughen or tan that translucent skin, but it was in places healthily if delicately pink, even rosy—her nipples, her knees, the narrow small of her back and the twin dimples at the top of her buttocks. And under one breast was a tiny ruby birthmark.

"Will you please, please tell me what you're doing?" There was now a rather plaintive note in her voice. Markey glanced at her and returned his attention to his sketches as if they were more alive than she.

"You're unbelievable, Mrs. Bishop," he remarked calmly. "You're quite possibly the most perfectly formed woman I have ever seen. To be candid, you're as perfect as an idealized sculpture of the Polycletus Greek period and just as boring."

"Boring?"

"I can't do a portrait of you. It would have all the personality of the Venus of Milo. Stone, Mrs. Bishop. No, I'll have to paint your beauty in the abstract."

"My god, do you mean one of those four-eyed Picasso things?"

"No. One of Cabot Markey's things, Mrs. Bishop. You may put your coat on for the time being. There's coffee if you want it. Have you had breakfast?"

"At eight in the morning?"

She had arrived promptly at eight, wearing nothing but a long blond mink coat. "It's my bathrobe," she explained. She had been disappointed in Markey, expecting the artist to be in paint-smeared jeans and smock, finding him instead in pressed gray flannel trousers, gray cashmere sweater and plaid shirt with the collar points neatly tucked under the crew neck of the sweater. He had smiled and politely instructed her to move into the light of the big north windows and said, "Nude, if you please, Mrs. Bishop." She had dramatically dropped the mink coat from her shoulders and, lifting her chin proudly, waited for his reaction. There had been no reaction other than a studious consideration of her body and then he had gone directly to the drafting table and begun to sketch.

Now she gathered the mink coat about her too perfect shoulders, hips, legs and arms, feeling an odd resentment of that perfection for the first time in her life. It had not pleased Cabot Markey, and Markey was one of those special people whom others strive to please.

"Order whatever you like," invited Markey, and while Clarice, on the phone, described a breakfast that would get a longshoreman's day started, he arranged a canvas on an easel, donned a bibbed apron made of denim and with many pockets, and began to assemble his palette.

The tray for Mrs. Bishop arrived with the usual fired-from-a-gun service of the lodge, piping hot and served on blue china on a damask tablecloth with damask napkin and an opening *rosa damascena* in the glittering bud vase, and while Clarice stuffed herself, Markey studied his sketches again and made some preparatory lines on the canvas in pale yellow pastel chalk. And as he drew the lines, he was not seeing in his artist's inner eye the perfections of the beautiful, spoiled woman in a blond mink coat she used for a bathrobe, presently poking browned and aromatic kippers into her mouth; he was seeing another woman, a lithe, smaller woman striding down a Welsh footpath with sturdy walking shoes on her feet, wearing woolen hose and, on her head, a green tam-o'-shanter.

In his career, Markey had painted only two murals—one in the statehouse of the state of his birth, Iowa, and the other in the Grand Hotel Camelot in London, the first because when asked he felt he should leave something by a Markey in Iowa, the signs on the barns his father had painted having long since weathered away or the barns fallen and burned. The second, and one of his most famous paintings, his "Morte d'Arthur," he had agreed to paint because besides being offered a staggering sum for the work, he had become intrigued with the shape and size of the wall in the new hotel's lobby. It was as wide and as high as the end of the barn near Lexington, Kentucky, where Dockweiler Markey had laid on his biggest letters for CARTER'S LITTLE LIVER PILLS, the one you could see for five miles.

The mural in the Camelot has become so famous and the visitors to it so numerous that the hotel finally, in desperation, gave that lobby over to the painting and its viewers and constructed another lobby where hotel guests arrive and depart. The Markey Lobby, as it is called, is open from ten o'clock in the morning until five o'clock in the afternoon, seven days a week, and there is never one of those hours without at least a handful of awed tourists or art lovers standing in the big room staring at that strange, glowing depiction of the death of King Arthur. One seems to view it through the gathering mists of time, a black barge with high scarlet prow bearing the silver-armored body of Arthur being thrust out into the fog on a lake, while on the shore there kneel his weeping knights, and beyond and all around them are mountains which are contorted with majestic grief. Malraux, in his study of the work, wrote: "It is blinding— blinding with tears."

In preparation for the mural, Markey had exhaustively researched Arthur and had come upon one rather obscure legend of the great man's death, a legend for which he could find no proper source; it seeped out of the folk tales of Wales, where myths are as common as the quiet rain that falls almost daily in that land of long, green slopes and twisted crags and peaks.

In Snowdonia, an ancient jumble of mountains in North Wales topped off by the Yr Wyddfa peak, more commonly known as Mount Snowdon, there lies on one of the paths that crawl up from the watery vale of Nant Gwynant, a ridge called the Pass of the Arrows. Here Arthur was pursuing a defeated foe down toward the lake named Llydaw when a flight of arrows came from the bows of the enemy and Arthur fell, and it was on Lake Llydaw that his body was drifted off toward the magical island of Avalon. Markey chose that legend and Snowdonia as the model for his mural in the Camelot Hotel. In Nant Gwynant vale he leased an old stone farmhouse which had been refurbished for vacation rentals and which provided a large, well-lighted room for his work and was within walking distance of the footpath that led up to the Pass of the Arrows. And it was there on that storied ridge that he met Lord and Lady Callam and their party of seven, including two footmen who carried on their backs the necessaries for picnicking, a folding canvas table and stools and iced packs for wine and perishables.

It was a jolly party, jolly with the wine they had consumed on the top of Mount Snowdon on that unusually sunny day. They had gotten to the top of the mountain via the electric tram that climbed up from Llanberis and were now walking happily down the ancient trail through the Pass of the Arrows, and, at the end of the trail, they would be met by cars from Callam Hall.

Callam Hall stood (as it had been standing for a hundred years) on the bank of the pretty lake of Mymbyr, about fifty kilometers from the trail's end along the road to Capel Curig. Traditionally, the Callams spent a few weeks in the summer at the hall and, with his wife, the fifth Lord Callam, called Boysie by his intimates, was now in residence.

"Do you know who that is—there, along the path?" Lord Callam was peering through his binoculars and, since no one in the party offered to guess who it might be there along the path, Lord Callam informed them. "I do believe it's the artist—the American—Markey." The binoculars were passed around and there was much cheerful agreement. Yes, it might be the American artist.

Some one hundred yards away and just off the path, he was leaning over the flat-topped rise of stone where he had his big sketching pad open and he was working in charcoal on the conformations of the mountains about Lake Llydaw, which lay shining in the sun.

"I'm sure it is," said Lord Callam. "I once met him, you know. Oh, I don't expect he'd remember, but it was at a show of some of his recent work in Paris, oh, three years ago. Remarkable man, you know. Oh yes, quite."

And Lady Callam, wearing the green tam-o'-shanter and tweed walking suit, said, "Well, in any case, Boysie, I don't think we ought to disturb him. He does seem to be working, doesn't he?"

"Yes, umm, yes," said Boysie. "Artists don't like folk peering over their shoulders, do they? But, dammit, I would like all of you to meet him. Well, suppose we trot along and give him a wave and, if he encourages us, we'll just barge in. Yes." And he led off, striding along on straight, knickered legs, a handsome man, tall and dark-eyed, a man with a real future in the diplomatic field, it was said. And behind him came his pink-cheeked friends, the two footmen and Lady Jael Callam, who would die on the end of a nylon rope in the French Alps and whose portrait, painted from grieving memory, would hang in the Tate Gallery, signed C. Markey.

Such are the accidents that shape lives and lead to death or love or both. As with the happenstance of a great storm and a great earthquake arriving simultaneously in the high Sierra and closing crushingly on Kirbo's Lodge, so the happenstance of Markey being on a footpath in Wales where the Callams were descending was an accident that changed his life and Jael Callam's life irrevocably and, if you wish to trace the coincidence to its logical conclusion, it led in its long and tortuous way to the gun in Markey's traveling bag and his cynical determination to die and leave behind a tantalizing "Unfinished Woman," based upon the too, too perfect body of Clarice Bishop.

Markey dined with the Callams at Callam Hall, and before the evening was ended he knew that he wanted Jael Callam and he knew that Jael Callam wanted him. It was nothing she said or did or even looked, but Markey knew. He had never married, largely because he had not had the time. He wanted marriage and children, but not just now or not just then—wait until after this or that adventure, when the right one would come along. He was thirty-three when he met Jael and the right one, if there had ever been a right one among his affairs, had not had the chance to make herself well enough known to him.

Markey was an aggressive man when he desired something, to get a painting down or a mountain climbed, a river run or a woman in bed. It was done quickly, expertly, and obstacles were brushed aside, climbed over or pierced, and he proceeded with Jael Callam without changing his modus operandi. Finding her closed against him, yet knowing she wanted him, he wasted no time trying to get around her; he literally, and with premeditation, raped her.

It happened almost a month from the day they met. Boysie and Jael had visited Markey's farmhouse several times at his invitation to see the progress of his preparatory work on the mural for the Grand Hotel Camelot. They had first been shown the charcoals and had watched as Markey began to experiment with the colors he might use. Lord Callam had actually posed as one of Arthur's knights—not in costume—but posed nevertheless, holding a bumbershoot in lieu of a broadsword, and Jael had sat in rather awed silence as she watched the transformation occur between model and canvas under the long, swift fingers of the master artist. Her aristocratic, if mildly and forgivably fatuous husband, had become a thick-wristed warrior with a bloody sword in hand and face wrought with grief.

As she was hypnotized by Markey's skill, so she was hypnotized by Markey himself, his easy grace, his clear eyes which sometimes seemed to look directly and questioningly into her thoughts, and she would feel pressed and uncertain. She vowed that she would not be alone with Markey, not from fear of him but from fear of the opportunity for intimacy. She suspected that he would say things that would be better unsaid. She had no comprehension of a man like Markey—a man of action, of sudden driving impulse. She was not forewarned.

Through these weeks, Markey was watching Jael as she was watching him, and he saw the quiet clarity of *her* eyes, the firmness in her face and body, the aliveness of her when she talked or listened, the way her close-cut hair curled on the nape of her neck, the way her lower lip was sometimes damp and shining from a charming habit of smoothing it with her small white teeth before she would burst into laughter.

On a Sunday, Lord Callam was called to London for a Monday

conference in the Home Office. Markey had been invited for dinner on that Sunday evening and Jael called him to cancel the invitation. He suggested, since she was to be alone, that she have dinner with him in Bangor, the centrally largest town near them. Jael found herself agreeing to that arrangement.

They had a pleasant candlelighted dinner at an inn in Bangor and started the drive back to Capel Curig. "Shall we stop at my place?" Markey asked. "I've some new work you might like to see."

And against her better judgment, she found herself agreeing to this.

In the big work room of the farmhouse, he displayed several new details for the mural and poured two glasses of port wine, which they drank while he explained how the details would fit into the overall pattern of the mural. When this was done, she turned away from him to place her empty glass on a mantel and felt his arms go about her. "Please," she requested calmly, and felt one of his arms leave her waist and then, in panic, felt his freed hand go up under her skirt from behind while the remaining arm about her waist tightened, its muscles hardening as she was pinioned against him. The hand under her skirt found the top of her panties and, in one ripping motion, he had them down and about her knees. She tried to kick back at him, but found the panties to be hobbles and realized that was what he intended them to be.

Jael did not cry out. She fought silently, wrestling with the arm about her waist, trying to break its grip, and was frightened by its strength and the man behind her as silent as she was. Her breath was coming hard now, but she knew that it was easy for him and that he was using only a fraction of his real power. She felt herself lifted and, trying to kick as she moved, saw that she was being carried not to a sofa or a couch but to a table. She was placed at the edge of the table and his free hand lifted her skirt from behind, then pressed on the back of her neck until she was bent over the table and held there by his chest against her back. She flailed awkwardly at her attacker over her shoulders, once catching his hair in her fingers only to lose it as he jerked his head away.

She sensed that with his free hand he was loosening his trousers and she felt warm bare skin against her buttocks and now she yelled, "No, goddam you, no!" Then he was inside her, easily, quickly, and she heard the breath of a laugh escape his lips and a new fury assailed her, one born of embarrassment. She had been ready for him, slick, wet and softened, and when he filled her she could not stop the orgasm. She stopped struggling and fell forward on the table, covered her face with her hands and let him work at her body.

He placed his hands on her hips and lifted her until she was properly seated against his groin and gently he ground himself inside her, knowing instinctively when to drive harder and catch the welling of her passion and then the sound of his muscular groin slapping against her roundness became a part of the pleasure of her orgasms. Four more times he brought her to coming and now he withdrew and moved away and she knew she was free. Half on the big table, she now crawled the rest of the way and lay there with her face buried in her arms, not caring that she was still naked from the waist down.

She guessed that Markey was fastening his trousers because she heard the jingle of a belt buckle against a zipper and, in a moment, she felt his hand on her bare skin again, a caress from its calloused palm, then she felt another touch, warm and soft, and she knew he had kissed her at the base of her spine. The hand pulled her panties up and her skirt down.

"Well," she mumbled into her crossed arms, "I suppose every woman wonders what it's like to be raped." There was no answer but she heard the rasp of a match as he lighted a cigarette. "You didn't come," said Jael.

"I didn't know your situation—the pill, your time, all that," he said.

"Well, if you didn't mean to come"—her face was still against her arms—"why the hell did you do it?"

"For you," said Markey.

She started to protest, then realized that as she lay there, lethargic in her satisfaction, the lady might indeed be protesting too much. She sat up on the side of the table, dangling her legs, and saw that he was sitting on a sofa near the fireplace, smoking. She ran her fingers through her hair and studied the floor for a few moments, then scooted off the table and crossed to the sofa and knelt before him, opened his trousers and, finding him still ready, took him in her mouth. It was over almost immediately. Now she closed his trousers and sat, still on the floor, with her back against his legs.

"I guess we're for it," said she.

"I like that English expression—and I guess we are."

"Well, let's not muck about. We'll tell Boysie when he comes back tomorrow night."

"Whatever you say."

"This is what I say and you'd best listen, C. Markey. It's not going to be, as you Americans say, a 'sometime thing.' It's going to be every day and every night from now on to the end of time or something approximating that. The only place we won't be together, and I'm not so sure about that, is when we go to the WC. How do you feel about the WC?"

"I think we might spare each other the WC."

"Very well," said Jael. "But that's the only place we'll spare each other. Now, suppose we begin by taking off our clothes and going to bed and doing this business in the proper way. Or aren't you up to it now?"

"Let me rest for three seconds more," said Markey.

"Time!" said she, and laughed her wonderful laugh.

If nothing else, and he was much more, Boysie Callam was a gentleman in the most romantic sense of the word. He heard Jael's plea for her freedom with gracious attention and pretended to no outrage or other sorts of surprise. Schooled from birth in the virtues of equanimity, he stuffed and lighted a pipe and exhibited only one moment of frowning distaste, and this because his hand that held the match was shaking.

"You know," said Boysie, "she doesn't have anything of her own. She's not, well, landed."

"Boysie, he's not asking for my dowry!" Jael exclaimed.

"No, of course. Yes, that was an odd bit, wasn't it?"

There was silence now, the three of them just sitting there in the library at Callam Hall while rain fell against the tall windowpanes. Finally, Boysie looked at Markey and said, "Well, old chap, I can't compete with you. I'm not in your league. Like trying to compete with Lawrence of Arabia, isn't it?—dashing, daring and all that. But let me tell you something. She's not all that much of a bargain, you know—forgive me, darling—headstrong and rather a bit too intelligent for her own good. Always was much sharper than I."

"Don't try to make yourself out as stupid, Boysie," said she.

"Oh no, not stupid—but I do think in organized patterns while you snap and pop about like a whip. Look out for that, Cabot, that snapping and popping about. Well," he concluded, "my blessing upon you. When will you be leaving, Jael?"

"Now."

"So soon?"

"I don't want to muck about with it, Boysie."

"No, of course. You were never one for mucking about with anything. All right. Good." He extended his hand to Markey.

He remained their friend, occasionally writing to them wherever they were, the salutation always reading, "Dear Jael and Cabot." And when Jael died, he wrote one last letter to Markey in which for the first and only time he revealed a little of himself. "I cannot grieve as I know you are grieving, because she had not been mine for a long time, but as we remember things of true worth in our lives, so I shall never forget her laughter. I hear it in my dreams."

Markey and Jael were together for three years. Though she was divorced, they did not marry. "I want you as a lover," said Jael, "not a husband."

Markey protested that he wanted children and she said, "When the time is right, and it isn't yet, then we'll do things properly. For now, I just want you."

And after she was gone, Markey felt rage inside that he had not made her pregnant against her wishes. He then would have had something of her other than the memory of her laughter.

It was after her death that Markey found Kirbo's Lodge and climbed the Scoop alone and painted the Gornaad. His painting was no longer a compulsive work, it was an escape. His climbing was no longer an adventure, it too was escape, a concentration that took him out of himself. Seven years had passed in this manner. The lodge more or less had become his home, his base, something he had never had before. And he kept a small apartment in San Francisco which he used on occasional visits to the city for concerts, the theater, his broker or the dentist. He and Jael had lived as he had always lived, because it had pleased her to be a gypsy with him.

Dock Markey had never given up his sign painting, even after Cabot became rich, and the old fellow had died in a fall from a scaffolding while he was painting the V in one of those sky-high signs that advertise the delights of Las Vegas above elevated automobile speedways. Cabot's mother had lived for a few years after Dock and then, quietly and without warning, died in her sleep of heart failure.

In the bloodlines that had produced the artist, there was, unfortunately, one strain that carried with it a weak heart muscle. Delo Markey's mother and her grandmother had, like Delo, died of a weakening heart a few years before or a few years after the age of fifty. Markey was struck well before the half-century mark. He was forty-three. It had not happened, as you might expect, on a mountain peak, but as he stood in Green Park in London, England, feeding the friendly wild birds of that park from a bag of roasted peanuts. He had felt a curious enervation and had stumbled to a bench and sat there quietly with pigeons and sparrows gathered about him waiting for more handouts. When the spell passed, he stood up and walked to the nearest boulevard, hailed a cab, got in and died in the back seat. The cabby was a resourceful man and he had puffed into Markey's mouth and thumped on his chest until Markey began to breathe, and then rushed with him to the nearest hospital. In the emergency room, Markey had recovered consciousness and his one request had been, "No publicity, please," and that request had been honored by the hospital. Since the cabby had not recognized him, he spent two weeks lying in without even a note in the London newspapers.

After a heart scan, Markey's doctor had come into the hospital room all smiles and good cheer and then proceeded to tell his patient that what was indicated was heart failure. The heart had suddenly, instead of dutifully and steadily beating, begun to squirm, and that had caused Markey's temporary demise. A pacemaker would be necessary and, of course, Markey's career as a hardy adventurer had come to an end. He could work, but with suitable rest periods, and he might live for another ten years or so with luck.

"I'm terribly sorry, Mr. Markey," the doctor said, "but you've got a congenital situation. Astonishing it hasn't developed before, considering the punishment you've put your body through on those climbs you've made."

So Markey was fitted with a pacemaker, given a supply of digitalis and warned about heights where the thinness of the oxygen might produce unwanted palpitation. He completed his business in London, the sale of half a dozen canvases which he had stored there in a bank vault some time before to gain value with the years, as vintage wine gains value, and had gone as directly as possible, with the stop in San Francisco to pick up his revolver, to the nine-thousand-foot altitude of Kirbo's Lodge.

"May I see what you're doing?" asked Clarice, naked in the north light of his studio with the blond mink coat fallen in lush folds about the stool on which she sat.

"Not yet," Markey said, and dipped the stubs of his chopped-off fingers into a glob of pink paint on the palette and, with the stubs, worked the color into the canvas before him.

"Do you always paint with your fingers?" asked Clarice.

"Sometimes I paint with my penis," said Markey.

He didn't smile and he did not expect her to smile. In effect, he was putting an end to her pointless questions. Clarice shrugged her beautiful shoulders, lifted her beautiful chin, looked up through the north windows with her beautiful eyes and watched the light snow scatter down from the heavy sky.

If there was a question of any consequence that could be asked about Clarice, that spoiled, self-adoring creature, it would be this: is self-love sustaining; will she love herself at fifty, sixty, seventy as she does at thirty? Would she be faithful through those descendant years or would she in that passage find a more appealing lover, perhaps in the shape, color and sweetness of death? Likely not, thought Markey, she would probably thrive on memories, something he could not do. He envied her.

With the alertness of the self-aware, Clarice felt Markey's appraisal and turned to find his penetrating gaze upon her, sensed there was no admiration or genuine interest behind it and mentally dismissed him, indifferent now. What did this celebrated man know about her or the quality of her life? She turned her attention back to the falling snow and saw another window, the big bay window in her family's home with the built-in seat where as a child she used to sit gazing out at the carefully tended grounds beneath spreading oaks, broken by formal gardens and stretching for a great distance to the boundary which separated the estate from a smaller property owned by a family named McGonigle.

On the McGonigle land there was a pond and, on that day, as a light snow fell, the boisterous McGonigle children—seven of them ranging in age from four to thirteen—were sledding down a small hill and across the frozen pond, sometimes sprawling and occasionally pummeling each other with high exuberance. The rowdy Irish youngsters had been scrutinized by her parents and her severe British nanny, Mrs. Tewksberry, formerly of Liverpool, and deemed unsuitable companions for the dainty Clarice. She had been forbidden contact with them, but the lure of the snow and the sight of the frolicking children were irresistible and, finding herself for the moment unsupervised, she had dashed for the door and stumbled in snow up to her knees toward the lively group, excited by the whoops and laughter now clearly audible.

Mrs. Tewksberry captured her as she reached the stone wall that separated the properties and dragged her, kicking and howling, back into the house.

"You'll catch your death of cold," Mrs. Tewksberry said, and, once inside, changed Clarice's clothes from the inside out. When she continued to cry, her nanny placed her on a stool before a large mirror and, with a thick towel, dried and brushed her gleaming red hair.

"See how beautiful," she crooned to the little girl as she worked with comb and brush. "Look at your lovely, soft hair."

And, as the tears dried on her pink cheeks, Clarice had looked at her image in the mirror and, finally, smiled.

She was then six years old.

15

We cannot accept the truth about the birds and the beasts, the truth being it is not we who are superior. That we can kill them without danger to ourselves, can reduce them to a relict, does not prove our superiority, only our cruelty. They were here long before we were and, if they can only survive the blight of our temporary presence, they will be here long after we are gone, because they do not make war upon each other or carry in themselves their own destruction. And they have a knowledge, a wisdom that is beyond our understanding because their superiority is beyond our understanding.

Now, you take the black bear that was denned in a dry cave in a canyon at the seven-thousand-foot level a few miles away from Kirbo's Lodge. It was a perfect winter den. It had been used by bears for that purpose for thousands of years and she was pleased to be its occupant and had driven off other bears who had come nosing about at its entrance.

She was young and was carrying cubs in her womb for the first time. They would be born in that fine, dry cave come February and she would bring them out in the spring melt. On this afternoon, while the earthquake instruments at the lodge were patiently registering nothing, the bear waked from a deep sleep and for a time remained motionless, listening, or feeling, or sensing something that those sophisticated instruments could not hear or feel or sense. She stood up and felt the cubs move in her belly and shuffled to the cave entrance and for a few minutes watched the snow fall. It was coming fast now because the stalled storm was unstalled and sweeping down across the mountains.

She left the fine, dry cave where bears had denned for thousands of years and went out into the wet snow. She trotted along unseen trails and in unerring direction toward a ridge where lay a great *fallen pine that was hollow. She smelled of the entrance to the hollow and growled and the growl fetched from the pine a shrieking ball of gray cat fur that raced off into the storm. The bear entered the hollow and went to the far end, which was surprisingly commodious, having been enlarged by the claws of cats, bears and coyotes through many seasons. The bear lay down and put her paws on her belly, where the cubs were restless, and after a while she dozed, to come awake again as dark fell and she perceived movement at the entrance to the hollow. It was the bobcat again. The cat, cold and white with snow, cautiously, politely, stepped into the hollow and waited for the growl to come. The bear instead closed her eyes and slept, and the cat curled up and got warm, not six feet away.*

In the night the quake would strike and that fine, dry cave where bears had denned for thousands of years would have its entrance sealed by millions of tons of granite.

CLARICE

Clarice had noted the stubs of the two fingers on Markey's right hand as he worked swiftly and with intense concentration as if he were alone in the room. She was only mildly curious about the mutilated fingers and about the artist himself. So consumed with herself was she that her interest in others was limited to an assessment of their response to her. She was not impressed by Markey's fame or his genius and was hardly aware of his considerable charm, but she was unsettled by his completely impersonal attitude toward her and his matter-of-fact appraisal of her body. She was not prepared for such a reaction in the initial stages of any relationship with a man. Indifference, in her experience, came much later. She shifted impatiently.

"Please turn into profile, Mrs. Bishop," Markey asked without looking up, and she sighed and turned.

Clarice hoped that posing for Markey would relieve her boredom and distract her, keep her from thinking about the architect in San Francisco who had not been on the plane. She dimly realized that she really did not care, that only her ego was bruised—and that not for long. She was not actively unhappy alone, could be pleasantly content in her cocoon, but the world was made up of pairs, as in Noah's Ark, and she had always felt she was missing something.

"Yours is a classic case of arrested sexual development," Dr. Allan Goldberg, her current psychiatrist, had explained, "an extreme narcissism. You must force yourself to grow, to reach out, to establish a relationship with a man." He frowned. "Or even a woman," he added desperately.

In addition to her other extraordinary features, her feet were exquisite and were of continuous delight to Dr. Goldberg, who frankly admitted to a foot fetish. They had a symbiotic arrangement during her visits to his study, wherein he massaged her high insteps and coral lacquered toes with cocoa butter as they delved into her problems. It had a marvelously relaxing effect on Clarice's troubled mind and provided the good doctor with a guiltless satisfaction.

Dr. Goldberg really could not help Clarice. All he could do was sympathize with her unhappy attempts to want someone other than herself and advise her not to be ashamed of therapeutic masturbation when the pressure for release became too much. Therapeutic her masturbation was not.

All the current, stylish group therapies and courses in human sensitivity had not made a dent in Clarice's love affair with herself. The British motion picture star who preceded the architect had stated the case most succinctly. "Honey," he had said, "you're a dead-ass."

The truth was that, as Dr. Goldberg had pointed out, no one—man or woman—was as physically perfect as Clarice. She could not help making comparisons and those comparisons led her back to herself.

From the time she was a tiny jewel of a child, she had been made conscious of her beauty. Her mother and father, the DeReigns of Delaware—old, established money—had been in awe of her. They were both DeReigns by birth, third cousins, and in searching the family records as far back as paintings and photographs would go, they had not found an ancestor who, by Mendel's law, could have provided the genes that produced Clarice. They were themselves on the homely side of plain and they had watched in fascination as their only child had grown from what had seemed to be an ordinary redheaded baby into a vision.

They had guarded her the way a collector would guard a Yung Lo Ming vase. They felt that no other hands were clean enough to touch her, that no other eyes were pure enough to look upon her. The choosing of her playmates was a matter of important consultation between them, and her tutors were scanned and probed and poked until those poor teachers were as awed by Clarice as were her parents.

The end result of all this was that that beautiful child had been like a prisoner in solitary and had found her only happiness in a closed room before a mirror with the companionship of her own reflection.

At nineteen her marriage had been arranged with John Paul Hammond, who was a suitably sanitized young man with enormous inherited wealth and a family that had somehow been derived from Captain John Paul Jones.

For parents other than Clarice's, he would have been deemed the catch of the century, but instead he was treated like the grocery boy who had somehow snuck into the parlor when the cook wasn't looking. They sniffed him, peered at him, discussed his pros and cons in front of him, marched him about like a buck private on inspection and even demanded that he produce a health certificate from his doctor that proclaimed him free of venereal disease.

Young John Paul endured all this because at the end of it he would have that wildly beautiful creature named Clarice DeReign in the bed with him.

They were married in the spring with a wedding that was spoken of reverently for years by the society editors of the eastern newspapers, and set out upon their honeymoon in a grand stateroom aboard the splendid *Queen Elizabeth II*. On that first night at sea, Clarice became hysterical and told him she could not bear the thought of his ugly organ touching that precious pink-haired portal that was such a secret, beloved part of her. This was, of course, long before she had turned in desperation to psychiatrists.

She and John Paul remained together for an extremely short time, the time it took for the *Queen Elizabeth* to sail to Southampton. They flew back to the United States in separate planes. John Paul's plane missed the end of the runway at the international airport in New York and its passengers died in the cold waters of the swampy approach. Clarice Hammond became an extremely rich young woman the moment the Boeing jetliner exploded. Young John Paul Hammond, for his trouble, had not once dipped his wick into that luscious tallow.

Clarice had grieved, not so much for his death as because she had discovered on that journey that she was afflicted. In the thirteen years that had followed, she continued to try, marrying three more times—a prominent criminal lawyer, a furniture designer and an investment banker—not one of whom was able to puncture the protective bubble of self-love within which Clarice was wafted through life. All three marriages ended within a year or two, leaving her more relieved than unhappy, and each time much richer than before. Two of her husbands asked her for a divorce and the other, the investment banker, some years her senior, obligingly died, presumably of disappointment.

It was with her third husband, Harlan Cones, that she at least enjoyed a short period of companionship. A designer and owner of a chain of furniture stores featuring the modern-colonial John Adams line, Harlan was attractive, witty and an unhappy closet queen, a misfortune he had concealed more or less successfully all his life.

He made Clarice laugh and he worshiped her beauty almost as much as she did. At first sight of her, Harlan became convinced that if any woman could reverse his sexual proclivity, it would be she, and he wooed her in the most tasteful and courtly manner. His touch was as light as an eyelash kiss and she felt no pressure, urgency or demand behind it.

Harlan selected her clothes, consulted at length with her hair stylist and taught her how to walk with that devastating swing. They shopped together, gossiped together and entertained lavishly. The social columns in the newspapers and chic magazines titillated their readers with their comings and goings at opera parties, pre-Columbian art galleries and charity events for the starving of Bangladesh. And they were an astonishingly beautiful couple, he so tall and elegant and she, on his arm, a ravishing sexual adornment who served to still the question Harlan thought he had seen in the eyes of some of his associates.

On their honeymoon at Cozumel, that so devilishly expensive resort off the Yucatan peninsula, he complained of an old back injury for which he was receiving treatment and suggested they have separate beds until he recovered. He was abject in his apologies and

Clarice was so understanding and solicitous that he felt enormous contrition. She became quite stern and assured him that she would not allow him to attempt anything that might jeopardize his health.

The truth was that Clarice's second husband, the lawyer Maxwell Donner, had almost totally exhausted her, so determined had he been to arouse some response in the pale and perfect body that lay, unmoving as a plastic mannequin, beneath him. At first overjoyed simply to have her beside him, he soon began to feel like a necrophiliac. Once, in extreme frustration, he had shouted at her, "I ought to pray over your goddam twat and write an epitaph on your stomach!"

He had cajoled, massaged, kissed and murmured endearments and obscenities into her ear and she had clenched her teeth and waited until he had finally satisfied himself and released her, panting and defeated. Afterward, she always fled to the bathroom, where she sat for an hour in a scented tub with legs apart until she felt purified and untouched again.

Max bought every "how to" book he could find on the subject of sexual satisfaction, reading them aloud to her until she fell into a bored sleep. When every orthodox method failed, he visited shops that featured erotica and brought home an assortment of sex aids that terrified her. The exception was a vibrator, which only served to facilitate her affair with herself, a result that was the exact opposite of his intention. It was that same vibrator she now carried in the secret compartment of her luggage.

Together they visited a marriage counselor and that baffled woman recommended that Clarice see a psychiatrist, her first. Thereafter, until she found Dr. Goldberg, she changed psychiatrists more frequently than she changed husbands. "You make my feet feel so good," she told Dr. Goldberg.

Max Donner urged Clarice to try various forms of group therapy and she endured the processes of est, among others. Then together they had visited a resort on the California coast—a new "experiment in living" group where, in the company of a lot of flat-chested women and potbellied men, they soaked nude in hot sulphur springs. The men (and most of the disbelieving women) had all stared at the magnificent Clarice until the enraged Max engaged one of them in a fight and they had rolled on the grass, a tumble of naked arms and legs, until Max realized the absurdity of it all and, with bloodied nose and a curious dignity, apologized to the man and walked, wang waggling, back to their quarters, an undulating and impassive Clarice beside him.

After eighteen months, he asked her for a divorce and shortly thereafter married a plain but passionate young law student who had been working in his law firm during her summer vacation. Clarice received a generous settlement and went away for a six-week stay at a health spa where, for three thousand dollars a week, she was wrapped in cellophane and hot towels, pounded and pummeled and bathed and dried. She had manicures, pedicures, facials and body facials, hand massages and contouring massages and heat treatment for cellulite. She ate carefully supervised meals consisting of as few calories as the dietician and the kitchen staff could devise, she did not smoke or drink and, at the end of her stay, she emerged looking exactly as she had when she arrived—absolutely breathtaking.

Clarice was without resources, altogether lacking in any inner energy and completely without any competitive drive. Had she had any of these qualities, she might have been a fine athlete, for she was blessed with perfect co-ordination. She was a good sailor, played a graceful game of tennis and acquitted herself well enough on the most difficult ski slopes. In her affluent world, these skills were expected of her and she performed proficiently but without enthusiasm.

Between marriages she traveled alone, always to those places of secret swank known only to the very rich and well connected, like Kirbo's Lodge, where even royalty received no special treatment, where privacy was protected and anonymity preserved. Though she had no close friends, her circle of acquaintances was wide and her credentials impeccable, hence she could be found on the pink courts of the St. Albans Club in Washington, at the remote and cushy Mill Reef in Antigua, at the sun-baked Del Zorro in the Anza-Borrego or languishing in the lush seclusion of Le Barringtonia on Bora Bora.

It was in Austria's Arlberg region, while staying at the elegant Gasthof Post hotel in Lech, that she met Harlan Cones, who had stared in disbelief as Clarice, in white pants and jacket with a navy stripe, her red hair beneath a blue cap streaming like a ribbon of fire behind her, skillfully and indifferently negotiated the long, winding slopes.

Following Max Donner as he did, Harlan was a tremendous relief to Clarice and she soon became quite fond of him. He talked to her about something other than sex, which few men had ever taken the trouble to do, and he amused her. He became, in truth, the first real friend she had ever had.

Harlan was dedicated to physical fitness and when, in the second week of their honeymoon, Clarice came upon him engaged in vigorous push-ups, perspiring and counting aloud, he was forced to declare his back improved and that night, his head full of images of deeply tanned and muscular beach boys, he took her to his bed. So tentative and delicate was his approach that Clarice not only suffered no trauma on the occasion, she hardly knew he was there. The disappointment was Harlan's, but in himself, not Clarice. A sensitive and kind man, Harlan took to drink, staying up very late at night and pleading too much alcohol as the answer to a question Clarice never asked. When she began to understand her new husband's problem, she was undisturbed.

"It just doesn't matter, Harley," she told him. "We have a good time and I hate the whole messy business anyway."

Harlan was incredulous. "You don't care that I'm gay? It doesn't bother you that I don't want you?"

"Harley, it's a relief."

"I wanted to want you," said Harlan sadly, "and I almost did, but I guess the truth is that what I really want is to *be* you—the most beautiful, most desirable woman in the world."

"Please don't be upset," Clarice said. "I'm happy."

Unfortunately, Harlan was not happy. They traveled for more than six months, staying at the Grand Hotel Camelot in London, at the Raphael in Paris and at the small and exquisite La Chèvre d'Or in the hilltop village of Èze overlooking the Mediterranean Sea. Through it all, Harlan was secretly distressed and when they were back home and living together in Harlan's home, once an old stable on Tenth Street in Greenwich Village which he had made a showplace (featured twice in *Architectural Digest*) and which was luxuriously comfortable, he began to receive telephone calls at odd times and disappeared for hours in the middle of the night. He became preoccupied and distant and the early companionship they had shared disappeared. Finally, he told Clarice he was in love with a young playwright (of dubious talent but with strong legs) and asked her for a divorce.

"A divorce isn't necessary," said she.

"It's necessary for me," said Harlan. "I'm really coming out of the closet. We're going to get married. In Denmark."

He deposited a large sum of money to Clarice's account and recommended that she see his old psychiatrist, who had moved to the West Coast. After their divorce, she took Harlan's advice, moved to San Francisco and had her first session with Dr. Allan Goldberg. Harlan was married to the young playwright and sent Clarice a framed photograph of the wedded couple. Harlan wore a white veil.

Clarice had always insisted on marriage, not from any moral sense, for she was completely amoral, but because it had postponed the inevitable moment when she would have to lie down with the man with whom she was involved. Two years after her divorce from Harlan, she was married one more time, to Bradford Bishop, the banker. Forty-five to her twenty-eight, Brad Bishop was no more successful in exciting her than his predecessors had been, and when he died of sudden pneumonia precipitated by sudden alcoholism only nine weeks after their marriage, Clarice swore she would never marry again. The only thing she learned from her affair with the thrice-married British actor and her recent relationship with the architect was that, for her, sex outside of marriage was no better and no worse than the conjugal variety.

She had not seen her mother or her father for years, and those disappointed and lonely people knew nothing of her life except what they learned from the gossip columns and society pages, clippings from which Mrs. DeReign carefully pasted in large scrapbooks bound in Venetian leather. For a few years after her first marriage, Clarice had returned for brief visits with her parents, but she felt stifled and depressed on the large, gloomy estate where she had grown up, and unable to bear the endless advice her mother forced upon her. The advice always ended in tearful sessions during which Mrs. DeReign blamed herself for the apparently cold and indifferent young woman her beautiful child had become.

There was also the inevitable question of grandchildren, which Clarice's mother wanted most anxiously, and that led to more advice about the rewards and joys of motherhood and lectures on what really produced happiness in women. Clarice would gaze at her mother's distraught and tear-ravaged face and clearly recognize the irony of it all. She finally stopped going home and never even wrote.

If her self-content was the cause of her isolation, it was also her salvation, because Clarice was truly alone.

Now, with Markey's permission, she came to stand behind him and was at first puzzled by what she saw on the canvas—a labyrinth of connecting lines in pastel chalk, the spaces in between the lines being filled in with color by Markey's fingers, brushes and knife. But as she studied the sprawling design, she began to recognize the lines of her body—unmistakably her lines, those she was so intimate with on the surface of her mirrors—from different angles of view, side, front, back, as if she were being painted in stop-frame instants as she pirouetted in full circle.

"It has no head," said Clarice.

Markey worked on, not answering.

"I want to be recognized. That's the least you could do." Petulantly, she scrounged into the pocket of the mink coat and produced a cigarette and lighter, began to smoke. But as she watched Markey's quick and certain hands, saw one of her shoulders emerge pinkly from the mass of lines, then the fullness of a breast, she forgot to smoke and stood entranced by the developing creation on the man. Clarice, who never really *looked* at anyone, began to look at canvas. And now her entrancement shifted its point of view, from this great man, she was also a surprise. She could not remember Markey. And Clarice, who never had any wonder about anything except her own wonderful self, began to wonder about Markey. Why had he agreed to paint her at all, and then why with no head? He didn't need her body to paint the kind of painting he was making— anyone's, the chambermaid's, would have done as well.

"Why did you have me pose?" she asked.

"You offered."

"No. Give me a better answer. Why are you painting this picture?"

He turned to look at her and found her to be seriously asking the question. "It is what I do, Mrs. Bishop. I paint."

"That isn't a painting," said Clarice, "it's an exercise." She knew that she had caught him.

He stared at her for a long moment, then smiled. "You're a surprise, Mrs. Bishop."

She was pleased. She was more than just a too perfect body to the painting to the painter, for after all, the painting's source was the

when anyone had ever complimented her so. She pushed for more.
"Why so?"

"Because you're right. It is pointless and that's enough of it."
He moved to the sink near his worktable and began to scrub the
paint from his hands.

"Aren't you going to finish it?"

"That may be the only point it has—that it's unfinished."

Clarice puffed on her cigarette and squinted at him through the
smoke. As a rule, she was bored by enigma. She liked things plainly
put, preferred the obvious, disliked the arcane, but, despite herself,
she was intrigued by Markey and that curious painting.

"On my way to pose this morning, I stopped in the library and
looked you up in the *Encyclopaedia Britannica*. You've got two
whole columns almost. One and a half, anyway."

"Did you find me interesting?" He dabbed paint remover on his
fingernails.

"Not especially," said Clarice, "but then, I'm not much for art
or artists, even ones as famous as you. One of my husbands tried to
teach me—always dragged me off to museums and galleries. He's
the reason I was in the Tate in London when I saw that portrait you
did. Lady something."

"How many husbands have you had?"

"Four. That one was gay. The one in the Tate. Why is the only
point that it's unfinished?" She got back to the present, sat on the
stool in the north light and crossed her legs. The mink coat fell away
and her smooth white thighs came into view. She left them that way
without deliberation.

"I shouldn't have started it. False start, it's called."

Clarice bounced this off her wall of common sense and found it
soft. "Your kind of artist doesn't make false starts."

"Then I don't like it."

"So I'm not to be finished. Story of my life," said she.

"I'd have thought you had a very complete life."

"Ha," she said, got up and stubbed her cigarette out in a tray.
She folded her arms and, standing there, settled into the blond mink,
eyes fixed on the ashtray, lost in herself.

Markey was reminded of the ride up from the landing strip with
Clarice beside him, unaware of his presence. "Mrs. Bishop?"

She looked at him, not really seeing him, her eyes opaque and
staring.

"What are you thinking, Mrs. Bishop?"

"That I'm grotesque," said she. She walked to the door, opened it and went through without another word.

And Markey let her go, but not without guilt. In her curious, almost backward way, she had opened herself to him and his response had been frosty. He had suppressed his charitable impulses. After all, what could he do? She was almost lost in her neurosis, gone feral; in a few more years, perhaps months, she would shut herself away in some den of a hotel room and, aestivating, begin that slow rot of the recluse.

In her room, Clarice lay stomach down across the huge bed and considered how she might spend the rest of the day. The morning had been wasted being nude for a painter who didn't like what he was painting. How could she make the afternoon count? Dr. Goldberg had said that she must do constructive things. She tried to think of constructive things—and went to sleep. And even as she fell into sleep, she knew she was sleeping too much.

16

On that morning, while the snowstorm was fooling around by itself a few hundred miles away, twenty-six guests checked out of the lodge and were conveyed by tram and limousine to Kirbo's Landing, where they collected their Rolls Royces or Lear jets or boarded the northbound or southbound morning commercial flights and by nightfall were comfortable in their homes or in other hotels far from the high Sierra.

Seven new guests arrived before the snowstorm finally pierced the feeble high-pressure area, and three more arrived afterward on the northbound afternoon plane, which was grounded at the Landing and its through passengers given emergency bus transportation to Carson City, Nevada. The three who took the limousine through the storm up to the lodge were, of course, bridge players, who, like postmen, are not daunted by the elements.

That evening the total number of guests in the lodge was one hundred and four. Seventy-one of that total were housed in the west wing and thirty-three in the north wing. There were no guests in the suites of the old main lodge because Arly had closed those grand accommodations for redecoration.

When the first quake bolted through the mountains, only twenty-eight of the guests in the north wing were in their rooms, the others being in the lounge or the cardroom, and thus it was that only twenty-eight died in the north wing.

Of the seventy-one guests in the west wing, fifty-nine were in their rooms and all survived the first quake, but some were injured from falling plaster or being heaved about by the movement of the floors and furniture. The guests who were in the main building for whatever reason, to eat, drink or play cards, not only survived the first quake but none was injured.

And all survived the second quake (7.2 on the Richter scale).

There were sixty-three employees (not counting Francine and Harry Ames) in residence on that night. Of these, at 2 A.M. in the main building, there was one telephone operator on duty, one room service operator, two sub-chefs in the kitchen, two room service waiters on duty, one waiter in the cardroom, a bartender (Paul) and a cocktail waitress (Diane) in the Earthquake Room, one clerk on the front desk, one maintenance man in the furnace room, and one housekeeper in the laundry room. These twelve survived. The fifty-one employees abed in the dormitory were killed in the first shock.

It is fortunate that the disaster occurred in the autumn change-over period or there would have been more than one hundred employees in the dormitory at that hour of the morning and three hundred guests registered at the lodge, of which number one hundred and thirty-two would have been alseep in the totally destroyed north wing.

Harry Ames was safe because his apartment was in the main lodge, and Francine was secure in her new quarters next to Arly's apartment. The lodge's doctor in residence also had his apartment in the main building next to the small infirmary, but he had gone into the town of Bishop for the night, where he was enjoying an affair with a pretty young anesthetist in the local hospital. The registered nurse at the lodge was killed in the dormitory, but fortunately Dr. Friendly was one of the uninjured guests and knew what to do about broken bones, and he found competent assistance in a bridge player who was an oral surgeon from Chicago.

PAUL

In the beginning he slept through the days and the nights, drug-induced sleep, heavy and without dreams, wasted weeks of his life. Later, when the pain eased, he slept from exhaustion, of mind and body, but he was only twenty-one and as his body healed, his mind cleared and the days and nights arranged themselves in proper order.

Through eyes half closed the folds and ripples of the green blanket became the gently rolling country of Wyoming in the spring or, when he was too warm and impatiently kicked the blanket to the hospital floor, the white sheets were a fall of heaviest snow laid upon the rich grazing land in the bleakness of a Wyoming winter.

"I'll come back soon," she said. "I promise." She kissed him quickly and waved over her shoulder as she hurried toward the car and the impatient man behind the wheel, his hand heavy on the horn. Three blasts, two long and one short, and the seven-year-old Paul ran after her, stumbled on the steps to the front porch of his grandparents' clapboard ranch house and sprawled on the path, not hurt but watching in shocked disbelief as the rear end of the blue car moved at high speed down the long, deserted road that stretched ahead it seemed for as far as he could see.

His grandfather picked him up and turned a face tight with anger toward Paul's grandmother, who shook her head warningly. The new trousers his mother had bought him for the trip were torn at the knee and his grandmother mended them while his grandfather brushed Paul's new jacket.

"When will my mother be back?" he asked his grandmother over and over, and she baked cookies and talked of other things. His grandfather took him outside to see the baby pigs and that night he ate dinner at a round table with his grandfather and his grandmother and two weathered ranch hands who gently teased the solemn-faced little boy still in his city clothes and urged him to eat his dinner. He tried but he couldn't swallow and he strained for the sound of a car's engine in the country silence to which he was not accustomed.

After dinner his grandmother took him to the small bedroom she told him had been his father's room. Her voice was steady, but as she unpacked the bag his mother had prepared for him that morning, the trembling of her lower lip betrayed her and in that instant the sensitive child relived the moments of that first loss ten months before, heard the sound of the door bursting open, felt his father's arms as he was hugged tightly a moment before he was dangled dangerously far out the window and dropped, felt the rushing air in his ears as he fell, choking from the smoke in his lungs, into the waiting arms of Sam Johnson, the big black man who was their neighbor. From the safety of those arms he had turned to look up at the window and had seen nothing but flame and black smoke curling on the early evening breeze.

Told that his father had been taken to the hospital for burns and smoke inhalation, he had waited for hours in the Johnsons' living room until his mother arrived. Pale and frightened, she sat the rest of the night by the sofa where he lay, her hand cool against his forehead each time he awoke crying in the early hours of the morning. Many days had passed before he understood that his father had died on the way to the hospital.

His grandmother laid his pajamas on the bed, but Paul refused to undress and fled downstairs to sit in a big chair by the front door. He must wait for his mother, he explained politely, and would not budge. Defeated finally, his tired and troubled grandparents went to bed and Paul sat alone throughout the long night. At six o'clock the next morning, his grandfather found him asleep in the chair and carried him upstairs.

For a week he sat by the door long after his normal bedtime but on the eighth night he had his supper and went directly upstairs to the room that would be his for the next twelve years of his life. He never asked about his mother again.

But he did not forget her and somewhere inside he continued to wait. Nose pressed to the window of the bus that took him to and from the country school, he examined each car on the highway searching for the blue car with a crumpled front bumper.

One night outside the door of his grandparents' bedroom, he heard his grandfather exclaim, "I knew he should never have married that bitch!" and his grandmother answered, "She was only a child herself, Frank," and she shushed him. Paul ran so he would hear no more. He didn't understand his grandfather's words, but he recognized the tone and sensed that they were discussing his mother and did not doubt that they were wrong. His beautiful mother loved him and she would come back to get him soon. She had promised.

Paul had voted for two Presidents and almost died in the rain forests of Vietnam before he began to understand how his life had been shaped by a twenty-three-year-old mother who had not come back.

"You have no mama and papa," the sheepherder said. "You must grow up faster, become a man—a strong man who does not depend on others."

His name was José and he was born in the Pyrenees. Dark and slender, with the straight-lined, regular profile of the Basque, he spoke English, French and Spanish and he lived in a trailer with his black and white sheep dogs.

At first attracted by the beautiful dogs, Paul soon became José's shadow, walking the green meadows beside him as he tended his flock of more than a thousand sheep, watching the intelligent and well-trained dogs react immediately at a hand signal from José, rounding up strays or herding potential wanderers back into the fold. Most of the time they walked in companionable silence and occasionally José would sing in a fine, pure tenor voice songs Paul could not understand. Sometimes when the sheep were near, Paul's grandparents allowed him to have supper with the sheepherder. They sat by the campfire while José prepared a rich and fragrant Basque stew and the coyotes harmonized on the ridges. It was peaceful and mysterious in the long, dark land and Paul was happy except for the hard little knot of anxiety that had not left him in the two years he had been on the ranch.

"I have a mother," said he. "She had to go away but she's coming back to get me."

His mother had sent him a sweater for his ninth birthday. The package had carried a New York postmark, but there had been no note and the sweater was too small and Paul would not wear it.

"And you are waiting." There was disapproval in José's voice. "You must learn all you can learn and become very independent. When you are independent, you are free and you wait for no one."

"My mother has long, blond hair and she is very pretty," Paul responded, and José murmured *"Por Dios"* and handed him a pewter bowl full of steaming stew.

In bed that night, Paul squeezed his eyes closed tightly and tried to find his mother's face, but he could not remember how she looked, only the blond hair he had described to José and the sound of her voice as she had said, "I promise."

When he was ten, Paul discovered his grandfather's library. He began with the horse and gun stories of Zane Grey and graduated to *Oliver Twist,* which he read twice because it was about a boy who had no parents, then discovered the adventure stories of Robert Louis Stevenson and, mesmerized, spent hours after dinner bent over the leather-bound volumes until his grandmother sent him to bed.

"I don't know what he's thinking," she worried to his grandfather when they were alone. "He keeps things to himself and it's not normal in a boy his age."

"Could be he's a little smarter than's good for him," his grandfather said, "but books won't hurt him. You don't have to worry that he won't grow up to be a man." He looked at her with quick perception. "Does his share of the chores and he rides that horse like a Comanche."

"He never mentions her, Frank," his grandmother said, and his grandfather snorted.

"Been a long time and, smart as he is, he's had the sense to forget all about that trashy bit."

"He hasn't forgotten." There was a sad note in his grandmother's voice. "He's lost his trust."

They had given him the horse for his tenth birthday, a fast red mare he named Rojo. He groomed her with care and rode for miles whenever he had the chance, delighting in his control of the horse, loving the distance behind them and the freedom of the distance ahead. As he rode without a saddle, boy and horse all of a piece, he sometimes caught sight of José and his sheep and guided Rojo toward them, and the sheep parted like a woolly sea as he rode through them and he lifted his hand in salute to the Basque, who waved in return, an understanding smile creasing his leathery cheeks.

Through his eyelashes, Paul watched the young blond nurse with the large gray eyes read the thermometer with practiced ease and evident satisfaction.

"How am I doing?" he asked, and the lazy smile was a rusty tool, unused for a long time but still effective, and the nurse, who was only a few years older than he, looked up in surprise and for a moment lost her efficient composure, her answering smile tremulous because he had been there for more than two weeks and it was the first time he had spoken. She had been present when they brought him in, when the tired doctor had looked down on the gurney and exploded, "Oh, Jesus," and sagged before he rallied and said, "We can try."

"Pretty good," said she. "That's how you're doing. An absolutely perfect temp of ninety-eight point six."

He smiled again and this time it came easier. The fresh-faced, dedicated little nurse considered her patient and her expression reflected genuine pleasure in his dramatic improvement plus a little something more that she did not know was the common reaction of women exposed to Paul's direct gaze.

"The Pope must have blessed that medal around your neck,"

said she, and walked casually out of the room, but once outside she ran down the corridor to find the doctor, blinking rapidly to ease the unprofessional stinging behind her eyes.

A few minutes later, an orderly wheeled in Paul's dinner, and while he ate he touched the gold medal at his throat, absently traced the engraved initials with the sore tips of his fingers and allowed himself to remember Ellen Walker.

"I'm Miss Walker," she said, and surveyed the class of thirty students who gazed back at her with curiosity.

Twenty-three years old and fresh from her summer vacation in the south of France, she was beginning her second year teaching the seventh grade at the consolidated junior and senior high school in Chugwater, Wyoming.

Ellen Walker was a good teacher and she searched the unfamiliar young faces before her and hoped this class might yield some bright students to make her days interesting in the coming school year. Last year's crop had been willing but unremarkable and, while she had enjoyed their high spirits and grown quite fond of some of them, she looked forward to a more challenging group this year.

By the end of the day, she had begun to sort them out and evaluate their potential, but she had been struck by only one, a curiously adult boy with remote eyes shaded by thick, dark lashes and an air of intensity that was unusual in a twelve-year-old. She had asked the class to write a brief paragraph telling about themselves, writing their names and seat numbers in the upper right-hand corner of the page. Class dismissed for the day, she shuffled through them until she found the one that read, "Paul Binns, Seat 3, Aisle 2."

> I live on my grandfather's ranch and I am not much of anybody but I like to read and learn and I will try to be a good student.

Young though she was, Ellen Walker was not too young to be moved by this succinct summary from a twelve-year-old boy and she reread the sentence several times before she turned to the other, more ordinary papers before her. Her interest in Paul Binns was engaged at that moment. It was a responsible interest, the kind a good teacher is charged to have for a pupil, and while it was certainly properly extended, his response was to be exceptional. Miss Walker would not ever forget Paul Binns.

On her way home that afternoon, she stopped by the principal's office. "What information do you have on a boy named Paul Binns?" she asked the plump, redheaded girl who registered new students.

"Just typing the cards," was the answer as the clerk checked under B in the square file box. "Binns, Paul, age twelve, completed sixth grade at John Colter Grammar School. Lives on a ranch, Rural Route Three. That's about twelve miles south."

"May I see his grade sheet?"

"Sure." The clerk checked another file and handed her Paul's scholastic record.

She read it quickly, saw that he had received an A in every subject but mathematics, which was marked B. There was a note attached from his previous teacher: "Exceptionally bright but with a tendency toward aloofness. Well-liked by his fellow students but should be encouraged to mix."

"Trouble?" asked the clerk.

"No trouble," Miss Walker replied. "Thanks."

As she drove home to the comfortable room and bath she rented in a private home in the little town of Chugwater, Ellen Walker wondered why such a bright and attractive boy had described himself as "not much of anybody."

By the end of the second week, Miss Walker had established a classroom routine and opened communication between herself and the youngsters in her class. She had identified Chuck Wilcox, a big-for-his-age town boy, as the harmless class bully, and had recognized that the seventeen girls in her class were, as usual, generally more responsive and better students than the thirteen boys. And had confirmed her reaction to Paul on that first day as accurate. Paul Binns possessed an oddly mature air of independence and she saw an element his previous teacher had not noted in the assessment of Paul's character and personality. It was not that he was not a mixer, it was that the other children seemed to be cautious around him as if he were an unknown quantity. Miss Walker was perceiving in the child that Byronic mysterioso Diane and other women later in his life would always find so arresting. And more than a few of the giggling little country girls gazed on him with secret admiration.

She felt it was important to give individual attention to each student and, at the end of the day, often called one of them to her desk to chat for a few minutes before the school bus departed. On Friday afternoon she asked Paul to stay for a moment.

"What do you raise on your ranch?" she asked.

"Sheep, mostly—and a few hogs."

"I grew up in a city—Denver—and I always wanted to live in the country because I wanted a horse."

"I have a mare," Paul offered. "My grandpa gave her to me for my birthday two years ago."

"Weren't you lucky." Miss Walker smiled. "And your mother and father didn't think you were too young to have your own horse?"

"My father died—a long time ago," he said quickly, and looked at the wall clock. "I'll miss my bus."

She picked up her briefcase. "We still have five minutes. I'll walk out with you."

Warned by his sudden evasion, Ellen did not ask about his mother, but outside she put a hand on his shoulder. "You know," said she carefully, "sometimes people who grow up in special circumstances become very special people. Remember that."

Paul stood silent for a moment and then he ran down the steps and boarded the school bus. Just before the door closed, he turned and waved and he could see that she was pleased—and all the way home he thought about Miss Walker and what she had said.

Several days later, as the rest of the class filed out for gym period, Paul stopped at her desk and from a paper bag took a stone the size of his small fist and placed it on her desk. "Here," he said.

She examined the rock, which here and there contained small blue transparent crystals. "Why, Paul, it's beautiful."

"It's only quartz," he replied, "but the blue could be kyanite, and that's rare. I found it in a field. You keep it."

"It's not just pretty, it's useful," she said, and placed the rock on a stack of papers. "Thank you." She looked at him curiously. "You seem to know something about rocks."

"Geology interests me," said he. "That's the most unusual rock in my collection."

"Then double thanks," she said.

He remained beside her desk watching her and she felt an odd discomfort. "Well, see you after gym," she said.

He nodded and walked away.

Too good a teacher to permit a show of partiality toward any one student, Ellen acknowledged to herself that Paul's presence in her class contributed in large measure toward the satisfaction she drew from teaching that year. She worried that the level at which they were working was not challenging enough for him, but there were twenty-nine others of whom that was not true, so she prescribed an advanced reading program for him. During the year, he worked his way through the list and, since they could not discuss these books in class, he wrote reports, which she read and returned with her comments.

In the beginning his reports were the usual formal school book reports in which he proved that he had read the story, and her comments were upon his presentation of what he had read, but as the months passed, he began to make his own comments on the books, expressing his likes and dislikes. Once he asked her a question in his report on *A Farewell to Arms:* "Why did you think I would be interested at my age in a love story between two adults?" Miss Walker thought for several days before she answered the question. "You see," she wrote, "the love story is not the most important thing. It is Mr. Hemingway's view of the tragic consequences of war that is important." Paul gave the report back to her and under her comment he had written, "Nonsense, Miss Walker."

For several days she found herself avoiding Paul's eyes, which were always attentive, and she began to wonder why, indeed, she had suggested the novel. Finally, she convinced herself that she was amused. In spite of his intelligence, he was only twelve years old. Going on thirteen. And growing.

Paul celebrated his thirteenth birthday in January and he brought her a large slice of the chocolate cake his grandmother had baked for him.

In the spring Miss Walker took the class on a field trip to identify the profuse wildflowers that waved like grain in their great masses. They spent the early afternoon wandering the meadows and the ridges and later she sent the boys over the hill and the girls into a grove of woods.

"You know why," said she, "and no peeking!"

The boys took off up the hill with rowdy good cheer and the girls giggled their way into the woods. Miss Walker sat on a log, smoked a forbidden cigarette and enjoyed the sunny spring day.

When, after fifteen minutes, the girls had all returned but there was no sign of the boys, she became aware of a peculiar silence beyond the hill and she left the girls, climbed the hillside and through the tall brush saw the boys.

They were standing around a small clearing where, in the center, two of them stood circling each other, fists doubled, and she recognized the larger boy as Chuck Wilcox and was not surprised. Responsible teacher that she was, she started forward to break up the fight, suddenly realized the other boy was Paul and did not ask herself why she hesitated and stayed behind the concealing brush.

As she watched, Chuck Wilcox began to swing wildly and Paul, on his toes, neatly sidestepped and, coming up close and inside, connected twice with short, straight, left-handed blows to the bigger boy's chin, followed by a right that landed hard on Chuck's nose. Chuck sat down, blood from his nose spotting his T-shirt and, stunned and surprised, he began to cry. The other boys stood staring down at him in startled silence.

"Now"—Paul turned to face the watching boys, voice low but clear in the country quiet—"anybody else want to call me teacher's pet?"

Miss Walker turned quickly and moved halfway back down the hill, waited a moment, then started up again, calling to the boys as she climbed. One by one they appeared, filing past her with expressionless faces as they trooped down the hill, Chuck one of the last, a handkerchief held to his nose as if he had just sneezed. Paul was the final boy to top the rise as Ellen Walker stood waiting several feet below.

She was tall for a woman, but now as he stood above her, the late afternoon sun at his back, the illusion of height and the shoulders that were already wide, the not quite arrogant tilt of his head, the proud stance and bold masculinity of his features, the unconscious grace of this strange boy struck Miss Walker and in a quick flash she saw the man in the child. She was disturbed by her vision and then he walked down to her level and he was again a child, the top of his head just above her shoulder.

But the hint of challenge in his gaze as he stood at the crest of the hill remained in her consciousness. Paul Binns had looked at her the way a man looks at a woman.

From their occasional correspondence that summer, Ellen gained no insight into the inner workings of Paul's mind, no clue to his private emotions. His letters were short and not of a confiding nature, rather full of endless questions about Ellen.

She was spending the summer at her parents' home in Denver and attending the University of Colorado in Boulder, working toward her master's degree, which had been interrupted the previous summer by her trip to France.

How many hours did she spend at the university and what was she doing with her free time? She had mentioned dancing—did she go with different men or did she have a special friend? (Ellen did not respond to this query.) How did she dress, in skirts or pants? Did she drink? What did she drink? Did she go out to dinner? What kind of perfume was her favorite? He liked her blond hair long and straight and he hoped she would not cut it or tease it in the manner of some of the dancers he saw on television. He liked some of the new rock music but preferred the songs of Edith Piaf. He had ordered her record albums from a music store in Cheyenne and had sent away for some recorded lessons in French.

About himself he volunteered the information that he was learning to take Rojo over the jumps and was reading John Steinbeck's *The Red Pony*. He had gone to Yellowstone National Park with his grandfather and had been impressed by the Obsidian Cliff and the travertine terraces at Mammoth Hot Springs.

On the first day of the new school year, classes were dismissed early. Lean and tan, the suggestion of hard new muscles beneath his short-sleeved white shirt, he stood unsmiling before her desk and she rose to find they were on an equal level. Her surprise delighted him and he smiled then. Miss Walker saw that, for the most part, the child was gone. Paul had grown more than three inches during the past summer, his voice had changed and there was a new confidence in the way he moved.

They ate together in her classroom, shared the lunches they had brought and talked about the summer just passed. When he left to catch his bus, she sat in deep thought for a long time before she gathered together the papers written by her new class and walked out to her car. She knew she would miss Paul's lively intelligence in her classroom this year.

He came by her room frequently in the months that followed. And since he was no longer her pupil, she sometimes forgot he was a schoolboy still. The eyes behind their tangled lashes were older than his years, and they were waiting, waiting for her.

She went home to Denver for Christmas and the florist's box with a corsage made of a single large gardenia was delivered Christmas Eve with a card that read simply, "From Paul."

On his birthday in January, she gave him the complete works of William Shakespeare and told him to save them until he was eighteen. A month later, he gave her a written report on *Romeo and Juliet* in which he made it clear that he was much impressed with Romeo's evaluation of Juliet—that she was the sun. It seemed to Miss Walker that everything she cast upon the waters came back to haunt her.

One afternoon in middle February, she found Paul standing on the steps of the school when she left at the end of the day. He had missed his bus and she drove him home. It was a gray day, windy and cold, and on the dashboard she pressed the button marked "heat." Outside dark clouds threatened snow and in the warmth and intimacy of the small car they drove the twelve miles in silence, each aware of a shift in the relationship, a strangeness in this first time together outside the confines of the classroom. At the junction of the highway and the farm road that led to the ranch, Paul spoke.

"I can walk from here," said he. "It's too muddy to drive."

Miss Walker braked and they sat in the car with the motor running. She did not look at him but knew he was looking at her and the current that flowed between them crackled with an energy as real as it was bizarre and, as she wondered what might happen if she switched off the ignition, Paul opened his door and the cold air swept through the car.

"Thank you," he said, and looked up at the sky. "It's going to snow. Be careful."

He pressed the lock and closed the door and even as he moved toward the road that led to the ranch, the first white flakes touched his dark hair. Ellen turned the car around and drove slowly back to town and did not try to identify the disappointment she felt.

On a Sunday afternoon Ellen and another woman teacher went to the movie house located on the main street of the little town. This day was dry but cold and as they stood at the box office she spotted Paul in the doorway of the drugstore across the street, the collar of his heavy plaid jacket turned up against the chill. He stood motionless, his eyes fixed on her. When they came out of the theater, he was gone and she drove her friend home, but when she turned into the street where she lived, she saw him again, sitting on the wall that surrounded the town's library. She drove the three blocks home, parked the car and switched off the ignition but did not get out. She sat indecisively for a few moments before she turned the key and started the car again. She would make one swing past the library.

He was still there and she pulled in at the curb. "How did you get to town?"

He remained seated on the wall. "I caught a ride."

"How do you propose to get home?"

He shrugged. "I'll catch a ride."

He made no move and Ellen knew suddenly what she was going to do. She leaned across the front seat and opened the door.

"Get in."

Neither spoke as she drove out of town and, when they reached the main road, she turned north rather than south toward the ranch. Almost an hour later, she drove into the parking area of a motel and left him sitting in the car while she registered. She returned to the car, handed him a room key and swung around to the back of the building, where she parked. Silently, they got out of the car and Paul opened the door, standing aside politely to allow her to precede him.

It was just dusk and Ellen switched on the bedside lamps. The room was pleasant, clean and warm and she removed her coat. Her gray wool dress buttoned down the front and she turned away from Paul to unbutton the dress.

"No," he said. He touched her on the shoulder and she faced him. He began to work on the buttons with shaking fingers, but he got the job done. He took the dress from her shoulders, knelt and drew her half-slip down about her feet. She stepped out of it and stood looking down at him in speechless wonder. It was not going to be the way she had thought it would be, that she, the older, the experienced one, would take the lead. He seemed to know her thoughts and looked up at her and smiled, then firmly pulled down her panties. Now he stood, turned her about and managed to fumble her out of her bra. He stepped away and studied her.

"Do you approve of me?" she asked lightly, and heard her voice tremble. No, it was not going to be the way she had thought it would be.

He nodded, moved to the bed, drew down the thick comforter and the blankets and turned out the bedside lamps.

"That isn't fair, Paul," said she, again with attempted lightness and hearing again the tremble in her voice.

"Kids aren't anything to look it," said Paul. "You are."

She lay on the bed and waited until he undressed. He lay down beside her in the darkness and for a little while, as they caught their breath, neither of them moved.

"I'm not a virgin," said Paul.

"No?"

"I haven't been since I was thirteen."

She was astonished that she felt a flash of jealousy.

"I thought you should know that," said he. "I'm not jail bait." And he laughed and bent to kiss her mouth. His lips were sweet and childish but then they seemed to harden. They moved to her breast then to her belly and into the dark triangle.

"Now wait a minute," Ellen said.

"I love you," said Paul. He kissed her again and she felt as if she were melting.

"By how much aren't you a virgin?" she asked.

"Not much," said Paul. "Once. But I've read an awful lot about it and I want to do it all with you, everything I've read."

And that is what they did, everything that he had read, by the book, and finally she gasped, "Paul, that's enough. Please."

He turned on a bed lamp and sat up on the side of the bed, watching her with a reverence that frightened her. She looked at her watch and could not believe that more than two hours had passed, and as he reached for her again, she rolled away and was quickly on her feet.

"It's almost nine. Your grandparents will be worried."

They dressed and she dropped the room key on a table, closed the door softly behind them.

Ellen drove faster than she liked to, concentrating on the road, conscious of his hand which lay possessively on her knee. Paul sat relaxed, head back against the seat, eyes closed. He sensed she was looking at him, opened his eyes and smiled at her, a smile that held nothing back, a mixture of pride, trust and adoration.

When she let him off at the end of the road leading to the ranch, it was suddenly as if the motel had not happened. They were as awkward as they had been the first time she had driven him home. He stood beside the car, looking at her through the window, and she stared back at him.

"You're angry," said Paul.

"Why should I be angry?"

"At yourself," said Paul.

She was unable to reply.

"Please don't be," he said.

She tried to smile and he stepped back to let her drive away.

Halfway back to Chugwater, tears blurred Ellen's vision and she pulled off the road, stopped the car and wept aloud. She did not know why she was crying and that made it worse, the confusion. But as she got hold of herself, she spooned one clear fact out of the mess she had cooked up for herself and Paul. She must run away from it as fast as she could go.

Students and teachers were caught up in midterm exams in the week that followed and she avoided the possibility of seeing Paul alone, lunching with other teachers and leaving quickly at the end of each day.

On Monday at noon, when normal school routine had resumed, Paul stood in the doorway of the seventh grade classroom.

"Yes?" The gray-haired lady in her fifties who sat at Ellen's desk looked at him alertly.

Paul knew before he spoke. "I'm looking for Miss Walker."

"Miss Walker is gone. Illness in her family, I believe. I'm Mrs. Dexter. May I help you?"

He shook his head, turned to go, remembered to say, "Thank you." The letter he wrote Ellen late that night said only, "You have left me with nothing."

The small package arrived in the mail two weeks later. A simple gold disk, his initials engraved on the back, was accompanied by a short note in which she said he must believe that her affection for him was genuine and it was that affection that had dictated what she had done. Paul hurled the medallion on its gold chain into the fields behind his grandparents' house. At dawn the following day, he searched for hours before he found it shining in the tall grass.

In time, he forgave her and even came to understand, but now the twig was truly bent and the gentlest hands could not straighten it.

He graduated from high school but he did not, as was expected, enter college in the fall.

They were hustling along now, getting close to the LZ where the Huey would come in fast and take them out fast. Joey was on the point with Ho and Corporal Paul Binns was now in command and bringing up the rear because Sergeant Correll had got it five miles back. They had buried the body and cross-checked the position on the map just in case Graves Detail had a chance to pick it up while there was something left to pick up.

The fern brush was thick and not much sunlight came through the forest canopy and they felt better about being in the shadows and the brush than they would have if they had been crossing a ridge and making nice targets against the white clouds. The sound of a single shot somewhere off stopped them in their tracks. It was not aimed at them because it didn't have that telltale crack of a gun aimed at you.

"What you got?" Paul called it in a hoarse whisper and the question went forward and came back from Joey.

"Clear. All clear up here."

"Move," said Paul, and the men moved, seven of them, four Americans and three Vietnamese, five days in the rain forest, mapping the trails, sleeping in their clothing, drinking iodined water and eating canned rations, shitting between their heels and hating every goddamned minute of those five days. And the sergeant got it. They kept hustling.

Now they heard voices, off to the left, and they froze and their thumbs moved on the AR-15s, moving the selectors off safe. The voices were louder and Paul was facing the voices. Charlie in a hard hat came into view and his eyes found Paul's eyes. Charlie's mouth opened in surprise, but in the time it took for him to open his mouth in surprise, Paul's gun was firing. You don't hesitate out there, you don't take the time to be surprised or open your mouth, you fire, and Paul fired first and Charlie curled up against a tree and went to his knees.

Paul and the boys were running now and around them came the crack and snick of chasing bullets. Paul, in the rear, would turn and fire until his magazine was empty. Then, running again, snapping a new magazine in the AR-15 without looking at his hands. He could change magazines in the dark or running or rolling or standing on his head.

Charlie was not running after them now. He was coming on but not running. Nobody runs after an AR-15 in the hands of a soldier who knows how to use it and Paul knew how to use it.

Paul could hear the jackhammer clatter of the Huey coming over. On time—just right—they were going to make it. "Joey!" he called, and Joey yelled, "Here—here—here!" and Paul ran in that direction.

He caught sight of the Huey as it paddled down toward the LZ and he knew he had to give it a chance, so he stopped and waited on one knee, a full magazine ready and one in his belt. Charlie had heard the Huey and was coming on faster and Paul began to fire, sweeping the muzzle back and forth like a man sandblasting paint. It was empty and he snapped the new mag in and plunged on through the brush. Now the Huey was settling and Paul knew they had it made. One more minute. He turned and went again to one knee and watched for Charlie and saw Charlie coming, maybe twenty of them, hard hats and French rifles. He began to fire and Charlie took cover and the French rifles cut loose and Paul was almost lifted off the ground when he took the stuff from the French rifles. He rolled and came up firing and started to the LZ and fell and came up again and kept going.

He was under the chopper blades and they were slapping faster as Joey and Ho came for him and lugged him aboard and now the Huey's fifties were talking and that would sure as shit stop Charlie.

Joey was holding Paul against his chest and saying, "Oh, my god, oh, my god," and Paul said, "What the fuck are you doing? Turn loose of me," but Joey kept hugging him and saying, "Oh, my god," and Paul went to sleep.

And now the brigadier general was coming into the ward with his aides and they were all smiles and the nurses and the doctors were all smiles and Paul watched them come directly to his bed. The brigadier general explained the purpose of his visit and Paul said, "Thank you, sir, but I don't want it, sir."

The brigadier general asked the doctor, "Does he understand what I'm saying?"

"Yes, sir, I understand, sir," said Paul.

"This is the Silver Star, young man," said the brigadier, who was a sad-faced old boy when he was not smiling. When the smile dropped, the whole face dropped with it right down into the jowls as sad as a bloodhound's jowls.

Paul felt a little sorry for the brigadier general but he said, "I know what it is, sir, but I refuse it, sir," and he rolled over and would not look at the sad-faced brigadier general again. He heard them go away.

The soldier in the bed next to Paul's, the one with his left foot gone, said, "You'll get yourself a bad paper discharge, buddy," and Paul said, "I'll take any kind. Just get me out of this war."

But, of course, he did not get a bad paper discharge but a perfectly honorable discharge that even made note of the Silver Star but not that he had not accepted it. On the record, he was a hero.

He went home to Wyoming and for a time he did nothing but help José with the sheep and ride his mare and sit quietly in the evening with his grandparents and watch television. But he knew what he had to do. In the fall, he packed a valise and kissed his grandmother, and his grandfather drove him into Chugwater, where he caught the Greyhound bus. Finally, at the age of twenty-two, he was going to do it.

He found her three months later a few miles outside of Beaumont, Texas, in the crowded cocktail lounge of a motel that catered to oil men. In the low light, she looked as he had remembered, blond-hair worn long and straight to her shoulders, straight legs in high-heeled sandals, figure trim in the ridiculously short, blue costume.

"What'll you have?" Her smile was mechanical and she did not really look at him.

He ordered a beer and when she brought it, she said, "That'll be one-fifty."

He gave her two dollars. "Keep it."

"Thanks," said she, and produced the mechanical smile.

"I'm Paul," he said.

The jukebox shook with loud country blues and she turned. "I'm sorry?"

"I'm Paul," he said again.

Her expression did not change. "Paul? Paul who?"

"Paul Binns."

She looked at him closely now but he could read nothing on her face. Across the room, somebody shouted for service and she waved acknowledgment. A moment of silence then as she studied him.

"My break is at nine o'clock. If you want to wait."

"You want me to wait?"

"There's a restaurant off the lobby. I'll be there."

In the garish light of the large, empty restaurant, she looked not old but older, a slight dimpling of the skin at her throat, faint lines between her eyebrows and at the corners of her eyes.

They ordered steak sandwiches from the listless waitress and she asked about his grandparents. He said they were fine and knew there was no interest behind the question, that she was searching for something to say.

"He never liked me much—your grandfather," his mother said. "Even before what happened—to your father, I mean."

"He never mentioned it," replied Paul.

"You've got his eyes—your father's."

They sat in uncomfortable silence for a while and he wondered about their food. They were the only customers in the ugly dining room, its floors uncarpeted and decorated with big, dusty plastic trees. Their waitress was sitting at the far end of the long room, slumped in a chair, painting her fingernails.

"You in school?" she asked.

"I just got out of the Army—almost two years in Vietnam."

She nodded without interest or comprehension. "I lost track. I used to hear from your grandmother sometimes but she stopped writing way back."

The waitress, being careful about her wet nails, brought the sandwiches, ill-smelling and soggy with grease.

"I've got two other kids. A boy nine and a little girl. She's three years old," said his mother.

"What does your husband do?"

"I divorced him," said she, and left it at that.

And Paul thought it was not going to be easy. She was almost thirty-nine years old now.

"But I'm doing okay. Tips here are good. I can pick up four or five hundred a week most weeks."

Paul pushed his food around on his plate and watched her eat, realized he felt nothing he had thought he would feel and knew it was the same for her.

She looked at her watch and said she had to get back. She wanted to sign the check, so Paul left a tip and walked with her to the door of the cocktail lounge, where she hesitated. "You want to stay a few days, you can stay with me. If you don't mind sleeping on the sofa."

"Thanks, but I've got a job waiting for me in Florida." He smiled. "I was just passing through and wanted to say hello."

She searched his face then and he saw relief in her eyes. "You're not bitter or anything, are you, Paulie?"

He suddenly remembered she had called him that and he studied her and knew why he had loved her so. She was kind and gentle.

"I knew you were all right. I wouldn't have left you there if I hadn't known you would be. A ranch is a good place to grow up. It wouldn't have been easy with me. I worry about the two I've got now."

"Write me if you ever need help," said Paul. "Write to the ranch. I'll get it."

"I'll remember that." She touched the gold disk at his throat. "It's pretty."

And Paul reached up and removed the gold chain and disk, pressed it into the palm of her hand, kissed her on the cheek and left the motel.

Outside the cool air was heavy with the smell of crude oil. The taxi took him past the pumping wells that lined the streets on both sides. He knew he had laid two ghosts in Beaumont, Texas.

To make his lie true, he did go to Florida, and found a job as a lifeguard at a hotel in Palm Beach and stayed until the spring. He had discovered the resort circuit and found its ethos to his liking. He was free and uncommitted and while he did not tend sheep, he tended bar or worked as a lifeguard in Palm Springs, California, in Sun Valley, Idaho, on St. John in the Virgin Islands, on Maui and in Honolulu. His jobs were as temporary as his personal relationships but his employers were as well satisfied as were the ladies in his company for whatever time he gave them.

When he left Greece in September, he had stopped in Paris for one day before catching a plane for the States. The money the Englishwoman had put in his pockets had amounted to eight thousand, nine hundred dollars. At Cartier's, he purchased a gold cigarette case inlaid with a small circle of emeralds and asked that it be engraved, "With affection from a constant companion," and sent to the Englishwoman in Greece. The cost, including the engraving, was a little more than nine thousand dollars. The inscription was sincere. He had liked her and hoped to see her again at some time, in some place. And unless that happened, he would seldom, if ever, think of her at all.

17

On that morning of the stalled storm, the lodge vehicles hurried up and down the road from the valley or to the valley and the snow that fell was fretful and quickly swept away by gusts of wind. At the road maintenance garages, the first located five miles up and called Snow One and the second at ten miles and called Snow Two, the crews idled about in the warm garages—six men to each location—and drank coffee and kept an eye on the lowering sky. They all knew they were in for a good one but it would not be the first and their machinery was in top condition, each garage equipped with one big caterpillar tractor with snow blade and two smaller, faster snow-dozers. And the men knew from experience where the drifts would collect, at which bridge or on which curve, or at the entrance to which tunnel, and they were prepared to do battle around the clock if necessary to keep the road passable. The limousines and the lodge service trucks were equipped with snow tires now and their wheels keened against the pavement as they passed the garages.

In addition to Snow One and Snow Two, the tram station had a snow-dozer to clear the limousine parking areas in front of the station. The tram station was well heated and designed not unlike a firehouse, there being living quarters above the waiting room for the night limousine chauffeurs and the cable machinery maintenance men. It was fortuitous that the station was so well appointed, because it would serve a desperate need in the next forty-eight hours.

In the valley, the interstate highway maintenance crews were also gearing up to clear drifts and the county sheriff's substations had alerted their volunteer rescue teams. In any snowstorm, there would invariably be a few foolish hikers to be found on mountain trails and saved from death by exposure. The rescue teams were practiced and skillful, composed of men who understood snow and *its terrors and were not afraid to go into it. Their courageous drive to reach Kirbo's Lodge after the quake would become a storied legacy for all the mountain rescue teams of the world.*

DIANE

People who are without cynicism, who remain hopeful, who see only the best side of us or of life, who believe love to be a pure element, these people we call incurable romantics—as if those positive factors were germy and diseased. Diane was an incurable romantic. She fell in love, when she was sixteen, with a lad named Percival (Perce for short) Hochstetter because he reminded her so much of Lord Byron, with whom she had been in love since she was fourteen. Between the ages of nine and fourteen, her most ardent affair had been with Jesus Christ and she had permanent scars to show for it, tiny black streaks in the flesh of both knees caused by so much kneeling in the alley behind the house where she lived. The alley had once been a railroad bed from the period of coal-burning engines and the cinders had tattooed her knees as she thanked her heavenly lover for all the good things he had given her, health and nice hair, a sweet mother and father and a baby sister and brother, and a new dress for Easter. And if all her prayers did not keep her sweet mother and father together, her passion was not lessened by one tot until she began reading poetry and discovered limpy, beautiful George Noel Gordon Byron.

> Ye spirits of the unbounded Universe!
> Whom I have sought in darkness and in light—
> Ye, who do compass earth about and dwell
> In subtler essence—ye, to whom the tops of mountains inaccessi-
>   ble are haunts,
> And earth's and ocean's caves familiar things—
> I call upon ye by written charm
> Which gives me power upon you—
> Rise! Appear!

Indeed, it is likely, even after her disenchantment with Perce, if that miserable episode can be so dignified, that at least part of Paul Binns's attraction for her was his Byronic heroism—like Manfred, he was mysterious, lonely and defiant.

Diane was the first-born of the puzzling and unlikely coupling of Harold and Margaret Haynes and she had arrived on Margaret's twentieth birthday, July 4, 1955, exactly nine months and two weeks after her parents' marriage. Independence Day, and for Margaret at least, the beginning of the end of personal independence.

The young couple had only two hundred dollars on the day Diane was born, and twenty-five dollars on account was paid to the doctor who delivered the baby. His total fee was two hundred and fifty dollars and they paid off the debt over a two-year period. Like an automobile, Diane was purchased on time.

Margaret was tall, handsome, optimistic and intelligent and it was from her mother that Diane inherited her good looks and ebullient disposition. She owed her nearsightedness to her gentle and pessimistic father. For the thirteen years that they lived together, people frequently wondered what Margaret, with her energy and love of life, had ever seen in Harold Haynes, and indeed, Margaret herself could not have answered the question if it had been put to her except to acknowledge that he had seemed to need her.

Harold was a kind and inoffensive young man who loved his wife at the same time that he was intimidated by her. At nineteen, he had come to Los Angeles from a small town in Nebraska and he viewed the sprawling and competitive city with alarm and a total lack of ambition. He was the quintessential country boy and, if he had not met Margaret, he would probably have gone back home within weeks of his arrival. Drawn to her strength and vitality, he had somehow mustered the courage to marry her and it was as if that giant step had depleted his store of positive energy, dried it up once and for all, leaving him to coast and Margaret to carry him. Although she had several years at Los Angeles City College before their marriage, Harold had barely scraped through high school. Without education or its equivalent, business acumen, he was unable to secure any but the dullest work and, at various times, he sold shoes, drove a taxi, was a salesman in the men's department of Sears, Roebuck & Company and a clerk in a liquor store. During those years, Diane's younger brother and sister were born.

The family lived in a tiny rented house near downtown Los Angeles, a safe but drab neighborhood of stucco houses and neglected lawns. When her father was between jobs, Diane's mother would brush her good suit, polish her one decent pair of shoes and go downtown to find temporary work as a legal secretary, reluctantly leaving her husband to take care of the children. It was on a day when both her parents were at home that Harold Haynes, at the bedroom window that looked out on the alley, saw Diane, on her way home from school, drop to her knees to offer up a brief prayer. This was not the first time he had watched his daughter's strange behavior and Harold did what he always did when troubled. He shouted to his wife.

"Maggie!" he bellowed. "Come in here. She's on her knees in that filthy railroad dump again!" he shouted desperately when Margaret, who had left her huge stack of ironing, rushed into the bedroom. "Why does she *do* that?" Harold moaned. "We're raising a religious fanatic!"

Margaret laughed. "If she never does anything worse than pray, we'll have no problem," she remarked.

"It won't be funny in a few years when she shaves her head and starts pounding a drum and handing out religious pamphlets," he predicted darkly.

Diane could not have explained why she prayed except that it seemed she had been born appreciating what she had and wanting nothing so much as to keep it. Not that she didn't want more. She had once prayed twice a day for a bicycle, and it was only when her mother suddenly grew dangerously ill with pneumonia (a condition that was worsened by her worry about money) and, at the same time, the family dog gave birth to one sickly puppy, that she willingly relinquished all dreams of a bicycle and prayed only for the health of Margaret and the puppy. When antibiotics and her God saved both her mother and the tiny dog, Diane felt the bicycle well lost and her bargain with the Almighty a good one.

In spite of the shortness of cash, the constant struggle to pay the bills and the increasing bickering between Margaret and Harold Haynes, it was not an unhappy household, full of lively youngsters and dogs and cats. For all his inability to cope, Harold loved his wife and his children and he worried about them all the time. Worried that they would get sick, or injured in an accident, worried that he and Margaret would not be able to scrape up the rent, that he couldn't get a decent job, worried about crime and violence, about traffic and germs, his bowels and his headaches. When Diane was twelve years old, Harold finally worried himself sick and, when he recovered, packed his bag and went home to the little town of Nebraska. He begged Margaret to come with him.

"This is no place to bring up kids, Maggie," he argued. "Nothing but crowds and smog and sex fiends in the streets."

But Margaret was a practical city girl who had always dreamed of living in New York City and considered Los Angeles itself a hick town. "There's nothing bad here that can't be found in Nebraska," she said. "I don't want the children growing up in the backwoods. They have to learn about the world and they'll learn faster here."

She remained adamant and one day they went to the bus depot to see Harold off. They all cried as they watched him climb the steps of the big bus, tears in his eyes and his old suitcase in one hand. Diane's mother went home to the rundown little house, threw herself into an orgy of housecleaning and, in the following week, found herself a permanent job as a secretary with a legal firm in downtown Los Angeles.

Diane was given the responsibility of supervising her younger brother and sister when they trooped home from school and this she did, under the careful eye of a friendly neighbor who dropped in from time to time. She wrote long letters to her father and he replied, warning her to be careful on her way to school and on her way home, to stay away from crowds and to look after her brother and sister. He wrote Margaret separately, sending her a little money when he could.

It was during the several years that followed that Diane began to read everything she could find and became acquainted with Lord Byron. By the age of fifteen, she had a clear picture of the kind of man she would one day marry. He would be sweet like her father, and kind, but he would also be strong, masculine, bold and mysterious and, at all times and in any circumstances, able to cope.

When she was sixteen, her brother twelve and her little sister ten, Diane, with the permission of her mother, got a part-time job after school at a pie and sandwich shop in the neighborhood. The pies were thick and glutinous and the hamburgers fat and watery as in most pie and sandwich shops, and an unimportant point since the customers really did not know the difference. Costumed in a red micro-miniskirt that showed off her slender, pretty legs and a white ruffled blouse that defined her narrow waist, Diane made the rounds of the noisy room, delivering Cokes and pecan caramel pie to the after-school groups who piled into the small shop at about three-thirty every afternoon—long-haired girls in skirts as short as her own and skinny, equally long-haired boys, all collecting as many cavities in their teeth as the pies could produce. At ease with the loud hilarity of these, her peers, Diane laughed and joked and took an active part in all the good-natured banter.

In the center of the brightly lighted room was a long counter and, as she moved about among the tables surrounding it, she was conscious always of the beautiful young man on the corner stool, drinking coffee and writing in a thick notebook. When the school crowd thinned out, Diane would take her place behind the counter and, heart racing, walk to him and silently fill his coffee cup. He seldom spoke or ate anything, just drank coffee and wrote in his book, but sometimes he looked up at her and she would feel the heat of the hated blush rise beneath her fair skin, spreading from her upper arms to her neck and streaking up to her hairline as she felt his eyes upon her. If there was a slight madness in those eyes set in the pale, handsome face framed in curly auburn hair, the young Diane did not recognize it. She was a romantic sixteen years old, an A-student, her head full of poetry and music, and she responded to him in much the same way as she would respond to Paul Binns almost a decade later. All she saw was his unbelievable physical perfection and his air of mystery and she was consumed with curiosity about what he wrote in his fat notebook. Usually, he slipped away while her head was turned, but one day her eyes followed his back with its broad shoulders and finely sculpted buttocks in jeans from which the back pockets had been excised, and she detected that he walked with the slightest suggestion of a limp. Astounded, she knew that fate had surely delivered her own Lord Byron. What she did not know was that the romantic limp was caused by one flat foot.

With the built-in awareness of the young woman she was fast becoming, Diane knew the handsome older man had begun covertly watching her, and her confidence grew. "You're a spy!" she said one day as she refilled his coffee cup for the eighth time.

He had been sitting on his stool for more than two hours and they were alone except for the cook, a scrawny, sixty-year-old Bulgarian who sat at the table behind his serving counter, reading the paper and drinking sweet muscat wine he kept hidden in the huge refrigerator behind the crocks of pie dough.

Twenty-six years old and very cool, Perce Hochstetter looked at the clean young girl before him and allowed himself a small smile. "A lovely aura," he said.

This was more than she had bargained for, and Diane stood silent, fighting that awful blush she felt starting from her very toes.

"Lovely," he repeated. "White, pure, unspoiled."

"A writer, then," Diane blurted as she felt the fire rise in her face.

"Perhaps you don't appreciate the importance of man's aura," Perce said softly, lips parting now in a smile that revealed his very white, perfect teeth. "Yours is very large, very unusual." He reached out and removed her glasses, looked solemnly into her pretty myopic eyes. "Energy," he said. "A great energy in your eyes." He replaced her glasses, dropped a bill on the counter and moved toward the door, turning once to look back at the stupefied Diane. "I'm a poet," he announced.

In the sixties, when rebellion jelled (or curdled) after the assassination of the nation's youngest President, and in which junk, meaning drugs, began to soar in popularity, other forms of junk also became immensely popular, i.e., broken-down school buses. They could be found up and down the California coast, parked in woodsy canyons and on the beaches, painted in frenetic designs and psychedelic colors and housing clusters of strung-out drop-outs.

It was to his Chevrolet bus, vintage 1941, painted in Day-Glo purple, yellow, orange and red, parked in the cluttered backyard of a friend and surrounded by cannibalized motorcycles, old tires and dirty mattresses, that Perce Hochstetter took Diane to live with him. If it is true that revolution arises among those who have nothing to lose, Diane did not qualify as a rebel. Too young in the early years of tumult to be aware of the Flower Children, the communal living and the general dissatisfaction that erupted in the sixties, she was, in 1971, a happy sixteen-year-old who loved her family, liked school and bounded through each day with youthful joy and enthusiasm. Perce was like the bicycle she had prayed for at the age of twelve, the something more to add to what she already had. She tried hard to communicate this to her mother.

Margaret herself was only thirty-six, a working mother, exposed to those a decade younger than herself and only that far removed from the "hippy" movement as it spread across the country. She had in the last three years begun seeing men, and, as she grasped for a personal life of her own, she felt stodgy and old in Diane's eyes, and guilty because she wanted some life away from the children she loved so much. She tried reason and fought tears and finally, bewildered like so many other parents in that troubled time, let Diane go because she did not know what else she could do. She tried hard to believe that she had instilled in her daughter the right values and that these values would see her through. To no avail, she begged Diane not to leave school.

"I can learn more from Perce. And we'll travel," said Diane in her innocence, and she took her clothes, her books and Beppo, her old cat, and moved into the dirty bus with Perce. She persuaded him that they should leave the ugly backyard and see the country, working their way north up the coast, so they started along the Pacific Coast Highway, the ancient bus groaning and straining and, midway between Santa Monica and Oxnard, a distance of twenty-two miles, the motor popped, then roared and spluttered out altogether. Perce pulled it over to the beach side of the highway and there they stopped and set up housekeeping.

The California Highway Patrol viewed the buses, vans and campers parked along the highway with a benign tolerance, at regular intervals instructing the drivers who lingered too long to move their vehicles within the prescribed time limits of the law. Most of them drove a few miles north or south and settled down again. When the uniformed officer stopped by and spoke to Perce, Diane called a tow truck and had the bus towed to another place that offered a better view of the sea.

Her mother's daughter, it was the dirt that bothered Diane the most and she scrubbed and painted the inside of the ancient bus, filling it with big pillows and wildflowers. She bought a battered bicycle from another waitress at a beach restaurant where she had found a job on Fridays, Saturdays and Sundays, and rode several times a day to a state park up the highway, bringing back leather canteens of water for cooking on the Coleman kerosene stove. She showered and used the restrooms in the park, while Perce "cleansed" himself in the ocean.

Perce worked on his leather headbands—punch, punch, punch —twenty-one punches exactly in every band, a mystical number, he told Diane, and he wrote in his notebook and meditated. On a battered portable radio, he listened every day to a sepulchral British voice discussing the miracles of meditation, with much talk of energy and auras, truth, reality, mind power, out-of-body experiences, self-realization, wisdom, beauty and on and on. Diane sat silent, understanding not a word, petting Beppo and worshiping Perce, content to be in his wise presence.

They slept on a mattress on the floor of the bus, on sheets and with blankets that Diane washed and dried twice a week, using a battered washtub, an old-fashioned washboard and the sun. If the time they spent there was not Byronic in its passion, nor as lovely and healing as she had expected, she really had nothing to compare it with and she adjusted her dreams and continued to adore Perce for his mind. The truth was that in matters of sex, Perce was as listless as Diane was to discover he was in other areas. His lovemaking was brief and infrequent and he was sometimes impotent. When this problem occurred, Diane was quick to blame herself.

Perce had never heard of Ken Kesey or his Merry Pranksters (or Lord Byron, for that matter, as Diane would learn to her horror), but he was still "into" the rhythm of the mid-sixties, the psychedelic life-style, the dress, the vocabulary, *I Ching,* the cabala, meditation, yoga, eggplantism (sliced, diced and squashed) and a smattering of all the other innumerable and forgettable isms. Fortunately for the bedazzled Diane, he used neither drugs nor alcohol. He had tried them years before, he told her, and found that he did not need them. "I'm always on a natural high," he explained.

Diane was puzzled by the fact that Perce, a poet, owned no books, and she arranged her own volumes on a rickety old table she had picked up at the back of the restaurant where she worked. Perce never looked at them. Sometimes in the evenings, he read her his poems.

> i go now to the sun,
> go, go, go, go, gone—
> burned like an asteroid
> falling into that furnace
> in the cosmos, i shriek
> with joy as i plummet
> to burn is peace, to burn
> is love, to burn is truth

Mesmerized by the resonance of his deep voice, Diane sat entranced and worshipful, feeling like Elizabeth Browning. One night she responded with some sad lines from the sad works of Edna St. Vincent

Millay, another of her heroes (or heroines, if you want to be old-fashioned about it).

> Time cannot break the bird's wing
> from the bird.
> Bird and wing together
> Go down, one feather.
>
> No thing that ever flew,
> Not the lark, not you,
> Can die as others do.

When she finished, Perce sat in silence just looking at her and she felt put down, felt the suggestion of a reprimand in his glance.

"I didn't write it," Diane said, confused. "It's called *To a Young Poet*—by Edna St. Vincent Millay."

When he didn't respond, Diane felt her face burn and, grateful for the dim light in the bus, resolved not to repeat her mistake. It was only later that she realized Perce knew nothing about Edna St. Vincent Millay, not even who she was.

Unlike Diane's father, Perce worried about nothing at all, including money, which he believed would in time simply come to him through meditation along with all the other good things in life. "Go with the flow" was his motto, and it was only when Diane pointed out that until the bus was repaired, they could go nowhere at all, not even with the flow, that he obtained a job at a feed and grain store in Malibu, thumbing his way to work five days a week.

Almost immediately, he began to complain about the job and his boss, a clod with a dark aura about him that Perce, with his built-in ability to detect evil, recognized. At the end of the second week, he quit or was fired. Diane was afraid to push for details.

"He was stealing my energy," Perce said, and went back to making headbands.

And Diane endured and was not unhappy. She loved the sound of the surf and the smell of the sea and the exciting feeling of freedom. Sometimes she turned on the old radio, swept the stolid Beppo up in her arms and danced with him, whirling round and round in the bus until Perce looked up from his notebook, frowned and said, "Diane," in a "that's enough" tone that served to quell her high spirits. She accepted this, as she had accepted discipline from her parents, feeling suddenly childish and unworthy of Perce, conscious of the ten years between them.

Perce had a friend he called Beaver, a big, overweight man about thirty with oily blond hair that was already sparse on top but swung in a defiant ponytail between his shoulder blades. Beaver painted, in dreadful thematic imitation of William Blake, and often appeared in the doorway of the bus, his latest work under his arm. The awful paintings all looked alike to Diane, full of Beaver's dreams, with lambs and moons and virgin mothers with bulging eyes and bellies scattered across the canvases. He and Perce talked to each other, ignoring the silent Diane, who tried not to notice the ugly roll of fat that surged around Beaver's middle, pushing up above the top of his jeans. He paced the length of the bus and back, talking and occasionally placing his hand on the clock, "stopping time," he said, or on Beppo's broad head, "feeling the energy." Diane picked up her cat and walked down to the beach, leaving Perce and Beaver to stop time and grope for their energies.

Some of her school friends came by occasionally and she tried once to entertain a new friend, a student at Pepperdine University in Malibu who worked with her at the restaurant on weekends. Perce sat silent on these occasions, refused to take part in the conversation, seemed to be judging her friends, who always became uncomfortable and made excuses to leave quickly.

"They're stealing your energy," he warned Diane when they were alone. It was his daily habit to light a white candle, draw the ragged drapes on the windows of the bus, fire up the incense and lie back on the mattress to meditate, closing his eyes and repeating the sacred mantra from Tibet. "Ohm mane padme ohm, ohm mane padme ohm, ohm mane padme ohm," he droned for more than an hour sometimes, striving for the stage of meditation known as the Alpha state, he explained to Diane, who usually left the bus and walked on the beach until she felt he had reached Alpha.

Margaret came twice, bringing with her Diane's brother and sister, who at once raced to the water's edge, leaving Margaret to try to chat with Diane and suffer Perce's silent and judgmental appraisal.

Diane tried to persuade Perce to arrange his poems in a volume to be submitted for publication.

"I don't write for others," he said, his pale face sullen. "I write for myself."

She sensed that he was afraid to try for publication. "Then let's take a booth at a crafts fair," she urged. "People will buy them."

"How much will that cost?" Perce asked.

"It doesn't matter," Diane replied. "I'll use my money and we'll sell enough to get it back." She was momentarily conscious of a new irritated edge to her voice. "I'll display the headbands, too." Diane was firm. "We need the money, Perce."

She heard the echo of long-ago conversations between her mother and father. The subject had usually been money and she shuddered inwardly, reminded of the romantic and completely harmonious life she intended to be hers. She softened and leaned down to kiss Perce. When he, who had also noticed the slight change in her attitude, did not say an emphatic no to her suggestion, Diane bought some thick white cards and spent many hours transferring the poetic material in Perce's notebooks to the cards, printing carefully with a blunt-tipped black pen. Doubt pricked her as she worked. Reading Perce's outpourings at high noon, without the benefit of a little wine, the darkness and the soothing sound of his mellow voice, she grew uneasy, feeling a touch of the same kind of flickering sense of distaste she felt while examining Beaver's paintings. Dismayed by her disloyal thoughts, Diane suppressed them and worked on.

On a Sunday, she called the restaurant and reported that she had the twenty-four-hour flu, gathered together Perce's poems and a supply of headbands and pedaled into Santa Monica to set up a booth in the park atop the palisades. Booths lined the edges of the lawn of the long, narrow park, house plants (too much philodendron), paintings (too many clown faces and pea-green seascapes), sculptures (too many frogs and roadrunners), mobiles (too many fish) and leather work (too many headbands), all for sale to those who wandered aimlessly about in the bright sunlight, picking things up and putting them down and, infrequently, buying something.

At her stand near the end of the lane, Diane arranged Perce's headbands in neat rows, the white cards on which the poems were inscribed stacked in front. She propped up a hand-printed sign which read: HEADBANDS—$1.50. POEMS—$2.00.

Poetry not being a common commodity at such affairs, some of the strollers stopped, curious, and picked up the white cards. Sometimes kindly but more often incredulously they looked at the nervous Diane, replaced the cards and moved on. By noon, she had sold no poems and only two headbands and decided on a new strategy. She reversed her sign and printed: POEMS—FREE WITH ONE HEADBAND—$2.00.

A literary sort in horn-rimmed glasses, slender and tweedy, idled up to Diane's booth, selected a poem and read it quickly, frowned and picked up another, squinted at it, head cocked. "You write these?" he asked, staring hard at Diane.

She flushed. "No."

"A friend of yours?"

Diane's voice was small. "Yes."

He bent to study the headbands. "Are these yours?"

Diane shook her head no.

"The same friend?"

"Yes."

The man studied her a moment. "You're a good friend to have," he said with a smile. "You'd better tell your friend to stick with the headbands." He bought one and moved away, leaving his free poem behind.

She sold three more headbands during the afternoon and watched as the buyers walked away, tossing the poems into a trash barrel a short distance down the street. She did not bother to retrieve them. At four o'clock, she packed up her wares and pedaled the long miles back to the bus. Perce was meditating when she got home and she silently started chopping eggplant for dinner. "Nobody was buying much," she told him later when he asked about the fair. "I sold five poems." It had been an expensive day and she did not mention that she would have made a lot more in tips if she had gone to work.

Later, with Beppo in her lap, Diane was sitting on a flat-topped boulder watching the surf as the pickup truck arrived and parked beside the bus. It was almost dark, but she caught a glimpse of the bearded, muscular man in run-over Mexican boots, accompanied by an almost emaciated woman with long black hair that hung below her waist. The man carried a gallon jug of mountain red in one hand and he pounded on the door of the bus with the other. When the door was opened by Perce, he and the woman went in. Diane waited for a few minutes and, when they did not leave, she picked up Beppo and walked to the bus.

They were all sitting in a circle on the floor, on her pillows, drinking wine from paper cups, even Perce, who did not drink. The beefy man was speaking and he stopped to roar, "Welcome," at Diane, poured her a cup of wine and continued to talk, wild talk it seemed to Diane, about "trips" and authoritarianism, about the high old times in Haight-Ashbury and the meaning of time itself. He quoted from Nietzsche, which caught her attention for a moment, and from Allen Ginsberg, which did not, and Diane looked into his eyes and they weren't focusing. The ravaged woman beside him stared off into space, laughing to herself now and then, and Diane was afraid. She looked to Perce, silently beseeching him to get rid of them, and he avoided her eyes and she knew that he was afraid, and that was worse. Time passed and the man, burned out and considerably older than Perce, continued to talk—about op art and pop art, Vietnam, economics and world peace—and the woman continued to laugh and Diane lost her fear and began to feel a compassion she did not understand. Suddenly, the woman stood and turned the radio up to full volume and the vibrations rocked the old bus. The loud music pounded and Beppo jumped up and streaked the length of the bus to hide under the driver's seat. The man asked Perce if he had any paint and Perce meekly supplied what he had and the man and his woman lurched out into the night to paint the rocks and splatter the bushes, singing and shouting. They were still singing when they crawled into the pickup truck and roared off into the darkness. Diane went silently to bed, too tired to notice that her cat was missing.

At dawn she looked for Beppo and he was gone. Perce shrugged and said cats wandered and went back to sleep. Diane spent the morning calling and searching. She prowled the hills and canyons across the highway from the bus, heedless of possible rattlers, calling for Beppo, stumbling and falling and, finally, she heard the hoarse meow and found him, huddled in the mesquite, quivering and dusty. She sat on the side of the hill, crying into Beppo's soft fur, now full of burrs, and knew that she had never been so lonely in all her life.

When Perce opened his eyes at noon, Diane was packing.

"What're you doing?"

Diane faced him squarely. "I don't want to live here any more." She neatly rolled a pair of jeans and stuffed them into her duffel bag.

"You leaving?" Perce asked groggily.

"I'm going home."

He sat up on the mattress and looked at Diane. "You blaming me for that old head from up North?"

"No, but you could have tried to get rid of them and you didn't."

"What'd you expect me to do?" Perce shouted. "I never saw either of those zonked-out characters in my life!"

"You were scared, Perce. All that mumbo jumbo you talk about and you're afraid of the real thing. He was freaky and kind of sad, but he was real. Ten years ago, he was what it was all about." She looked at him levelly. "You're a fake, Perce."

He was on his feet now, pale and a little ridiculous in his jockey shorts with one hairy testicle hanging out. "You'll find out what's real when you're back home being mama's little girl—all of them stealing your energy!"

There was anger now in Diane's voice. "I'll tell you who's stealing my energy—you are! You don't do anything, you don't want anything, you don't give anything and you're never going to *be* anything!" The tears started and Diane rubbed her eyes angrily. "I'm tired of eggplant and this bus, I'm tired of hauling in water and I'm tired of going off in the bushes with a roll of toilet paper under my arm!" She looked at Perce, standing white-faced and astonished before her. "Perce," she said, "I'm tired of you."

A horn tooted cheerfully outside and Diane recognized it as belonging to her mother's old Buick. She picked up Beppo in one arm, her duffel bag in the other and walked to the door of the bus, hesitated a moment, then turned and managed a smile. "See you," she said, and slammed the door shut behind her.

Finally, the short period she spent with Perce became like a dream and she never remembered anything except that he was such a bad poet. She was glad she had not told him so.

At home again, and relieved to be there, she returned to school in the fall. She developed an insatiable desire to learn and nurtured it, graduating with honors and enrolling at UCLA, where she worked her way through, thrilled with the feminist movement, involved and happy to be young at a time when life was changing for women. A romantic she still was, and so she would remain, but she prepared herself to stand on her own feet. To be a teacher was compatible with her interests and she planned to be the best.

There were several relationships with men in those years, but they were more companionable than passionate. She became involved for a time with an associate professor of literature and, later, had a brief affair with a young man who was studying to be a veterinarian, their mutual love of animals being the strongest source of attraction between them. But she did not stray from the course she had planned for herself, or allow any distraction until she met Paul Binns.

On this night, at Kirbo's Lodge, after their walk in the garden, Paul left her at her door with a kiss on her cheek. Diane brushed her hair and her teeth and did not see the flushed cheeks and shining eyes reflected in her mirror. In a long flannel nightgown she knelt beside the narrow bed in her small room and began her prayers and did not ask God to give her Paul because she figured that if He knew anything at all, He knew what she really wanted.

18

At eight-thirty in the morning of that day, Arly stood at the window of her apartment, watching as the first tram docked and a dozen employees who lived in the valley arrived to start their day's work, bundled up in heavy coats and scarfs and wearing galoshes in anticipation of snow. The day was raw but still the storm was only a threat, an occasional flurry of minute snow crystals from the murky sky.

The last passenger to step out of the tram was Francine, trim in her tweed coat with its false fur collar, her light hair covered by a black fur hat, and Arly was reassured as she noted the small overnight bag Francine carried in one hand. Arly saw her speak to a porter, who boarded the tram and emerged a moment later with a matching larger suitcase.

Arly turned away from the windows quickly so that she would not be seen. She did not want to mark the new residency of Francine in the lodge as being in any way out of the ordinary and she put a suede jacket over her shoulders and left the apartment. Passing swiftly through the lobby so that she would be out of the area before Francine entered, she heard the insistent buzzing of the switchboard that was housed in the long room to the left of the desk. The telephone operators were deluged with calls and three reservation clerks were handling requests from skiers prompted by the certainty of snow within the next twelve hours. Most of the callers would be disappointed. The lodge had been almost completely booked for months in advance, "first snow" reservations.

Arly entered the great hall, where the activity was centered at this early hour. The designer she had employed to transform the hall into the disco it would become for the next five months shouted instructions to the electricians who were installing the strobe lights for the extravagant lighting.

"The red!" he roared to one electrician, who was placing a blue slide on one of the projectors. "Not blue over there—red!" And Arly thought, Why must he bellow like that?

The carpets had been removed from the center of the room, exposing the gleaming parquet floors, and workmen were arranging tables and chairs around the big oval dance area. Earth tones dominated the furnishings, plush velvet sofas and chairs of cocoa brown scattered about behind the tables.

On a platform erected high above the dance floor, a slim-hipped, frail young man with a crew cut was seated before his amplifiers and, as Arly stood surveying the activity, he turned one of the knobs and the music exploded at the pandemonium level for which the DJ was noted. Arly had lured him away from Studio 54 in New York City on the recommendation of a frequent guest at the lodge who owned discos on both coasts.

"He's a master of the segue," the man had told her. "Song to song without showing the weave. No seams. He'll keep 'em on the floor till they drop."

Arly, whose taste in music leaned toward Mozart, put her hands to her ears, hurriedly left the lounge and walked outside, moving briskly toward the chalets, which were being readied now for the skiers who would begin to crowd into the lodge within the next few days. She was grateful for the busy schedule and the endless detail that would require her attention. It would make the day pass quickly and subdue the excitement that stirred just beneath her efficient composure. The dainty Francine had accepted her invitation.

A short distance away from the water so they would not frighten the birds, Jessica and Dr. Friendly, dressed warmly and wearing hiking boots, watched as rosy finches, mountain bluebirds and pine grosbeaks fed around the hot pond, their bright plumages striking in the cold light of the overcast day. After a few minutes, the doctor and his wife moved on and headed up the trail beside the Gornaad Creek and into the pines. There was time for one last walk before the storm got down to serious business.

The aerial trams hummed smoothly across the gorge and back again all morning, depositing departing guests and their luggage at the station and returning with arriving winter employees or occasional new guests.

During the morning hours, the lobby had been alive with exuberant greetings among employees returning for another winter at the lodge and now, in mid-afternoon, most of them were gathered in the hall, where the snowtime bar was being made ready for the coming weekend. Behind the bar, Paul racked the bottles, stacked the glasses and checked off the necessary supplies that were kept in the portable refrigerators. Diane and several other girls were busy setting up the buffet area. The winter buffet at the lodge was famous for its hot and plentiful food, which was available almost around the clock since skiing here was not only for the day but also for the night, the runs being illuminated by mercury lights atop tall aluminum poles.

From behind his bar, Paul saw the first big, lazy, meaningful snowflakes fall a few minutes after three o'clock and thought that now it would be the real thing and crossed to the windows. The grounds of the lodge, already dusted with a light icing of crystals, were being blanketed and, even as he watched, the white curtain gained density. He turned and shouted, "Here it comes!" and the young people in the lounge crowded cheerfully at the windows to gaze at the silent fall that, in just a few minutes, turned the branches of the trees into white lace and began to drift along the garden paths.

In the sealed and silent cardroom, the players sat in concentration over their cards, oblivious to the growing storm outside, but from his studio, Cabot Markey saw it begin and walked out onto the deck, where he heard the rush of wind high above the lodge's protected cove and watched as a flock of band-tailed pigeons came down through the snow and settled into the broad-limbed sugar pine trees about the lodge.

At four-thirty in the afternoon, a young Japanese who spoke little English and was employed as an assistant gardener, squatted in the snow beside the hot pool and stared with puzzled interest at the bubbling current that danced across the water, became still and then began again. When all movement stopped, he shrugged and turned away toward the greenhouse, where he would not try to explain to anyone what he had seen.

At seven-thirty that evening, the maître d'hôtel pressed a switch that lowered the eighteenth-century crystal chandeliers and waiters with long tapers lighted the eighty candles in each of them, after which the fixtures ascended to cast their soft and magical glow down upon the linen tablecloths of purest white, the glittering vermeil flat-ware from Tiffany's, and the Royal Copenhagen china, hand-painted with the wildflowers of the Sierra and made especially for the lodge. On each table were charming arrangements of miniature red and white roses and a pink candle that burned with a gentle fragance from Patou.

In an alcove behind a black, patterned scrim, the summer musicians, two violins, a cello, a piano, a bass fiddle and a flute, began to play unobtrusive melodies to dine by and now the tall mahogany doors of the dining room were opened and the corps of waiters stood at easy attention as the guests came quietly, reverently into that temple of grace.

Among the first diners to be seated were Dr. Friendly and Jessica, slender in a floor-length beige silk dress, her only adornment a tear-shaped fire opal on a gold chain (a gift from her husband) that blazed in the cleavage between her small breasts.

Thirty minutes later, Clarice Bishop maneuvered the length of the dining room a few steps behind the maître d'hôtel, who proudly brought her to a table at the far end of the room, knowing that the diners sat, forks suspended, in gaping appreciation. She wore a long white gown of Athenian design, discreetly split on either side to reveal an occasional glimpse of a perfect thigh, and her smooth red hair swung loose below her shoulders, swept back from her face with platinum-mounted sapphire clips that duplicated the flashing blue of her eyes.

"My god," Jessica gasped, "she's Circe—or a circus."

"And more than a slightly potted one," Dr. Friendly remarked, his sharp physician's eyes having noted the unsteadiness of Clarice's passage. He knew from his years of work with women that excessive beauty could be crippling, could make a woman's life a limited experience, could retard her emotional growth. He said as much to Jessica.

"I'd chance it," she replied.

"Heaven forbid," the doctor answered, momentarily bemused by the thought of Jessica's dedicated sense of purpose and energetic intelligence wrapped in Clarice's packaging. Staggering!

Apart from the extensive a la carte menu, there was the dinner with suggested wines recommended that evening by Chef Henri Bertranou. For the interested gourmet, that last culinary creation of the famous chef (who died in the quake) can be presented here because

the menu survived as a souvenir in the handbag of a guest who also
survived.

TABLE D'HÔTE
Pâté de Veau et Porc avec Gibier
Céleri-Rave Rémoulade

Soupe Gratinée des Trois Gourmandes

Salade à la d'Argenson
avec
Graves 1976 Chateau Carbonnieux

Caneton Poêlé aux Navets

Gratin de Pommes de Terre Crécy
Pointes d'Asperges au Beurre
Endives à la Flamande
avec
Clairet 1953 Chateau Lascombes

Coupe Perrichon Glace Myrtille
et Vanille Fruits Vodka
Cafe

It is interesting to note that a claret was chosen to accompany the
duck and turnips. The price of the dinner? Who knows? There were
no prices on the lodge menus and no one ever asked.

At ten-thirty Clarice was the last to leave the dining room, having eaten her way through the recommended dinner with two en-
cores of the coupe perrichon, accompanied by six double Hennes-
sys and half a pack of extra strong New Orleans Picayune cigarettes,
which she favored in her periods of disappointment.

Two captains and the maître d' anxiously escorted her from the
dining room, expecting her either to fall backward or tumble forward, neither of which she did but instead rather handily made her
way back to her rooms. She kicked off her shoes, fumbled with the
hidden hooks on the shoulders of her gown, which fell in snowy
folds about her feet. Altogether nude now, having forgotten to put
on panties and not needing a bra, she stepped over the dress and
collapsed upon the big bed, instantly asleep. And Clarice Bishop
was perhaps the only person within a radius of a hundred miles to

sleep through one of the most memorable and powerful tectonic disturbances ever to occur in the chronicle of the planet Earth.

In their afternoon game with the English lady and the Pole, Cora and Lorenzo had recouped a good part of their loss of the day before to Emil and Archie and on this night did not eat in the main dining room but instead gobbled sandwiches in the coffee shop and hurried back to the cardroom, where they had a game lined up with the sloe-eyed Peruvians.

Still locked in the game with the Japanese, Emil and Archie were ahead $176,000 and Emil was refreshing himself with his usual nosh of caviar in potato skins, chased down with ice-cold vodka.

Markey, as he often did, had dinner sent to his studio and now he lay sleepless upon the bed, watching the snow melting on the panes of the windows and knowing with satisfaction that tomorrow would be the day that he would walk off into the storm with the gun in his pocket.

Arly had invited Francine to share a light supper as her guest on this, her first night at the lodge. In the small kitchen of her apartment, she prepared an omelet and green salad and they ate in the dining nook, from which they could see the lighted trams alternately appearing and disappearing into the snow.

Arly was warm yet impersonal as she encouraged Francine to talk about herself, and Francine further promoted the modest image she had presented to Arly. Demure and soft of voice, she sketched a background of poor gentility in which she grew up alone with her widowed and ailing mother and, as she talked, carefully avoiding any suggestion of self-pity but rather creating an image of extraordinary virtue and delicate strength, her cool mind, as calculating as the computer with which she worked, correctly assessed the effect of her recital on Arly, who, in spite of her sixty years and real sophistication, was as unsuspecting and admiring as she had been in the company of Elsa Geising, almost a half century before.

Some three hundred and fifty miles away in Idyllwild, California, a small, wiry man sat watching the eleven o'clock news, intent on a report of the storm smothering the Sierra. George "Peck" Nordo knew that wild and beautiful terrain perhaps even better than did Cabot Markey, and when at eleven-thirty he flipped off the television set and retired for the night, he could not know how severely that knowledge would be tested on the next day.

At about the same time that Peck Nordo was falling asleep, the summer musicians who played for the season boarded the tram with their instrument cases. They were the last passengers to leave the lodge before the quake.

On the road to the valley, behind their powerful yellow lights, the snow-dozers from Snow One and Snow Two pushed on through the heavy snowfall, clearing the way for delivery trucks loaded with meat and fish, with delicacies flown in from around the world, with fresh produce and dairy products, all moving on schedule up the twisting course to the tram station, deliveries made by special arrangement between the hours of 10 P.M. and midnight to eliminate the possibility of inconvenience to the guests of the lodge.

Shortly after midnight, trash men loaded the big cardboard cartons containing the lodge's refuse on carts and wheeled them to the landing dock and onto the trams. On the other side the cartons were transferred to a truck and carried through the storm and down to the trash dumps in the valley.

In the Earthquake Room at one o'clock that morning, a few scattered guests sat in low-voiced conversation over their drinks and only Paul and Diane remained to serve them. Diane sat on a corner stool at the bar, writing a letter, glancing frequently toward the last drinkers to see if she was needed. Across the room a guest beckoned and she moved quickly to take his order, returning with a request for two brandies. Paul poured the drinks and watched as she carried the tray to the table, reminded of his mother. He had not seen her since Beaumont, Texas, eight years before, but they wrote occasionally and he had heard from her not long ago. She was still working as a cocktail waitress but she had married again—a good man this time, she said. He hoped it was true.

And all this was the way it was on the last full day and night that Kirbo's Lodge existed.

At 1:59 A.M., through the band-tailed pigeons all warmly fluffed on their roosts in the sugar pines, there swept an irresistible impulse and they rose in flock and circled higher and higher into the snow until they were caught by the fierce and freezing winds of the storm and borne away into the night.

At 2:01 A.M., the mountains moved and the sugar pines were cast down and splintered.

19

And, behold, the Lord passed by,
and a great and strong wind rent
the mountains—but the Lord was
not in the wind; and after the
wind an earthquake; but the Lord
was not in the earthquake:
And after the earthquake a fire;
but the Lord was not in the fire;
And after the fire a still small
voice.

First Book of Kings

It began with lights, a mysterious phenomenon that sometimes occurs with strong quakes. The engineer on duty in the control room on the second level of the lower tram station caught a glimpse of the first jagged streak and, only mildly curious at first, moved close to the windows, but as he watched, more lights danced below, flashing here and there through the snow above the lake, and in alarm he shouted at a second maintenance engineer asleep in an upper bunk across the room.

Even as he spoke, the sound began, a low moan from deep in the earth followed by what sounded like rapid bursts of distant artillery fire, and the building began to sway, trembling in the first seconds but quickly convulsive, a violent jolting accompanied by anguished creaking and the loud splitting of windows and buckling of doors. A coffeepot on a small table shot into the air and fell with a tinny crash. Dishes tumbled to the floor and shattered and, across the room, doors sprang open and the cabinets spewed out their contents.

The man in the bunk jumped awkwardly to the floor, lost his balance and sprawled, cursing, in the jumble of broken glass and books and papers.

Awake in his bed, Cabot Markey heard the first ominous rumble and knew what it meant and was not surprised. More than anyone except Arly, he had known it could happen, would happen eventually, and he felt no fear, rather a surging excitement at being there when it finally came. Instantly on his feet, he got from the bedroom to his studio as the rocking vibrations began. The room seemed to tilt and each step he took was like the first step on a moving escalator. As he lurched through the big room, the building trembled with successive violent shocks, bucking on its foundations. The lights went out, heavy furniture slid in crazy patterns across the uncarpeted floor and, as he grasped the doorknob and plunged out onto the sheltered deck, he heard the implosion of the big studio windows behind him and the fall of chunks of glass spraying the polished wooden floors.

The outside lights dimmed now and went dark and on the deck he grasped the twisting rails and stared into the snowy darkness. As the convulsions abated, from the direction of the Scoop there came a sound indescribably greater than any that had come before, a rock-roar that stunned the senses, prolonged and relentless. Because of the falling snow, Markey could not see the curving bow of friction fire that was avalanching down from two thousand feet, but he knew the overhang of the Scoop had crumbled and he threw himself on the deck and heard the rock-roar reach a crescendo as it came off the concave base of the wall and exploded into the dormitory. Shards of granite pelted the deck about him and in the deafening blast he thought he heard a thin, piping scream.

As the quake had begun, in the basement of the main lodge the maintenance man on duty, napping on the cot in his small room, leaped to his feet and when the lights went out, dropped to his knees and crawled across the waving floor, groped in a desk and found a flashlight. On his feet again, he made his way as quickly as possible down the long hallway, feet spread wide in a sailor's walk, arm extended against the wall to maintain his balance as the floor continued to shake beneath his feet. He reached the door of the emergency diesel generator room and found it buckled, rammed a broad shoulder against it until it gave. Inside he jumped to the starter button on the wall and pressed it and the big diesel engine turned over but did not fire. He pushed the button again and the diesel fired and settled down into a steady, comforting rumble as the generator raced and the light above the engine came on.

The outside lights on the main building of the lodge suddenly blazed again into the darkness and Markey, on the deck, could see that nothing remained of the dormitory but debris strewn across the back acreage of the grounds in the path of the rock avalanche. The chalets, stables and greenhouses were gone and smoke was pouring from the crushed north wing of the lodge where the massive boulders of the avalanche had come to rest. As Markey watched, flames licked out of the smoke and, forgetting his breath, forgetting his pacemaker, forgetting his heart, he raced down the steps to the next level, jumped over the railing and ran toward the north wing.

He could hear shouts coming from the lodge, but Markey was the first to see the awful destruction. The north wing was barely recognizable, two walls and the roof gone, the falling snow already smothering the flames. Most telling and frightening was the total silence except for the spluttering fire, and he made his way through the huge boulders and wreckage, hoping for a moan or a cry of pain, anything but the chilling quiet. Inside what remained of the wing he saw the remnants of a bed crushed beneath an enormous boulder, and in the darkness he could distinguish a motionless leg in striped pajamas, all that was visible of the occupant of the bed. He turned as Paul Binns arrived at the scene and moved searchingly past him into the darkness of the ruined north wing.

And now they were all there—Arly in a wool robe, Harry Ames, a couple of sub-chefs, the housekeeper, the maintenance man and a stricken, white-faced Diane.

Arly looked at Markey and he shook his head. "There's nothing you can do here," he said, and she nodded and spoke to Harry Ames.

"The tram, Harry," said Arly. "And the road."

Without a word, Harry Ames turned and moved rapidly toward the main building.

Too much wine gave Jessica headaches, but at dinner she had been unable to resist and, at a few minutes before two o'clock, an insistent pain over her left eye finally awakened her. She had risen quietly, careful not to disturb her sleeping husband, and gone to the bathroom for aspirin. Back in the bedroom and at the foot of the bed when the temblor began, she stood still for a moment in sleepy surprise, then looked up, caught the movement of the ceiling and, as the plaster rained down upon the bed, instinctively hurled herself protectively upon the sleeping figure of her husband. Awakened abruptly, he felt her arms around him, her cheek against his forehead, heard the roar of the quake, the crash of windows and, in that instant, felt the impact and extra weight as the heavy beam crashed down.

Jessica had cried out in pain then gone limp on top of him. "My back," she whispered.

He put one arm tightly around her shoulders and with the other reached through the darkness and felt the trembling beam lying across them as the rock-roar and the quake abated.

"Don't move!" he said. It was a fierce command that instantly controlled her. He had eased himself from beneath her, swept the pillow to the floor so she was not elevated and warned her not to lift her head. He stepped to the wall and pressed the light switch but the room remained in darkness. He turned, and as he crossed to the bed the overhead lights suddenly blazed as the emergency generator cut in. Dr. Friendly stooped, put his shoulder against the beam, raised it and dropped it to the floor. "Lie still," he cautioned her again.

Jessica was face down on the bed, arms above her head and only the left side of her face visible, tears streaking her cheek. Dr. Friendly sat beside her, his hand lying lightly on her shoulder. She was wearing only a pajama top and he lifted the shirt and examined her back. The skin was unbroken but the entire lumbar region was scarlet and already beginning to discolor. Fear churned inside him but when he spoke it was with a doctor's authority, his voice calm and reassuring.

"Don't turn your head. Don't move at all except when I ask you to."

"Please, I want a drink of water." Jessica's voice was weak and muffled. "My mouth is so dry."

"Try to move your toes," said he, and ignored her request.

"I can't."

"Try."

He watched tensely but there was no movement in her toes. A

cold wind whipped through the broken windows and he stood up, brushed aside plaster that had fallen on the bed and pulled blankets gently over Jessica, stepping around and over the six-by-six, eighteen-foot beam that lay on the floor beside the bed.

"My mouth is so dry, Alfred," Jessica said again.

He dampened a tissue in the bathroom and moistened her lips, then picked up the phone and found it dead. Afraid to leave her, he chose the only sensible course. Wait. The management would check the rooms.

In the hotel's switchboard cubicle, the frightened operator was bravely doing her job. The outside lines were dead, she told Harry Ames, but he could reach the tram station by intercom. Harry picked up the desk phone and dialed.

"What's your situation over there? Are the trams operable?"

"The one on our side is damaged," the engineer replied. "It smashed into the tower and the floor's gone. Better check the one over there."

"Take a look at the tram!" Harry shouted to a waiter standing near the desk, and turned back to the phone as the man ran for the door. "Can the damaged car be used for ballast?"

"It's good enough for that," replied the engineer.

"I'll get back to you."

Damage to the lobby was minimal—a few pictures had fallen, standing ashtrays were upended, plants and flower arrangements overturned, their containers shattered. The room was beginning to fill with shocked and tearful guests and a man Harry recognized as a bridge player from Houston, Texas, ran to the desk, bleeding from a deep cut on the side of his face.

"Mr. Ames, my wife's hurt. I think her arm is broken!"

Harry spoke to the desk clerk, his voice low. "Why isn't the doctor here?"

"He hasn't come back from the valley yet," the desk clerk answered.

"Go back to your wife, sir, and wait," said Harry. "Someone will be there to help you."

The pacified Texan hurried away.

The waiter who had gone to check the tram was back, panting his information. "Tram looks okay."

Harry nodded and spoke to the desk clerk. "All right, Johnny, take Binns and Diane and two others and check all the occupied rooms in the west wing. Quickly."

"Yes, sir." The clerk darted from behind the desk and a moment later he and Paul, with Diane and two waiters, left at a run.

In the office there was built into the wall a powerful shortwave radio that, like the diesel generator, was ready at all times for emergency use. Arly sat at the radio, Markey standing beside her and an anxious Francine hovering nearby.

"Snow One. Come in please, Snow One."

The radio crackled and a voice answered, "Snow One."

"This is Arlene Kirbo. We have no outside power here. Can you give me a road report?"

The voice on the radio was excited but clear. "We believe bridge number three is down, Miss Kirbo. It would have taken the cables with it."

Another snapping crackle and a new voice spoke. "This is Snow Two. The tunnel under Satan's Hill has collapsed, Miss Kirbo. There's no way anybody can get in or out by the road."

As Arly questioned Snow Two on the tunnel collapse, Francine was beside her, a mug of hot coffee extended. When Arly did not acknowledge her, she attempted to place the coffee before Arly, who waved her back in irritation. Francine sank down on a chair, pale and chastened.

From the radio a third voice broke in loudly. "This is the Landing, Miss Kirbo. We're okay here. What is your damage?"

"There are injured people," replied Arly, knowing that it was pointless at this time to detail the extent of the catastrophe. "You've heard the road report from Snow Two?"

"Yes, ma'am. We've got radio communication with the sheriff's office and you can depend on them to set up a rescue operation."

Arly leaned back and closed her eyes and Markey, watching her, thought that for the first time she looked every one of her sixty years.

"You're not responsible," he said.

Arly opened her eyes and her gaze was level. "If I'm not," said she, "who is, Cabot?"

In the lobby the desk was crowded now with bruised and bleeding guests frantically requesting medical assistance for members of their families still in their quarters and unable to walk to the lobby. Arly came from the office.

"Have you called Dr. Friendly?" she asked Harry.

"The phones are out on that side of the wing," he replied. "I'm having all the rooms checked right now."

A brisk middle-aged man, dark-haired and with a long English jaw, pushed his way to the desk. "Dr. Rushton, Miss Kirbo—Bert Rushton. I'm an oral surgeon but I have some medical training. May I be of some assistance?"

"You're a godsend, Doctor," Arly said gratefully. "Let me open the infirmary for you. You'll find bandages and drugs, anything you need."

She picked up a ring of keys and as she and the dentist pushed through the crowd toward the infirmary, Harry watched her go, concern in his eyes. In spite of her quick step, she looked ill from shock.

One of the sub-chefs hurried into the lobby. "Mr. Ames, we have buffet dishes ready in the main kitchen."

"Bring the food up here to the coffee shop." As the man rushed away, Harry felt a grim satisfaction that, in spite of the wreckage around them, the system was still functioning.

Like everything else at the lodge, the infirmary reflected Arly's dedication to the care and comfort of her guests. There was a comfortable, cheerful room with two hospital beds, a spacious, well-equipped examining room and the doctor's office with its large desk, on one wall a locked cabinet containing medicines and drugs and on the facing wall floor-to-ceiling bookshelves. The entire infirmary was well ordered and shining with cleanliness.

In the doctor's office cabinet doors had swung open, framed medical diplomas had fallen and most of the medical textbooks had spilled from the shelves and lay in bent disorder on the floor. From a closet in the examining room, Arly produced a sanitary white coat for the dentist and, as she turned, it seemed to her that the room tilted and the lights dimmed. She leaned against the door frame and gripped it hard with both hands.

"Miss Kirbo!" Dr. Rushton grasped her arm and led her to a chair.

Arly felt as if her chest would burst and she leaned her aching head against the back of the chair, fought to regulate her breathing.

"You'd better lie down," said Dr. Rushton.

Arly shook her head impatiently. "You know I can't do that. Can you give me something?"

The dentist studied her strained, white face and turned to the drug cabinet. The glass door was broken but inside the medicines and drugs were so carefully arranged that there was no breakage. Bert Rushton examined labels and chose a small bottle of tablets, returned to the examining room and handed Arly a glass of water and two tablets.

"Take these now and put this in your pocket." He gave her the small plastic bottle. "Ten-milligram valiums. Don't take more than four in the next twenty-four hours."

Arly swallowed the pills and forced herself to stand up, her color slightly improved now. "We're trying to locate a guest who's a doctor—Alfred Friendly."

"You'll need him. I'll do what I can, but—"

He broke off as a tall blond woman, panic in her face, appeared in the doorway, half supporting a man Arly recognized as the Swedish bridge player. His face was wet with perspiration and he was obviously fighting nausea.

"My husband," the woman gasped. "Chest pains."

With one quick stride, Dr. Rushton was at the man's side and he caught him as his knees sagged. "Find Dr. Friendly!" he barked, and Arly ran.

In the west wing, Dr. Friendly opened the door to one of the waiters.

"I'm checking rooms, Doctor. Are you and Mrs. Friendly all right?" the young man asked, and knew immediately from the doctor's face that they were not.

"My wife's hurt."

Then Arly arrived and it was she who asked, "How bad?"

Dr. Friendly shook his head mutely.

"I'm so sorry," Arly murmured. "So sorry."

Dr. Friendly turned immediately back to the bedroom.

"Miss Kirbo, can I do anything?" the young waiter asked.

Arly sent him on his way to finish checking rooms and she moved into the bedroom, saw the fallen beam and was stabbed with a sense of responsibility so heavy she felt faint.

"I have to get her to a hospital," the doctor said.

"We're cut off from the valley." Arly looked at Friendly and knew his pain and hated what she had to ask of him. "Dr. Friendly, our doctor is there. The lobby is full of injured people and we have an immediate emergency—a possible heart attack."

He stood silent for a moment, his face gray, then he drew a shaky breath. "Can you find someone completely responsible to stay with my wife?"

"I'll stay," Arly answered without hesitation.

He went to one knee beside the bed. "Jessica." His voice was low and urgent. "I have to leave you for a little while. Other people are hurt. Miss Kirbo will stay with you. Don't try to move at all." He placed a hand on her cheek. "Promise me."

"Yes," Jessica said weakly, and he thought she smiled.

He hesitated indecisively for a moment, then kissed her wet cheek. At the door he spoke to Arly. "Don't give her water and please find me if there's sudden pain."

When he was gone, Arly drew up a chair and sat beside the bed. The tranquilizers had calmed her only slightly and unable to take any immediate action now, worried about the activity in the lobby, deferring grief over the loss of longtime employees and guests, many of whom she had thought of as friends, she was gripped by the enormity of the disaster and she could feel her body trembling. Jessica looked up at her with frightened eyes and Arly fought for control, forced reassurance in her voice.

"We'll do as the doctor says," Arly said, and was hurt by how young Jessica looked, like a child, small and still beneath the blankets.

Jessica would not have been as frightened if she had been in pain. It was feeling nothing at all that terrified her now and she lay motionless on the bed, trying not to think about the veterans' hospital in Long Beach, California, where she had served as a volunteer aide for two summers when she was on vacation from Vassar. She had learned something about spinal injuries there, had spoon-fed patients and read to them, lowered and raised their beds and pushed a few of the luckier men around in wheelchairs. She remembered that hospital where the slightest movement of a finger or a toe was a triumph, where miracles almost never happened. And she remembered believing—when she was twenty years old—that she would prefer death.

As Dr. Friendly hastened through the corridor toward the lobby, he was computing the possible damage to his wife's back. Not an expert in the field, he still did not doubt that it was broken but he knew that the measure of the break, its exact location and innumerable other variables would determine treatment and the extent of recovery possible. Keeping her absolutely immobile was all that could be done immediately. The slightest movement of her head could sever nerves, possibly even cause her death. And there could be kidney damage. Cold with fear, he forced his trained mind to evaluate all possibilities as if she were a stranger and, difficult as that was, it was easier than confronting the reason she had been so critically injured. That it had been to protect him was to Friendly almost unthinkable. He had lived the greater part of his life and she was only beginning hers. He was not important, she was everything.

Paul had been pounding on the door of Clarice Bishop's room for several minutes. There was nothing but silence behind the door and, alarmed now, he used a passkey and entered, leaving the door open. There was a strong scent of expensive perfume and in the lighted bathroom he could see broken bottles of scent and bath oil lying in glittering heaps on the floor. Plaster had fallen from the ceiling of the large room and a big window to his left was broken; snow was on the sill and collecting on the floor below.

Across the room Clarice lay face down on the big bed in all her glorious nakedness, motionless, her face buried in the pillows.

"Mrs. Bishop!" Paul called loudly from where he stood.

When there was no response, he walked to the bed, looked down on her and saw she was breathing evenly. Paul had first seen Clarice in the limousine and on the tram when he had arrived at the lodge and, before dinner that night, she had seated herself briefly at his bar and downed four fast martinis. There were no circumstances so extreme as to make it possible for a man to look unmoved upon the nude perfection of Clarice Bishop and, even in the emergency of the moment, Paul was no exception.

"Mrs. Bishop," he said again, and when she still did not stir, he leaned down and gingerly grasped her bare shoulder, shaking her lightly.

Clarice moaned, turned over and opened her remarkable eyes. She squinted up at him a moment, focused with difficulty. "I know you," said she groggily. "You're the cool-assed barkeep. What're you doing here?"

Clearly, she had slept through it all.

"There's been a bad earthquake. I'm checking the rooms to see if anybody's hurt."

Even in the dim light it was apparent that there was not even a bruise on her flawless body, that she was simply drunk.

"I'm not hurt," she muttered. "Do I look hurt?" She made no move to cover herself. "Go away. For god's sake, just go away." And she rolled over and was immediately asleep again.

Paul had learned to be patient with drunks. She was not injured and there was no reason she should not sleep. He bent over her and pulled a soft yellow blanket to her shoulders. She felt its warmth and snuggled deeper into the bed with a little sigh of pleasure and Paul left her there.

By 3 A.M., the panic in the lobby had subsided and some order was established. The check of the rooms in the west wing had turned up three possible concussions, a dislocated knee, a broken ankle, a broken hip (possible) and one case of hysterical paralysis. Waiters with wheelchairs were dispatched to those rooms and Paul Binns was assigned the job of scheduling the order in which guests would see the doctor. A calming influence, he moved easily about the lobby, taking names and noting the nature of injuries, quietly seeing that those most in need of medical attention were given priority.

Inside the infirmary Diane was assisting Dr. Friendly and the dentist. When the quake had struck, Diane and Paul had been alone in the Earthquake Room cleaning up for the night. He had shouted, "Get in a doorway!" and she had stumbled to the door and braced her buttocks against one side of the door frame, both hands against the opposite side as they had been instructed to do by an earthquake expert at a meeting Arly had insisted all lodge employees attend and which, Diane remembered, nobody had taken seriously.

Paul had ducked under the bar gate as the mighty shake broke loose. The giant photographs of wreckage from famous quakes toppled off the walls and the glassware behind the bar sprang from the racks and showered down like splintered ice. The famous ringing wine glasses in their special cove collapsed immediately in a crystal heap as the green light gave way to red, then went out altogether. The shaking subsided in less than a minute but in the darkness it seemed to last for a thousand heartbeats and in the roar of the avalanche that followed, Diane shouted, "Paul!" and he had answered, "Stay where you are!" Their hearing was numbed as the avalanche detonated against the dormitory outside, and suddenly the lights came on. Paul came up from under the bar gate, saw that Diane was whole and raced outside on the decking. She had followed, and when she saw that the dormitory had disappeared, she started to scream, but Paul touched her and said, "No," and she caught the scream in her throat.

Cora and Lorenzo had left the cardroom and were on their way back to their suite when the quake began. In the corridor of the west wing, Lorenzo had flung himself to the floor, arms over his head and his face buried in the carpet. Cora slid to the floor, back braced against the wall. When the shaking stopped and without a word to the still cowering Lorenzo, she had scrambled to her feet and, driven by the instinct to flock in times of peril, hurtled on her short legs toward the flocking place, the lobby. She had been halfway down the corridor before he had gained his footing and run after her.

They stood at the desk now among other guests demanding attention, each intent on assuring their mothers of their safety.

"Mr. Ames," Lorenzo began, "I must get a message—"

He was cut off by Cora, who maneuvered herself in front of him.

"My mother is old and very ill," said Cora. "She'll be worried. Can you radio Los Angeles?"

Harry Ames spoke to the group around the desk, indicating paper and pencils on the counter. "Ladies and gentlemen, if you'll all write down your messages, they'll be dispatched as quickly as possible."

Cora and Lorenzo grabbed for paper and began writing immediately as Emil von Rothke stepped forward. "Mr. Epstein and I are unhurt, Mr. Ames. May we perhaps be of some assistance?"

In these two men, witnesses of and participants in stunning horrors perpetrated by men upon their brothers, calamities of nature, no matter their proportion, produced no shock. During the quake they had, with their partners, crouched calmly beneath the steel bridge tables, silent except for Emil's shouted, "Gentlemen, keep your cards!" Now, assured by Harry that they would be called upon if needed, Emil glanced across the lobby toward their Japanese partners, looked questioningly at Archie, who understood and nodded indifferently. Emil strode purposefully toward the Japanese.

"Gentlemen," said Emil. "Shall we resume our game?"

The prosperous Orientals, equal to the moment, bowed and smiled, and the four men proceeded directly to the bridge room, dusted plaster off their table and began to play.

When the last cut was bandaged and the final bone splinted, Dr. Friendly literally ran to his room and his injured wife. The guest who had suffered what the doctor believed to be a slight heart attack was resting comfortably in one of the infirmary beds and Bert Rushton occupied the other so that he could keep an eye on him.

Guests whose rooms were greatly damaged had been assigned other quarters and the lobby was quiet as Diane went to Harry Ames, still at the desk, and asked what else she could do to help.

"Get some rest, Miss Haynes," said Harry kindly, and they both looked away for a moment, reminded of the tragedy of the dormitory.

"This is a master key to the west wing. Take any room on the second floor between numbers fifty-six and sixty-two. Try to find one without broken windows."

As Diane thanked him and turned away, the switchboard operator, who was now tending the radio, called to Harry.

"I have the sheriff, Mr. Ames!"

"Wes Pankey, Harry!" the sheriff's gravelly voice over the radio charged the communications room with energy. "We've got three big choppers coming in from Edwards Air Force Base. We'll send 'em up at daylight, weather permitting. With doctors and nurses."

"We'll be ready for them," said Harry. Above all else, he had an old-fashioned respect for efficiency and he knew the tough, competent sheriff would do exactly what he had said—and more, if need be.

Diane passed the coffee shop on her way to the west wing and caught sight of Paul through the open door. With several other people at the counter, he sat on a stool at the end, nursing a cup of coffee. Tired beyond any fatigue she had experienced in her short life and with nothing to occupy her mind now that the immediate emergency was over, Diane felt the full weight of the past hours and, in search of strength, companionship and comfort, she entered the coffee shop and took a seat beside Paul as one of the sub-chefs brought a plate of scrambled eggs, toast and bacon for him.

"What'll you have, Diane?" the chef asked.

Diane felt her stomach squirm at the sight of Paul's plate. "Just coffee, please." She turned to Paul. "Mr. Ames has given me a room in the west wing," said she. "Do you want one?"

Paul shook his head. "No. I'm fine."

Her coffee came. Diane took a sip, set it down, and stared into the hot liquid. Paul was attacking his food with good appetite and she wondered how he could eat.

"They're all dead," she said.

He didn't answer and Diane looked at him, puzzled by his apparent indifference. They had both known almost everybody who died in the dormitory, had worked and played with them in the last winter.

Paul felt her appraisal. "Things happen," he said then. "Wars, fires, earthquakes. That's the way it is."

He proceeded calmly with his breakfast and after a silent moment Diane got up and turned toward the door.

"Sleep well," said Paul.

She barely nodded and as she walked to the west wing she groped for the reason behind his detachment and the little chill it inspired in her. Paul was no different than he had ever been and what he had said was true enough. Things happened. The earthquake had happened and Paul was hungry and she could not have swallowed a bite of food. That was the way it was and Diane felt a confusion that was almost a pain.

At the far end of the west wing, she opened the door of Room 59, flipped on the lights and saw that the furniture was disarranged, a few objects toppled and broken but with the windows intact. She opened the doors to the decking and walked outside.

At the railing she looked out upon the grounds, where the strewn wreckage of the dormitory and the dismembered bodies lay covered by snow, thicker and softer now, and she thought how merciful that was. Then she sensed a movement at the top of a flight of stairs that led to the decking above her. She recognized that decking as being an extension of Cabot Markey's studio and saw that Markey was sitting in a chair at the top of the stairs, arms crossed and head bowed.

"Mr. Markey," she called softly, and he raised his head. "Are you all right?"

"Quite all right," Markey answered. He stood and came to the stairs and took a step down, recognized her, searched his mind quickly for her name and found it. "Thanks for asking, Miss Haynes."

She continued to look up at him and he asked, "And you? Are you all right?"

"I'm fine. Mr. Ames gave me this room to get some sleep."

But she stayed on the decking, silently looking up at him and making no move toward her room. She was wearing only a light sweater and she looked cold and too young and lonely.

"It's a bad time to be alone," he said, and when she did not reply immediately added, "Come up here."

He had sensed what she had not realized herself, her need to be with somebody, and Diane, responding almost automatically, climbed the stairs. Markey took her inside his studio and seated her on a long couch with large velvet pillows.

"Can I offer you a drink? I think there's a bottle of scotch that hasn't been smashed."

"Not a drink, thank you," Diane replied. "Maybe coffee?"

"Of course. Wish me luck about a cup that isn't busted."

She sat unmoving on the couch as Markey prepared coffee in the kitchen in the corner of the studio, and the rattling of dishes and his cheerful call, "Found one!" seemed to be coming from far away as a numbing sense of detachment crept over her. She felt the trembling begin in her knees and then seize her entire body and she began to shake convulsively.

Markey came from the kitchen and reacted immediately after one quick glance at the ashen-faced girl on his couch. From a nearby chair he picked up his topcoat, draped it around her and moved swiftly to the bar, where he poured two fingers of scotch in a surviving glass. "A drink after all, I think," said he and, with one arm tightly about her quivering shoulders, he pressed the glass to her lips. "Drink it all," he said firmly, and Diane swallowed the liquor. She gagged and coughed but kept it down and Markey handed her a handkerchief.

"I'm so sorry," Diane whispered, but she could not stop the deluge of tears that flowed uninterrupted as she fought the sobs that threatened to follow. Markey lifted her to her feet and without a word wrapped his arms around her and held her tightly. She clung to his warmth until her tears dried and the shaking was gone. When she was quiet, he settled her in a big, comfortable chair, went into the kitchen and returned with coffee and a plate of English biscuits. The coffee was hot and strong and this time she was able to drink it, warmed by the scotch and relieved by her tears.

"So," said Markey, "where were you when the spaghetti hit the fan?"

His tone was matter-of-fact and intentionally light. Diane's head snapped up in surprise and he smiled. "In a doorway," she said, "in the Earthquake Room," and found she could smile in return. "I'm sorry about the flood," she said again.

"The only unforgivable tears are the ones we shed for ourselves."

Tension gone, Diane yawned suddenly, and Markey grinned and said, "And that's the proper response to a trite remark."

"Oh, I didn't mean—" Diane began.

"I think you should stay here," he interrupted. "If you won't accept my bedroom, you can use the sofa."

Diane had found comfort in an unexpected place and, feeling grateful, watched as he took pillows and blankets from a closet. When she lay exhausted on the couch, he removed her shoes and pulled the warm blankets over her.

"Good night, Miss Haynes," he said, and she murmured in return, already almost asleep. Her last fleeting, drowsy thoughts were that a man who was a legend should be older and that if Mr. Ames or Miss Kirbo should want to find her, they would not know where to look.

When he returned from the infirmary, Dr. Friendly had brought flexible rubber tubing and allowed Jessica water, followed by two strong tranquilizers.

She woke as he was carefully inching a clean sheet beneath her and knew she had not slept long. She lay for a moment with her eyes still closed, searching for some sensation below her waist and finding none. She could hear him moving about the bed, opened her eyes and saw the pile of rumpled sheets on the floor beside the bed.

"I wet on myself, didn't I?"

"Lie still," he said, and did not answer her question.

"Didn't I?" she demanded.

"That's not important," he replied, and thought her voice was stronger and that was good.

From the corner of her eye, Jessica could see him bent over her. "What are you doing?"

"I'm cleaning you up with a sponge and warm water. Can you feel anything?"

"Not a damn thing." She fought to keep the fear from her voice.

Jessica's lower back was bruised almost black, but it was the vaginal bleeding he could not tell her about that was the source of the doctor's immediate terror and his mind screamed kidney damage. "Loss of feeling can be shock," he said, and heard in his voice the echo of countless reassuring speeches to frightened patients and knew the words this time were as much for himself as for Jessica.

"I can't stay in this position much longer, Alfred. My arms ache."

"Helicopters will be here in a few hours. You'll be fine."

"I won't be fine," said Jessica. "Why do you tell me that?"

"Because I won't have it any other way," snapped Friendly.

"Then I'm with you, daddy. Would you get sore if I asked for a cigarette?"

She sneaked cigarettes and he knew she did. It was a poorly concealed, seldom acknowledged secret between them.

"I'd just as soon you didn't."

"Okay," she said.

"Where do you keep them?"

"In the corner of my makeup case."

He found the cigarettes and lighted one, put it between her lips and let her take a drag, removed it, gave her another puff when she exhaled the first one. "That's all," he said.

"Thanks," said Jessica. "You're a real prince of a fellow."

And Friendly began to cry. He cupped his hands over his mouth and hurried into the bathroom, ran a lot of water and flushed the toilet three times, all until he could control himself. He checked his watch. Two hours till daylight. Two hours until the helicopters would come, then another hour to the nearest hospital. Toxicity resulting from damaged kidneys could be fatal and a sudden move could bring death or permanent paralysis. Numb with frustration and despair, Dr. Friendly splashed cold water on his face and returned to the bedroom.

"Now we're going to have something to eat," he told Jessica sturdily. "How would you like some caviar?"

"And champagne!" she replied. "Let's have a party."

They played the mindless game that people sometimes play against the threat of death. A bantering game learned in dark motion picture houses from the brave characters facing 70 mm deaths. And Friendly thought of this and yet pressed on with it because it was an alternative to panic.

"Bacchanalian," he said.

"With lots of screwing," said Jessica.

In her luxuriously appointed little room, Francine Sharpe huddled on the bed, a soggy heap of self-pity that quickly developed into a fierce and childish rage as she recognized that months of her careful strategy had collapsed along with the lodge.

There would be no time now for the cautious cat-and-mouse campaign she had planned to pursue in her conquest of Arly. She had counted on propinquity, a slow day-by-day growth of intimacy. Now the lodge would be evacuated and she and Arly would go their separate ways and Francine would once again be a loser.

The unfairness of it all produced an ache in her throat that almost choked her and Francine clenched her fists and beat on the pillows in frenzied frustration. After a few moments, she forced relaxation, rolled over and stared at the ceiling. It could not all be a waste. There must be a way to save the situation and she would simply have to find it.

There was no sound from the rooms next door but she knew Arly would come upstairs soon. Francine got off the bed and walked to the full-length mirror mounted on a closet door, shuddered as she surveyed her swollen eyes and disheveled hair. With a tissue she dried her eyes, then plugged in an electric curling iron on the dressing table. Decision and determination in her movements now, she entered the bathroom, scattered a liberal measurement of perfumed milk bath in the shining pink tub and turned on the tap full force, tested the temperature and was pleased to see that the pipes still worked and that she could get water that was at least warm.

Almost an hour later, composed and with skillfully applied makeup, dressed in well-cut jeans and a soft blue sweater, she was putting a final touch to her hair with the curling wand when she heard Arly enter her apartment. Francine was ready.

In her living room, Arly switched on a table lamp and immediately poured a stiff jolt of scotch and splashed a little water in the glass. She worried briefly about mixing alcohol with tranquilizers, then shrugged wearily. What difference did it make? She was sitting with her drink, staring out into the snowy darkness above the lake when the knock sounded on her door. Too tired to stand up, she called, "Please come in," then realized she had locked the door and rose heavily, crossed the room and opened the door to Francine.

"Am I intruding?" asked Francine. "I wondered if there might be something I could do for you?"

Arly looked into Francine's clear green eyes and realized she had completely forgotten Francine was next door and had not in fact thought of her at all for hours. Right now, the young woman seemed a very unimportant part of a long-ago past.

"That's kind of you, dear," Arly replied, "but I'm perfectly all right."

There was polite dismissal in Arly's voice but Francine held her ground. "I thought you might not want to be alone," she persisted.

And Arly, who wanted nothing so much as to *be* alone, thought that Francine was young and probably frightened and saddened by the death of her co-workers. "Come in for a few minutes," she said kindly.

Francine moved quickly inside and this time accepted the drink Arly offered her. Even in the dim light she noted how old Arly suddenly looked and she fought against a twinge of distaste at sight of the loose flesh beneath Arly's upper arm as she prepared the drink. Still she did not waver but felt only a surge of confidence in the power of her own firm young body.

They sat side by side in twin chairs, sipping their drinks.

"What will you do now? Will you rebuild?"

Arly shook her head. "The lodge is finished."

"But it may never happen again!" Francine protested.

Arly smiled sadly. "No, it's finished."

The lodge was gone and with it most of her life. Arly felt a tension at the nape of her neck and she rotated her head uncomfortably. Francine grasped the opportunity eagerly, set down her glass and, moving quickly behind Arly, began to massage her neck, a skill she had acquired and perfected on the stiff muscles of the harried v.p. at the SoMo Oil Company.

There was strength in Francine's small hands and as she worked on Arly's neck Arly relaxed slightly and accepted the relief gratefully. Francine continued the soothing massage for an extended time and when she stopped, Arly leaned her head on the back of the chair, her eyes closed. Francine studied her thoughtfully.

"I think you should lie down," she suggested.

Arly opened her eyes. "Maybe I will," said she.

Francine accompanied her to the bedroom, plumped up the pillows, and Arly sank exhausted on the bed. "Thank you, Francine. I'll be fine now. Get some sleep yourself."

Francine nodded and moved from the bedroom to the living room, where she acted swiftly, pulling the sweater over her head, unzipping her jeans and removing her shoes. She folded the clothing neatly on a chair and, nude, moved quietly back into the bedroom to stand at the foot of the bed. Arly lay with her eyes closed, her pale face drawn in the light from a bedside lamp.

"Arlene." Francine's voice was soft. "Arly."

Arly opened her eyes and at first her expression did not change. She considered Francine for a long, silent moment before she spoke. "What exactly do you think you're doing?"

Francine smiled. "I want to sleep with you," said she. "I think we should hold each other."

Insulated by exhaustion, the sedatives and the alcohol, Arly did not react immediately, but she realized instantly that she had been played again, that the demure Francine was nothing Arly had believed her to be and her bizarre behavior at this moment simple desperation. She continued to stare at her until the girl's smile wavered and soured and was replaced by a look of stubborn defiance.

"It *is* what you wanted," said Francine. "I want you to be happy after this terrible night."

It was then the hot rage rose and Arly felt a sharp explosion in her head, a pop like the bursting of an abscess, and the poison of fury shot through her.

The cane stood in an umbrella stand beside the bedroom door and a great surge of energy propelled her off the bed and across the room. Cane in hand, she turned upon Francine and began to beat her, and Francine's first startled whimper became a squeal as, arms protecting her breasts, she jigged about in a mad and naked dance while Arly, using the cane like a saber, pursued her relentlessly from the bedroom to the living room. The stinging blows striped Francine's pale skin with scarlet as she absorbed her own punishment and that of Tati and Jeannette and, most of all, Elsa Geising. She was crying now, panting with real fear as she saw the maniacal anger in Arly's eyes. Dodging and begging, she spun about, plunged into a coffee table and fell sprawling on hands and knees. Arly raised her arms high and, gripping the cane like a baseball bat, delivered a mighty blow to Francine's defenseless buttocks, reveled in the satisfying crack at contact, then blinked with surprise as the cane snapped in two.

In the sudden quiet, Francine scrambled to her feet and, protecting her burning bottom with her hands, ran for the door that connected her room with Arly's apartment. She threw one frightened look over her shoulder toward the motionless Arly and then slammed the door and bolted it.

Papa's cane. She had broken Papa's cane. Arly picked up the half that had fallen to the floor and slowly, carefully fitted the ends together. It was a straight, black-lacquered cane with a silver tip and an ivory grip on which Caiphus' initials were engraved in silver. He had brought it back from the Far East, a gift from Maharaja Man Singh of Jaipur, and had carried it on the gala occasions when he wore his white tie and tails.

Arly found mending tape in her desk and, remembering her father's stories of tiger hunts and elephant safaris in India, remembering her father mostly and his gleaming boots and whiskey smell, she pasted the broken ends of the black cane together and wept. Francine was not any part of these lachrymose memories. She was forgotten.

20

Diane slept quietly, on her back, one arm curved above her head, slender fingers curled. Markey stood for a moment looking down on her. It had been a long time since he had been capable of that kind of restorative sleep and he studied her face, the clean jawline, firm chin and sensitive mouth, its corners upturned even in sleep. A pretty girl, making her own way, an interesting girl perhaps who once might have caught his attention. When he was young, when he had casually accepted health and his great strength as permanent assets. Before that day in Green Park.

Even as these thoughts rippled through his mind, Markey felt that they were not true. He added the self-denigrating thought that he would never have paid note to the girl asleep now on his sofa, a girl who waited on him in a bar. He accused himself of having been too busy building the legend he credited others with inventing for him, a legend he had told himself he viewed with detached amusement. That was false, too, and he acknowledged now that it had pleased him to be so romantically set apart and he had nurtured and perpetuated the myth. It seemed to Markey at this moment that ego had dominated and directed his life, that perhaps only his work and Jael Callam had been real. Jael was gone and his work no longer interested him. Never difficult for him, it had become too thoughtless now and he knew anything he painted would be enthusiastically praised.

He turned from his concentration on Diane to the easel on which rested the unfinished portrait of Clarice Bishop. How trivial it was. She had called it an exercise but it was less than that. Galvanized by this sudden self-contempt, he picked up a palette knife and slashed across the painting again and again until it hung in tattered pastel ribbons, then tossed the knife aside and entered his bedroom.

He pulled on a wool cap, zipped up a padded jacket, dropped the .38 revolver in one of the deep pockets and walked back to the studio. He looked once more at the sleeping Diane and walked out onto the decking, closing the door quietly behind him.

Outside he descended the stairs and walked through soft snow that rose to the tops of his boots, past the ruined north wing to the snowmobile garage near the ski shack. The roof of the garage was askew and inside the snowmobiles had been tossed about like toys. He righted one and slid it outside into the snow. He straddled it, started the motor and began a steady ascent up the zigzagging ski slope toward the glacier level. It was not quite daybreak and the palest light barely found its way through the falling snow. Twenty minutes later he could feel the wind as he neared the top. The floodlights outside the pavilion were dark and the building was hardly discernible until he was upon it. As he turned the snowmobile in order to go around the end of the pavilion, he suddenly decelerated and let the machine stop, cut the motor and, in astonishment, watched the decking of the structure.

In the half-light of dawn, the broad, snow-covered decking was buckling and, as he watched, a board sprang up and clattered against the railing. Although he knew instantly what was happening, Markey was incredulous. He fired the snowmobile's motor and, keeping well clear of the pavilion, guided the machine around the end of the building. Now, through the brightening day and a sudden gust of wind that opened a window in the thick snowfall, Markey saw it. It reached high into the snow, higher than the range of his sight, and was plainly filling the gorge from wall to wall. The ancient Gornaad was rising from its prison—rising silently, easily, towering far above the pavilion, its blue ice smoking in the warmer air. The shock of the mighty earthquake had moved the mountains enough to tilt the balance that kept the glacier locked in and now Markey saw the pavilion begin to break up under the steady, deadly creep of the glacier. His nature being what it was, even as he recognized its awful threat to the lodge far below at the base of the long, smooth ski slopes, Markey cheered the freedom of the great, blue beast that was at last bursting from its prison of twenty thousand years.

He knew that he must take the alarm quickly to the lodge, but he was reluctant to leave the extraordinary and magnificent spectacle before him. As the daylight grew brighter, he could see that the moving wall of ice was more than a hundred feet tall and still rising as it pushed through the boulders of its dam and gnawed hungrily at the frail wooden pavilion. And it was not as silent as he had thought. It made eager, squeaking whispers as if it longed to roar triumphantly but was not yet sure of its escape.

With full freedom it would first stretch out on the upper slope of its dam until, in the way of glaciers, it would break—and that portion, if it were breaking into the sea, would become a massive floating iceberg. Here, that berg would begin to descend toward the lodge and the lake—and on the steep slope it would gain speed and move faster and faster . . .

He was held in thrall, his purpose all but forgotten, and now it nudged his memory and Markey's thought was that death could wait, and if it was dying he wanted, then why a furtive shot in a snowstorm? Why not a ride to glory? How much more Markey-like it would be if, having warned the lodge of its peril, he returned to this dramatic junction and, as the ice began its lunge to ultimate freedom, found a crevice on its great, cold shoulder and, like Ahab aboard his white whale, was borne on a wild roller coaster to extinction.

Markey laughed aloud at the thought, and started the snowmobile's engine again. He accelerated on the downward journey and, for the first time in years, he felt a charge of happiness. He spoke to himself. He told himself he was mad but still he could not chide away the merriment he felt in his electronic heart.

On her bed, Arly stared up at the ceiling that had become a screen on which flickered faces long forgotten or only half remembered, concentrating dreamily as events from the past were reenacted now, and familiar voices spoke so clearly she hardly heard the immediate knocking on her door. A second, sharper knock roused her and she felt a moment's irritation, resisting this anxious summons that was an intrusion on the security of memory, its comforting joys, griefs blunted and less painful for having been overcome or endured.

But the terrible reality of the present won this inning and she rose miserably from the bed to admit Cabot Markey and Harry Ames. She listened in stoic silence to Markey's recital of the situation and when she did not respond he continued.

"I'd suggest you tell guests and employees that helicopters will come in at the lower tram station. And start immediately to move them all across the gorge. They'll be safe until the storm passes."

Arly still did not speak and Harry Ames glanced uneasily at Markey, wondering if it was his imagination or if the artist also sensed that she was losing touch. After another moment, Arly spoke.

"How long do we have?" she asked Markey.

"I don't know. It may not happen at all," Markey answered carefully, "but you'd better assume it will happen suddenly and today."

The sense of responsibility so strong in Arly showed itself now. She moved quickly to the windows and opened the drapes to the gray day and the still falling snow. She stood for a moment looking across the lake, and when she turned to face them, the worried Harry recognized with relief that she had rallied.

"How safe are the cables?"

"We'll put a test load on the car," Harry replied.

"Then get the guests organized to go. Cabot's right. Don't tell them about the glacier. We don't want a panic."

"I'll get on to Sheriff Pankey," said Markey. "They'll have to know this new emergency."

Harry left quickly but Markey stayed briefly with Arly. Like Harry, he had noted the signs of shock a few minutes before and now he gauged her carefully.

She connected instantly. "Don't worry about me, Cabot. Just help me get everybody safely out of here. I'll be fine."

"I'll depend on that," said Markey.

He moved to the door.

"Cabot, what does the thing look like—the Gornaad?"

He smiled. "It's of a proper size, Arly. As big as the Sierra."

When he was gone, Arly splashed cold water on her face, brushed her hair quickly and left the apartment. On her way downstairs she checked her watch. It was five minutes past six.

In the terminal at Kirbo's Landing, they were waiting. Members of the volunteer rescue team had started to arrive within an hour after the quake and now they were all there, experienced men, coolheaded and courageous veterans. But they had never been part of a natural catastrophe of a proportion even comparable to the giant temblor just passed and there was an air of excitement edged with grave concern for the people trapped at the lodge.

A newspaperman from Bishop and one from Carson, Nevada, were also present in the crowded room, the only representatives of the press close enough to make the scene this quickly.

Sheriff Wes Pankey and his deputies stood at the window watching for the helicopters due in from Edwards Air Force Base. The tall sheriff was the first to hear the stuttering sound of the engines and he immediately plunged outside and onto the airstrip, bareheaded and heedless of the wet and silent snow falling in the valley.

The first big troop carrier put down and the two pilots and crew of four climbed down. The first pilot, a stocky man with captain's bars on his shoulders, shook hands with the sheriff and shouted over the noise of the second helicopter just descending.

"Took us longer than we planned. We had to fly the highway to get here in this damn snow!"

They hurried toward the terminal and the second chopper landed and disgorged uniformed doctors and nurses. A hundred yards away the third helicopter settled down and Wes Pankey smiled as he saw with its crew one civilian passenger moving toward him through the falling snow, a slight figure whose quick pigeon-toed walk identified him immediately.

"Glad you got the message, Peck," Pankey said.

"Sheriff's office in Idyllwild brought me to the Air Force Base in a bubble," Peck Nordo replied in the deep voice that was always a surprise coming from a small man. He was balding and had a crumpled nose that belonged on a punchy fighter. Another surprise was the size of his hands and the length of his arms. He could be described as misshapen, but it all somehow came together in a knot of efficient muscle.

As Pankey greeted Nordo, an urgent call came from the terminal. "Sheriff, the lodge is on again. It's Cabot Markey."

Pankey and Nordo hurried toward the terminal. "At least you've got a professional on the other end," said Nordo.

Nordo and Markey had climbed together and served together on rescue teams, and in the field of rock climbing Nordo was as famous as Markey. The very name, Nordo, was in fact a label on climbing equipment manufactured by its owner. Nordo nylon rope,

Nordo chocks, Nordo pitons, Nordo ice axes were prized by knowledgeable climbers, and in the village of Idyllwild, which was at the base of the granite walls of San Jacinto Mountain, Nordo operated a school for advanced climbers.

Nordo liked Markey but he did not approve of him as a climber. There are two kinds of climbers, the classic athlete who assaults a mountain by its most practical vantage, and the new school of enthusiast who tackles it by its most dangerous. Nordo was classic, Markey was maverick. But Markey was a climber of consummate skill and strength and, besides, he seemed to have a charmed life. Too many lesser talents had tried to emulate his daring and had died for their efforts. Granted, it was not Markey's fault that others wanted to be like him, but in principle Nordo thought the artist set a bad and parlous example. And he felt that Markey had paid a price for his foolhardy climbs. He had been in Chamonix when Markey brought Jael Callam's body down and a Swiss guide who had been leading a party near the place of Markey's ascent had made a later observation to Nordo—"The poor dear shouldn't have been on that treacherous wall with Cabot."

Knowledge of Markey's presence at the lodge had brought the newspapermen to their feet and they pushed closer to the radio, notebooks in hand and pencils racing as the sheriff, with Nordo beside him, spoke to the artist.

"This is Wes, Cabot. We're all here, including Peck Nordo. What can you tell us?"

Through the crackle on the radio Markey told them, clearly and succinctly, and when the conversation was concluded there was a stunned silence. There was no one present who had not seen the Gornaad and each grappled now with his own mental picture of the situation Markey had described, found it almost impossible to believe or accept that the glacier was moving and, indeed, had it come from anybody but Markey, would have rejected the story as being entirely preposterous.

The helicopter captain who had greeted the sheriff spoke first. "Sheriff, there's no way we can get up there until the snow slows. That's a hundred-knot wind over those peaks and flying blind we'll go right into the side of a mountain."

Wes Pankey knew he was right. The choppers could not follow the road up the canyons as they had followed the interstate highway to the Landing, because the canyons were too narrow. They would have to climb more than twelve thousand feet and go over the escarpment. The captain was only being sensible, not too cautious.

"The snow may not slow for another twenty-four hours," the sheriff said. "Moving the people across the gorge, including the injured, will take a little time. All we can do is hope Markey's wrong or that they all get across before the thing comes down."

"If Markey says that ice is coming down, it's coming down," Nordo said, frowning concentration on his beaten-up face.

"We'd better put a backstop team up there in case the tram breaks down," said Pankey. "Will you take it?"

"Backstop for what, Sheriff?" asked the newspaperman from Carson.

"To winch survivors up the east wall of the gorge," replied Pankey.

Nordo was already moving through the press of men, quickly and quietly choosing the youngest and the strongest from among the men he had worked with before. All of the volunteers were eager to go, but Nordo knew the fewest would travel the fastest. As he selected the men, he was planning the assault. A truck would move them and the climbing equipment to the bridge that was down. They must cross that gorge, then Snow One bulldozers would race them to the collapsed tunnel, where they would rope up for the climb over Satan's Hill, and from there Snow Two bulldozers would speed them up the road to the tram station.

Starting from there, if it became necessary, they would have to work in the howling wind and driving snow on the sawtooth ridge that led precipitously up for three thousand feet to the rim of the east wall above the lodge.

The danger did not lie with the gorge, the ridge or Satan's Hill so much as with the speed with which those obstacles would have to be taken. And with those triple risks, the rescue party might even then not be needed. But Nordo and his volunteers knew this. Still they would go.

When Markey had spoken to the Landing, he had been alone in the communications room and, as Arly had ordered, no one except she and Harry Ames and Markey knew of the danger hanging far above them.

Now mattresses, blankets and foodstuffs were being loaded on the one remaining tram car for the test run across the gorge and inside the lodge guests were being calmly instructed to pack a small, single bag and come into the lobby, where there would be an orderly arrangement of departure.

Paul Binns had helped load the car and now joined Arly and Harry Ames in the upper station as Harry used the phone to notify the engineer in the opposite station that they were sending the test car over.

"You'd better have somebody ride it across, Mr. Ames," cautioned the engineer. "To check the cable. We can't see it in this snow."

"Isn't that dangerous?" Harry objected. "If the car gets there, can't we safely assume the cables are okay?"

"Quake might have parted some of the cords," the engineer explained. "The car might make it over here but, if there's a bad spot, the wheels might stick the next time and you'd have a carful of hysterical passengers stalled over the lake."

Harry relayed the suggestion to Arly and Paul immediately volunteered. "I'll ride it over," he said.

Harry turned back to the phone. "We'll have a man on the car."

Arly and Harry moved with Paul to the door of the tram. He stepped aboard and Harry closed the doors and pushed the button. Paul waved jauntily at them through the window and they watched anxiously as the car moved smoothly away until it was lost in the snow.

Through the sloping, snow-free windows in the top of the car Paul could see the cable and he stood relaxed in the center of the tram, watching for any evidence that the cables were not intact, for any sign of broken strands springing up. He knew that Arly and Harry thought him brave, but Paul also knew that bravery had nothing to do with it. Where another might have been afraid, he felt nothing at all and was curiously bothered by that fact, as he had been inwardly disturbed by Diane's earlier appraisal of him in the coffee shop. He knew she had expected something more from him and he had had nothing more to offer her.

Paul was aware that he was not capable of the emotional responses he detected in others. He simply did not feel the things they felt and he had long since recognized and accepted this. He did what he believed was expected of him and that was his sole motivation.

At eighteen, he had viewed the war in Vietnam as an adventure, and although he had not found the experience to his liking, he had been relatively untouched by the death and the terrible destruction around him. Still, he had performed as he thought he should and he had been baffled by the social outrage the war had provoked.

The tragedy at Kirbo's Lodge had left him unmoved. After Diane had left him in the coffee shop, Paul had walked outside and into the snow to look at the place where the dormitory had stood. He had conjured up the faces of the dead he had known and tried to will himself to feel something for them. Bored with that rare moment of introspection, he had turned away in sudden impatience and returned to the main building. His own inner workings were of no more interest to him than were the emotions of others.

The ride across the gorge usually took eight minutes, but with the decreased power from the emergency generator, the crossing with Paul dragged out into almost double that. It was almost fifteen minutes before the tram docked and he stepped out and into the station to greet the waiting engineer. "Slow as hell but smooth as honey," he said. "No problems."

And when the car was unloaded, he got back in for the return trip.

The engineer looked at him in surprise. "You're not going back over there!"

Paul said, "Close the doors and push the button."

The engineer shrugged and closed the doors and in a minute the car slid silently out again into the storm.

Dr. Friendly had not been deceived by Jessica's brave front. He knew that terror gripped her and he had given her an injection of Demerol to calm her. Now she slept and he sat beside the bed watching her apprehensively, checking for any sign of disturbed breathing, his terror greater than her own because of his medical knowledge.

His skilled surgeon's hands were shaking and frustration and rage choked him. He was a doctor who could not help this very young woman he loved more than life. As she lay removed from him by sleep, he remembered his loneliness before Jessica and he again felt withered and empty and fifty-eight years old. The feeling of youth and pleasure in living he had enjoyed with her had not been an illusion. Those had been her gifts to him and he had greedily accepted, and because he had, she was here, at Kirbo's Lodge, in this room, on this night.

Dr. Friendly stared grimly at the fallen beam and up at the ceiling from which it had come. In the entire west wing, why that particular beam? Had it been a poorly driven nail or had one more nail been necessary? Was Jessica the victim of shoddy workmanship completed years before she was even born? Aware of the futility of such thinking and helpless to take any constructive action, the doctor sat and waited.

Jessica grunted suddenly—a short, animal sound. Her breath caught and Friendly jumped to his feet. For a frantic moment, it seemed to him her breathing had stopped and he felt for the pulse in her neck, found it rapid and weak and her skin cold and clammy to his touch. Panicked now, he looked at his watch, saw it was almost seven o'clock, reflexed nervously at the sound of a sharp knock and hurried across the room to open the door to Arly.

"How is she?" Arly asked immediately.

Dr. Friendly shook his head. "No better."

"The helicopters will pick up passengers at the lower tram station. We're moving everybody across the gorge immediately, the injured first."

"That won't do!" His words were curt and his tone sharp. "They'll have to pick her up on this side."

"I'm afraid that may not be possible, Doctor."

Friendly's voice was unyielding and cold. "You will have to make it possible, Miss Kirbo. My wife cannot be moved more than one time and that move must be directly to a hospital."

And now Arly was seeing the other side of the quiet and undemanding doctor on holiday she had believed she knew so well. The exacting and uncompromising surgeon so familiar to his operating team stood before her and Arly responded to his strength and knew he deserved nothing less than the truth. She told him then about the glacier and when she was finished he was silent for a moment.

"Are you sure?"

"Not sure, but we have to believe it will happen."

"How long?" he asked.

"We don't know that, either. Perhaps just a few hours." Arly hesitated. "Dr. Friendly, the helicopters can't get up here at all until the blizzard ends and, according to the reports, the storm won't pass for another twenty-four hours."

There was quick comprehension in his eyes but his composure remained unshaken.

"We'll wait here," he said quietly after a moment. "We have no choice but to risk it."

"It's your decision, Doctor," Arly said slowly. "You still have a little time to think about it."

Jessica cried out suddenly and Friendly whirled about and moved swiftly to the bed. "I'm here, Jessica," he said.

"My head," she whimpered. "My head aches! I feel as if it's going to burst."

He reached for a hypodermic needle and bent over her. "The helicopter ambulance is on its way," he said. "No time at all, my dear."

Arly had followed him into the room and he looked up at her. Their eyes locked for a moment, then Arly nodded slowly and left the room. When she was gone, Friendly pulled the chair closer to the bed and sat beside Jessica. She was quiet again, her eyes closed, and he reached out and touched her hair, brushed it gently off her damp forehead. Her condition was critical and steadily worsening but she was not in severe pain and, if she were, he could control that. He would not subject her to the hazardous move by tram across the gorge and the indefinite wait on the other side. Twenty-four hours was too long. Jessica needed expert medical attention now.

So they would stay where they were. The doctor's shoulders sagged and he leaned back in his chair and tasted a bitterness of frightening depth as he forced himself to accept the unacceptable. They were waiting for Jessica to die.

The deep and easy, almost instant sleep into which Diane had plunged was of short duration, her spirit too troubled to permit escape for long. Disturbing dreams soon intruded, dreams of falling and of running, and though she slept still, she was but slightly removed from consciousness, turning and twisting restlessly until she woke suddenly, shivering in the frigid air that flowed through the broken studio windows, the warm blankets tangled about her feet. Groggy and disoriented, she sat up and pulled the blankets about her, lay down again and closed her eyes, waiting for the chill to pass.

And then, in swift pain, she remembered the events of the night just past. Her eyes opened again and through the windows above her she saw daylight behind the falling snow. She rose quickly and stood still for a moment in the silent room. She wore no watch and as she glanced around the room searching for a clock, she saw the easel with its mutilated painting and crossed the room to stand before it, curious and puzzled. Distraught though she had been a few hours before, she dimly remembered seeing the painting and was reasonably sure that it had been intact. Now it hung like curling serpentine and Diane studied it and wondered and after a few moments turned away and moved toward the bathroom. In a small cabinet she found a supply of antiseptically sealed toothbrushes provided by the lodge. She brushed her teeth, hesitated, then decided circumstances warranted the small impropriety, picked up Markey's tortoiseshell comb and ran it through her tumbled hair. The celebrated Cabot Markey's comb. Diane suddenly grinned at her image in the mirror, then inexplicably thought of Paul Binns and their brief encounter in the coffee shop. She sobered at once, a small frown replacing her smile. Paul had for a long time dominated her thoughts, waking and sleeping, producing an undercurrent of excitement, a feeling that anything could happen, buoying her up and brightly coloring her days. And now she thought of him for the first time without pleasure and did not know why. Just yesterday he had agreed that she hardly knew him and, although she had said it first, Diane had not really believed that. A new, odd intuition told her it was true and she felt uneasy and let down. Then as she stared at her reflection, she was suddenly ashamed.

She and Paul had survived the cataclysm and she recognized that her preoccupation with a romantic attachment—and a feeble one at that, existing as it did only in her mind—was trivial to the point of absurdity. She made a disgusted face at herself in the mirror, tossed the toothbrush in a wastebasket and turned away. She had slept too long and Miss Kirbo would need her. Diane opened the bathroom door and moved rapidly down the short hall to the studio, where Markey was just coming in from the deck.

"Good morning, Miss Haynes," Markey said. "Feeling better?"

"A lot." She indicated the painting. "Who did that? The knife work, I mean."

Markey turned away and pulled off his cap, did not answer the question. Diane knew something of Markey's life and of his work and she watched him curiously as he unzipped and removed the padded jacket. There seemed to be so many Cabot Markeys and Diane, composed now and somewhat astonished at being where she was, struggled for a composite, a blend of the legendary figure she had in her school days pictured as a venerable old gentleman, of the tired-looking middle-aged man she had spoken to on the day he arrived, of the understanding and gentle person who had comforted her earlier that morning, and of the apparently vigorous young man she saw before her now. He looked up and caught her appraisal and Diane was reminded of the way she had clung to him a few hours earlier, remembered the hard-muscled feel of his body and felt color rising beneath her skin. She looked quickly away and Markey, oblivious, moved to the kitchen and busied himself with the coffeepot.

"Miss Kirbo has asked everybody to come to the lobby," he told Diane. "You have time for coffee if you'd like some."

"No, thank you," replied Diane. "I'll go now. They may need me." But her eyes returned to the easel.

"It wasn't good," Markey said.

"It looks like the work of vandals," Diane observed. "Do you always vandalize a painting when it isn't good?"

He laughed. "Only once in a while."

Diane moved to the door, paused. "You've been very kind to me, Mr. Markey," she said formally.

Markey discounted this with a wave of his hand. "It was a difficult night. I'm sure you lost friends, people you liked."

"I feel bad about those I liked"—she faltered briefly, appeared to be struggling to understand her own unexpected emotions—"but somehow I feel worse about the ones I didn't like." She smiled a sad little smile. "I guess that doesn't make much sense."

"It makes sense, Miss Haynes," said Markey.

"Did you know any of them?" Diane asked.

Markey shook his head. "Not much, I'm afraid."

"That makes me luckier than you, I guess," she replied obscurely. "At least I knew them." She was silent for a thoughtful moment, then turned and, with a quick "Thanks again," she was gone.

Markey sensed that Diane was the kind of girl whose energies and interest flowed outward rather than turned inward, making her under more normal circumstances a happy person to be around. An uncommon type in Markey's experience and, he believed, in an ego-ridden world, but he had known one such woman and memories of Jael Callam suddenly assailed him.

As Diane hurried down the corridor of the west wing heading for the lobby, she was indulging her own curiosity about Cabot Markey. He had been surprisingly easy to talk to but she recognized that he was not as easy to know and, perhaps, could not be known, at least not by Diane Haynes of South Los Angeles. Still, she was teased by a premonition that she might be on the verge of a tremendous discovery, like Columbus, who sailed for India and found instead a far richer bourne. But this is no time for poetry, thought Diane, and walked faster.

The bridge that had collapsed on the road up to the lodge had been a suspension structure more than sixty yards long that swung across a deep and narrow gorge. On the trip from the valley, the day limousines often stopped on the bridge to give new guests a first look at the inner splendors of the Sierra escarpment, because from the bridge they could discover a wispy white waterfall in the rising distance and, far beyond it, a tantalizing view of a snowy crag.

Now the bridge dangled down into the canyon, one pier cruelly torn from its foundations by the earthquake, and at about the same time that Paul Binns was riding the tram on its test journey from the lodge to the lower tram station, trucks bearing Peck Nordo and his stouthearted rescue team arrived at the site of the collapsed bridge.

The members of the Snow One road maintenance crew were already waiting on the other side of the canyon. A line was immediately fired across to them and they hauled in the thin steel cable attached to the line and made it fast to a snow-dozer. The dozer then took up the slack in the cable and another line was fired and Nordo fastened himself to the cable by a carabiner on his belt and was tugged across the chasm by the second line in the hands of the men of Snow One. Quickly, his eight team members made the crossing in the same manner and then the rescue equipment was brought over, almost half a ton of it, cable, winch, tents, rope, climbing hardware and stretcher-type carriers designed to be supported by four men to each carrier.

The men and equipment were transported by the snow-dozer up the winding road through snowdrifts and rock falls until the mouth of the crashed tunnel through Satan's Hill was reached.

Satan's Hill was so named by the construction crews who drove the tunnel through the hill. Three men had died in the building of that tunnel and a score had been injured. It had been the most difficult of the obstacles in the way of Caiphus Kirbo's road, being not a hill at all but a great, solid granite dome thrusting up from the side of the canyon where the road was to pass. There had been no way around it; they had had to go through it.

And now, with its tunnel fallen in, Nordo and his crew had to go over it.

From the road to the top of the dome was about a thousand feet, most of it a perpendicular wall until it began to curve suddenly toward its summit. There were no chimneys to make it easy, but there were plentiful cracks, which showed themselves by the snow they were catching as it drifted across the face of the stone.

With carabiners and pitons clanking from his belt, Peck Nordo walked to the base of the wall and, playing out his nylon rope behind him, began to climb. Even to those with him who were excellent rock men, it was instruction to watch him. Somehow, his fingers and boots found purchase on the rock face and he was almost one hundred feet up before he drove his first piton into the granite.

There was a uniform and audible sigh of relief from his waiting team as he secured his rope to the piton by carabiner, leaned out from the precipice and waved the second climber up the rope and immediately moved on to the next pitch.

From the time he took his first step up the rock face until he stood on the dome's summit, approximately one hour had passed. Then another thirty minutes for his team to arrive and fifteen minutes to bring up the equipment and Nordo rappelled down the other side of the dome, where the drivers of Snow Two were waiting to carry the team through the storm to the tram station.

At the tram station, it would seem that their rush to get there was needless, but as they warmed themselves in the station, drank hot coffee and talked to the lodge guests who had arrived by the cable car from across the lake, they would in only minutes find it necessary to go forth and climb that sawtooth ridge in a brutally cold wind that peeled skin from their faces as they lugged the equipment three thousand feet higher into the blizzard.

Their concentration on their cards not diminished one whit by the destructive event of that morning, Emil and Archie continued to trounce their Japanese opponents and it was only when Paul appeared in the cardroom with word that Miss Kirbo insisted they come to the tram station that the four ceased playing and broke up their game. Emil pocketed the playing cards and Archie the score-cards and they separated with the promise that the game would be resumed on the other side.

The Japanese hurried directly to the tram and caught the next car, but Archie and Emil went to their rooms to pack the single bags they were allowed to take with them.

With other anxious guests, Cora and Lorenzo waited for the next tram across the gorge. Lorenzo was pale and visibly trembling, his small moustache quivering, and his eyes darting fearfully about the station. Cora was resolute, jaw set, keeping a sharp eye on Lorenzo, who sat on the edge of a bench, poised for flight. It had been a battle getting him this far.

"Go!" Lorenzo had shrieked. "You go—and enjoy your swim. I won't put a foot on that tram!"

"You," Cora had replied coldly, "are ridiculous."

"Being here at all is ridiculous," Lorenzo shouted. "It was your idea to come to this godforsaken top of nowhere! I wanted to go to the tourney in Acapulco."

And at the thought of the warmth of the climate and the safety of the seashore, Lorenzo had moaned aloud and buried his face in his hands.

"Why, you lying prick!" Cora exploded. "We never go to the tourney in Acapulco!"

She stared at him contemptuously for a moment, then picked up her small bag, stumped toward the door and snapped, "If your mother could see you now, she'd throw the goddam pastafazoola on the floor."

Lorenzo's head had snapped up. "You leave my mother out of this!" he squealed after Cora, who had stalked away and down the hall. But her last shot had worked. The thought of home and his mother's table drove Lorenzo to his feet and he had unsteadily fol-lowed Cora to the station.

Now he peered into the falling snow, dizzy with fear, convinced that they would all end in the freezing lake. The returning car, emptied of its last load of passengers, emerged suddenly and silently from behind the thick snowfall and docked slowly and smoothly. As the other guests moved forward to board the tram, Cora rammed an elbow in Lorenzo's ribs.

"Up!" she hissed, and rose to stand above him. He inched back on the bench, cowering, eyes glassy with terror.

"Move, goddamit!" Cora roared. And Lorenzo moved. He scrambled to his feet and snaked around Cora, pushed through the boarding passengers and raced up the steps of the main building toward the lobby. Cora chased him to the foot of the stairs and screeched, "You fucking jellyfish!" at his retreating back. She started back to the tram car, slowed indecisively at the entrance, considered the possibility of a twenty-four hour wait on the other side without a bridge partner and balked in exasperated rage. One of the waiters just ahead of her turned and politely motioned that she should precede him. Cora blinked, muttered, "I'll take the next car," turned and stamped back toward the stairs and the lobby.

Since Dr. Friendly was determined to risk the danger of the glacier rather than move his wife, Arly had no choice but to remain at the lodge. She did not even consider the choice. She was the innkeeper and as long as there were guests she would keep the inn. Her mind was playing odd tricks on her, disconcerting memories still flooding in if she gave them the least vacuum to fill. After her hysterical anger with Francine when the first mnemonic gate opened she had been lost in maudlin recollection. Brought back to reality by Markey and Harry Ames with the awful news of the moving Gornaad, she had then pushed herself desperately, fearful of being drowned again in those vapors from the past.

From Friendly's room, she had rushed from place to place, guest to guest, smiling, frowning, encouraging, reassuring, commanding, the officer in charge of the retreat to the tram station across the gorge.

"I'm not going to leave you here," said Harry Ames.

"Harry, you're getting on the tram and going across! You're needed over there! Now, that's an order, Harry!"

And Harry was too accustomed to being in his proper place in the scheme of things to disobey. He bowed his head politely, squared his shoulders, pursed his lips and took the next car across the lake. It was the last car to make the crossing.

Francine was also on that car and Harry, even in the turmoil of the moment, allowed himself a soupçon of satisfaction at her crestfallen appearance. His intuition told him that somewhere in the midst of the horror and confusion of the last few hours, Arly had ticked off that saccharine little bitch.

And Arly had seen Francine one more time. From the basement where she had ordered the maintenance man to leave his post by the generator and take himself to the cable car, she had climbed a narrow backstairs that brought her to the floor of her apartment. She had personally checked the guests and the employees off the list of survivors as they embarked on the tram for the other side and Francine was not yet accounted for.

Arly knocked on the corridor door to Francine's room and in a moment it was opened by pale-faced Francine.

"You have been told to go to the tram station, haven't you?" asked Arly, and Francine nodded. "Then please go," said Arly.

"I was waiting for you," said Francine. "I thought—I thought you might need me to help you."

"Help me to do what?"

"I don't know exactly."

"Well, I'll say this for you," said Arly, "you don't give up easily, and that's a good quality. Now, all you have to do is find a more practical use for it. Don't waste it on old lesbians. We're a hard-boiled lot. Try an old man next time. They're weaker prey." She patted Francine on the cheek and hurried off toward the main stairs to the lobby.

Francine turned back into the room, picked up the small valise she had packed, hurled a Wedgwood ashtray at the mirror of the pretty vanity and both shattered in a burst of blue and silver. She stalked down the corridor to the outside fire stairs and glumly found her way to the tram. She avoided Harry Ames's probing gaze and did not look up from her clasped hands when Arly came from the lodge to check the names of the passengers on the car off the list on her clipboard. She heard Arly mutter the name Francine, along with the names of others on the car, and then heard her speaking to the tram engineer on the telephone.

"Take the car away," Arly said, "and I'll have everybody who's left ready for the next trip."

The tram moved slowly, heavily away into the snow-white day and Francine dabbed at angry tears with a little snow-white handkerchief that matched her snow-white gloves.

Without a backward look, consulting the list as she went, Arly walked quickly up the steps to the lodge. Besides Friendly and poor

Jessica, there remained Emil von Rothke and Archie Epstein, Cora McElvain and Lorenzo Dante, Clarice Bishop, Cabot Markey, Diane Haynes and Paul Binns. Diane was in the office, charged with attending to the radio, Paul had gone off to stir Clarice Bishop into action, Cora and Lorenzo were in the great hall fighting about taking the tram, and Emil and Archie were having a leisurely breakfast which Emil had cooked in the coffee shop.

Emil had insisted in his aggravating if graceful manner that they be on the last car. "Women and children first," Emil had declared, and Archie had nodded agreement with this gallantry.

"Really, Emil," Arly had said, "the ship isn't sinking, for god's sake."

But he had waggled a finger at her and smiled and gone off to the coffee shop, where he placed a chef's tall cap on his head and announced that the Chez von Rothke was open for business.

And there you are. Of all the people in the lodge on that gentle night before, only these eleven were left on this harrowing and luckless day.

The tram bearing Ames and Francine and fourteen others grumbled along its cables without mishap and docked perfectly. When the car was empty, the engineer pressed the switches to reverse its journey and watched it move wearily once again out into the falling snow. It disappeared in the murk and only his instruments told him that it was rolling steadily on its way back to the lodge. As he watched the instruments, he heard a faint grinding sound, like pebbles being crushed beneath auto tires. The sound grew louder and he was suddenly horrified to see through the big windows in the control room the tram cable tower beside the station toppling in slow motion from its foundations. It struck the shoulder of the gorge and the weight of the cables dragged it off the shoulder and down, down into the gorge and the lake. Damaged by the earthquake, the foundations had heroically persevered until this moment, and the engineer gave silent thanks that the tram car was empty as, somewhere out there in the storm, it dropped into the void.

21

When Arly and Harry Ames had discovered that Clarice Bishop was missing from among the guests who had been mustered in the lobby and were being transported to safety, Paul, knowing something of the reason for Mrs. Bishop's absence, volunteered again for service above and beyond the call of duty.

He knocked on her door and, expecting no answer and getting none, let himself in and found her in precisely the same position under the yellow blanket. She had not moved since his last visit. He shook the bed with his knee and called her name. He found her shoulder through the blanket and shook that and called her name. He bent over her and shouted, "Goddamit, lady, wake up!" and Clarice said, "Huh?" without opening her eyes.

"You have to get up, Mrs. Bishop."

"In my whole life," said Clarice, "I've never *had* to get up. Who are you anyway?"

"It's the cool-assed barkeep again, Mrs. Bishop, and you still have to get up. All the guests are being moved across the gorge to the tram station there. For the helicopters."

This piqued her interest and she rolled over and looked up at him. "What helicopters?"

Paul again explained about the earthquake that she had slept through and the now present need to transfer everyone to the lower tram station.

Clarice responded to this urgent information by remarking upon her awful hangover and would he kindly get her a split of champagne from the refrigerator.

"Mrs. Bishop, you're going to get up and put some clothes on."

"Get out of my room," said she.

"Will you get dressed?"

"If you don't get out of my room, I'll have you discharged."

"Lady, there's nothing left to discharge me from and I'm only here in your room on a mission of mercy to get you started toward the cable car." He swept the blanket off her with one flinging gesture. "Now move or I'll put you over my shoulder and take you jaybird naked into the lobby of this hotel."

She stared at him. "It's cold," she said, "and I have to go to the loo."

Paul stepped into the bathroom, grabbed a terry cloth robe from its hook and brought it to the woman on the bed. "Do what you have to do, but hurry."

Clarice labored to her feet and, dragging the robe behind her with one hand, went into the bathroom and closed the door.

He heard its lock click into place and crossed to yell at its panel, "Five minutes and I break it down!"

He went to the refrigerator, opened a split of champagne and dumped it into a big tumbler, crossed to the bathroom door and shouted, "I've got your champagne!"

In the bathroom, Clarice was seething, not only because the cool-assed barkeep was ordering her about, but also because he had not seemed to notice that she, perhaps the most beautiful woman in the world, was naked—except to catalogue it under the heading of "jaybird."

For a bartender, he was an oddly attractive specimen. She had noticed that before in the last day or so when he had appeared for duty in the Earthquake Room. Fuzzily, it occurred to her that perhaps there was some emergency in the lodge or they would not have sent this man to roust her out of bed, but still she was not going to be treated in so cavalier a manner without extracting some revenge. She would show him a thing or two.

The door shook as he banged on it and she heard him say, "Don't you want your champagne, Mrs. Bishop?" and she thought, Aha! He thinks I'm an alcoholic needing my morning jolt. She did want the champagne, needed it desperately, but also she had to show him that thing or two.

She started the shower and, when it was warm, unlocked the door and then walked down the steps to stand under the running water. Again he struck the door and now rattled the doorknob and, after a moment, opened the door.

Clarice had assumed her best pose, one knee bent, her arms

raised, hands clasped in her hair, and she knew she made a glistening and statuesque spectacle with the light over the huge Roman tub spotted directly down upon the body in the shower.

Paul stood in the doorway and, while he could not help but admire this living reproduction of a Bernini fountain, he almost burst into laughter. The drunken beauty was actually trying to play a game with him. Not one word he had said about the emergency in the lodge had penetrated her vacant head. She was angry because he was bossing her about and doubtless expected to bring him worshiping to his knees.

Paul stepped forward to the bath console on the marble wall beside the tub and turned off the shower. He presented wet Clarice with the tumbler of champagne and said, "Okay, Mrs. Bishop, I'll admit you have cute tits and a dynamite bottom. Now drink up and let's go." He left the bathroom.

Well, Clarice thought bitterly, I showed him a thing or two all right. She chugalugged the champagne and immediately felt better, then stalked from the bathroom, still naked, and smiled at Paul. "You sure you don't want some, baby?" she asked.

"No, ma'am, I'm not sure," said Paul with a grin. "But they're waiting for us."

Clarice began to dress, drunkenly humming a bright tune as she pulled on pantyhose and pants. Paul felt a brief, dispassionate pity for her. This woman had everything and nothing. He had known so many like her in the rich resorts where he had worked, but perhaps none so beautiful and for that reason, none so sad.

Arly had told Markey of Dr. Friendly's dilemma and he knew that she would not desert her guests. In consequence, Markey also knew that he could not desert Arly and go off to do the dutch. He was needed and his quietus would have to wait or, at least, accept the company of others. With this view in mind and after the tall and pretty cocktail waitress with the clear, honest and slightly enlarged (by her chic bifocals) eyes had left his studio, he made a sandwich from various exotic ingredients he found in the studio refrigerator, washed it down with strong coffee and hurried off to where he had left the snowmobile. He brushed the snow off its seat, started the motor and gunned the machine up the ski slope as fast as it could climb. If Arly and the good Dr. Friendly and wife had to risk the fall of the glacier, the least he could do was try to make another assessment of that risk. Was the thing coming down or wasn't it? More than an hour had passed since he had first discovered the looming presence, and the exodus to the other side of the gorge was moving along as swiftly as the crippled tram system could carry the people.

He knew that Peck Nordo and his rescue team were by now on their way over Satan's Hill to the lower tram station, and that if the tram should stall, they would push on up the ridge with a portable winch and enough cable to snake survivors up the east wall to safety. All that being pendent upon the glacier. If it failed in its escape, there was nothing to fear; if it was succeeding, then even as Markey drove the snowmobile higher into the blizzard, it might begin its plunge and he would have his ride to glory without the asking.

The snow seemed heavier and Markey could find his way on the steep ski run only by steering close to the trees that bordered it. He cursed himself for having forgotten goggles, a carelessness for a man with his experience, and he swept the snow from his eyelashes with his gloved hand, bent his head against the white crystals and pressed on. He wasn't sure how far, how high he had come, but a few minutes later he felt prescient hackles rise and he stopped the snowmobile and listened.

It was there, just behind the thick palisade of snow, moving, making a giant paw-fall sound, rattling stones, scuffling, and then there followed a hungry crunch, as if it had bent to gobble up a tree.

Markey started the vehicle, geared it down to its slowest speed and inched on up the slope. And there it was. It had obliterated the pavilion and crept on across the leveled ground to the ski tram terminus, which had been knocked over and was being flattened. The smoking blue face of the Gornaad now stood by Markey's estimate nearly three hundred feet high and it was beginning to thrust out over the down slope. He steered the snowmobile to within a few yards of the base of the thing and felt the ancient chill of its frozen bulk as he determined that it was coming on at about one foot per minute.

With a megatherian grunt, it gave a sudden lurch forward that sent a shock of fright racing along Markey's nerves and he turned the snowmobile downhill and went as fast as he dared back toward the lodge. It was no longer a matter of risk. Unless a miracle occurred to stop the ice, it was hell-bent to begin its slide into the gorge where it rightfully belonged and from which it had been separated an aeon ago.

Markey had expected to find only Arly and the doctor with his injured wife still at the lodge, but when he strode into the lobby, almost a snowman from his journey, he found Arly with seven additional marooned souls in various states of collision with the brutal facts of the danger on the slopes above them. With the collapse of the tram cables, Arly had felt it necessary to prepare those left for the probability of perdition and she had told them about the Gornaad.

And when they gathered hopefully about him after learning that he had been reconnoitering the glacier, the only hope he could offer was the information that Peck Nordo and his men were surely on the march up the hill to the sawtooth ridge and that he believed (though he did not) that they would arrive above the east wall in time to lift all out of the path of the glacier.

Markey knew that under the best conditions the ridge hike was an hour's trip, and in the blizzard and wind it might be two hours or even more. In a race with the glacier, the glacier was a sure thing.

From habit, as he explained how the rescue would be effected by a slender steel cable with a harness on the end of it, he read the faces of his listeners. Arly's black eyes knew that he was lying about the rescue chances and, curiously, he suspected that the bartender Paul Binns also doubted his assurances. There was in Paul's eyes a tiny, hard point of amused cynicism. Lorenzo and Cora grasped avidly at his words, Lorenzo's teeth fairly rattling with fear, and relieved, milky tears filling Cora's red-rimmed eyes.

Emil and Archie, those inseparables, were at ease and Markey, knowing little about them, felt sure they had been in tight places before. Sleepy-eyed, fur-swathed Clarice viewed him from some distant place, probably did not believe that she was awake. Diane was at his mercy. He had come from the wilderness to save her and if he had said they should all take wing, she would instantly have started flapping her arms. Markey was helpless before the total trust in her scared face and he knew then that no matter how wasted it might be he must make an effort to try to save these lives.

Arly's cave where the sophisticated earthquake machinery was installed, the tunnel she had driven into the wall of the gorge, might have been a temporary haven from the onslaught of the glacier. When Arly had first learned of the perilous situation from Markey and Harry, she had thought of the tunnel as a refuge and had sent the maintenance man to check its condition and been told that its entrance had fallen in from the mighty quake. And there was no escape into the lake because there were no boats and it was too cold for swimming. In the early days of the lodge, a mother and child had drowned there and, like Arly's father's, their bodies were never found in the strange, deep currents. Arly had had the stone steps that switchbacked down through the talus torn out. And even if there had been boats, there was no place for them to go where they could escape the plunge of the berg and the mountainous waves it would create.

Now Markey considered the frightened faces before him. "I think it might be well if we get a jump on the rescue team," said he, making it seem merely logical. "Meet them partway. There's a good wide ledge about four hundred feet up on the east wall. Any of you done any climbing?"

"I've done enough to know the principles of it," said Paul.

Markey knew principles would not be enough. Speed was the key here and only he was capable of that. Had been capable. He felt anger at the implanted batteries that kept his heart on course. In the last few hours he had been taken out of himself by the excitement of the events, had almost forgotten that he was crippled. For him to go up the rock face might be impossible even if there were no urgency, but to do it fast and unerringly was not imaginable. He would collapse on his rope and hang there dying, hidden by the snow, while these people, this girl with the big eyes behind the glasses, waited for him to help them. Still, it was at least a useful way to go as opposed to the egomaniacal suicide he had planned, and if he could by some miracle reach the ledge, he could belay Paul Binns up the wall and from there they could lift the others up one by one on the end of the nylon rope.

With Paul following and Diane traipsing along, Markey left the lobby and went into the storage room behind the lodge store where climbing equipment was kept. In minutes he had laid out the tools he would need and, with Paul and Diane to help him, had set off for the east wall, first admonishing Arly to get the others to the ski shack which was near the point where he would begin to climb.

"I think I can manage that," said Arly. "Maybe not much more, but that." She made a mock salute and turned away from him.

"Wait," he said.

She moved on as if she had not heard. With four long steps he caught her, seized her arm and turned her to face him. "What does that mean, Arly?—maybe no more than that."

She looked up at him and smiled. A kind and patient smile. "It means," she said, "that I'll be staying here with Dr. Friendly and his young lady. So maybe we should say good-by—just in case."

Markey did not protest. He knew her too well, knew the temper of that metal. He bent and kissed her on the mouth. "Just in case," he said, and left her there.

She watched him lope away and briefly covered the kiss with her fingers, then turned away quickly and went about her business. She got her charges started on their way to the ski shack after taking them into the store and equipping them with padded ski jackets, thick ski gloves and wool caps to cover their ears along with galoshes to buckle over their shoes. If they were to be hoisted up the east rock face, they would need the proper clothing for it.

Since they were obviously more competent than Clarice or the Madame Cara Loves You pair, Arly instructed Emil and Archie to fire up the ski shack's fireplace when they arrived since the heating system might not be working. Emil bowed and clicked his heels and stated that he and Archie would build a fire that would do honor to Prometheus.

Arly, keeping busy, and thinking not only of her guests but of the rescue team that would eventually reach them if Markey was able to get them temporarily out of danger's way, dashed into the coffee shop and raided the refrigerators of packages of pre-sliced ham and cheese and loaves of sandwich bread. She dumped it all into an empty burlap potato sack and, carrying it over her shoulder, rushed to the west wing to inform Dr. Friendly of the new plans for rescue. New plans, of course, could have no effect upon Friendly, but Arly wanted him to be aware that she was still there to serve him in any way she could. Earthquakes and galloping glaciers might change the topography of mountains but they could not alter the rigid devotion to the rules of hospitality that had governed Kirbo's Lodge for forty years.

Arly turned into the long corridor of the west wing and so deserted was it and silent, some of its ceiling lights broken by the quake and making it gloomy for all its bright decor, that Arly felt she was entering not a familiar hallway but a strange passage to an unknown place. She could hear her steps brush against the carpet and she could feel her breath becoming short. It was with relief that she reached Friendly's door, dropped the potato bag and softly rapped on the panel instead of pressing the buzzer.

The door opened and the doctor was there in the darkness of the foyer. She could see that behind him the blinds had been closed over the windows of the room. His face was touched by the dim light from the corridor but his stolid expression gave no clue to the state of things in the room.

"Your wife?"

He nodded. It could mean anything—that Jessica had recovered, had died, was improving. Arly did not insist on clarification. She quickly told him of the tram's collapse and of the rescue team and he nodded again in much the same way as before.

"Can I get you anything, do anything for you—anything?"

Friendly shook his head this time but with the exact same tempo as he had nodded.

"I'll continue to check in with you," said Arly.

"Thank you," said Friendly, "but it won't be necessary."

And while he remained there politely looking at her, she knew he was not seeing her but was only waiting for her to go. She nodded this time and turned away, heard the door close and its night lock snap into place. Against what? thought Arly, and why? Then she was occupied again with the length and depression of the deserted corridor. Shifting the bag of victuals from one shoulder to the other, she hastened toward the welcome, brighter lights of the distant lobby. It was a hundred miles away and she was being followed by things she could not see or hear, but they were there just the same and she was cold even in the thick ski jacket she was wearing.

When Friendly closed the door and twisted the night latch, he was making a tomb for himself and Jessica and he was quite nonchalant about it. He moved back to the chair beside the bed, sat and crossed his legs and folded his arms. He was unaware that she was watching him through her eyelashes. And she thought, How strong he is, the strongest man in the world, that's why I wanted him so much. She opened her eyes wider and smiled at him.

"Hey," she said.

"So you're awake."

"For a minute I wasn't sure. It's so dark."

"A dark room is more restful."

"For who, you or me?"

"Both of us."

"Bullshit," said Jessica.

"You know I don't like that word in your mouth."

"But you'll forgive me."

"I'll forgive you anything, my dear."

"Anything?"

"Anything."

"Forgive me if I die?"

"No, I wouldn't forgive that. That's the unforgivable."

"You'd carry a grudge about that."

"Indeed I would."

"To the grave?"

"To the grave and beyond. On to China."

"Well, since you're not going to forgive me, does it matter how I do it?"

"Ah, you're getting at something. Something very sneaky. You're trying to pull something on me. I know the approach."

"Yes. Could you turn me over? I mean, if I'm going to pop it, can't I do it face up? I'm tired of lying in this same position."

"I'm sorry. I can't do that."

"Then you don't love me."

"Then I don't love you."

"But you do."

"Yes, I do."

"And I am dying. Tell me, Alfred. I mean, I might want to leave a will or think of something snappy to say or maybe pray to little Jesus."

"No, you're not dying."

"Well, something peculiar is going on in here. My voice doesn't sound right and, listen, I'm not breathing so good."

"That's because you're talking too much."

"Yes. I'm tired now."

"Sleep again."

"No. I'll keep my eyes open. I want to see you." She watched him. He remained very still, his legs crossed, his arms folded, the strongest man in the world. And then she could not see him and yet she knew her eyes were open.

"Jessica?" She did not answer. He bent forward and took her limp wrist between his fingers and felt for life. It was there, still. She had that quickly gone into a coma. And he sat back and folded his arms again. Thinking as a doctor, he concluded, as he had many times before, that the mind makes it so easy for us to die, closing little secret doors against pain and terror.

Because so few were left at the lodge, the Nordo team could shed some of its equipment before it started the ascent to the ridge that would take them to a point above the east wall of the gorge where they could spin out the rescue cable. Shelter for so few rather than many meant the welcome loss of several hundred pounds of nylon tenting. But the residual burden was still heavy even when divided between and lashed on the two stretcher carriers and its weight supported by four men to each stretcher.

The beginning of the climb was relatively easy, a fairly smooth uphill grade through pine forest, but as they came above the timberline and without the protection of the trees, their ordeal began in earnest. Nordo could see the long streamers of snow flung out by the hard wind on the crest of the ridge, and as he came close to the crest he set his goggles in place and saw that his companions did the same.

They were roped together in fours and further attached to each other by their grips on the stretchers, and they were strong men and fit, but when they came from the shelter of the mountain's flank and stepped on the ridge they must follow, all were struck to their knees by the force of the blizzard's gale.

For long and precious moments they knelt there, leaning into hurricane wind, and finally got their balance together and rose to start the walk on the ridge. They could not talk to each other, for their voices were snatched from their lips by the wind, they could only dimly see each other through the driving snow. The four men carrying the rear stretcher simply followed the four men carrying the first stretcher and those men were guided by Nordo. Their leader, crouching against the storm, his legs moving like steam pistons, led them along the narrow top of the ridge at a pace that would have killed lesser men. The distance to the point on the ridge where they could move down and out of the wind to set up their rescue camp was now a little more than one mile and some twenty-five hundred feet gain in altitude, but one member of the team later reported, "That was the longest mile and the highest climb I'll ever make in my life. The only reason we made it was because Peck Nordo dragged us up behind him."

Trudging through the snow toward the ski shack with the potato sack slung over her shoulder, padded against the storm, wearing a wool scarf over her head and galoshes on her feet, Arly looked more like a babushka than the fashionable owner of a famous hostelry, and she felt bent and old and haunted. On the bridge over Gornaad Creek she paused and looked down into the swollen, raging stream and heard the roar of it where it pitched off into its long tumble through the talus into the lake. Her father had carried her across this bridge on his shoulders, had tipped her carefully forward over the rail and let her spit into the water and then pretended he might let her fall and, when she squeaked in delight, he had pranced on with her into the fragrant pinewoods where fairy lanterns bloomed.

Hot tears flooded down Arly's cold cheeks and she stumped on through the storm with her load of ham and cheese and bread. "You've got to stop this, stop it, stop it," she spoke aloud, and mopped at her tears with her mittened hand.

In the shack, Emil and Archie, true to their boast, had a cheerful fire going in the big center fireplace and with Cora and Lorenzo they were sitting on the benches around the fire. Clarice was off in a corner of the room by herself on a sofa, buried in her sables with her knees drawn up against her stomach. The ski jacket Arly had issued to her was discarded on the floor beside the sofa with the galoshes and wool cap. Clarice peered out from her furry nest like a startled blue-eyed owl.

"We're of good cheer," Emil proclaimed, and Archie nodded and Lorenzo sniffed and Cora tried to smile.

"Are you all right?" Arly asked of Clarice, and Clarice blinked and moved warily deeper into the protecting sables. I'm not the only one who's lost her marbles, thought Arly, and opened the potato sack on the bar and began to make sandwiches.

The shack door opened and Diane entered and slapped the snow off her clothing. "He's up there," she said. "Completely out of sight in the snow. He just began to climb straight up and in a few minutes he was gone."

"Of course," said Arly. "He's a human fly."

"He's the bravest man I ever saw," Diane commented with childlike wonder, and she took off her jacket and automatically began to help Arly with the sandwiches.

"We have to make enough for the rescue team," said Arly.

"That'll be nice," said Diane, and Arly knew they had all become unscrewed.

Suddenly Cora yelled at Lorenzo, "You goddamned wop sonofabitch!" and then was silent, her stubby fingers stuck between her puffy lips. Lorenzo paid her no attention. Diane looked up in shocked surprise but she continued with the making of sandwiches. Arly shook her head sadly and Clarice's beautiful white face poked out. She stared glassily about and then withdrew again. Archie shrugged at Emil and Emil blew his nose into a large monogrammed handkerchief.

"Why don't we have some music?" asked Arly, and Emil waved the handkerchief in approval and boomed, "A brilliant idea! And we will sing."

Arly pressed some buttons under the bar and the disco tapes laid in for the ski season blared forth from the amplifiers about the room and Emil shouted, "I don't know the words to that, Miss Kirbo!" and Arly began to laugh and laughed until she cried.

Diane punched off the music and went back to slapping ham on cheese on bread for the grand arrival of the rescue team.

Outside the shack and fifty yards away, Paul stamped his feet to keep the circulation going and squinted up into the snow where he could still hear Markey on the rock face. He could hear the rasp of chocks as Markey wedged them into cracks and now and then the clink of a hammer against the granite. Once Markey shouted, "Heads up below!" and a shower of stone chips came rattling down through the snow.

Paul watched the spool of heavy cord on the ground unwind inch by inch as the other end of it, attached to Markey's belt, moved higher and higher. When Markey reached the ledge, he, Paul, would cut the cord and tie it to a prepared loop on the end of the nylon rope that lay in a great coiled pile at his feet. Markey would then pull the rope's end up to the ledge and Paul was to fasten the rope to his climbing harness and begin to climb, placing his toes in the webbing slung to the carabiners that Markey had clipped to the chocks anchored in the granite. With Markey pulling and Paul giving what help his climbing experience would allow, Markey hoped to have Paul beside him on the ledge in a reasonably short time.

"Then we'll get the others up in a matter of minutes," Markey had said confidently, but Paul had noted the older man's heavy breathing just from the quick hike from the lodge to the wall and twice now the spool of cord had stopped for minutes at a time and he could hear no sound from the precipice above. He had called, "Are you all right?" and not immediately but moments later the reply had come down to him, "Yes—okay." Paul knew that it was not okay, that up there unseen, pressed against the stone, the famous Cabot Markey was fighting something other than the problems of the solo face.

Emil and Archie came from the snow shack, looked up into the snow as people will do when something other than sunshine falls from the sky, and strolled to where Paul was monitoring the spool of cord that turned in fits and jerks as Markey climbed.

"How is he doing?" asked Emil.

"He's up there," said Paul.

Emil and Archie squinted up into the snow again as if they expected to catch a glimpse of the man on the wall. "Can we do anything?" Archie inquired.

"I don't know what it would be," said Paul.

"No, that is true," said Archie.

"Thanks just the same," Paul said.

All three men watched the spool of cord as it patiently unwound itself.

"He is a remarkable man," said Archie.

"That's what everyone says," replied Paul.

The spool stopped for a few minutes and all silently watched until it started again.

"How far do you think he is?" asked Emil.

"More than halfway now, I'd think," answered Paul.

"You will let us know when it is time?"

"You'll be informed, sir."

"Thank you," said Emil, and he and Archie wandered away along the path to the creek. Paul looked after them with approval. Cool, those two. No panic there.

And cool they were. They were not afraid. They knew beyond doubt that death was the end. Mathematically, the punishment of afterlife was quite impossible. Try as the faithful might, no equation could prove that S for Soul $+$ G for God $\times$ P for prayer would $=$ I for immortality: it would always come out Z for zero, and zero was not to be feared. Emil and Archie walked out upon the miraculously undamaged roofed bridge over the rushing creek and watched the water meditatively. They were not reviewing their lives. What was done was done and they were accustomed to the burden of guilt. It was always there, that encumbrance, and they were devoted to it. If, when their concentrations on games were concluded, they had not had that weight to assume, their lives would have been empty and that they knew.

"I am having intuition," Emil spoke in German.

"You have no belief in intuition," sniffed Archie.

"Allow me please a temporary belief. We will not be leaving here."

"That is the intuition?"

"Yes."

"Since you never have had one before, I suppose I should place some value on it."

"I don't know that it would gain you anything."

"No, especially since there is nothing I can do about it."

"But there you are. We are completed."

"Finished, you mean."

"No. Completed."

"Yes, I see what you mean."

"There is a difference."

"Decidedly."

And they nattered on comfortably about the proposition of death while Markey climbed desperately and Peck Nordo and his men fought the blizzard's blast and Dr. Friendly kept vigil over his wife's shallow breath. And far above them, the Gornaad pushed its great blue mass closer to the breaking point.

On the granite face, Markey had stopped again, his weight hung against a chock rammed into a crack and on its fitted wire loop a carabiner through which his climbing line was threaded. He was less than halfway up the four hundred feet to the ledge and fifty agonizing minutes had passed. There was no pain to his climb, only a frustrating and sickening weakness. He rested now and listened to the thudding of his heart, fearful that each clamoring beat would be the last—but it slowed and became metronomic again, one per second, and Markey moved on up the wall and found a niche for another chock, that climbing device that looks like a metal nut and serves in place of the heavy iron piton. He tapped the chock home with the point of his hammer, attached the aluminum snap-gate called a carabiner, worked his line through the snap-gate, fastened a webbing loop to that, stepped into the loop and gained another three feet on the wall.

Through the snow he could see a fissure off to his left and he tried to visualize its place on the wall. How high did it go? Was it deep enough to facilitate his climb? He cursed his unfamiliarity with this side of the gorge. In all the years at the lodge, he had climbed it only one time, and that to amuse himself for an afternoon, so simple was the ascent. He could not remember that inviting fissure. Still, in his enfeebled condition it was worth trying.

He found a crevice for his boot edge and crept out to begin the traverse. At full reach he could see a hairline crack that would serve to anchor the traverse and he reached into his pocket and took out a rurp, a tiny metal sliver invented by the mountaineer Yvon Chouinard. He hammered the rurp into the crack and clipped his line to it with a carabiner.

With a good thought for Chouinard and the rurp, Markey swung down and toward the fissure. His fingers missed the edge and he fell. It was a short fall, no more than six feet to the end of his rope, but it seemed to him in slow motion and bottomless and as he fell there was nothing at all in his mind but a picture of the tiny rurp in the thin crack. He could see it there in the front of his head, the carabiner turning with the line as the line swung back, and in his imagery the rurp slipped from its crack and Markey's fall became a plunge that tore supporting chocks from their places and left him a heap of broken bones at the bottom of this simple schoolboy's climb. Disgraced.

The rurp held and Markey was not disgraced. He was still for a few moments on the end of the rope until his breath returned, then he began to swing back and forth and finally his fingers caught the edge of the fissure and he found a toehold for his boot and was enormously pleased to find that the fissure was deep and fairly wide.

He rested again and then worked his way up through the fissure, increasing his protection with quickly placed chocks in cracks that fanned away from its rough edges. And now Markey began to believe that he might actually reach the ledge only a little

more than two hundred feet above him. He realized that in his enthusiasm he was climbing too fast and he forced himself to stop, to
breathe deeply and regularly and to wait for his heart to stabilize its
beat. But he was pleased with the flow of strength he felt in his arms
and legs, and where he had been cold and his skin dry, he was warm
now and sweat trickled pleasantly down his face from under his
watch cap.

"Okay up there?" Paul Binns's voice came to him from below,
muffled by the snow.

"Okay!" shouted Markey, and found a sharp point in the fissure
for his boot cleat, thumbed a chock into a crevice and lifted himself
another four feet. Yes, he was going to make it and he felt that perhaps God had finally discovered that he was there and had offered
him a Michelangelesque hand. Who needs it? thought Markey, and
climbed on.

22

For Arly finally, there was nothing left to do. The ham and cheese sandwiches must stand as a last and absurd contribution to the comfort and welfare of her guests and she stared at the sandwiches now, neatly stacked on trays by Diane and placed on the shack's bar, where they sat untouched and ignored by the mismatched souls stranded there.

There was, however, one more courtesy to be extended to two of those who had trusted her and for that reason Arly must return to the main building, but still she paused and compassionately considered the wretched little group in the shack. Cora and Lorenzo were huddled on separate benches and Clarice remained in her hermitage of furs and still upright on the sofa. Diane sat on another bench, nervously alert and ready to help in any way she could.

Arly beckoned to her and Diane moved quickly to her side. "I've an errand, Diane, and while I'm gone I must depend on you to take care of things here. You might make coffee."

"Yes, ma'am," said Diane.

"If Mr. Markey is successful, you'll have to move quickly," Arly cautioned her. "Look after Mrs. Bishop and Miss McElvain if I haven't returned." She glanced at Lorenzo, who sat with his head in his hands. "Mr. Dante, too. I'm afraid he won't be much help, but you can count on Mr. von Rothke and Mr. Epstein."

"You can depend on me, Miss Kirbo," Diane replied earnestly.

Arly considered the fresh and trusting young face before her and was wrenchingly reminded of the others who had died and the conviction that their deaths were her fault was an unrelieved sickness. "Thank you, Diane," she said, and unexpectedly offered her hand. The surprised Diane shook hands with Arly and Arly left quickly. Diane stood for a moment thinking about that puzzling handshake and she wondered what errand Miss Kirbo had to do and whether she should have offered to do it for her. But no employee of the lodge had ever questioned that lady's decisions and it had not immediately occurred to Diane to question this one. Still, there had been an odd finality in Arly's manner, as if she expected they might not meet again, and Diane felt suddenly and truly frightened. She seized upon her promise to look after the others to quiet her own anxiety.

"How does a cup of hot coffee sound?" she asked cheerfully, and, ignoring the silence of her morose charges, measured coffee into the large urn that stood behind the bar, hopefully plugged it in and was rewarded by a red light as the electrical connection was made.

Arly walked swiftly to the west wing and found a room two doors removed from Dr. Friendly's quarters. She removed her jacket, sat at a small desk and wrote a note to Dr. Friendly telling him her room number. She would be just down the hall and he was to call her immediately if he needed anything. She folded the note and went to Friendly's door. There was no sound from within and Arly slipped the note beneath the door and returned to her chosen room.

At the windows she looked out at the falling snow. One window was broken and the room was cold. She pulled the drapes, removed her shoes and crawled into the big bed, drew the luxurious satin comforter to her shoulders. It was over. There was no more she could do. Her whole life had crumbled about her so swiftly and she could not control whatever might happen from this point forward. In the silence of the darkened room Arly relaxed and while it could not be said that she was experiencing a sense of peace, still she was quite calm now, a calm that accompanied the relinquishing of control. She closed her eyes and almost immediately slipped again into welcome memory, and, in the way that an inconsequential song or an inane jingle sometimes become trapped in the mind, an old rhyme from her childhood bounced about now in her head, repeating itself over and over.

> Oh, she jumped in bed
> And kivered up her head
> And then they couldn't find her.

There was a game her father had invented to persuade her into bed at night. When she was very young she had scrambled into bed, covered her face and waited for his footsteps and his call as he came toward her room. When he approached the bed, she had thrown off the blankets and shouted, "Here I are, Papa, here I are!" and Caiphus had exclaimed in mock astonishment before he kissed her and tucked her in for the night.

A smile curving her lips now at the recollection, Arly pulled the comforter over her head and let the past have its way with her.

The warmth from the fireplace penetrated Clarice Bishop's fur cavern and she dropped the hood of the coat and let the fur slip lower on her shoulders. Hungover as she had been earlier, she had hardly listened to Arly's explanation of the danger of their situation and had simply let herself be shuttled to the ski shack. Clarice was not conditioned to react to impending disaster because she had never in her entire life been threatened by anything at all, but she was fully awake now and there was certainly something ominous in the air. She glanced around the room, studied glum Cora and quaking, gray-faced Lorenzo, shuddered with distaste, rose to her feet and walked to the bar behind which Diane stood.

"Would you like coffee, Mrs. Bishop?" Diane asked politely.

Clarice started to ask for a beer, then changed her mind and nodded. "Black, please."

When Diane placed the steaming cup before her, Clarice added three lumps of sugar, considered the sandwiches and reached for one.

"What exactly are we waiting for?" she asked Diane.

Diane studied the gorgeous Clarice and guessed that she had not really understood everything Miss Kirbo had told them earlier and thought perhaps she should explain again. "Mr. Markey is climbing the east wall to the ledge now and there's a rescue team coming over the ridge," she finished, and when Clarice calmly continued to devour the ham and cheese sandwich she added, "You musn't be frightened, Mrs. Bishop. We'll be all right."

Clarice laughed then, the low gurgle that surprised Diane as it had Cabot Markey the day before. "Aren't you?" she asked.

"What?"

"Frightened," said Clarice.

And Diane started to protest. She was, after all, entrusted to take care of these guests in Miss Kirbo's absence and reassuring them was important, but it had been a direct question and something honest in Clarice's eyes made her hesitate and she blurted, "I'm scared to death," and Clarice laughed again. Diane refilled her coffee cup and Clarice took another sandwich. If she was lucky enough to be hauled up the wall of the gorge, she would need strength, and if she wasn't, the calories would not matter. Appetite as ravenous as always, she gulped her food and searched for somebody to blame for the outrageous situation in which she found herself, and she thought of the architect and the fact that she would not have been here at all in this damn early winter blizzard except for the lodge's proximity to San Francisco. For months he had pursued her and then lost interest in a few days when, at the unveiling finally of his unremarkable weenie, she had not become crazed with passion and unhinged with gratitude. Even mustard and the works would not have helped. What did they expect? she wondered. Standard equipment, like windshield wipers, and every man sported one. Even you, you little worm, Clarice thought, and glared venomously at poor, terrified Lorenzo. Make no mistake about it, you romantics, Clarice thought, cocks—not love—make the world go 'round. Well, she had had too little love and too much of the other and she was convinced that each man went from cradle to grave seeking proof that he alone had something more than the regulation issue.

This revelation seemed in her hapless condition to be worth sharing. "Cocks," she muttered aloud. "That's all it's about."

"Excuse me?" Diane turned a startled face toward her and Clarice grinned, flashing the white, capless, filling-free teeth that had stunned every dentist who had ever examined her mouth. And at that moment Emil and Archie stamped in out of the cold. Two more, thought Clarice, one circumcised and one un, and reached for another sandwich.

Across the room Cora sat rigid on the bench, every soft muscle a hard knot of fear. Not fear of pain or even of death, which was Lorenzo's problem, but stark terror at the possibility of leaving her poor invalid mother alone in an indifferent world. The problems would not be financial and she supposed she should be grateful for that. Everything she had—and what she had would take care of an army of old ladies—would go to her mother. Cora had seen to that, but it was not enough. Who would really care for that wracked soul, who would keep her company when she could not sleep at night, who would rub her back? Who would love her?

As for herself, Cora anguished, who but her mother loved her? Who but her mother would miss her and mourn her? And if she died, it would place a final oppressive grief on Mama. At the thought, Cora moaned aloud and directed such a look of loathing at the wretched Lorenzo that it jarred him out of his trance and he flinched as if she had struck him.

Diane watched the cheerful fire that crackled in the fireplace in the center of the room and she was sharply aware of the good pine smell of the burning logs, the fragrance of the fresh coffee. She had loved her winters at the lodge and the merry hours spent here in the ski shack, and she strained now to recapture the faces of friends, the sound of the music, the mood of those evenings, consciously putting it all in deep storage, for she knew with a sudden and painful maturity that it would not come again.

On all those nights her attention had been riveted on Paul and Diane considered now the sense of disappointment she had felt about him earlier and, in this contemplative mood, forced herself to acknowledge another truth. The Paul with whom she believed herself to be in love was her invention and she did not know the real man at all. She had been captured by his reckless smile, his physical grace, his independent air, and had imbued him with qualities of her own romantic imagination. He had offered her no encouragement beyond a casual friendliness and it was her problem, this Byronic quest. For the first time in years, she remembered poor comical Perce and reflected glumly that more than ten years later she was still afflicted.

Markey had done what he had believed he could not do, but now as he reached the ledge and rolled onto its angular security, he could not take the time to feel triumphant. A few moments of rest in the snow on the ledge, breathing deeply, storing oxygen, and then, gulping a mouthful of snow to quench his thirst, he got to his feet and began preparations to bring Paul Binns up the wall. The ledge was comfortably wide, almost five feet, created by a fault that had caused a great slab of granite to shear off in weathering. This side of the gorge was stair-stepped and the ledge on which Markey stood was the first of the giant steps.

He climbed above the ledge to a point about double his height and there drove an iron piton into a firm crack in the stone. To this he fastened a pulley and descended to reel in the cord that was still attached to his belt. On reaching the ledge, he had signaled Paul by jerking on the cord and he could now expect Paul had tied the end of the cord to the end of the stronger rope that would stretch the whole distance from the base of the wall to the ledge. In a matter of minutes, he had the rope in hand and he climbed up, threaded the rope through the pulley and scrambled down to the ledge again. And he was ready now to bring Paul up, the pulley giving him the advantage of his own weight on the rope in addition to the strength of his arms. With the webbing loops on the rock face at intervals of fifty or sixty feet where Paul could cling to give Markey a breather now and then, he expected to lift Paul to the ledge without mishap.

Markey brought the rope through the metal snap-gates on his climbing belt so that he could control the rope's slippage by feeding it around his body, then signaled Paul again with three jerks on the rope. At this point, Paul, with the other end of the rope fastened to his harness, was to begin climbing.

But as if the forces in the earth were playing a game of tease with Markey and with those below who were depending on him, as if Markey's scorn for the helping hand his God had offered had enraged that frivolous deity, the 7.2 aftershock chose that moment to wrench the mountains.

It came without warning; no opening salvos of artillery, no distant crescendo of thunder; it struck suddenly and viciously and with a single thrust. On the ledge Markey was thrown off his feet and showers of stone rattled down off the rock face above but his luck held and he was not hit.

On the ridge, Peck Nordo's team grabbed for earth and hung on. Those in the ski shack were tossed up and fell down with no injuries and Paul Binns, at the base of the gorge wall, had the presence of mind to get away from the wall before broken pieces of granite came pouring from above. In the crowded lower tram station, there was momentary screaming panic that ended as quickly as did the quake itself. In the almost deserted lodge, unbroken windows shattered and the diesel engine that powered the emergency generator was shocked into a fit of coughing and, with no one to adjust its fuel injection, coughed itself to death.

In her room, Arly staggered out of bed and started to rush efficiently into the lobby to take command, then realized there was nothing to be done and lay back down. Dr. Friendly remained in his chair beside his unconscious wife and had the lodge crumbled about him, he would not have moved from her side.

The screaming in the tram station had scarcely become a whimper and Arly had not gotten her time machine revved up again when the Great Sound was heard. Even though muffled by the snow, it was heard as far away as the terminal at Kirbo's Landing, as if the earth were made of glass and had split open like a clingstone peach, a strangely musical sound, its echo chiming across the Sierra. It was a sound perhaps never heard before because it had never been made before. It was the breaking of an escaping glacier and where or when had it happened before? And after the Great Sound the one-hundred-yard-long, two-hundred-yard-wide and one-hundred-yard-high chunk of ice hit the slope above and shook the lodge almost as much as had the earthquake.

Those who knew of the glacier's extrusion had no doubt about the source of the Great Sound. Arly drew the comforter over her face and Dr. Friendly lowered his head as if to take a blow and pressed even more firmly against the seat of his chair.

On the ridge, Nordo and team scrambled faster and on the ledge Markey pulled on the rope and, finding no weight on its other end, jerked it furiously as a signal to Paul to for god's sake get started up the rock face.

At the base of the gorge the granite chips had stopped falling and Paul leaped through the snow to the rope dangling from above. At the same time, all those in the ski shack came plowing through the snow to this only point of reference, this only way out of the trap they knew was finally and irrevocably closing its teeth.

Besabled Clarice was the first woman to reach Paul, quite naturally without the rough weather equipment given her by Arly but wearing French custom-made boots of some poor crocodile's skin. Paul seized her, pushed her arms into the harness, lashed the climbing belt over her sable coat and sent Markey a signal on the rope. Clarice rose like a fallen angel being returned to heaven as a bountiful gift from Mammon to St. Peter. All watched breathlessly as she silently vanished into the snow.

On the other end of the nylon rope, Markey was astonished at the ease with which he was lifting Paul Binns. He knew that he must now get Paul up to the ledge without the planned rest stops on the webbing and he had expected the task to be herculean. He was breathing heavily and his arms were beginning to ache as he took the rope in hand over hand through the fixed pulley above him, but he had to stop only once to let his heart stabilize itself. And then he knew the catch he was reeling in from below could not be Paul Binns, whose weight he estimated to be at least 175 pounds. Markey judged the weight he was lifting at no more than 100 pounds (112, to be exact, and a perfect 36-24-36), and when he hauled her onto the ledge, his strained heart almost gave up in anger.

"Goddamit, I needed a man up here!" shouted Markey.

"Relax, Mr. Markey," said Clarice. "I may be a dead-ass in some departments, but I'm not feeble. Just show me what to do."

Markey pulled her quickly out of the harness and, leaving it attached to the rope, tossed it over the side, letting the rope run through his fingers as it dropped into the gorge. When it had reached the bottom and Paul's signal came to lift the next refugee, Markey stood Clarice beside him and instructed her to place her hands just behind his on the rope and pull as he pulled, measuring her rhythm to his. And Markey was relieved to find that in Clarice's perfectly formed body there was also some firm muscle. She laid into the job with a will and between them they had Lorenzo Dante up in no time at all. As a man, he turned out to be useless, at least temporarily for he had not only lost control of his bladder, he could not stop vomiting long enough to help them on the rope.

As Markey flung the harness and rope back into the chasm and waited for it once again to reach the people below, he became conscious of an insistent and pervasive sound, a soft brushing occasionally punctuated by yet faraway shrieks of pain and joy as the escaping ice ground against granite. The berg was presently moving down the slope with a proper glacial speed, but it would gather momentum as it came. A jerk on the rope alerted Markey and he and Clarice bent their backs and began to pull. After this one coming up, there would be seven left on the lodge level, counting Arly and Dr. Friendly and Jessica Friendly. Discount Friendly, who would not leave his wife, discount Arly, who would not leave Friendly (or was it perhaps the lodge she could not bear to leave?), and four were left. There might yet be time to get them all to safety, but there was no time to mourn those who would be left behind.

Markey's heart was missing beats again but he could not stop now to rest. Under his clothing he was wet with perspiration and he knew Clarice was also steaming under the sable coat, for he could smell the hot, sweet odor of perfume mixed with the scent of champagne that was in the little clouds of her warm breath.

Lorenzo had been the second to reach the ledge because he had fallen weeping into the snow at Paul's feet, the craven sight of him so disgusting to Cora that she had begun kicking him, cursing him for having gotten her into this mess so far away from her poor old twisted wire of a mother. Emil had seized Cora firmly and, murmuring pacifications in German, drawn her away from the prone Lorenzo.

"Take him," Archie had said, as much to save Lorenzo from Cora as from the threatening glacier.

Paul had lifted him, fastened the harness and belt, signaled Markey and, like a battered Peter Pan, Lorenzo had gone soaring off on the end of the nylon rope. As he rose he blubbered as many Hail Marys and Glory Bes as he could get his mouth around, weaving in as much of the Lord's Prayer as he could remember, and when he reached the ledge and began to vomit, he swore by the Holy Trinity that he would go to confession every week in payment for his life.

When the rope and the harness descended again through the snow, only Paul, Diane and Cora were waiting. A moment before, Diane had suddenly remembered and gasped, "Miss Kirbo!" and Emil and Archie had rushed off toward the main building to see what was keeping Arly. Only Markey and Arly knew that Dr. Friendly and Jessica were also among those left behind by the fallen tram. It had been Archie's idea to go in search of Arly and Emil had insisted on accompanying him. "If she is hurt, you will need help," he had said, but the truth was that Emil feared his lifelong companion might not return in time and he, Emil, did not want to face even one more day ever again without Archie. The Jew was his talisman and, more than that, living proof to Emil that he had done one good and humane thing in those egregious Nazi years.

Paul had sent Cora up next. A blob in her dark green, padded ski jacket, she appeared to be a stuffed bag of trash with short pegs protruding from its bottom.

"You're next," Diane said firmly, and he smiled. "Paul," she insisted, "Mr. Markey can use some muscle up there."

"He's doing fine," said Paul. "Didn't you see how Madame Cara Loves You, Just You, went flying away from us, just us?"

"Are you always funny?" snapped Diane.

"Wall-to-wall jokes," said he. And then they tensed alertly and fell quiet as from the direction of the shrouded slope came an audible, if distant, crash of falling trees as the glacier moved forward. Paul looked up into the snow and murmured, "Hurry."

Diane was suddenly trembling and she whispered, "There I go again," and wrapped her arms about herself trying to contain the terror.

The rope whipped down from above and Paul caught it. "Hang on, kid," he said. "You'll be okay."

And he guided her arms into the harness, buckled the belt at her waist and signaled her for go. "See you upstairs," he said, and as she rose she caught a last glimpse of his smile and raised one hand in an awkward good-by gesture. She was drawn swiftly up past the snow-rimed rock face, rising with almost breathless speed, for on the ledge Markey now had not only the aid of Clarice and Cora but even of Lorenzo, who had recovered enough to help. Diane was dragged sprawling onto the ledge and a hand with two short fingers caught her hand, pulled her to her feet, skinned the harness off her shoulders and threw it out into space.

And through Diane's fright and trembling, the discovery that had waited out there on the edge of darkness thrust forward suddenly in blinding light. This man, this one so removed from her by fame and legend, was truly Manfred, and with him were the Seven Spirits at his beck and bidding, and Markey said, "Welcome to purgatory, Miss Haynes. Here you're expected to help bring up the other poor souls. Take your place on the end of the rope."

Diane stumbled past him to join the others, who were ready, one behind the other with the rope in their hands. She positioned herself next to Lorenzo and accepted the rope, then looked back through the snow at Cabot Markey, who stood nonchalantly on the very lip of the precipice looking down into the storm, waiting for the signal from below. Awed and comforted by his confidence, Diane thought he looked like the Rider of the Wind and then she immediately felt ineffably foolish because in this awful hour she was playing with poetry.

Paul was alone. He could clearly hear the moving mountain of ice, hear the shrieking friction of the berg against the stone sides of the gorge, hear the rifle-crack reports as tree trunks were snapped off, but still he could not determine how far away the thing was. Sound in the gorge was trapped and amplified by the high rock faces. The glacier might still be half a mile up the slope.

He was not afraid of being alone; to be solitary was natural to him, but he was torn between the urge to remove himself immediately from danger and the responsibility he knew he should feel for the others somewhere off in the snow, Arly and the two men who had gone in search of her. Could they hear the glacier, did they know how close it might be, were they now hurrying to where he waited with the harness and the rope in his hands?

He felt no deep personal interest in whether they lived or died and, as he stood motionless now, it was a replay of that day during the war in Vietnam when he had held off the Cong attack, delaying his own safe departure because he knew he should feel passion for the safety of others.

The rope jerked in his hand, Markey asking for response, and Paul dropped it and plunged off into the drifting snow toward the lodge. He reached the bridge that crossed the creek and could see no one coming on the path on the other side. He shouted, called out for Arly and Mr. von Rothke and Mr. Epstein. There was no answer but the plowing sounds of the oncoming berg and Paul could feel the ground, cushioned even as it was by new snow, moving beneath his feet from the impact of the still hidden force.

Again he shouted the names into the driving snow and still there was no response and then he ran back past the ski shack toward the gorge wall. The harness was dancing off the ground as Markey signaled pleadingly for a weight to be put in it. Paul slipped his arms into the harness, buckled the belt about his waist and answered Markey's plea. The rope tightened and he was lifted and as he was borne swiftly higher and higher he saw through the snow the advancing enormity of the ice. Vapors fumed off its jagged blue front and the top of its colossal precipice was yet far above Paul even at the speed with which the nylon rope was lifting him. It seemed now to be coming on fast and in silence for all its clumsy and ponderous bulk and Paul knew he had waited too long. He was enveloped by the fierce coldness that rushed ahead of it and then it struck him and he bounced away and swung back and bounced out again and knew he would fall the next time between the ice and the rock face, where the mighty molars of the berg were at work.

Mercifully, a shutter clicked in his mind and the scene changed to one of a land as long and flat as a calm sea across which white sheep moved like a regatta of little sailing vessels and were followed by a rider on a red mare named Rojo, and all drifted off the edge of the world to where dragons be.

On the ledge the nylon rope went limp and they stopped pulling. "Oh, dear God, who was it?" wailed Diane, and they all pressed back into the angle of the ledge and watched the geysers of pulverized blue ice gush up from the grinding teeth of the berg, and in one geyser there spewed unnoted a gout of color like pulped red roses.

Emil and Archie had not found Arly and as they were hurrying back to Paul on the path that led to the bridge the ice monster loomed out of the snow and bore down on them. "We overbid the hand!" yelled Emil above the roar of the sliding ice, and Archie shouted, "We can't win them all, Herr von Rothke," and contemptuously turned his back upon death. As he turned, his sister's face, the fairest face in his family and one he had not envisioned for forty years except as a convulsed dead thing lying among the tortured bodies and splattered fecal matter on the floor of the gas chamber, that face now came to him as it had been in life, sweet and gentle in its concentration on the cello in the sunlit music room of their home in Leipzig—and from the soul of the cello swelled the grace and gaiety of Schumann's *Fröhlicher Landmann*. Archie felt no pain as he was scooped up with Emil against the face of the berg and they began the wild roller coaster ride Cabot Markey had planned for himself, down over the talus to the lake a thousand feet below.

Emil had looked death in the face and stood ramrod straight as behooved a Prussian officer and for him there came a grand blare of trumpets and a mighty roll of drums as he rode the glacier beside Archie, and while Archie dreamed of Schumann and his fairest sister, Emil goosestepped to crashing martial music down an endless Unter den Linden lined forever with curling red and black flags.

In the room where Arly was hiding with the comforter over her head, enjoying the warm darkness beneath it, she became vaguely aware of the sound of the approaching berg. But it seemed no more than and rather like the step of her father as he searched for her, and when the lodge was rammed and its walls collapsing, Arly threw down the comforter and popped up in bed. "Here I are, Papa, here I are," she cried, and he came to her and, laughing, took her up into his arms.

A moment before impact, Dr. Friendly had lifted his wife's limp hand and pressed it to his lips and suddenly her eyes were open and she had looked at him with a most profound expression of love. This once his heart was closed by selfishness as he snatched that love to himself like a thief and ran with it into eternity. He was the happiest man in all of space and Jessica, in whom consciousness had flickered for that short and precious moment, saw that he was happy and she slept in comfort.

Now, if some who died on that day were the bravest, the noblest, the kindest and the most loving, and some who survived were the craziest, the most quarrelsome, the most cowardly and the most vain, well, those are the breaks.

23

After the berg had passed and with elephantine leaps thundered down to the lake, raised gigantic waves, displaced the water so that its level rose to within a few hundred feet of the lower tram station, the survivors huddled together on the ledge, exhausted and silent. "There'll be someone along to pick us up," Markey told them, and no one doubted his assurances. Here on this precarious place high on the gorge wall, the rest of the world blotted out by the falling snow, Markey was the center of their lives. They watched him, his every movement; watched his hand brushing snow from his face, watched when he removed his gloves and breathed warm breath on his cold fingers, when he now and then looked up to where the top of the precipice hung unseen more than a thousand feet above. Once he seemed to hear something and their ears pricked up to catch the sound he had heard. Once he turned to them and smiled and they were instantly happier.

Now Markey heard the sound he had been waiting for, a faint, metallic singing sound, like wind through telephone wires, and he cupped his hands to his mouth and shouted, "Here, here, here!" The singing stopped and Markey shouted again and the singing began, then stopped again and he bellowed, "Here!"

Moments passed and a small clatter of falling stones was heard from somewhere and from the white murk a figure appeared, swinging easily above the chasm on the end of a thin steel cable, bounding across the rock face and landing with catlike precision on the ledge beside Markey.

"So here you are," said Peck Nordo.

"What's left," said Markey.

It was not necessary for Nordo to explain to Markey how desperately hard the rescue team had tried. Nordo's face and clothing were rimed with ice and he seemed bent into a shape the wind had made. He fumbled a compact walkie-talkie from his pocket, pulled out its aerial and spoke into it. "I've got them. Five. We'll be coming up."

Even Lorenzo was, relatively, fearless about the next steps in the rescue; at least, he did not throw up after being whisked to the top of the cliff via the steel cable. And Cora was so relieved to know with reasonable certainty that she would be with her mother again that she was in a constant state of tearful sniffling. Cora, who had not cried in thirty years.

In the midst of all the discomfort of being a survivor on this wet, cold day, Clarice was ebullient, tremendously pleased with herself. She had discovered the satisfaction that being of service imbues and she played the scene again and again in her mind where she had stood beside Markey and thrown her strength into the rescue effort. She was prouder of the little pink blisters in the palms of her hands than she had ever been of the azure irises of her eyes.

Diane remembered the pile of sandwiches left on the ski shack's bar and regretted that she had not had the presence of mind to bring a sackful for the rescue team. It would have made Miss Kirbo happy, a last hospitable gesture from her lodge. Diane grieved for Miss Kirbo and felt sadness for Emil von Rothke and Archie Epstein, but it was only when she was alone in the small tent assigned to her by Peck Nordo that she allowed herself to think of Paul. As she fell into exhausted sleep, and before the tears dried on her cheeks, she saw again the snowflakes in his dark hair, the white flash of his smile as she floated up and away to safety, and she marked his image for memory.

Cabot Markey had come back from the edge of extinction. He felt almost like his old self-sufficient self, give or take a few grievous losses. Jael. Arly. His spirit was alive again. He was not sure why. Perhaps because he had climbed the rock face despite his bum ticker, perhaps because he had discovered again, as Clarice had discovered for the first time, what it meant to be of service, what it meant to be strong enough to offer life to others. He was not so anxious now to waste himself. There were still things to do, hills if not mountains to climb, canvases to take the colors of his brush, causes to be championed and even, yes, even women to be loved. Jael would have cursed his chastity. "You're a goddam silly fool. I'm dead, Cabot, dead." She spoke to him as he lay behind the nylon fabric of the tiny mountaineering tent fixed between two saplings in the rescue camp above the gorge. The wind beat about outside the tent looking for entry and Markey listened to the voice in the wind and finally, there in the darkness of a stormy Sierra night with Peck Nordo snoring beside him, he began to think not of the past but of the future.

The wind huffed and puffed until almost midnight, trying to rip through the tough little tents staked there on the side of a mountain, but it grew tired and lost heart and skittered away to the south, where it had more fun breaking branches off live oak trees in the San Joaquin Valley. With the wind gone, the snow had the Sierra to itself and added a few inches more just to touch things up, then followed the wind to the south and turned into rain, caused some flash floods in the Mojave Desert and finally became an unhappy drizzle over downtown Los Angeles. Rarely can a storm be successful in Southern California. It was like most of the other hopefuls who arrive on that scene and find it ain't what it's cracked up to be.

At daybreak, the wonder of the high Sierra in its winter ermines began to unfold. The rescue team had the Primus stoves going to celebrate the occasion, coffee perking and freeze-dried food bubbling when the survivors of Kirbo's Lodge crawled out of the warm tents and rediscovered the miracle of being alive.

Except for the ever present mists drifting aimlessly about the highest peaks and lying doggo in the deepest canyons, the day was clear and splendid, and splendid too was the mighty if murderous Gornaad, seen now from this eagle's view. The glacier was still gliding majestically out of its immemorial confinement and it treated its watchers to an encore of yesterday as its massive forward peninsula ringingly broke off and began with a grand rumble to slide to the lake, which was hidden by the deep ground fog.

And the fog also kept kindly concealed the raw scars where the lodge had stood.

The first laser beams of sunlight were shot from behind the mountain ranges to the east of the Sierra, and with them came the Air Force helicopters, engines laboring in air almost too thin to support the heavy craft. There was no safe place for the choppers to put down near the rescue camp, but they all circled over the thirteen people, who jubilantly waved welcome before the pilots tipped the big slapping blades toward the tram station, where there was space to land and people waiting to come aboard.

Nordo's men packed up their gear and, with Nordo and Markey on the point, the whole party began their descent to the tram station along the knife-edge ridge. It was not difficult, even for Clarice in her crocodile boots, for the wind had kept the ridge clean of snow.

Despite the terrifying and grisly past twenty-four hours, the survivors were in good spirits (and feeling a little guilty about that) as they trailed behind Peck Nordo and Cabot Markey in the surprisingly warm aftermath of the blizzard, the sunlight making sequins gleam in the long slopes of snow beneath them.

Diane was first behind Markey, but taking care not to make her presence noticeable. It was enough that she walked near him for this short duration and she was overwhelmed by the knowledge that not only had he saved her life, he had actually held her in his arms. That would be something to tell her grandchildren when she escorted them through a museum where hung glorious paintings signed C. Markey. She did not occupy her mind with notions that he might discover her for himself—Diane the cocktail waitress can wear the glass slipper please step into my pumpkin coach. She was finished with idealizing and idolatry. Cabot Markey was probably, when you got to know him, as vain as old Perce and as impenetrable as poor, sweet Paul, Diane reflected, and then was ashamed of her judgmental thoughts. I'm too critical and I expect too much, she told herself, and if I can't think constructive things about people, I simply won't think at all any more. She stumbled then and almost fell, but Markey had heard the misstep and quickly turned, caught her flailing arms in his hands and set her right.

"Not too much farther, Miss Haynes, and then it's all over."

"You'll be glad to get rid of me, I bet."

"You're a very brave young lady, Miss Haynes."

And, dear grandchildren, he said to me, you're a very brave young lady, but it was an impersonal remark and left me feeling insignificant, which I was.

The Air Force helicopters delivered all the survivors to the nearest jet airport, in Reno, Nevada, and from there they dispersed to all points of the compass, although some had no particular destination, that being the reason they were at Kirbo's Lodge in the first place. And so for a few days Reno enjoyed a bonanza of rich folk who shopped the best shops to replace their lost wardrobes, occupied the largest suites in the hotels and scattered money about on Reno's gambling tables the like of which Reno had not seen since its rival, Las Vegas, became the hub of American foolishness.

As quietly and unobtrusively as possible, Markey slipped away from newspaper reporters and boarded a plane for San Francisco. Diane was without funds and needed a job, so she called a friend from college who was working in the nearby winter resort of Mammoth. She waited for hours in the terminal until the other girl arrived to pick her up and, after a good night's sleep, found a job at The Ski Bum, a restaurant at the resort.

Clarice Bishop wasted no time in Reno but flew by chartered jet to San Francisco, raced by limousine to her condo, bathed and exchanged her sables for snow leopard and rushed to her psychiatrist, who was eagerly waiting with the cocoa butter, ready to massage her feet and listen to her woes. Instead of woes, he was chagrined to find her Gestalt doing nip-ups of happiness as she told him of the fantastic release she had found not in a new lover but in pulling on a rope. He could see that he was about to lose not only his favorite pair of feet but, worse, his most remunerative patient. He tried to reason with her, using every undefinable psychiatric term and psychologic jiggery-pokery he could think of to explain that the rope she pulled on was really nothing more than a sublimation of penis envy. Dr. Goldberg succeeded only in enraging Clarice, who fired him on the spot and gave him a lecture entitled Cocks and All That Bullshit that he would not soon forget.

Lorenzo's mother was waiting in the driveway of their mansion as the electric gate swung open and admitted the limo bearing her boy. She announced that lunch was on the table and that it consisted of caponatina Sicilianese, minestrone Genoese, eel Anguilla, ossobuco Milanese and chocolate ice cream with cherries. Lorenzo was home.

Cora's arrival at her mansion was heralded by a truckload of flowers for her mother and when Cora rushed into her mother's huge room, the old thing was lost somewhere amongst the gladiolus plaintively calling for help. Cora battered her way through the blossoms and picked Mother up out of the wheelchair, carried her to a sofa and cuddled Mother on her lap as she told her she would never, never leave her alone again. Mother wanted a cigarette and Cora lighted it for her and then told her of the disaster at Kirbo's Lodge.

Mother wanted a sip of Southern Comfort and Cora supplied that, then Mother went to sleep as Cora sang a lullaby Mother used to sing to Cora. Cora was home.

Harry Ames had scarcely gotten a night's sleep when a trans-oceanic call came in from Horace Calley, Arly's old beau who now operated the world's biggest hotel chain. Harry could name his own price if he would undertake the supervision of the Grand Hotel Camelot in London, recently purchased by Calley. And so Harry, too, went home.

While waiting out the blizzard in the lower tram station, Fran-cine struck up an acquaintance with Bert Rushton, the oral surgeon from Chicago, who was not an old man (as suggested by Arly) but was past fifty and old enough to be rich. White-gloved hands com-posed on knees pressed primly together, she told him she did not know what she would do now that the lodge was gone. The dentist was sympathetic and, besides, was interested in her pretty teeth, and when she obligingly opened her mouth wide to give him a better look, he told her she had the cleanest mouth he had ever seen. Fran-cine encouraged him to think that she was the purest lass who ever came down the pike—except that she was afflicted by an unnatural lust. They wound up in the same hotel suite in Reno and when the doctor left for Chicago, he gave her a sweet gift of five thousand dollars. Francine realized that all along she had missed her calling and she eventually became the neatest and most expensive little hooker in Reno, offering specialties that entailed the use of white silk gloves.

Cora McElvain and Lorenzo Dante, as you might expect, went on much as they had before, getting richer on Cora's goops and en-joying their hatred of each other even more.

For those who thirst for reform, it would be slaking if Clarice Bishop, because of her revelation on the mount, had become Major Clarice of the Salvation Army or engaged in other good works, but instead, after dismissing her faithful psychiatrist, she fell in with a group of wealthy devotees of Swami Gupta Atman, a teacher of kundalini yoga whose ashram was in a village on the sacred Burhi Gandak River in Bihar Province, India. Clarice made the pilgrimage to sit at the feet of Gupta Atman, which was not as uncomfortable as might be imagined. Gupta charged approximately two hundred dollars a day for room and bath with breakfast, and the appoint-ments at the ashram were not unlike those of a good Holiday Inn.

And you really did not have to sit at the swami's feet, only at his breakfast table, which was comfortable John Adams modern colonial.

Clarice did not find much salvation in listening to Mr. Atman, who gave his lectures with his mouth full of breakfast cereal, but she was discovered by a cult that worshiped Uma, that creature of light and beauty, of globular breasts and hourglass hips. They perceived Clarice as the reincarnation of Uma and set up camp outside Gupta's hostelry to be near her. She humored them by occasionally showing herself on the little balcony attached to her room, and even went so far as to dress as Uma, wearing strands of pearls about her throat, a beaded loin cloth and nothing else. She looked more like a goddess than Uma ever hoped to look and she even began to find a satisfaction in the worship she engendered. The cult members actually rolled on the ground and spoke in strange tongues, so enchanted were they by Clarice's perfection.

Things went on like that until Clarice granted an audience to the leaders of the cult and was horrified by their request that she save her urine in bottles they had brought so that they could sprinkle her essence on their heads. What with the swami's cereal-sprayed incantations and her own messy converts, she had had enough, and flew to London, was checked into the Grand Hotel Camelot by old friend Harry Ames and settled down to hiding out again, keeping company with herself.

For months the lake in the gorge looked like a dump for used glaciers, great hunks of ice thrusting up at disreputable angles, but considering the vast quantity of the stuff that had suddenly fallen into the pristine waters, it melted with surprising swiftness. By the end of the next summer, there was nothing left of the Gornaad but several floes that drifted aimlessly about on the mysterious currents in the lake and, mysteriously also, there was no surplus of water from the melted ice. While a connection could not be established, the Owens River, which had gone dry during the earthquake, began to run fulsomely again, and yet the new stream in the Tehachapis continued to flow. The Los Angeles Water and Power experts were baffled by this turn of events but suiting their action to their motto, the more the merrier, they kept all of the water.

When the flock of band-tailed pigeons came billing and cooing back from warmer parts and found their favorite nesting and roosting pines were gone along with the feeders maintained for them by the lodge, they circled about in a lost manner then very sensibly flew off in search of other accommodations.

The bear's cubs were pretty, as bear cubs go, but not especially well behaved and they led their mother quite a funny chase as they tumbled about in the spring sunlight on the greening slopes above the chasm where the glacier used to be. She did not lead them down into that empty place because it looked not new, as you might expect, but forbiddingly old and maybe haunted by the ghosts of strange, snouted creatures that had grazed there before the ice age began.

Hikers who came over the trails to look at the site where the famous lodge once stood were also depressed by the curious character of the deep, wide hole in the earth that had been the Gornaad's prison. After a while they stopped coming and the trails were lost.

As for Cabot Markey? That will take a little longer . . .

There are some elderly men who arrive at a certain station of decline and seem to remain there without further change for the rest of their lives and their lives seem to go on forever. "You mean he's still alive?" "Yep, and looks just like he always did." Phillip Bongart was like that. He was middle-aged when he bought young Cabot Markey's entire first show of paintings for a wealthy client and, in effect, christened Markey's career. It pleased Mr. Bongart to use the term "christened." He preferred it to "launched" since he thought of himself as the high priest of art who baptized the chosen.

He had christened not a few noted painters of the century, but Markey was his greatest discovery and he assumed an air of ownership about the artist which was graciously permitted by Markey. And now that Markey was seriously and industriously painting again, Bongart expected to be the first invited to view the work and, indeed, he was. Looking a portly sixty-five (he was seventy-nine) and clearly in firm charge of all his faculties, he boarded a transatlantic plane in Paris for the initial lap of the journey into Markeyland.

Markeyland was currently somewhere on the west coast of Mexico—exactly where was not clear to Bongart since his sense of geography had always been poor, but he trusted the fat book of plane tickets prepared for him by his secretary to get him there.

In New York he tended to other business for two days, then flew to Mexico City, changed planes and winged to the capital city of a Central American republic, changed planes again, this time to an ancient DC-3 which carried him to a smaller city in that country, the name of which when translated to English became Poor People Town. In Poor People, an Indian with one white eye and teeth that appeared to have been filed to points met Mr. Bongart and guided him to a dilapidated taxicab, rode with him in silence on a road full of chuckholes for approximately five miles down the coast to a fisherman's cove, where Bongart was helped aboard a listing twenty-five-foot vessel with a wooden mermaid on its prow, her nose and one breast knocked off in some long-ago collision. The craft set sail with Bongart ensconced in a canvas chair under a tattered tarpaulin on the stern deck, the man with filed teeth at the wheel in the pilot house and a deckhand, small and brown and about twelve years old, who tied a hangman's knot in a length of deck rope and pretended to hang himself for Mr. Bongart's amusement. He accepted all of this without surprise and even with some pleasure. Through the years he had found Markey in even more outré places and it was encouraging that the artist was up to his old tricks again after the listless years that followed Jael Callam's death.

The sea off this coast had a curious purple tint caused by a rare kelp that grew nowhere else in the world and for an hour the boat held a southerly course not far off the shore and finally reeled in from the purple sea to a cove where on the end of a long pier Cabot Markey was waiting. Behind Markey and the pier, a large villa was set like a block of pale chalcedony against the peridot green of the tropical jungle.

As Markey led Bongart toward the villa, he explained that it presently belonged to the general of the military junta that ruled the country, expropriated from the dictator who preceded him, who had in turn inherited it from another dictator. It sort of went with the territory. Its current owner was in need of dollars for his Swiss bank account and for that purpose he rented to rich Americanos who fancied getting away from it all.

Markey had fancied it for a painting spree and in six months' time, he told Bongart, he had produced more than twenty canvases. The art expert salivated at the thought of twenty Cabot Markey canvases that he would be the first to see. He felt like an explorer approaching a new land as they climbed the steps to the long cool veranda, where a table had been set with a frothy iced punch made of bananas, oranges and coconut milk. A pet coatimundi leaped from the veranda's railing to Markey's shoulder and a spectacular blue and yellow macaw swung on its perch and inspected Bongart with a friendly golden eye.

"Paradise," said Bongart, "nothing less."

And in walked the long-legged woman who was Markey's companion in paradise. Bongart, knowing nothing of her at all, knew instantly by the easy swagger of her walk that she was American. She grasped his hand firmly, smiled and said, "Hi," and then said, "Hey," when he bent to kiss her hand and explained she had never had her hand kissed before. It was a tan, strong hand and smelled a little doggy because she had four dogs of assorted colors and sizes who stayed close to her bare legs and feet. She was wearing rolled-up duck trousers and was braless under a blue chambray shirt with sleeves cut off at the shoulders. Her hair was dark and short in a self-scissored style, she wore no makeup and on her nose were the kind of glasses that go dark in the sunlight and become clear in the shade. They were clearing now since she had entered the veranda from its sunny end and Bongart could see that her eyes were brown. She was altogether, if not stunning, certainly vital. There was confidence in her eyes and when she spoke, her voice was in a low key and flatly positive.

She pointed at Markey with her thumb and said, "He's been waiting anxiously for you. He needs approval, ha-ha," and poured a frosty glass of punch for Bongart.

"Are the paintings good?" asked Bongart.

Said she, "I'm a pushover for any kind of smudge he makes."

Bongart glanced at Markey and saw tolerant affection for the informal young American woman who was so unlike the exquisitely finished, sensual Jael Callam.

This pair in this remote place, this narrow corner of the earth, were like characters from a Maugham novel come to life. Bongart made a mental note of that for use in *Bongart's Notes on Artists and Art,* the voluminous journal he had kept that would be published before his death, that is, if he could time that event properly. In it were the never before revealed accounts of his personal relationships with such luminaries as Picasso, Matisse, Braque, Markey, Klee and many others, as well as his comments on their careers and their works. He made further note of Markey's appearance—healthy, tanned, dressed in corduroy shorts, espadrilles on his feet and a paisano straw hat on his head.

"Do you want to see the paintings now?" asked the casual young American woman, whose name was Diane and who wore an oldpawn turquoise necklace about her throat.

"Not until morning," said Bongart. "In the morning, when the light is fresh and I'm fresh."

She showed him to his room, which had big screened windows that looked out into the jungle where vines of red blossoms and pink and gold parrots decorated the branches. "How long have you known Cabot?" he asked, and she said, "Not long. Can I get you anything?"

He thanked her, no, and she left him and Bongart knew he would have to woo her before she would volunteer anything he might use in his journal. He bathed, shaved, patted cologne on his jowls, took a nap, dressed in whites and appeared for drinks and dinner. Dinner was served by quick, smiling Indian women who moved noiselessly about on bare feet, and afterward he sat with Markey in the thick tropical darkness on the veranda. The coatimundi clung to the veranda rail and watched Markey with its luminous eyes. Diane had found an excuse to leave them alone and that gesture pleased Bongart. He and Markey could now talk in shorthand about things past and fondly remembered. And after a time, with Bongart's encouragement, the talk got around to Diane.

"She was a student working at Kirbo's Lodge," said Markey. "We went through that harrowing experience together and she bore up quite well, I thought, with a little nervous weeping now and then. I didn't think too much about her at the time, mainly I suppose because the circumstances didn't allow much study. When it was all over and I was in San Francisco, I found myself wondering about her, her job gone, all that, but more than that, I realized she'd made an impression on me. You know how it is, you meet someone in passing and then discover they've stuck to your ribs, you don't forget them. Well, I kept thinking about her off and on for a couple of months.

"My thoughts were random at first, but then they began to take a shape. I wanted another woman in my life. Candidly, it didn't have to be Diane, but as I said, she had stuck to my ribs for whatever reason and I finally made some inquiries—the lawyers handling the lodge affairs, they had a list and addresses of the survivors. She was working in Mammoth, the ski resort just up the road from

Kirbo's Landing. I went to Mammoth. Looked her up. She's not a person to be trifled with. She asked right away, 'Is this accidental or did you come here to see me?' I told her the truth and she said, 'So you're shopping.' I agreed that in a way I was shopping and she said, 'Well, a libber's pride goeth before a fall. You can buy me cheap. I don't want anything but affection.' She packed her suitcase and went to San Francisco with me. She's a delight, Phillip. Dead-on honest like Jael Callam."

Markey paused and they sat listening to the musical sounds of the jungle and the gentle slap of the surf as it rolled in through the pilings that supported the pier. Bongart knew instinctively that they were not finished with the subject of Jael Callam.

"I killed Jael," Markey said. "My carelessness killed her. I shouldn't have had her with me on that rock face in Chamonix. It's taken me a long, long time to admit that to myself, that I killed her. She was there because I wanted her there. She lived for me. Well, I've turned that around. I live for Diane. Everything is for her. The paintings you'll see were painted for her. I never painted a canvas for Jael. Not one."

Bongart was making notes for his journal. Diane was in fact a surrogate for Jael Callam. It was Callam who still occupied Markey's heart.

Bongart slept well that night and rose to prepare himself for the viewing of Markey's new work. He selected a seersucker suit, a white shirt of the softest Egyptian cotton, a gray silk tie and white shoes. He ate a hearty breakfast and announced that he was ready. He was not as ready as he had thought. When Markey unlocked the door to his studio and allowed Bongart to enter, the great art expert was so overwhelmed by the paintings hung on the walls that he did not even realize he had been left alone in the studio until he turned to exclaim his excitement to Markey and found the door closed and Markey gone. He turned back to the paintings and knew that he was breathing as fast as if he had been running. This was not just a show of the expected Markey genius, this was an eruption of creative spirit. Volcanic, thought Bongart, yes, volcanic. Markey, who had always worked with a subdued palette, had here given freedom to color and the result was like a wildfire racing around the walls of the studio. He had painted the flaming blossoms of the jungle and the purple glidings of the sea and the dark, quick figures of the Indians who lived in the jungle and on the sea. But it was not derivative, not from Tamayo or Gauguin. It was pure.

Bongart drew a chair to the center of the big studio and sat down. For four hours he sat there, turning the chair about to give him a view of each quarter of the room, rising now and then to move to an individual painting and study it close at the end of his nose.

A soft knock on the door and Diane was there with a tray of fruit and cheese for his lunch. He stared at her until he became aware that he was making her uncomfortable.

"Don't you want lunch?" she asked.

"Do you know these were painted for you?" It was an accusation and Diane plainly was baffled by his manner. "For you, you!" he orated, and pointed a finger at her. "What have you done to deserve this?"

"I'm afraid not very much," said Diane.

He smiled. "No one could deserve this, my dear. No one."

Diane looked about the studio with grave wonder. "He isn't real," said she.

"Not real?" Leading her.

"He's—he's Manfred," said Diane. "Do you understand?"

And Bongart, being a man of vast knowledge, understood. She had found the romantic spirit created by Lord Byron, "half dust, half deity," the hero that all women want and never find, this woman had found him, and there was about her a glow that would have sent those who believe in personal auras into ecstasies.

"Yes, he's Manfred," said Bongart. Why should he dim the glow, fade the aura?

In the late afternoon, Bongart came from the studio feeling disoriented, as if he had been spun about blindfolded and was now finding his way. He walked slowly along the veranda, expecting to be discovered by Markey, but when neither Markey nor Diane appeared, he asked a servant for them and she pointed off toward the shore.

They were strolling on the beach beside the lavender effervescence of the surf. They were close together, hand in hand, and deep in intimate conversation. Surrogates both of them, she for another woman, he for a mythic knight, and if they were bound together by such frail lacing, well, the result was happiness, for a time, and that

K46

was not to be sneered at, Bongart knew. Besides, look what it had produced—the paintings—and when all else was gone, the paintings would remain as evidence that the artist and his inspiration had once lived and loved in this faraway place.

Bongart repaired to his room, opened his notebook and began to write.